"Anything you've seen before?"

I looked down at the cold body and then back to her, still confused about the whole situation and why I'd been brought in to share my non-existent expertise.

"Why are you asking me?"

The Detective came in close.

"Fetch, we know what you're doing."

"Really? Could you tell me?"

"You're looking for ways to bring the magic back."

By Luke Arnold

The Last Smile in Sunder City
Dead Man in a Ditch

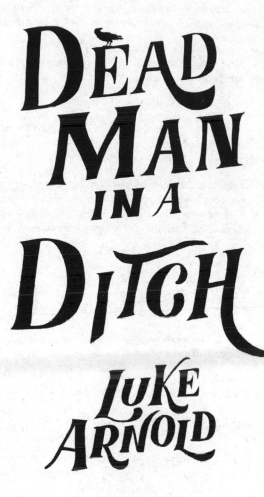

DEAD MAN IN A DITCH

LUKE ARNOLD

orbit

www.orbitbooks.net

Copyright © 2020 by Luke Arnold
Excerpt from *Spellslinger* copyright © 2017 by Sebastien de Castell
Excerpt from *Senlin Ascends* copyright © 2013 by Josiah Bancroft

Cover design and illustration by Emily Courdelle

Orbit
Hachette Book Group
1290 Avenue of the Americas
New York, NY 10104
orbitbooks.net

First Edition: September 2020
Simultaneously published in Great Britain by Orbit

Orbit is an imprint of Hachette Book Group.
The Orbit name and logo are trademarks of Little, Brown Book Group Limited.

The publisher is not responsible for websites (or their content) that are not owned by the publisher.

The Hachette Speakers Bureau provides a wide range of authors for speaking events. To find out more, go to www.hachettespeakersbureau.com or call (866) 376-6591.

Library of Congress Control Number: 2020933396

ISBNs: 978-0-316-45586-2 (trade paperback), 978-0-316-45587-9 (ebook)

Printed in the United States of America

LSC-C

1 3 5 7 9 10 8 6 4 2

For everyone who ever let me crash on their couch.
Seriously.

Prologue

They say the cold won't kill you if you can remember what it was like to be warm.

But when the hell was that? Back before we broke the world: when the streetlamps were full of fire and you didn't have to search so hard to find the spark of light in someone's eyes. Now there's just darkness and death and—

No. Remember.

Shoulder to shoulder on the Sunder City streetcar, crammed between fur-covered creatures and dirty workers done for the day. Music and mulled wine in underground clubs, before it all went rotten and silent and—

No.

The Ditch, after closing, alone with a mop. Warmer than you might imagine. The air thick with the memory of pipe smoke, folk songs and bad breath. Windows fogged over and the kitchen ripe with onions, mutton and sage.

I wipe the tables, warmed by plates and heavy elbows; clearing peanut shells, tobacco crumbs, gristle and spit. Working from top to bottom, I sweep and then mop, thinning down the sickening mix of food scraps, melted snow and spilt beer.

I throw the bigger pieces into the fireplace: a cast-iron sculpture in the center of the room, topped with a thick chimney. I watch the flames eat the leftovers, spitting grease against the glass door. For a moment, that fireplace is the warmest thing in the building. Then the front door opens and Eliah Hendricks arrives.

"Fetch, my boy! You have got to try one of these!"

The High Chancellor stumbled into The Ditch with both hands wrapped around a leaky paper bag. Brown oil dripped down his ringed fingers on to my newly mopped floor. His copper-colored hair, sprinkled with snow, was bunched up in the collar of his riding cloak. I was flattered: the leader of the Opus had traveled for days to get to Sunder City and I was his first stop.

Well, second. He'd stopped to get snacks.

I wiped my hands on my apron and made a move towards the bag. Hendricks pulled it away like he was saving a baby from a lion's jaws.

"Don't even think about sticking those filthy tentacles in here. Open up."

Hendricks reached into the bag and plucked out a sweet-smelling, crispy bundle. I opened my mouth and he pushed it onto my tongue.

"They call them Swine-o's. Fried plums wrapped in thin strips of fatty pork." I bit down slowly, feeling the mixture of fruit juice and animal fat fill my mouth. "Isn't it just marvelous? This right here is the miracle of Sunder City. Most people on the continent can't see it. They're so set in their ways they don't understand what's so special about this place. This," he pointed an oily finger at my full cheeks, "is a modern marvel. The old magic would never have conjured this up. Not in hundreds of years. I ought to know: I was there!"

He pulled another burgundy morsel out of the bag, held it under his nose, breathed deeply and shook his head in disbelief.

"Mizaki winter-plums, sweetened to perfection by the chilled winds of the north, cocooned in marbled pork-belly from the cocoa-bean-eating boars of Southern Skiros. An ingenious invention of Sunder City cuisine sold on a street-corner at midnight for the shocking price of one silver coin per packet." He popped it in his mouth and kept on talking. "This is progress, Fetch! This is something worth fighting for!"

He dropped the oily bag on my clean table and I dragged over a couple of stools. Hendricks went behind the bar and began the well-practiced routine he performed every time we were together.

First, he slipped two bronze bills into the register. It would not only cover the booze we were about to consume, but also encourage Mr Tatterman to overlook my debilitating hangover the next day.

There was no point trying to do any work while Hendricks was around so I dragged the mop bucket out back, took off the apron, washed my hands, and helped myself to some leftovers from the kitchen that wouldn't be missed: a quarter-wheel of hard cheese, a dollop of honey and some bread that was a day away from stale. When I brought out the plate, Hendricks had all his ingredients lined up like soldiers.

Burnt milkwood, like most cocktails, began its life as medicine. The sap of the tarix tree is cooked over an open flame till it melts into a bitter, caramel-colored syrup: good for sore throats and sinus infections but it tastes terrible on its own. Mothers with sick kids mixed in beet-sugar to balance out the flavors. Over time, more ingredients were added until the recipe became so rich that, if one was so inclined, it could hide a ridiculous amount of alcohol without anyone being able to taste it.

Most bars kept a pre-mixed bottle of tarix sap on hand, but Eliah preferred to make his own.

"My boy! How go the adventures of the biggest kid in Sunder City?" he asked, as he emptied a small vial of raw sap into a saucepan. "Still breaking hearts, banks and expectations?"

He always talked to me like that. For all our fondness of each other, I never quite worked out if he was teasing me about my struggles or whether he actually thought I was making good impressions around town.

"I've got a new room," I said. "Sharing with an Ogre who snores like thunder. I have to get my sleep during the day when he's working at the steel-mill but it still feels like I'm moving up in the world."

"No need to move up, Master Fetch, just around." He swirled the sap in the saucepan as he made his way over to the fireplace. "This is a marvelous city to play in but most people misunderstand the game. The beauty of Sunder is that it isn't some ancient kingdom bogged down with bloodlines and crowns where the leaders spend all their time trying to cut each other off at the necks. It's a market. A dance-hall. It's a laboratory of unstable chemicals reacting to each other in beautiful and unexpected ways. Don't look up. Look down! Take off your shoes and let the city squeeze between your toes. Wallow in it. Smell it and taste it until you've absorbed everything it has to offer."

Hendricks sat down in front of the fire, wrapped his cloak around his fingers and grabbed the handle of the glass door. When he opened it up, the heat blew back his hair. He pushed the saucepan inside, slowly shaking it in circles as the flames caught the sap. I took a seat at the table and dipped a crust of bread into the honey.

"There's not much time for wallowing when I have to work three jobs."

He pulled the saucepan from the fire, blew out the flames that were burning too quickly, then slid it back in.

"I suppose that all depends on who you work for," he said.

"It's different every week. I've been working for Amari quite a bit."

"Ah, yes. My Faery friend with her little Fetch wrapped around her finger. What does she pay you in? Batted lashes and hidden kisses?"

I blushed and ignored the question.

"Mostly, I'm just here. Sometimes I run errands for the apothecary or take one-off jobs from customers."

The sap turned a deep caramel so Hendricks pulled out the pan and brought it back behind the bar.

"But who do you really work for? The sleepy oaf who runs this place? He's the one who pays you and gives you your orders."

He was mounting the back of another one of his speeches and I'd learned not to stand in his way when he took off.

"I suppose so."

"Or are you really just working for the money? If so, then some would say that you're actually working for the Sunder City Bank. Perhaps we all are! But does the city serve the bank or does the bank serve the city?" It wasn't a question I was supposed to know the answer to, so I just shrugged. "Perhaps I'm underestimating you. Maybe it's not about the money at all. In your heart, perhaps you work for the customers. When you polish the bar and mop the floors and clean the glasses to perfection" — in jest, he wiped a smudge from the high-ball he was holding — "do you actually think about the patrons themselves? Do you see yourself as being in service to them?"

He stirred in the other ingredients, balancing his attention perfectly between drinks and discussion.

"Well, I wouldn't do it for free."

"*Wouldn't you? If you didn't need the money and this place couldn't function without you, wouldn't you help if they asked?*"

"*I suppose.*"

"*So perhaps the money isn't really what matters. Perhaps the money is working in service of the city just like you. You both play your part. Two of the many moving pieces that this city needs to function, the same as the smokestacks and the cobblestones and the newspapers and the fire.*"

He brought the two thick drinks back to our table and pointed at the fireplace behind me.

"*Who does the fire work for? All of us? For itself? Does it care? It burns just as brightly no matter what purpose we bestow upon it.*"

We tapped our glasses together and I took a sip. It was sweet, but unlike other cocktails (or the same one made by less skilled hands) the sugar didn't kill the more complex flavors underneath.

"*Fetch, you know what Dragons are, don't you?*"

"*I've seen pictures at the museum. Big, scaly monsters, right?*"

"*They can evolve into all manner of creatures but yes, common Dragons are just like you say: scales, tails and wings. Miraculous creatures, each and every one of them. We do our best to protect them now but two hundred years ago, Dragon-hunting was a highly regarded profession.*

"*Unlike most warriors, Dragon slayers had no national allegiance. This freedom allowed them to work in any land, for any species, and become rich as princes if they were successful in their craft. Towns would hire slayers for protection. If an attack had already happened, they would pay for their revenge. On top of that, Dragon scales and bones were precious commodities that the slayers would sell for a small fortune on top of their fee. Above all this, their most valuable prize was fame.*

"*It's hard to imagine now. Dragon slaying, like most mercenary work, has gone quite out of fashion. I take some responsibility: the Opus has made a concerted effort to cut down on the number of free agents out in the world, swinging swords for profit. There are so few Dragons left that killing one constitutes a crime but, back then, there was no career more heroic, exciting or profitable.*"

Unlike Hendricks, who had spent three hundred years exploring every *corner of Archetellos, I'd only seen two cities in my life. Weatherly, where I grew up, was surrounded by high walls that hid the outside world. Sunder was multicultural and ever-expanding but it wasn't without its limitations. After three years in the one place, stories of the outside world were starting to make my feet itch.*

"You've seen the way children here talk about sportsmen, or how ladies fawn over the troubadours singing at the playhouse. Well, Dragon slaying was all that rolled together and multiplied by ten. We knew their names, we traded rumors of their exploits and sung songs of their adventures. They had streets named after them and replicas constructed of their swords. They never paid for a meal, never paid for a bed, and rarely went to one alone. There was nothing else like it anywhere in the world. Every species and town had their heroes, but a Dragon slayer belonged to everyone.

"Of course, this brought an incredible amount of competition. As Dragon numbers dwindled, any rumor of a monster started a race without rules. Carts were sabotaged, meals were poisoned and swords were put through slayers' chests while they slept. Many fighters became more concerned with beating each other than the Dragons they'd been trained to battle.

"Then, one night, a group of merchants arrived in Lopari. They claimed to have seen a burst of flame in the Sunderian swamps that lit up the sky and shook the earth. The rumor had barely been spoken before a young warrior named Fintack Ro was leaving town on horseback. It didn't matter to Fintack that nobody was paying a bounty: his prize would be bones, scales and, most importantly, a boost to his reputation. Though there were hundreds of aspiring slayers in the world, only a handful had truly proven their worth. Fintack was younger than the others and he'd come to the game just before the Dragon population dropped.

"Older hunters could choose to retire: write a book, train princes for a ridiculous fee or open a tavern and bring in crowds by telling stories of their adventures. Fintack was still an up-and-comer. He needed that one great kill. He needed one of those tales that had wings of its own and flew from the tongues of travelers like a plague in winter.

"Fintack stocked up on rations, sharpened his weapons, and was the first warrior to arrive in Sunderia. He spent a whole week hunting

through the swamps, his socks always wet and bug bites rising on his arms. He traveled during the day, slowly and dangerously, and at night he'd stay awake as long as he could, searching for fire on the horizon.

"To his frustration, the first signs of life came from the camps of rival slayers: other top-tier warriors who were stumbling around the swamps, equally empty-handed. Finally, one sunrise, Fintack woke to find the ground rumbling around him. He opened his eyes to see a ball of orange flame rising from deep in the mangroves. He grabbed his sword and ran right for it.

"He had learned how to navigate the reeds and puddles, knowing which mud would hold his weight and which would eat his shoes. His hands grabbed branches that were black with soot, and he sensed that the creature must be waiting up ahead.

"When he cut his way through a web of vines, another burst of flame erupted right in front of him, but he still couldn't see the beast. He squinted through the mangroves, searching as he crept onward, but when he heard the others closing in on his position, he was forced to step out into the clearing and face . . ."

Hendricks took a long sip to extend the tension.

". . . nothing. No movement, no tracks, no sign of any Dragon at all. Fintack searched in all directions as two other slayers joined him in the clearing: a Wizard named Prim and a Dwarf called Riley. All three warriors looked around, confounded and frustrated. Then, from the center of their triangle, a stream of fire shot out from the swamp and up into the sky.

"There was no Dragon. It was a decoy, made by the land itself. The slayers were frustrated. Angry. Tired. They called a truce and set up camp. Fintack killed a water-bird and attempted to roast it on the next burst of flame but Prim gave him warning: as a Wizard, he could sense the power beneath their feet. This wasn't just some pocket of fiery swamp gas, it was a glimpse at something far more powerful.

"That night, the slayers didn't tell tales of past battles or trade information on different types of Dragon. Instead, they pondered what it might take to bring that fire out of the ground and use it for fuel. The warriors had spent their lives traveling Archetellos. They'd seen families, caught

without a home for the winter, frozen by the side of the road. They'd seen Satyr slaves up in the Groves collecting coal to warm the Centaur palace. They knew all about the Dwarven forges that were powered by lava and could only be worked while deep inside dangerous mountains.

"Until that night, these warriors had served nobody but themselves. You could not have found more prideful, ambitious cut-throats anywhere on the continent. But standing right here," Hendricks stomped both his feet on the stone floor, *"they saw an opportunity to make the world a better place. Those three slayers used their influence to build a city like nobody had ever imagined. They gave up everything that had previously defined them. They relinquished the prizes they had been working so hard to find and, in doing so, they changed history."*

Hendricks stared at me with that bright green glint in his eye and picked up his empty glass with a flourish.

"I'm ready for another," he said. *"Storytelling makes me thirsty."*

I reached for my half-filled cocktail too quickly and my cuff caught the table. I tipped over the glass and as I jumped up to grab it, my other hand swung back too far and hit the iron of the fireplace. I ripped my hand off as fast as I could but a piece of skin was left stuck to the metal, sizzling and bubbling and smelling like meat.

Hendricks had already jumped into action. He filled a bowl with water and some snow from out back and I rested my hand in it for as long as I could manage. He dried it, carefully, then took the honey from the table and spread it over the wound, telling me that there was nothing better for healing skin than a good coat of fresh honey.

"How is it now?" he asked.

"Better. Still stings a bit. I'm so stupid."

He laughed at me the way he always did, with an indistinguishable blend of fondness and patronizing amusement.

"We all burn ourselves, Fetch. It's the best way to learn from our mistakes. It's only when some part of you freezes that you cut the fucker off."

He cackled madly and made us another round of drinks. And another.

Soon, I was so plastered that I couldn't feel my fingers or the cold or much of anything terrible at all.

1

I was as cold as a corpse in the snow. Cold as a debt collector's handshake. Cold like the knife so sharp you don't feel it till it twists. Cold like time. Cold as an empty bed on a Sunday night. Colder than that cup of tea you made four hours ago and forgot about. Colder than the dead memory you've tried to keep alive for too long.

I was so cold, I found myself wishing that someone would fire up the lantern I was sitting in and roast me like a chestnut. Of course, that was impossible. There hadn't been fire in the lamp for over six years. The open-topped torch used to be one of the largest lights in Sunder City, shining brightly over the stadium during night games. Now, it was just a big ugly stick with a cup at the top.

The field had been built above the very first fire pit. During construction, it was an open chasm to the maelstrom below. Once they'd installed the pipes that carried the flames through town, they'd decided that it wasn't safe to leave a gaping hole to hell right at the entrance to the city. They covered it over, and nobody was permitted to build on that plot of land.

Instead, kids used it as a sports field. It was unofficial at first, but then the city installed stands and bleachers, and it eventually became the Sunder City Stadium.

When the Coda killed the magic, the flames beneath the city died too. That meant no heating in town, no lights on Main Street, and no chance of fire coming up between my legs. I was huddled in the cone at the top of the pole with my arms wrapped around myself, ducking down out of the wind.

I hadn't thought about the wind when I'd taken the job. That was stupid because the wind ruined everything. It pushed the cold down my collar and up my sleeves. It shook the lamppost back and forth so I was always waiting for it to bend, snap, and send me crashing to the ground. Most importantly, it made the crossbow in my hands completely useless.

I was supposed to be watching over my client, ready to fire off a warning shot if he gave me a signal that the deal wasn't going smoothly. But firing into this gale, it would be either pushed down into the snow or flung up into orbit.

My employer was a Gnome named Warren. He was down below in his trademark white suit, blending into the snowy ground. The only source of light was the lantern he'd hung off the gatepost.

We'd been waiting for half an hour, him down between the bleachers, me up in my metal ice-cream cone. I tried to remember if this is what I'd planned for when I became a *Man for Hire*. I thought I was going to help those whose lives I'd ruined. Do things for them that they could no longer do for themselves. I doubted that covering a Gnome during an illegal exchange reached the noble heights I'd had in mind.

I'd chewed through half a packet of Clayfields, knowing it was a bad idea. They were painkillers, supposed to make me numb, but the cold had already killed the feeling in my fingers and toes, so numbing was the last thing I needed.

Finally, from the other end of the field, a figure crossed the halfway line. She was wrapped up far more sensibly than I was: thick jacket, coat, scarf, beret, boots and gloves. The metal case she carried at her side was about the size of a toaster.

Warren stepped out from the bleachers, holding his hat in his hands so that it wouldn't blow away.

They stepped close to each other and it would have been impossible to hear their conversation over that distance even without the howling wind. I brought up my crossbow and rested it on the lip of the cone, pretending that my presence at the meeting wasn't a complete waste of time.

Back when there was magic, I would have had access to all kinds of miraculous inventions: Goblin-made hand grenades, bewitched ropes and exploding potions. Now the only thing that could take someone down over distance was a bolt, an arrow or a well-thrown rock.

Warren reached into his jacket and pulled out an envelope. I had no idea how many bronze bills were inside. I didn't know what was in the case either. I knew nothing, which put me on familiar ground.

The woman gave Warren the case. He handed her the envelope. Then they both stood opposite each other while she counted her cash and he unlocked the box.

When the woman turned and walked away, I dragged the weapon back from the edge and curled up into a ball, breathing into my hands.

Then, Warren was screaming.

When I looked back over, he was waving his hat above his head. That was the signal, but the woman was already halfway across the field.

"It's bullshit!" screamed the Gnome. "Kill her!"

Let's be clear about two things: one, I never agreed to kill anybody; two, shooting women in the back isn't really my bag. But if I didn't at least look like I was trying to stop her, I'd have to give up my fee and the whole night would be for nothing. I crouched down, aimed the crossbow a few feet behind the fleeing lady and fired.

I tried to shoot a spot in the snow that she'd already passed, as if I'd misjudged her speed. Unfortunately for me (and the fugitive) the wind changed direction while the bolt was in the air.

From out in the darkness, I heard a *yelp* and then a *thump* as she fell into the snow.

Shit.

"Yes! You got her, Fetch! Well done!"

Warren grabbed his lantern and ran off, leaving me in the dark while he cursed her and she cursed him and I cursed myself.

By the time I'd climbed down the ladder and made my way over to Warren, he'd already snatched back the envelope and was putting the boot in. I pulled him back, and he tumbled onto his ass. Since he was only three feet tall, it wasn't much of a drop.

"Quit it. You've got your money back, don't you?"

I'd hit her right calf. The bolt wasn't in too deep, but a good amount of blood was dripping onto the snow. When she tried to turn over, it twisted the muscles around her injury. I put a hand on her shoulder to hold her still.

"Miss, you don't want to—"

"No!" She span around, lashing me across the face. A line of pain ripped through my skin. Her claws were out, sticking through the tips of her fine gloves and shining in the lantern light. She was a Werecat. When I reached for my face, I felt blood.

"Damn it, lady. I'm trying to help you."

"Aren't you the one that shot me?"

"That was two whole minutes ago. Don't hold a grudge."

I crept closer again and, this time, she managed not to swat me. She looked Human, other than the claws and a glowing set of cat's eyes. No fur or other obvious animal traits. Her hair was long, dark and tied back in thick dreadlocks.

"Hold still for a moment," I said, pulling out my knife. She did as I asked, allowing me to slice the cuff of her trousers up to the point where the bolt had gone through them. The wind and thick material had slowed down my shot so that it only went a couple of inches into her flesh. I pulled out a clean handkerchief and my pack of Clayfields. "Anyone got any alcohol?"

Warren reached into his jacket and fished out a silver flask. I took a sip that warmed my insides.

"What is it?"

"Brandy. My wife makes it."

I splashed it onto the bleeding leg and wiped it dry with the handkerchief. The Werecat gritted her teeth but thankfully didn't attack.

I pulled one Clayfield out the pack and put it between her lips.

"Bite down on the end and suck. Your tongue will go numb but that means it's working."

Her eyes were yellow-green and full of loathing.

"I wouldn't mind getting my ass out of this snow," she said.

"Let me do one thing first."

I crushed the whole pack of Clayfields in my fist. There were still a dozen twigs inside, so when I pushed the cardboard together and rubbed it, I turned them into a paste. The goo slid out of the packet, onto the wound, and I smooshed it around the bolt, trying not to get it on my fingers.

"Is that helping?"

She nodded.

I helped her up onto her one good foot, put an arm around her back, and we stumbled over to the bleachers. She laid down on her stomach while I sat on the bench below and went about removing the bolt.

"Warren, what was she selling you anyway?"

The Gnome was sitting away from us, sulking, but he opened up the case. Inside, there was something that looked like a crystal flower with multitudes of thin petals that spiraled into a sharp point. It was sitting in the metal box on a velvet cushion and I had no idea what it was.

"Some kind of jewel?" I asked.

"Not even," said Warren. "Just glass."

"Then why did you want it?"

"I did not want it! I wanted the real thing."

"The real what?"

Warren slammed the box shut in frustration.

"Unicorn horn."

I stopped working. The Gnome and the Cat sent their eyes to the floor, rightfully embarrassed.

The story goes that there was once a tree whose roots reached so deep into the planet that they touched the great river itself. One spring, the branches bore a crop of rare apples infused with sacred power. When a herd of wild horses passed beneath the tree, they fed upon that fruit and the magic caused spirals of purple mist to spin out from their foreheads.

They were rarely seen and universally protected. The idea that someone would hunt one down to take the horn from its head was barbaric. I looked down at the Cat-lady.

"You've come to Sunder to sell shit like this?" I asked. She didn't say anything, so I poked my finger into her leg.

"Ecchh!" She pushed herself up on her hands and hissed at me. Her claws reappeared out the ends of her gloves, but it was only a threat. For now.

"Where are you getting Unicorn horn?" I asked. "And lie back down or I won't be able to get this bolt out."

She rested her head on her hands.

"I'm not getting it from anywhere. It's just like the Gnome told you. I made it with glass. It's a fake."

At least she hadn't actually been out in the wilderness slaughtering legendary beasts for a bit of bronze. But that was only part of the problem.

"Warren, what do you want with it?"

The little fellow was hunched over, grumbling away in his native tongue.

"Warren?"

He didn't look up, but he spat out an answer.

"I am dying," he said. The wind went quiet.

"We're all dying, Warren."

"But I am dying soon, and it is not going to feel so good." He lifted up his hands in front of his face, opening and closing them like he was squeezing two invisible stress balls. "I can feel my bones. My joints. They are . . . rusting. Cracking into pieces. Doctor says there is nothing to be done. We little folk had magic in our bodies. Without it, something inside does not know how to work." He put a hand on the case that held the false horn. "I found a new doctor who told me that there is power in certain things. He said that a horn is a piece of pure magic and if I bring him one, perhaps he can put some of that power back into me."

I bit my tongue to stop myself from saying the obvious – that he was a gullible fool who was only making things worse for himself. If he was sick, then the last thing he needed was to be out in the cold on a night like tonight, looking for a piece of the impossible.

I couldn't keep my mouth shut for long.

"Warren, you know that's ridiculous, right?"

He didn't say anything. Neither did the woman. I took out the bolt and tied up the wound so the woman could put some weight on it when we walked back to town. The Werecat and the Gnome didn't say anything else, and I finally learned to do the same.

We were back in the guts of Sunder City around midnight. Warren paid me what I was owed and sulked home. Then it was just me and the Cat.

"How's the leg holding up?" I asked.

"Lucky for you, it feels terrible."

"Why lucky?"

"Because I have a swelling desire to kick you in the teeth."

When we hit Main Street, she told me she'd be all right on her own. I guessed that she just didn't want me knowing where she lived. I was fine with that. I was freezing and fresh out of pain-killers, so I wanted to be fast asleep before the medicine wore off.

"Make sure you get a real doctor to look at that," I said.

"No shit. I can probably catch an infection just by looking at you."

She meant it as a joke, but she wasn't too wrong. My building hadn't had hot water since the fires went out. In winter, it takes a stronger man than me to wash every day.

"But thanks," she added. "If I had to be shot by someone tonight, at least it was a guy who was willing to patch me up afterwards. What's your name?"

"Fetch Phillips. Man for Hire."

She shook my hand and I felt the tips of those claws rest against my skin.

"Linda Rosemary."

The night had worked out about as well as it could have. She'd tried to put one over on us, we'd caught her out, she'd gotten an injury in exchange for our wasted time and we all got to go home to bed. It was fair, somehow. Fairer than we'd come to expect.

She walked up Main Street, one hand resting against the wall, and I thought she'd given me just the right amount of trouble as long as I never had to deal with her again.

But Sunder City makes a few things without fail: hunger in winter, drunks at night and trouble all year round.

2

The piss in my chamber pot was frozen.

I hadn't really been sleeping, just scrunched up, wearing every item of clothing I owned, pretending I was dead until the sun came up.

I slipped out of bed and forced my double-socked feet into my boots. When I first moved into my office/apartment/icebox, I'd liked the idea of being on the fifth floor. The view was high enough to make me feel like I was looking over the whole city, and the fall out the Angel door would be hard enough to kill me if I dived out of there head first. It's just one of those little touches that makes a house a home.

Sunder was a sprawling city, though not particularly tall. That meant that my building made an impressive lookout, but it also caught the full force of the wind. The breeze came in through cracks around the windows and the gaps between the bricks. It even forced its way into the room below and came up through the floorboards. I was going to patch the place up when I had the time. Just like I was going to get a haircut and stop drinking and sew up the holes in my trousers before they completely fell apart.

The cuts to my face had been worse than I'd thought. The morning after my trip to the stadium, I'd asked Georgio, the owner of the café at the bottom of the building, to put in some stitches. His shaking hands only made the blood flow faster so I told him to forget about it. Four days had passed since then. Now, I had four red-brown lines down the right side of my face and was hoping they wouldn't scar.

I didn't have my own bathroom. Hence the chamber pot. I picked it up and opened the door to the waiting room and almost bumped into a woman. She was standing there, caught out, like she'd just changed her mind about knocking but hadn't gotten away fast enough.

It was Linda Rosemary.

She was wrapped up in the same set of sensible clothes she'd been wearing the other night: red overcoat, houndstooth scarf and a black, woolen beret off to one side. The first time I'd seen her, it was night and she was covered in snow. I hadn't noticed how tired and broken everything was. On her hands she wore thick, black gloves that favored warmth over dexterity, and there was a flush in her cheeks that complimented the mist coming out of her mouth. Her eyes fell on the cold block of ice I was holding out between us.

"You making coffee?"

I lifted up the pot, attempting to hide the contents.

"Yesterday's. It's gone bad."

She wrinkled up her nose. "Smells like piss."

My embarrassed smile revealed the truth in her statement. We both stood there for a second with awkward expressions stuck on our faces.

"You . . . want to come in?"

She took a long, painful beat. Her eyes wandered from my face to the chamber pot to the office behind me. My bed was still down from the wall, unmade. There were dirty glasses on the desk and a trail of ants passing crumbs across the floor. I'm not sure what they'd found because I hadn't had a meal at home in weeks.

Linda stood rigid with indecision, like when you try to feed a wild animal from your fingers and it has to fight against all its natural instincts if it wants to take the food. Eventually she said, "What the hell," to herself and stepped inside.

She limped a little as she entered, then wiped down the clients' chair with a handkerchief. I ran around behind her, stuffing dirty underwear and tissues into my pockets.

"After the other night," she said, "I asked around—"

"One moment."

The Angel door was behind my desk. A remnant of the old days when the world was magic and a few lucky souls might arrive at your house by a set of wings instead of the stairs. I pulled it open and the wind hit me in the face like a hired goon collecting on a loan. I put the chamber pot out on the porch, wiped my hands on my coat and closed the door again. When I turned around, Linda's face was full of regret.

"Sorry," I said. "I rarely have guests so early."

She pulled a pocket watch out of her overcoat.

"But it's—"

"I'm sure it is. How's the leg?"

"Stitched up like a sailcloth. How's your face?"

"I think there's still some of it stuck under your fingernails. Isn't it fashionable to file those things down?"

She unwrapped the scarf from around her neck.

"I detest that custom. Werecats only trim their claws when they're around other species. My ancestors made their home in the icy hills of Weir. We had our own kingdom. Our own rules. Now that the Coda killed all that, I've been forced to come here."

I couldn't stop my eyes from wandering. Her skin was smooth, and every movement she made was graceful. Her teeth, though she barely showed them, all seemed to be accounted for.

"If you don't mind me saying, Miss Rosemary, you came out of the Coda pretty darn well."

It wasn't exactly a compliment and, from her expression, she didn't take it as one.

"My sister died halfway through the transformation with her brain trying to be two different sizes at once. My father's face was inside out. He lived for a week, silent, being fed through a straw till something in him snapped. There were twenty of us in our house. I cared for all of them, for as long as I could, till I was the only one left. I walked away from my home and eventually ended up here. I know that I'm one of the lucky ones, Mr Phillips, but I'm sorry if you don't find me jumping for joy."

There was a long pause as she let her story sink in to my thick skull. Outside, the wind picked up. The chamber pot scraped along the porch and slid off. A few seconds later, there was a clang down below and someone shouted a few obscenities to the sky.

Her expression never changed. When all was quiet, she continued.

"After the other night, I asked around about you. Heard some interesting stories."

"Really? Nobody has ever accused me of being interesting."

Not exactly true. The story of the Human who escaped the walls of Weatherly to join the Opus does have a few exciting moments. Not quite as juicy as the sequel, when that same kid handed the most prized magical secrets over to the Human Army. Then there's the big finale, when the Humans used those secrets to drain the world of magic.

"I've been trying to work out what it is you do," she said. "You're not a detective. Not a bodyguard. Then someone told me that you investigate rumors of returning magic."

I flinched.

"I don't know who told you that, but they're wrong."

That rumor wasn't just wrong, it was dangerous. Everybody knew that the magic was over and there wasn't any way to bring it back. My job might be a strange one, but I certainly didn't go around selling pipe dreams to dying creatures like she'd tried to do with the Unicorn horn.

"Apparently you found a Vampire a few months ago," she continued. "A professor who managed to find his strength again."

I wanted to lie, but the shock on my face had already given me away. Nobody was supposed to know about Professor Rye, the

Vampire who turned himself into a monster, and nobody was supposed to come knocking at my door looking for answers.

"Not exactly."

"I heard that the Vampire found a way to turn back the clock. He unlocked his old power and you're the one who tracked him down and discovered how he did it. You know a secret that the rest of the world would kill for," she put her hands on my desk, tapping her claws against the woodwork, "and I want to know what it is."

My body tensed. The determined look on her face had hardened and, I have to admit, she scared me.

"I'm sorry, but I can't tell you that."

We stared each other down and I hoped I wasn't going to have to fight her. Then, I realized that it wasn't hostility in her eyes. Not quite. It was something closer to desperation.

"I'm not here to cause you problems, Mr Phillips. I'm here to hire you. Whatever you know. Whatever you found out. I want you to use that information to make me strong again."

I sat back in my chair, happy that I didn't have to fight off a vengeful feline, but stumped about how to explain myself.

"Miss Rosemary, that's not what I do."

"Well, why the hell not? What are you saving up all your energy for? Helping little old Elven ladies cross the street? I want to be whole again, and I don't know who else I can ask for help."

I growled into my mouth and shook my head.

"It wasn't magic that came back into the Vamp. It was something else. He gave in to the same temptation you're feeling right now, and it destroyed him. I hate this new world as much as you do, but there's no going back. You got out of it better than most. Hold onto that, and be thankful."

She curled her fingertips, scraping eight little lines into the desktop, then lifted one hand up to her face.

"*This* isn't me. Your kind killed me. Everything I was and everything I had. I am not this person. In this place." She looked around, disgusted with where she'd found herself. "What even is this place?" A tear rolled down her cheek and the trail it left behind turned to ice. "You don't understand anything, Mr Phillips. Not a thing."

I tried to bite my tongue but after years of exercise it had learned to fight back.

"I know the magic isn't coming back. I know that when people try, it gets them killed. Move on, Miss Rosemary. Find something else to look forward to."

She looked like she was about to rip out my throat. Back in the old days, perhaps she would have. My soft Human flesh wouldn't have stood a chance against a Lycum like her. But that strength was gone. It had vanished the moment the sacred river turned to glass. Instead, she picked up her scarf, got to her feet and walked to the door.

She looked at the sign that was painted on the window: *Man for Hire*. She read it out loud to herself, rolling the words around inside her flushed cheeks.

"*Man*," she said, wrinkling up her nose. "I see what you're going for. You're a Human. You're male. I'm sure it made sense to you. But look at how you live. Listen to the way you talk." She didn't bother turning to look at me, she just stared at the pane of glass and tried to break it with her eyes. "You're a boy, Fetch Phillips. A stupid boy, playing with things that aren't yours. Put them down before you hurt yourself."

Then she was gone.

I looked for a bottle to wash her words out of my head. What did she know? She just wanted to be strong and she hated me for standing in her way. What was I supposed to do? Lie to her? Pretend I could go out on some quest and come back with magic that would make her whole? It was impossible. The magic was gone and the sooner we all accepted that, the better.

Ring.

I picked up the phone and heard the weary voice of Sergeant

Richie Kites. There was some kind of commotion happening behind him, but he kept his words to a whisper.

"Fetch, can you get over to the Bluebird Lounge, up on Canvas Street? Simms wants your opinion on something."

That was a first. Usually the cops tried to kick me out of crime scenes, not call me over so I could take a peek.

"Sure. Why the invitation?"

Richie whispered into the receiver. "We got a dead guy here with a hole in his head, and it wasn't done with any weapon we know about. I don't know what to tell you, Fetch. To me, it looks like magic."

3

I was having the kind of day that wasn't supposed to happen. Beautiful women didn't come knocking at my door before noon, cops didn't call me up to ask my opinion, and nobody blasted anyone else with any kind of magic. Not anymore.

The Bluebird Lounge was a Human-only members' club on Canvas Street in the inner west; a two-story granite building without any signage out front.

The entire Sunder City Police Department was crowded around the entrance. Usually, you were lucky to see more than a couple of cops at a crime scene. In our new, dark world, even murder had become mundane. So it was strange that these police were acting all excited instead of sad and half-asleep. Again and again, this day was different.

Sergeant Richie Kites stood by himself, leaning against the granite. His heavy Half-Ogre body looked like it could push the whole place over.

"What's going on, Rich? You cops so lonely you have to travel in one giant pack these days?"

He shook his head, obviously annoyed by the crowd.

"When they heard the story, every asshole made an excuse to come on down and take a peek. Come inside. You'll see why."

Richie led the way, waving off another cop who tried to protest my arrival.

"He's got clearance. Special request from Simms."

I was just as confused as the cop but I tried not to show it. Some part of me suspected I was being lured into a trap and they were all about to force my hand onto a murder weapon and frame me for the crime. That seemed more likely than them asking me for help.

The walls inside the Bluebird were covered in wooden tiles with white marble inlay. It was a warren of narrow hallways that led to small, private rooms for two to six people. Everybody was whispering. The staff, cops and other "specialists" hovered in alcoves already working on the rumors that would soon take to the streets. The crowd was bigger at the end of the hall and I followed Richie into the room that was getting the most attention.

The booth could barely accommodate two velvet seats and a square, black marble table. There was one empty glass and another half-full, held by the man sitting on the other side. He was impeccably dressed in a three-piece woolen suit with a blue cravat and pocket square. His fingers, wrists and neck were wrapped in garish gold jewelry. His hair was plastered back with shiny product and his eyebrows were groomed into narrow arcs. He must have been quite handsome before someone opened up his face.

One of his cheeks was ripped apart, revealing the bottom row of teeth all the way back to the molars. His fingers were curled in tight hooks, one hand around the glass, the other at his side. The blood had pooled on his jacket above his collar bone, overflowed, and cascaded down his chest. His eyes were open, frozen in shock, and the whites were red and wet.

He was only a dead man. Far from the first, and unlikely to be the last. Even so, there was something peculiar about him. Something more unsettling than the blood or the ripped flesh or the rigor mortis. I was still trying to work out what it was when I heard a voice that sizzled like water hitting hot coals.

"It happened in an instant," said Detective Simms as she sidled up behind me. "Look at the shock on his face. He didn't even let go of his drink."

She was right. Death, as we know it now, is slow. You get sick or too old or too cold, then you cling onto life for as long as you can until the darkness takes you away. Maybe someone beats you in an alley or you get stabbed in the gut and stumble around till your heart stops singing, but even then, you have time to take it in. This guy looked like he was halfway through a story when a bomb went off at the back of his throat.

It was just as she said: instant.

Detective Simms was rugged up in a thick coat, wide-brimmed hat and black scarf. It was the same outfit she wore all year round. Her yellow Reptilian eyes poked out from the dark material and, for a change, they weren't filled with disdain and loathing. Instead, they were asking me for answers.

"Anything you've seen before?"

I looked down at the cold body and then back to her, still confused about the whole situation and why I'd been brought in to share my non-existent expertise.

"Why are you asking me?"

The Detective came in close.

"Fetch, we know what you're doing."

"Really? Could you tell me?"

"You're looking for ways to bring the magic back."

"I don't know who's been—"

"Shhh. We'll talk about that another time. For now, I just want to know what kind of magic could have killed this guy in this way."

There was no point arguing. Not here. And the answer was obvious: no kind of magic, because there *is* no magic and everybody knows that. But, since my role had been explained so clearly, it would have been rude for me not to play along.

First, I focused on the face. That's where the story was being told. His mouth was open in two ways. First, at the front, the way you'd expect it to. Four teeth were missing. Two at the top and two at the bottom. The closest ones to the gap were all pushed back suggesting that the blast had gone into his mouth from the front. The second opening was through his cheek, jaw and even some of his neck. His lips were still together on the left side but the cheek was shredded, hanging open, and the back of his throat was a muddled mass of flesh.

Blood was splattered on the back wall like a celebration. A light spray covered all corners of the room but the reddest spot was right behind his head. There was blood on the table too. Less. Like he'd sneezed it out.

So, what happened?

I drew up a little mental checklist and tried to tick things off. Could it have been done with a weapon? Not a blade; the wound was too much of a mess. Anyone wielding a blunt weapon, like a baton or blackjack, would have brought it down on his head or the side of his face, not stabbed it through his mouth. Besides, it would have needed to be fired from a ballista to do this kind of damage.

I ran my mind through all the creatures I knew; those that had claws and talons, horns and tusks. I suppose it would be possible to strike quickly, so that your victim never saw it coming, but you'd need more than sharp fingernails to blow open a man's face.

A projectile? There was no bolt or arrow to be seen and, again, it was too messy. Besides, if the person you're drinking with pulls a crossbow out their pocket, you'd have to be tougher than a Dragon's dentist not to let go of your cocktail glass.

I got inches away from the horror-show and saw that part of the victim's collar was black and broken. Burned. On the table, between the blood and cutlery, there was a spattering of fine gray powder. Ash.

"Did either of them have a pipe?" I asked Simms.

"Can't smoke in here. The host would have known."

My list was getting frustratingly short. The only thing left was the impossible. So, I said the thing I knew they wanted me to say.

"Somebody summoned fire."

Simms nodded to confirm that she'd come to the same conclusion, but her expression told me something else. She was shocked, yes. She was scared. But beneath all of that, she was *excited*. In her old, golden snake-eyes, I saw the giddy expectation of a young girl ready for adventure.

That terrified me more than anything.

"Let's find somewhere quiet for a chat," she said.

We went into another room, away from prying eyes and ears. Simms sat in a booth, I sat opposite, and Richie stood in the doorway to keep watch.

The Detective unwrapped her scarf and let it fall over her shoulders. Her lips were cracked. The bottom one was bleeding and she licked it with the tip of her forked tongue. Usually, Simms was rigid with authority and impatience. Today, she sat back in the booth and picked at the edge of the table as if she was waiting for an idea to fall into her head. Eventually, I was the one to get the conversation started.

"Who is he?"

Her head snapped up like I'd woken her out of a dream.

"Lance Niles," she said. "New to the city. He's been sniffing around town, buying up property and making friends. Nobody knows much about him but he has plenty of money and already owns a lot of land."

That explained the jewelry on the corpse. Since the Coda, not many locals go around wearing polished stones or expensive suits.

"Any witnesses?"

"Only the host. Niles came in first. A few minutes later, a man joined him. He carried a cane and wore a bowler hat, black suit and thin mustache. They ordered drinks. The other man ordered a second. A few minutes later, the host heard a short, sharp explosion. When he came in, the scene was just like it is now, only fresher. The other guests say the same thing but with even less detail."

The worst thing about the story was that it was almost normal. Six years ago, before the world got shot to shit, those events wouldn't have seemed out of place. Two guys get into a drunken fight and one of them sets off a fireball in his friend's face. It happened. But not in a place like this. Even back then, this club was for Humans. It was the last place you expected to see a bit of sorcery.

"What did the killer look like?" I asked.

"He had some facial scarring, apparently, but the staff can't remember anything specific. No signs of magic: smooth ears, straight teeth, tight skin, flat shoulders, all his fingers in proportion. The staff here are trained to be discerning."

"So, he was Human?"

"Or someone that could pass. Wizard or Lycum would have the most luck. After the explosion, he took off out the back door and nobody dared to follow. No idea which way he went, whether he had a horse, or if anyone was waiting outside. Niles made the reservation and had the membership so the killer never gave a name. We only know what he wore, and I doubt that it will get us very far."

I nodded. It was nothing. Less than nothing. We were all picturing the outfit not the man underneath. Once he changed his clothes and had a shave, we'd be lost.

I finally had to ask the question that was tickling in my mind.

"Simms, why did you ask for me?"

She looked me over like I was the wrong food delivered to her table.

"Rumors move through Sunder like wildfire and you're catching a lot of heat. Whispers about what you found in the library. Things you might know. You're the new poster boy for magical mysteries."

"And you believe that?"

Simms scoffed. "Fetch, if I thought you had real secrets, we wouldn't be here. I'd have you tied up in interrogation with a hot poker between your balls. But if that story is on the streets, then people with rumors will find their way to your door. So, what have you heard?"

It was sound reasoning, I suppose, but a desperate move for a cynical detective like Simms.

"Nothing that would be helpful. Just misguided hope."

"Anything that could be connected to this?" I shook my head. Simms didn't seem surprised. "It was a long shot."

"If I hear anything that fits, I'll let you know."

"You bet you will. Because now that you've seen this, you're working for me. In an unofficial manner, of course."

"I'm confused again."

Simms chuckled, but I couldn't find the joke. "You're in a position to sniff around in places we can't. People will come to you, thinking you're the guy with answers to the questions we don't ask anymore. And . . ." She threw a look up to Richie "And we're gonna get hamstringed on this one. Lance Niles was making a lot of friends before he died. One of those friends was Mayor Piston. I've already been told to report everything about this case to his office. In a few hours, they're going to tell me to leave it alone and by tomorrow he'll have his own dumb thugs on the streets breaking down doors. When that happens, I want to have a dumb thug of my own."

"But why? The Mayor has kicked cases out of your hands plenty of times. You've never worried before."

She leaned in, and there was something in her face I've never seen before. It bordered on embarrassment.

"Because this looks like magic, Fetch. I know it can't be but, if it is, I want to hear about it first."

I nodded. I had to. She couldn't have looked more naked if her clothes were off.

"I can't pay you," she said. "But there will be a reward. You find the guy who did this, or information that leads us to him, and I'll make sure you get compensated. But come to me first."

It was a strange proposal. As earnest as Simms looked, I couldn't forget the dozen times she'd put her boots into my ribs. Then again, I was desperately out of work and it wouldn't hurt to have a couple of cops on my side. But those reasons didn't even matter. I was as curious as she was. After what I'd seen, I wouldn't be able to help myself. I'd be digging around town anyway. If Simms wanted to pay me to do it, I had no reason to stop her.

"Consider me in your service."

We shook hands and her fingers trembled against mine. I had a dozen tired lines I could have used on her. The same things I told every desperate creature who came knocking on my door hoping I could make them whole again. On top of that, I could have opened her eyes to the fact that only an insane person would see salvation in the bloody face of a dead man. I could have told her a lot of things. But I didn't. I nodded, got up, patted Richie on the back, and made my way out onto the street.

The cops outside watched me exit the building like they expected me to make some big announcement, but it was the same story we'd been hearing for six years: death is an ugly son of a bitch and he comes for us all in the end.

Simms was kidding herself. I couldn't prove that now but I would set her straight when I found the killer. The Human, non-magical killer.

Solving this case could fill up my wallet, get Simms on my side and put a murderous man behind bars, but most of all it would show everyone that I wasn't trying to make my living pretending that magic was still out there somewhere. There would be a reasonable, scientific explanation for this murder and I was going to deliver it right to their door.

4

I'd been avoiding The Ditch all winter. A few months ago, I got a whole group of Dwarves kicked out of their homes. In exchange, I was given the deed to a mansion with nothing in it but the frozen body of a long-dead Faery. It's one of those choices that feels wrong every time I think about it but if you gave me another chance, I'd do the same thing again.

To make matters worse, the Dwarves were regulars at my favorite bar and I'd been too scared to show my face there since. They say that time heals all wounds, but that's only if you sew them up first. Otherwise, when you come back, they'll be septic, infected and angry.

I kept my head down as I entered and only spotted one of them. His name was Clangor. His red beard and unwashed hair were twisted into braids and he still wore his steel-worker's uniform, even after years of unemployment. He was sitting at the bar, drinking the cheap dark ale that tasted like grease. He hadn't seen me and I wanted to keep it that way so I turned left towards the back of the building where they kept the dartboards, payphone and booths.

The Ditch wasn't warm anymore. Not without the fire. The patrons moved less than they used to. Laughed less. No dancing or folk music, just quiet customers drinking jars to block out the memories of better days.

The only noise came from Wentworth, one of the few Wizards who styled himself with a mustache but no beard. As usual, he was being a nuisance: leaning on one of the tables, yelling at a bunch of Banshees who, voiceless, had no way to tell him to shut up. My guess was that they were Boris's family. Boris was the post-Coda bartender who'd bought the place cheap after Tatterman retired. He spotted me from behind the bar and his look said, *I'm glad to see you, but you should probably get the hell out of here.*

I didn't like making trouble for Boris but I hoped that saving his family from Wentworth's onslaught might buy me some favor. The Wizard was in the middle of a rant when I approached.

". . . they'll tell you it was an accident, but who really believes 'em? Not me, that's for sure. A convenient bloody accident for them, I tell you what. Taking my powers away. Your voice. All those things that once put us above 'em. This was an attack, I tell you, and it ain't over yet. We're in the middle of a war but our side thinks it's over so we're laying down and letting them win. We need to wake up. We need to fight back with everything we've . . ."

The eyes of all the Banshees looked over his shoulder, up at me, and eventually he noticed.

"Hey, Wentworth. If you've got a moment, I'd love to ask your advice on something."

Some people might be embarrassed, being caught out like that. Not old Wentworth. He scowled right into my eyes to let me know he didn't care that I'd heard him talking about my kind.

"I could be persuaded," he said.

Boris was watching me carefully so I signaled him to bring over two drinks. He knew our usuals, and Wentworth softened his scowl when he saw the glasses being filled.

"Come over to the corner," I said. "I want to keep a low profile."

"Oh, I bet you do."

The family of Banshees nodded their heads in thanks once the Wizard had turned away. We got into the corner booth and our drinks arrived shortly after. Wentworth didn't give me his attention until he'd had a good sip.

"So, young man," he said, with froth falling from his wet mustache, "what brings you before me today?"

I looked down at the burnt milkwood that Boris had put in front of me.

"I want to know how magic worked. Back before it dried up."

"It didn't dry up, boy. Your lot cut it off."

I'd learned a long time ago not to argue with Wentworth over anything. Especially when he was right.

"Yes, before it was cut off. I want to know how spell-casting worked. Specifically, the kind that could be weaponized."

"Since you've had enough good judgment to come to the right source, I will give you the information you seek." He took another large sip, happy to be asked to speak for a change. "There are three types of spells, each performed by a different category of caster. Sorcerers make up the first two classes. Those are Wizards – who are trained, and Mages – who are not. You can tell a Sorcerer by his white pupils, white hair and flamboyant fingers. Most Sorcerers were born to Human parents. Nobody ever proved how or why they happened. The best we could surmise was that atmospheric magic built up in the mother's system and was passed on to the fetus before birth. Many twisted minds tried to force the process but, as far as I know, none succeeded.

"These white-eyed children could sense the energies in the world around them. Natural abilities varied, but the basic talents were often the same: pushing waves in water, conjuring gusts of wind, coaxing sparks to grow into mighty infernos. Sorcerers have an instinctual ability to listen to the magic inside the elements and give them a little push. These talents, when practiced in the wild, create what we call a Mage. Well, they *did*."

He wanted to have another dig but the ground he was going for was all mined out.

"A Mage with training becomes a Wizard. These are the most powerful, skilled and hardest to explain of all the spell-casters." He made a gesture, signifying himself, without any hint of irony. "Some say that only a student of Keats University is a true Wizard. That's where I studied, of course, but I've never been that much of a snob. What's important is the level of ability. Wizard training teaches a Mage to reach out beyond their immediate vicinity, latch onto the elements in their purest form, and summon them into the space between their hands. When I needed fire, I opened up a portal to a world of brimstone and flame. When I wanted to fly, I brought wind from the unknown to under my feet. If I wanted to hold a man in place, I would conjure gravity into my fingertips and draw him into my grasp."

There was no mistaking the relish on the old man's lips. His white-pupil eyes shrank into slits and he gritted his teeth, remembering the days when he had deadly powers at his disposal.

I saw plenty of Wizards cast spells while I was in the Opus. I even heard about the location of this *unseen place*. After I defected to the Human Army, and they convinced me that the Wizards were trying to wipe us out, I handed over that information. When the Humans went out there to dip their machines into the magic, it froze itself up in response.

"So, those are the Sorcerers," I said. "What's the other one?"

He blinked, like he'd forgotten where he was.

"The other what?"

"The other type of spell-caster. You said that—"

One of his fingers was tapping against his empty glass. I got the hint and signaled Boris for another round.

"Oh, the other spell-caster? Yes, yes, yes. The Witches and the Warlocks. Longer fingers than you lot, which gives them certain talents. I'm sorry I left them till last because they really are a disappointment by comparison. All they do, essentially, is play with the magic that has already seeped into the physical world. Like cooking. Mash one thing with another thing and sprinkle on some essence of whatever-you-call-it and, for a moment, it unlocks the magical energy trapped within. A poor substitute for real spells but I have seen a well-stocked Witch create quite a bit of trouble. More than—"

"No fookin' way!"

I looked back over my shoulder. Boris the bartender was halfway to our table, drinks in his hands, and grimacing in regret. He'd been caught out. Back at the bar, Clangor was red-faced, fuming, and pointing his finger right at me.

"What the fook are you doing back here?"

Boris gave me a look that said, *Sorry, but could you kindly fuck off before the little bugger starts smashing things?* I nodded to say that I would.

I hadn't even finished my first drink but I threw enough coins onto the table to cover them all. I stood up, raised my arms in submission, did a respectfully apologetic bow and made for the exit, but the Dwarf was more ale than brains and didn't want to let me go.

"I asked you a question!"

He was off the stool, trembling in anger, with a pendulum of spittle hanging from his lip.

"I just came to see a friend. I didn't mean to intrude."

His tankard hit the doorframe, splashing cheap beer over me and the welcome mat.

"Friend?" He did one of those laughs that's really just an audible sneer. "You don't have any friends, Fetch. Not in this bar. Not in this city. Not anywhere. You know that, don't you?" He stepped closer and I backed up the stairs towards the door. "If I was still as strong as I was before your lot fooked up the world, I'd cut you off at the knees, then the waist, then the neck, then put my foot down on your empty fookin' head and crack it open right here on the floor."

I looked around. I shouldn't have.

I'd worked at The Ditch. Then I'd drunk at The Ditch, every day. I'd bought my share of rounds for every regular in the place and they'd bought their share for me. But their eyes were down. Nobody said anything. Nobody looked up. Nobody was going to argue with the Dwarf.

"Fook off," he said.

And I did.

The last thing that happened to me in the Human Army was getting blasted in the chest by a bolt of pure magic. The scar had never quite healed and the pain occasionally tried to peel open my ribs. Once I was outside The Ditch, I opened a fresh pack of Clayfields and bit down on the end of the twig, sucking in the juice. It helped, but my breathing was still too shallow.

It had been stupid to go back there. I'd talked to enough Wizards in recent years to know that none of their powers were working. Not even a faint wisp of anything. The papers said that in Keats University there were still students and staff trying to unlock the old magic every damn day. If those dedicated experts couldn't crack it, I doubted an untrained Mage had any chance. Even if they did, it was unlikely that the first thing they'd do, when wielding their returned power, would be to blast a businessman in the face with a miraculous post-Coda fireball.

That left the Witches and Warlocks: long-fingered magic users who never summoned anything on their own but only dug the dormant power out of organic matter around them. As far as I knew, none of that stuff worked anymore either.

Well, not like it used to.

I pulled the Clayfield out of my mouth and examined the chewed-up end. It had been magical once. Powerful enough to numb my whole body. Now, it was only a shadow of its former self. Even so . . .

A hint of power remained. An echo that had been packaged up by folks who knew that a piece of old-world magic hidden in the plant might still have some use.

I put the Clayfield back between my lips and drank in the flavor.

Yes, it was something.

5

I called Warren's house and a woman answered the phone. She told me I could find him at Hamhock's Ceramics, a defunct factory in the middle of the manufacturing district. The wind traded shifts with the snow as I made my way across town, wishing that I'd taken the time to sew up the knee of my trousers.

Back when the fires were burning, the snow in Sunder would go brown while it was still in the air. Post-Coda, it waited till it hit the ground before soaking up the ash, rust and rubbish. At least it didn't stink so much. In summer, the sewers cooked like a casserole.

The manufacturing district was a ramshackle mess of factories and wholesale markets on the west side of the city. I did most of my shopping down there, rather than splurge on the Main Street vendors who charged extra for the same product if it was hanging on a better quality hook.

I'd passed Hamhock's many times but had never been inside. It was two stories high with a roller door that filled the whole front wall. Half a dozen chimneys sprouted from the roof, along with a large wind turbine that turned at a hypnotic speed.

The roller door was open and the inside of the building was a mess. Gray-brown slurry covered the ground, walls, machinery, and most of the workers. There were drying-racks full of unfired pottery: vases, bowls and plates. Some pieces were glistening wet, others dry, and a few were cracking into pieces. The turbine on the ceiling was connected to a huge vat full of slip, so that the spinning on the roof churned the mix below, occasionally sloshing it over the sides.

A lot of work had been done here, but something had brought

it all to a stop. The crew were sitting around, unproductive, while a small team gathered around a big metal box in the corner.

Warren, the well-dressed Gnome, was sitting by himself. Years ago, before I knew him personally, he'd been a legend of underground crime. The Coda killed the big players he'd put into power and took the muscle out of his muscle-men. He'd lost most of his savings since then trying to re-establish his empire, and had ended up as just another lone conman who'd seen better days.

Warren might have lost a lot of money and most of his business, but his pride was still intact. His suits were always clean, his hair never more than a week away from the barber, and he had a relaxed way of moving that suggested he had all the time in the world.

But he didn't have all the time in the world. He had very little time left and was scared about how he was going to spend it.

His hat was in his hands and his usual charm had withered. I pulled a stool up beside him and let him speak first.

"When there was magic, my friend owned this factory and he made good money selling plates and vases. That stopped six years ago. But when the autumn floods came through Sunder, and made great pools of clay downstream, I thought we could use the mud to start things up again. But the fire . . ." He waved dismissively towards the metal box. "We cannot make it hot enough. We have tried everything. Even if it costs more to heat the kiln than we could earn selling the pots, we could at least make *something*. But, no. There is nothing here. Just more waste."

We watched the mud-covered workers drag a tray of soggy ceramic cups out of the kiln and throw them to the side.

"Try something smaller," ordered Warren. "Some . . . some thimbles, maybe. And double the wood."

The disheartened potters nodded, and it was almost funny. They were criminals. Hard men who'd once made their living knocking people on the head. Now they were all standing around in aprons and gloves, disappointed that they couldn't complete their teacups.

Almost funny.

"I'm sorry, Warren. I wish I could help you but science was never my strong suit. If I hear of anything helpful, I'll let you know."

He looked up at me.

"So, that *is* what you are doing? Looking into magical powers? I thought you said it was impossible."

"It is impossible. But that doesn't mean there aren't new, non-magical things out there. Like whatever that doctor was trying to sell you."

He scrunched up the brim of his hat. The disappointment of the Unicorn horn was still raw.

"He just had an idea, that's all. He only wanted to help."

"Well, I want to help too. Can I talk to your friend?"

He gave me an expression I'd seen too many times on too many people: when someone knows I'm about to make trouble.

"He is just a chemist. A Warlock who is trying to make a new way in the world, like all of us."

"By selling you lies. How much was he going to charge you to mix up your Unicorn soup?"

Warren put one of his small hands on mine. It shocked me. We'd built ourselves a good routine of teasing and trading barbs. For some reason, he'd decided to break that with a bit of rare sincerity.

"Do not blame him for giving me a dream, Fetch. His heart was full of hope, the same as mine was. I will tell you where to find him, but do not go busting his balls. Just because you have given up, you don't need to bring down the rest of us."

Dammit. I'd done it again. I went to apologize, but Warren didn't need it. He'd said his piece and I'd listened. That would be enough. I tried to remember to do it more often. I put my other hand on top of his and held it. He breathed deeply, looking around at the useless warehouse and the dying business that he'd failed to resuscitate. I didn't need to remind him that things had moved on. He saw that clearer than I ever could. Whatever job I thought I was doing, it wasn't supposed to be going around slapping the last piece of hope out of someone's hands.

So, I said nothing. Warren told me that the chemist's name was Rick Tippity and that he worked a few blocks north. He told me that I should be nice to the Warlock because there were too many folks being mean in the world and they were all doing a better job of it than I was.

"So, be nice," he said. "These days, there is less competition."

6

When the Coda put Witch-doctors and Medicine-men out of business, pharmacists rose up to take their place. The cures are less dramatic, more expensive and not always reliable, but it's the only place left to turn when somebody gets sick.

Warren told me that Rick Tippity, on top of being a Warlock, had also trained as an alchemist. That gave him a rare understanding of the intersection of science and magic, and allowed him to adapt to the new world quicker than others. I'd been to his pharmacy once before: stocking up on Clayfields before they became easily available all over town. It was a tiny store up on Kippen Street; a narrow lane that was suitable for horses but not ideal during that brief period when automobiles made their way into town.

Business on Kippen was far from booming. The only open doors were a laundry, a noodle bar and the drug store in question, which stood out from the rest of the buildings by having clean windows, fresh paint and a sign above the door featuring a big green leaf.

When I walked inside, the first thing that hit me was the smell: a sharp mixture of smoke, chemical fumes and pollen that stabbed its way into my sinuses.

The place had recently been renovated and the chosen color palette was white on white with an extra big splash of white. A bold move in a city like Sunder where even the air can leave a smudge. A wood counter split the room and leaning over it, scribbling into a notepad, was the Warlock I was coming to meet.

Rick Tippity looked like he was in his early forties but his waist-length hair had lost all color. He wore small, silver-rimmed glasses and a white coat that matched the walls. When he looked up, his eyes had the intense focus of someone who was either wildly intelligent or just a touch insane.

He put down his pencil and stood up straight, resting his long-fingered hands on the counter. He had an air of confidence that bordered on arrogance, like he wanted you to know that the end of the world hadn't slowed him down at all.

"Good afternoon to you, sir. What can I help you with today?"

"Two soft packs of Clayfield Heavies, please. And," I pointed to the four cuts slashed across my face, "could you recommend anything to heal these up fast and stop them from scarring? My wife will be back in town next month and I don't think she'll believe that I got them at church."

He smirked to show that he understood, and turned to the shelves behind him. One of the things I'd learned after six years on the job is that if you go into anybody's business expecting help, you'd better be prepared to buy something. Doesn't matter if they're innocent, guilty or inconsequential, they all talk easier after seeing a bit of bronze.

He stood in front of a shelf that held five metal urns, each with a tap at the bottom. He turned one, and it dropped a dollop of pale green liquid into a glass bottle. Before it was full, he moved along the aisle, sprinkled in a couple of different powders, then gave it a shake.

"Rub it into the wound twice a day and again just before bed. The scabs will soften, which will look unpleasant while they're healing, but should be gone in a week."

He dropped the bottle on the counter with the packs of Clayfields.

"Thanks. I don't feel like being kicked out the house in this weather."

"One bronze coin for the Clayfields, another for the medicine."

I made a meal of the process: finding my wallet, not having any bronze coins or bills on hand, so digging around in my coat to make it up with coppers.

"You hear about that business up at the Bluebird Lounge?" I said. "Kind of spooky."

His eyes were already back on his notes, waiting for me to leave so he could finish whatever puzzle he was working on.

"What's happened?" he asked, seemingly uninterested.

"Someone got killed with a fireball to the face." Every coin came from a different pocket. I lined them up on the counter, slowly, as his sharpened eyes came back to the present. "Everyone's already spreading a lot of nonsense about it. I bet you hear that kind of stuff all the time, though, right?"

He knitted his brow so tight he turned it into a sweater.

"What stuff?"

"Folks coming in here asking how to make magic. Mostly to help. Maybe to harm." I picked up the bottle of pale syrup and examined the consistency. "I don't pretend to understand how you do what you do, but at least I know it's science. Other people out there think you're still playing with the good stuff."

He wasn't moving. He was spooked. I just didn't know why. Then he said: "I am."

The room was icy cold. Like someone had opened the door and let the winter wind blow in. But the door was still closed, and we were alone. Just me and the Warlock with the wild eyes.

"Oh, you are? Wow. That's uh . . . What do you mean?"

"There is magic in all things. Always was. Always will be. Your kind might have changed the way we use it but you cannot take it from us. No. Do not think yourself as important as that."

The bastard hadn't blinked in a whole minute. It was my turn to be spooked.

"So . . . you say that there's still magic in all this?" I gestured to the boxes and bottles behind him and spoke in my most frustratingly condescending tone. "But how powerful is it, really? You might be able to pop a few pimples but you can't use this stuff to kill somebody."

The Warlock took off his glasses and put them in the chest

pocket of his shirt. His hands dropped to his sides, below the counter.

"Who do you work for?"

"Nobody. I'm just a guy with some stupid questions. I didn't mean to hit a nerve."

He didn't act like I'd hit a nerve. He acted like I'd strung it over a violin and played it with a razor blade.

"You're with the police," he told me. An accusation that would have been absurd any other day of my life.

"No. Not really. I just want to prove to them that nobody could have—"

His hands came up from under the desk and there was something in his right fist. It looked like a coin-purse or a sack of marbles. As I stepped back from the counter, he tore the package open and a giant ball of fire appeared in his hands.

It roared like a wild animal and the warm air pushed the scream back down my throat. I tripped backwards. In the end, that might have been what saved me.

The back of my head hit the concrete. The fall didn't knock me out but it hurt enough for me to wish that it had. I could smell parts of me that were cooking: hair, eyebrows, and a little skin. I slapped my hands over my face and collar but luckily the flames hadn't set anything alight. It was just a flash. A hot, painful, uncomfortable moment, but over so fast that the damage was only superficial.

It wasn't a killing blow. It wasn't big enough to blow the paint off the walls.

But damn my soul if it wasn't magic.

7

Tippity was gone by the time I got to my feet and I can't say I was disappointed. I wanted to catch the bastard but I needed a moment to compose myself. I'd waited six years to see someone use magic but I hadn't expected it to happen two feet from my face. I wiped my hands through my hair and little burnt bits came off in my fingers. My throat was sore from inhaling a mouthful of hot air and my vision was full of white spots.

There was ash on the ground around me. I looked for the little pouch that had coughed out the flames but it must have been incinerated in the blast. There was a wooden door cut into the counter so I pushed it open and went through to the other side. There were shelves down where the Warlock's hands had been but there were no more magical pouches full of fire.

The notes that Tippity had been writing were indecipherable to me, so I left them for the police to worry about. I did find a metal tin containing plenty of cash so I refunded myself for my earlier purchases and paid for my impending trip to the barber.

There was a phone on the wall but I didn't use it right away. I'd come to the drug store to disprove the magic theory, not encourage the rumor, so I wanted to have something more to say than, *The magic is back and I've got the burns to prove it.*

The aisles at the back of the room were full of tinctures, seeds and bits of bark but nothing that resembled the explosive pouch. Nothing was labeled either, so my search was useless (other than the Clayfield stockpile that found its way into my coat pocket).

Behind the aisles, on the back wall, there was an open door

that the Warlock must have used for his escape. I took my knife from my belt and held it ready as I kicked the door open and looked inside.

It was just a storeroom, cluttered and dark. The only light came from the opposite exit that went out to the alley. My eyes were still sparkling from the attack, so I stumbled over a few boxes before I found a lamp hanging from the roof. I flicked on my lighter and held it up to the lantern. When the wick flared up, I jumped back in shock. Not because of the fire, but because of the giant block of ice at the back of the room with a screaming man trapped inside.

He was lying against the wall as if he'd slid down it after a big night out. The ice was coating his entire body but it was thickest around his chest and head. The water was perfectly clear, but the surface was spiked with tiny icicles.

I had no idea how long ago it had happened. With the storeroom door open, the air was cold enough to slow the melting process to nothing.

It was another Warlock. His long fingers were spread open and his arms were bent, like he'd been pleading with someone when the spell hit him. He was older than Tippity, with shorter hair and a trimmed beard, and underneath his overcoat he wore the same white uniform.

They must have been colleagues. If so, what went wrong?

His hands were empty. Looking around, I saw no signs of a struggle. Crates, bottles and canisters were stacked in abundance but the only things messed up were the boxes I'd kicked over myself.

I opened a few containers and searched for anything that looked more like magic than medicine. Neither of those things were my expertise, so I didn't come to any smart conclusions. I pawed through pots of red soil, boxes of bandages and vials of syrup. I found a bottle of light-gold liquid that looked familiar, so I opened it and had a taste. Tarix sap, and of a better quality than what you find at most bars. I slid it inside my coat. It was harder to hide than the Clayfields but far more valuable.

Nothing else seemed particularly interesting. I stood in the middle of the room, chewed on a twig and looked into the frozen eyes of the man in the corner. There was something familiar about his face. Not because I'd seen him before. It was his expression. The way it was stuck in a horrified moment of realization.

As if it had happened in an instant.

It was just like the body at the bar. Caught by surprise, except this guy had been blasted by ice instead of fire. Death was always busy in Sunder City but it was working faster than usual and with plenty of pizazz.

I went back out to the other room, called the police department, and asked for Simms.

"Can I ask who's speaking?"

"Her neighbor. I'm supposed to be taking care of her cats but one of them has started throwing up everywhere and she told me that if that happened I needed to give it one of the blue pills but the damn thing keeps throwing it back up and the carpet is a mess and I don't know what to—"

"Hold the line, sir."

Thirty seconds later, Simms was growling on the other end.

"Okay, wise guy. What's the deal?"

"Thought you wouldn't want the receptionist announcing my name in front of the whole department. I know the rest of the cops aren't as fond of me as you are."

She huffed, not wanting to concede that I was right.

"What's this really about, then?"

"I got another stiff for you. Drug store over on Kippen Street. I ain't saying it's magic but it's something similar to what we saw this morning. Ice this time."

There was a long pause while Simms ran through the repercussions.

"You know who did it?"

"Pretty sure it's the pharmacist, Rick Tippity. I came in asking questions about Warlock magic and the guy got so worked up he smacked me with a ball of fire."

"Hell. You all right?"

"You'll have to tell me that yourself. I haven't seen a mirror yet."

"Stay safe. I'm on my way."

When I hung up the phone, I heard myself laughing. The adrenaline was leaving my body and I was all giddy from the ridiculousness of Simms talking to me like she cared.

I went back into the storeroom and pulled the flavorless Clayfield out my teeth. There was a dumpster in the corner so I opened up the lid.

Then I stopped.

The room was dark, so I told myself I must be seeing things that weren't really there. I *hoped* I was seeing things that weren't really there, because I *thought* I could see bodies lying at the bottom of the bin.

Praying that it was all in my head, I pulled the lid all the way back and got out my lighter again.

When the orange light hit the shadows, I ran outside to be sick.

8

When Simms and Richie arrived, I took them through the events as quickly as I could. Others would be on their way and Simms didn't want them to see us acting all chummy. I showed them where I got hit, described the pouch and the fire that came out of it, and then took them out back to meet the ice man.

They didn't say much, just nodded along and tried not to jump to any wild conclusions. I'd been trying to do the same thing. There were plenty of ways to make fire. I had a little lighter in my pocket that did it every day. You didn't need magic for that. But ice? Well, ice is different. Sure, there's plenty of it around this time of year, and it wasn't the first time someone had been killed by the cold, but this wasn't some poor homeless guy left out in the elements. It looked to me like someone had summoned this ice the same way as the fireball. If Rick Tippity had opened up a little leather pouch and a frozen blue cloud came out and killed someone, then I didn't know what else to call it but the obvious.

Still, I was no scientist. Just because something is strange, it doesn't mean someone's unlocked the secret that makes magic flow again. And even if they did, I certainly wasn't going to be the first one to say it.

"Seen anything like this before?" I asked.

Both of them shook their heads.

"Not for a long time," said Simms. "The rest of the force will be here soon. Anything else you want to tell us before they let their imaginations run wild?"

"Yeah. I don't know how it's related but look in here."

I opened up the bin. The two stoic police officers peered inside and their faces cracked like china plates on a concrete floor.

The bin was full of little bodies. More than twenty of them. They were tiny: between one to two feet tall, and all skinny and stiff.

They were the bodies of Faeries. All dead. Dried up and devoid of magic.

"Oh God." Richie stumbled out the back door. Simms stared into the abyss.

"What did he do to them?" she asked.

She was talking about their faces. Finding a dumpster of Fae bodies would be bad enough, but they'd also had their heads split open. Someone had ripped open their faces, done something to their insides, and thrown the bodies in the trash when they were finished.

Simms slammed the lid back down. I sucked on another Clayfield. Richie stayed outside swearing.

There were plenty of magical creatures in the world but Faeries were different. In a way, they *were* magic. Pure pieces of the impossible that walked among us. They were limitless in their variety: Brownies, Imps, Leprechauns, Bogarts and Sprites, but when the Coda came, they were identical in their suffering. They froze up, just like the great river itself, and the life faded from their bodies.

Even in a steel-built city like Sunder, away from the forests, you could feel the empty space they'd once filled. I thought the tragedy of the Faeries was that you didn't see them anymore. It turns out that was a better feeling than finding a pile of their lifeless bodies desecrated and thrown into a dumpster.

Eventually Simms asked, "Do you know why there were . . .?" She waved a hand over her face.

I shook my head. "No."

We were quiet again for a while. Richie came back in.

"Was this yours?" he asked, wiping his shoes.

"Yeah. Sorry."

"No, I get it."

Simms wiped her eyes.

"When the rest of the team get here, I'm going to be hard on you, like the old days. I'll ask you why you were snooping around and threaten to bring you downtown if you don't tell me who you're working for. You know the routine."

"Sure."

"I'm sorry, Fetch. I'm sure you're as shaken as I am but the Mayor is already interfering in this case, asking for updates on whatever we find. We need to keep you isolated, free, and—"

The front door opened and the first of them arrived. Ten minutes later, every beat cop, detective, constable and traffic warden had filed in to get a look at the second miraculous kill of the day. Simms, Richie and I stuck to our plan, acting out the play we'd performed so many times before.

I was being a right smart-ass. It was more fun when I knew I wasn't actually going to get dragged downtown for it. I had to pull back my performance when I felt like Simms had stopped pretending to be annoyed and was actually pissed for real. With a warning to keep my mouth shut and not leave town, they eventually kicked me out of there. I was happy to go. I wanted to be as far away from that dumpster of broken bodies as possible.

The image of the Fae was burned into my mind. It was all too sad. Too tragic. Too familiar. My stomach swirled with every step and I couldn't work out if I was angry, afraid or about to weep.

But I knew exactly where I needed to go next.

9

I went past my office to drop off the Clayfields and the sap. I washed my face and brushed the burnt hair from my head. I looked in the mirror and found solace in the fact that only one of my eyebrows had been vaporized.

I dusted myself off. Used some mouthwash. I even put on a clean shirt.

As if it mattered. As if I wasn't going out to see a girl who hadn't had a thought in her head in six years.

I filled a pewter flask with whiskey, tucked it into my coat and made my way uptown.

Everything was perfect.

The gate to the mansion was closed and there weren't any footprints in the snow. The door was shut. The windows weren't broken. The roof hadn't caved in.

I climbed the stone steps, careful not to slip on the puddles that had turned to ice, and took the key from my pocket. I used to leave it under a pot on the front porch. It hadn't felt right to take anything away back then. Now, this place was all mine.

The new key slipped into the new lock and I pushed open the door that I'd recently reinforced. I stepped inside and quickly closed the door to shut out the wind. It was quiet. The air was almost completely still, but not quite. There was a breeze coming from somewhere above: a gap, up on the second floor, that I hadn't fixed yet. I'd already spent a solid week patching holes, covering windows and filling cracks. The house had been left to rot after the Coda and I was the first person to try to get it back in shape. There was always more work to be done but I was happy to do it. For her. For the woman who was waiting on her knees in the middle of the room.

Amari was a Wood Nymph. A Forest Sprite. Larger than the Fae back at the pharmacy but just as precious. Once upon a time, she'd been the most magical thing in the world. You can keep your sunsets, shooting stars and babies' laughter. All those birthday-card ideas of what makes life worth living. I'd trade them all if she could say a single word again.

Amari hadn't moved a muscle in six years. She was stuck in place. Turned to wood. Splintered and cracked. But she was safe. I'd made sure of that. I'd fixed the tiles on the roof and laid canvas in the ceiling before the snow came. I'd even cleared away the vines that had once been wrapped around her body. Unwound them from her waist, snipped them from her limbs and peeled them off the floor with more care than I'd ever put into anything. I'd taken off that rotten nurse's uniform. Cleaned her of bugs and dust. Scraped the moss from her legs and the dirt from under her knees.

She was in one piece, relatively speaking. The major threats to her body had been eliminated. She was still delicate. Too delicate to touch unless absolutely necessary. Even if all I wanted to do was put a hand on her cheek and remember what it was like when it was warm, it wasn't worth the risk.

She was wearing a new uniform. Just like the old one, but clean. I'd done everything that I could. More than was necessary. Because none of it was necessary. None of it mattered because she was gone. It was just her body, abandoned and empty, and there was nothing I could do to bring her back.

That's what I told myself. Over and over. It's what I told every lost soul who stumbled to my door with an idea of going back to a time when the best things in life weren't broken. I kept saying it till I almost believed it.

But then, there was Rye.

I'd been kicked around a basement floor by a three-hundred-year-old Vampire who shouldn't have had the strength to get out of bed. Some kind of power had slipped back into his body and if it could happen to him, then why couldn't it happen to her?

That's why I'd been keeping her safe. Because what would be the point of any of it if we fixed the world for everyone but Amarita Quay?

I sat down in front of her. The whites of her eyes were pale wood. Her pupils slightly darker but just as still. I took out my flask and drank a toast to her beautiful face and the beautiful soul that had vanished from behind it.

I'd seen something evil in the drug store that day. Some kind of unimaginable cruelty. But maybe I'd seen magic. Maybe it wasn't all lost after all. Maybe I was right to keep her safe. Forever.

Just in case.

10

Baxter Thatch was a one-of-a-kind Demon: Minister of Education and History, museum curator, sometimes friend, occasional enemy, an ageless expert on a variety of magical phenomena, and technically neither male nor female. Their magical expertise came not from performing magic, but by witnessing and studying its use throughout the centuries.

Baxter had been working tirelessly to get Sunder City back on its feet. I never knew where I was going to find them, so it was always best to call ahead to the House of Ministers. This time, they informed me that Baxter was over at the Sunder City Power Plant because, apparently, "The fucking thing is on fire again."

The power plant was built on the north-eastern side of the city, tucked behind a hillside like the city was ashamed of its presence. That was fair enough: the plant was ugly, dangerous and unreliable. Mortales, the Human-owned electronics company, constructed it in a rush after the Coda killed the fires. It was a sad replacement for the eternal flames that had founded the city. The plant couldn't produce enough energy to put the factories back in production or even keep the lamps lit on Main Street. It got the phones going and kept the lights on in most homes most nights of the week but if you pushed it too hard it was likely to shit itself.

There were always plans to fix it up but none of them ever eventuated. Every year, the Mayor talked about building more, but that never happened either. All the effort went on repairing the parts that broke or cutting down on the number of accidents, as the steam engine produced fatalities more reliably than it produced power.

The plant was pumping out even more smoke than usual, blackening the already dark sky, and I could smell the building before I could see it.

All the workers were standing on the street as members of the fire brigade ran in and out of the building carrying hoses and buckets of snow. The fire looked like it was almost under control and the crowd seemed more frustrated than panicked. It would likely be a day or two before the plant was up and running again, but every Sunder local had learned to keep a healthy supply of candles on hand.

It was a tired routine, nothing worth writing to the papers about. The plant workers were already making light of the situation and planning how to spend their time off. Baxter Thatch was the only one who looked truly depressed.

Baxter's body was a huge, red and black, seemingly indestructible piece of marble topped with two huge horns. When the Coda happened, nothing about Baxter changed at all. That led some, including Baxter themselves, to worry that they had never actually been part of the magic.

That might be why Baxter worked so hard. They dedicated their days to helping whoever they could. First as a traveler, now as a minister, they always managed to keep up an air of positivity and confidence.

Until now.

Baxter was across the road, sitting on a rock, with their head in their hands. Baxter's typically smooth suit was a crumpled mess. The tie that was usually on their neck had been tossed to the ground. I'd never seen Baxter emotional. Despondent maybe. Disappointed, sure. But nothing like this, especially in public.

"Something wrong, Bax?"

Baxter raised their eyebrows, pushing them into the red-and-black horns on their head.

"Only everything."

Damn. Baxter had been around for an eternity and something

had finally broken them. I took a seat on the rock, pulled out the flask and passed it over.

"It's pointless," they said, after a sip. "Without the fires or the factories, this place is nothing. Yet people keep coming here. Not because of what it is. Not even what it was. But because of what it was once supposed to be. They're coming in search of a story."

"Not all the stories were that welcoming."

They scoffed and passed back the flask.

"Sure, there was crime and poverty before the Coda. But there was balance. There was a reason to wade through the mud and pickpockets and the brown fucking snow. But now?"

Baxter sat back and looked at the sky. I took a gulp, and the lip of the flask smelled smoky.

"I had hope, Fetch. I saw a chance to make something happen here again. Not this . . ." Baxter waved vaguely to the smoldering plant across the street. "This bullshit. But real progress. Industry. Jobs. Now, it's gone."

"Because of this? It was just a little fire."

Baxter raised their hands and gestured to a big ball of nothing.

"He died!"

I looked back to the smoldering plant and the lazy firefighters strolling in and out. Nobody else was acting like there's been a fatality.

"Who?"

"The first person to come to the city with some foresight. With gumption. With fucking money!"

Baxter slammed their fist on a rock and I thought it might split in two.

"Oh. His name wasn't Lance Niles, was it?"

Baxter didn't raise their head. "You heard?"

"No, I saw."

I filled Baxter in about the fireball and the man in the bowler hat. Simms had been right about Lance making powerful friends.

According to Baxter, the Mayor had gone giddy about kick-starting industry in Sunder again and it was all because of the late Lance Niles.

Baxter might have been in a mood, but when I described the fire and the ice that Tippity had weaponized, the brimstone in their eyes flared with excitement. Like me, Baxter had tried to squash the dream of better days under their boots. Dreamers aren't much help to anyone these days. You need a firm jaw, cold blood, and a constant grip on reality to get anything done.

But when I described how flames erupted out of the pouch, Baxter actually smiled.

"I guess that's where your eyebrow went."

"Yeah."

Baxter looked up at the sky again.

"I never thought this day would come."

"Maybe it hasn't."

Baxter stopped, frustrated with my interruption, but smart enough to know that they'd been getting ahead of themselves.

"What else could it be?"

I pocketed the empty flask and chewed a Clayfield.

"I don't know. I never understood magic, even back when it was happening, so I'm the last person who should claim to be an expert on it now. But from how it was explained to me, magic flowed. It was alive. This feels more like the shadow of magic. A bit left over after life dries up."

"But you did see him conjure a spell, didn't you?"

"Maybe."

It wasn't all that I saw. I didn't want to describe what was in the dumpster, though. I had no problem talking about Lance Niles in the Bluebird Lounge with his head all blown out and bloody. It wasn't pretty but it was life. We're all gonna bite it someday, and none of us will look beautiful when it happens. But those perfect little pieces of magic, piled up on top of each other in the dark? That was a real tragedy. The kind of thing that sticks to you once you know about it. I didn't want to taint Baxter with that knowledge if I didn't have to.

"Where would someone find a Faery?" I asked. "And don't say the Governor's mansion because, if we've done things right, nobody is ever going to find anything there."

"Nowhere. You know that. They're gone."

"But what about the corpses? I never thought about it before, but I didn't see any Fae bodies after the Coda. I guess I assumed they'd just vanished; turned back into pixie dust or something. But that didn't happen to Amari and it turns out that didn't happen to a lot of them."

Baxter lost the last of their enthusiasm.

"What do you mean, a lot of them?"

I shook my head. Eventually, Baxter realized that they didn't really want an answer, so they went on.

"There were never many of them here. Most lived down in the slums: refugees from ruined forests who were trying to make a new start. Not high creatures, of course, but simple Fae like Imps and Bogarts. It really stirred things up when some of them tried to look for work in this industrial world."

"I remember."

"Well, something you won't remember because you were still locked up in Sheertop is that a few days before the Coda, all the Fae left the city."

I didn't know that. After I deserted the Human Army and was caught by the Opus, they threw me into a magical prison that was supposed to hold me for the rest of my life. Obviously, that didn't happen. The Coda crashed Sheertop's security system and I strolled out the front door without being stopped. By the time I got back to Sunder, the end of the world was a few days old.

"Where did they go?"

"South-east. Apparently there's an old Fae church in Fintack Forest. I have no idea why they all left together just before the world went bad. Maybe they sensed something the rest of us didn't know about yet."

It wasn't impossible. Faeries were a perfect blend of magic and matter, closer to the sacred river than any other creature. Perhaps, when a hundred Human soldiers marched onto the sacred mountain and attempted to harness its power, the Fae instinctually knew that something wasn't right.

"Can you point me towards the church?" I asked.

"Why?"

"So I can catch the man who killed Lance Niles."

The fire in Baxter's eyes turned blue behind their glasses.

"Come with me."

We went up to the House of Ministers and into a room marked *Maps and Planning.* The walls were lined with giant shelving units, stacked with long, thin drawers.

Inside each drawer was a map of the surrounding areas. Each design was different, depending on the race that drew them.

"The Fae didn't really keep maps of their own," said Baxter, "at least, not in a way that we'd be able to read. Luckily, a studious Elf went to the effort of translating them."

Baxter pulled out a large, faded sheet of paper and draped it over the desk. Sure enough, south-east of the city, a few miles from the entrance to Fintack Forest, there was a lone structure marked with magical runes.

"That's the church?" I asked.

"I believe so. Though I don't see what this has to do with Lance Niles."

"Good. You've had enough bad news for one day."

I copied down the location of the church and thanked Baxter for their help. I didn't want to imagine what was out there. The journey wouldn't be easy and there might be nothing but a nightmare at the end. So, I set my thoughts on Rick Tippity. If a trek into the wilderness to find a Faery graveyard in the middle of winter brought me one step closer to catching that killer, then there wasn't anything else I wanted to do.

11

There was no road to Fintack, just a path that peeled off from Maple Highway and rolled east over low hills. The sun had finally decided to show itself at the last minute of the day, like a date who acts coy all through dinner but blows you a kiss as they walk out the door.

I'd learned from my mistakes and stopped by a second-hand clothing store before I left the city. I was wearing four layers on top and some tights beneath my trousers. My socks were thick and the Chimera fur in my coat was still as dense as the day it was ripped from the beast's back.

Without the old lights illuminating it, Sunder soon faded into darkness. The clouds thinned out to let the full moon shine through and give me an outline of the path to follow. I made good time, only stopping to piss or get food from the bag. Georgio had caught me on my way out the building and been kind enough to pack me a midnight snack: nuts, dried berries and slices of chewy sausage.

After two hours of walking, a colony of bats crossed the sky overhead, following the path towards the forest. There were more than fifty of them, screeching like hags and flapping their leathery wings.

Over the next half an hour, the tension dropped out of my body. First, it was the tight little muscles in my brow. Then my jaw and down my neck and shoulders. Knots untwisted around my spine. My arms swung at my sides and I breathed deep, letting the cool air into my lungs. I was alone. Not alone like in my office, where someone could knock on the door at any moment. Not alone in a bar, where I might be lonely but was still surrounded by strangers. Properly alone. No Humans. No ex-magic creatures either. Nothing with memories or opinions. Nobody to judge the things I'd done or the things I was about to do. Not the mistakes I'd made or the stupid, naïve things I'd said. I didn't mean anything to anyone. I was just part of the scenery, shuffling along without a history or a future that mattered to anyone at all. The far-off stars couldn't see me and they didn't care. Nobody cared. I could lie down right there in the dirt until my breathing slowed and stopped and it wouldn't matter to anyone.

It was beautiful.

At the edge of the forest, I found an old hunter's cabin with nobody home but a family of spiders and a pink-nosed possum.

"Got room for one more?" I asked.

The residents didn't object so I closed the door. It felt good to step out of the wind for a while. There was a canvas hammock in the corner that was dirty but intact. I slapped off the dust and hopped in. It wasn't as comfortable as a bed and it didn't exactly hold the heat but it got me off the ground and raised my legs to ease the pain that had crept inside them. The cabin was dark and quiet and it didn't take me long to fall asleep.

Crunching. The rip of flesh and crack of bones.

Edmund. Albert. Rye.

I could hear him. His mouth full of broken teeth and bleeding gums, chewing the bones of young girls and sucking out the marrow. He'd wanted magic. Instead, he became a monster. A devourer of sweet creatures. A curse on himself and those he loved.

He was standing over me. Murder on his breath. Eyes full of oblivion. Laughing because he'd been freed from the burden of trying to put things right.

Then the darkness turned to red. Then gold. Sunrise. I remembered to open my eyes.

The possum was chewing on the biggest spider in the web. Little legs stuck out from her muzzle, giving her extra whiskers.

"Save some for me?"

The possum didn't respond but I'd slept with my bag in my arms so it was easy to reach inside for a handful of berries and have my breakfast in bed. The possum and I shared our meal, then I wished her well and hit the path again.

The mist and trees were thick but the path was clear enough that I could keep a nice pace and get my blood pumping. I had to watch the ground, though. If I stared ahead, into the white, I lost my sense of reality. There were noises all around. More bats and possums, probably. Maybe wolves. I had a knife but not much else. Worried that predators might smell the meat, I ate the rest of the sausage, threw away the paper it was wrapped in, and washed my hands on a patch of wet grass.

There weren't any leaves on the trees. Maybe because of the Coda. Maybe just because it was winter. I couldn't tell. Branches reached out over the path like Witches' fingers. I ducked under them, sometimes. Once, when I was looking down at my feet, a branch scratched a scab from one of the cuts on my forehead. I was just about to start swearing when I saw someone on the path, waiting in the mist.

They were right on the path, just ahead of me. I held my breath but my heart slammed against my ribs so loudly that I feared the figure in the shadows must be able to hear it.

He was looking right in my direction. Just a silhouette; gray against white. Shorter than I was. Not Tippity. A friend of his? A scout?

He hadn't said anything. He hadn't attacked. Perhaps he hadn't noticed me. Or if he had, he wasn't sure if I was friend or foe.

I bent my knees and dropped the bag as quietly as possible. The figure didn't react at all. I pulled the knife out of my belt, muffling the sound of metal against metal by keeping it under my coat. I tucked my right hand into my pocket and slipped my brass knuckles over my fingers, then I stood up and spoke deep, plain and clear.

"Hello."

Nobody answered but the wind. It shook my clothes and whipped against my eardrums.

"You waiting for me?" I asked.

Still nothing.

I moved closer, tense as a tripwire.

"I'd rather talk than fight, if I have a say in the matter. But I'm prepared for both if I don't."

I squinted, searching for features, but something was wrong. The mist swirled around the stranger. Loose clothing moved in the wind but the thing beneath them was rigid. He had one hand on a cane and the other was outstretched. His thin fingers were spread open, but they were too motionless to be alive. It was a statue, dressed up in fine formal clothes, left out in the middle of the forest.

Still, I couldn't make out its face.

I stepped closer again. He was even shorter than I'd first thought; only a few feet high. The outfit was tattered and rotten and insects had moved into the folds of cloth. I came through the mist, my knife at the ready, and realized why his face had been so hard to see.

He had no face. Not anymore. There were ears on either side and something that resembled a chin but everything in between had been peeled apart. It was a creature of the Fae. A poor fellow who had died when the Coda came, and then an unofficial autopsy had been committed on his body, just like the Faeries in the back of the pharmacy.

His cracked and open face was gruesome in a clean kind of

way. There were no organs or blood, like there would be if a Human had been ripped to pieces. It looked more like someone had carved out an old tree stump. The flesh of the Fae's head was firm, like petrified wood, but filled with tiny tunnels. Looking closer, I could see that his insides were marbled with silver; just the faint glimmer of something shiny, like spider's web or starlight, threaded into his muscles and bone.

I felt sick, but also kind of grateful. When I'd returned to Sunder after the Coda, Amari had been waiting for me. She'd been safe inside the mansion, not left alone, out in the wilderness, to be bug-eaten and butchered like this lost soul.

There was nothing to be done for him, of course. Nothing to be done for any of the creatures who lost their lives when the magic went away. Nothing to do but pat him on the shoulder and go further into the woods to see if he had any friends.

Then, I noticed that it wasn't a cane he was leaning on. It was a signpost, but the marker on the top had been broken off. The post was positioned on the right side of the path, beside a gap through the trees that might have once been a walkway. I followed the direction through an overgrown archway and soon found two more tiny bodies. Imps, I think. They were holding each other, half covered in snow, just as frozen as the first one. One of their faces was split the same way, the other was missing her head completely. These were forest creatures. That meant that, unlike the creature on the signpost, their bodies were still growing. Little vines had crawled out from their shoulders and back, wrapped around their bodies, and tightened, crushing their limbs. Under the snow, the foliage must have spread out to reach the nearest trees because there were leaves there; little ones, born from the threads of vine that sprouted out from the creatures decomposing on the floor. It was all too familiar. All too sad.

I pushed my way through the woods to meet more death and more desecration. There were statues lying in the path and leaning against trees, all with no eyes. No faces. Just empty heads on rigid bodies frozen in pantomime gestures of pain. The path opened up and the mist thinned out so that as I came into a clearing, I could see the whole silhouette of the church.

It was forty feet tall without a straight line to be seen. The walls were braided branches, woven together in unimaginable patterns all the way from the ground to the tip of a pointed tower. It wasn't just impressive for its size; it was a piece of art. There were shapes in the woodwork: faces, spirals, runes and words. All three-dimensional. All beautiful.

Forest Fae had power over plants. Usually, it was only used in small ways, like asking a flower to bloom early or ripening a piece of fruit. I had no idea what it would have taken to create this kind of miracle. Was it a group of skilled Wood Nymphs working in tandem or one particularly gifted architect with plenty of time on their hands? Birds had built their nests on the sills of the glassless windows and around the pointed spires that cornered the roof. Every inch was filled with minute, perfectly designed details. Past a certain height, I couldn't tell which shapes were part of the architecture and which were Faery inhabitants frozen in place.

The garden around the church was full of huddled creatures and I was relieved to see that some still had their faces. Whoever was tearing them apart, they hadn't yet finished the job. I stopped looking too closely and pushed myself forward, hoping that the bodies would all be whole after this point.

When I went inside, everything got worse.

12

More bodies. Hundreds more. Packed into the church like little sardines if someone left the lid off and they all dried up. Most were tiny, like children's toys. Others, for their size, could have been Human. The same pained expressions were stuck on all their faces and their bodies were cracked and wrapped in vines.

I didn't want to be there. The ones without faces filled me with hate for the man who broke them. The ones with faces made me hate myself instead. Some of them were screaming. Some of them were shattered into pieces. All of them were dead.

It looked like Baxter was right. The Fae must have sensed something. Somehow, they'd known about the Coda before it happened and decided to flee the city. But why? Why was it better to die out here in the middle of the forest rather than back in the city that had become their home?

There was a table in the middle of the room. High, like a podium. A few of the larger Fae were leaning over it. Others had collapsed against the base. It was covered in sheets of yellowed paper. Being a church, I thought they might be some kind of spiritual text. No. They were letters, orders and lists. The Fae hadn't just been hiding out here. They were preparing themselves for something important.

A small map sat at the center of their focus. As Baxter had explained, Fae language wouldn't be easily decipherable to an uneducated lug like me. They have their own ideas about space and distance and their sentences look more like snowflakes than speech. I flipped through the rest of the pages, trying not to tear the frail paper.

Everything was indecipherable until I turned over a letter that was different than the others. It was the same message written over and over again, translated into every language imaginable: Elvish, Dwarvish, Gnomish. Most shockingly, the handwriting was familiar. I blew away the dust and held the parchment up to the light.

> To Every Creature of Magic. Every Defender of light. Every Ally to the natural world.
>
> The Humans have attacked Agotsu, killing the Echoes and claiming the mountain as their own. We call on the assistance of every able body. Every creature connected to the source. We must take back the mountain, protect the river, and defeat the villains who have committed this crime.
>
> Ready your forces. Prepare yourselves. Meet us at the mountain.
>
> High Chancellor Eliah Hendricks
> The Opus

The letter fluttered in my shaking hand.

I was the one that had led the forces to the mountain. But when the fighting started, I'd fled from the battle and been captured by the Opus who threw me in prison till the magic of the world drained away.

We'd learned to think of the Coda as a single moment but, of course, there had been a battle beforehand. Or at least the preparations for one.

The Fae community of Sunder City had got word of the attack and come to the church to prepare their forces before heading off. But the end had come too soon. Whatever the Humans did on the mountain, they didn't waste any time.

There are some questions you try not to ask yourself. Even if you spend every second trying to push them away, they never quite leave. They sit in the shadows with sharpened teeth, waiting for a chance to bite down on the most tender little pieces of your brain. I'd found Hendricks' handwriting while my guard was down, and all those hungry questions scurried in.

Some part of me had secretly hoped that he'd never found out what I'd done. That the Coda took him out before he heard the news. But he was High Chancellor of the Opus. When the Human Army invaded Agotsu, he would have been notified first, and known in an instant that I was the one who'd shown them the way.

Was he still planning his response when the Coda happened? Or had he already marched off to the mountain, hoping to take it back? Maybe the battle had already begun. Perhaps he died in a skirmish before the great sadness stripped the world of its beauty. Maybe it would have been better that way.

Hendricks was three hundred years old. I knew younger Elves who didn't survive the first week. Hopefully that meant it happened fast. Nobody could dance to life's tune like Eliah Hendricks. The worst death I could imagine for a man like that would be to lie down by the side of the road and watch every beautiful thing fade from existence without saying goodbye.

At least the letter explained one thing that had been bugging me. Baxter had said that all the Fae left the city, but Amari was still there. If all the Faeries had sensed that something was wrong, then why was she the only one left behind? It turns out that it was all my fault, again.

It was no secret that "Hendricks' pet Human" had left the Opus and defected to the Human Army. But he wasn't the only one whose reputation I'd compromised. The magical population of Sunder City had seen me standing at Amari's side too many times.

As a precaution, I can understand why the rest of the Fae wouldn't have told her their plans. Maybe they thought we were still in contact. If so, bringing her to the church could have tipped me off to the incoming attack.

So, they left her alone, in an abandoned mansion, because she'd committed the crime of trusting me.

Just like every shitty thing that had happened in the last six years, these creatures were here because they'd hoped to stop the disaster that I'd started. They were dead because they hadn't done it in time. Their bodies were being ripped apart because . . . Why? That was the piece I still didn't understand. The one terrible thing that I still had a chance to stop.

Tick. Tick. Tick.

The sound came from all around the church, like every little creature was clicking their tongue in disapproval. Then it got louder. Faster.

Rain landed on the snow outside and the roof above. I waited for it to leak into the church but the walls were made of a million intricately wound branches and the architects had sealed them tight. The church stayed dry and almost warm. If I tried walking back to Sunder now, I'd end up like that frozen Warlock, trapped in a block of ice by the side of the road. Besides, it might just pay to wait.

If Rick Tippity was using Faery bodies for his experiments, he'd left them all behind when he fled from the pharmacy. He'd need to restock. He'd need to come out here.

And I'd be waiting.

13

I should have brought more food. I should have kept that cross-bow. I should have joined the circus when I was a fifteen, fallen off the trapeze, and saved everyone a lot of trouble.

I sat at the back of the house of horrors, blending in with the frozen Fae and doubting myself. Maybe the broken faces had nothing to do with the Warlock. Maybe it was some kind of animal. Perhaps there was something in the Faery heads that was tasty to a hungry woodland creature and they cracked open the faces like the shell of a nut to nibble at whatever was inside.

Maybe Tippity just came across a few discarded corpses and picked them up to mix into his potions. Just another strange ingredient in his collection of experimental odds and ends, same as the tarix sap and Clayfields.

I nodded off and woke up again countless times; hungry, angry and wishing I'd never seen this place that was too full of too many hard truths. When the rain eased up, I could hear the world outside. Birds were singing. The wind knocked branches from the trees. Then, finally, there were footsteps, slamming down the freshly thawed path.

Rick Tippity ran inside with a hooded cloak wrapped around him. He was wet, irritated and full of fury. When I'd seen him back at the drug store, he'd been wearing a thin mask of sanity. That was long gone. He was muttering to himself. Swearing. Angry at the world. Rick Tippity was an intelligent, prideful man whose plans had been thwarted, and that made him one of the most dangerous bastards around.

He wasn't expecting company. I hadn't covered my tracks but the rain had done that for me. Tippity searched the room, not for enemies but for victims. Like a gluttonous guest at a breakfast buffet, he surveyed the room for the ripest fruit.

A young female Sprite sat cross-legged in a group of already mutilated Imps. Her flesh was solid and dark, like burnt stone. She'd been a creature of fire, once upon a time; a Nymph that could move among flames, live in boiling springs, and spread forest fires beneath the trees to cleanse the floor of underbrush.

Tippity leaned over and examined her face in a way that made me uncomfortable. I felt like I was looking into a carnival mirror: familiar but warped, and not my best angle.

Tippity reached inside his cloak and removed a metal tool that was the love-child of an ice pick and bottle opener. He brought it up to the fire-girl's face and I realized with horror that he was deciding on the perfect spot to make his first incision.

I tensed but I didn't move. I wanted to stop him. Of course I did. But, as much as I hate to admit it, I was far too curious about what he was going to do.

The Warlock put the end of the object up against the woman's eye socket, then slammed the back of it with the heel of his hand. There was a tiny cracking sound as it punctured her head. Then, he twisted. The bridge of her nose snapped away and part of her face crumbled into her head.

My brass knuckles were on my right hand.

He put the thin end of the object inside her face and pushed back against her skull till something snapped.

I had my dagger in my left hand.

He pushed down with the sharp end, inside her skull, levering the tool against her jaw. Then he pulled, hard, and her face split down the center. Her cheeks hit the floor and the rest peeled back, revealing something shiny inside.

It was a jewel. Orange-red, with spikes coming out on all sides like a sea urchin. When it caught the light, it sparkled.

Tippity reached out with one gloved hand. His fingertips slid over it—

And I was running.

I surprised him but he was quick to react. He spun around and turned the tool into a weapon, holding it like a dagger. His other hand fumbled in his pockets, surely searching for another pouch of impossible magic. I ignored the metal instrument and went to tackle him before he found what he was looking for. Better to be hit with the weapon you know than the one you don't.

The ice-pick-bottle-opener came down on my skull and cut me open, probably down to the bone. I had to ignore it. I was already in the air with all my weight coming down on his body. I reached out, struggling to keep his other hand immobilized. We crashed through the fragile Faery statues and Rick Tippity landed on his back among the broken bodies. I crunched down on top of him with one hand around his throat and the other holding his right forearm. His hand scrambled around in his pocket, like he was going for a last-minute fiddle.

"Stop struggling," I said.

"Get your hands off—"

I pushed down on his throat, hoping to deprive his lungs of air or his brain of blood. His dancing right arm became more desperate, but I moved my knees across his body till I had him pinned.

Things settled down. I finally had control.

Then, Rick Tippity's crotch exploded.

It was blue and orange, all at once. A gust of hot air blasted past my face but, at the same time, my hand was suddenly covered in snow. I jumped off Tippity, fearing both burns and frostbite, while patting down the flames on my chest with my freezing left hand.

Tippity was screaming. There was steam shooting up from his body and half of his trousers were gone. Nothing looked fatal, just painful enough to stop him from running away anytime soon.

I held up my left hand and clenched my fist. I could move it, which was nice, but there wasn't a lot of feeling in my fingertips. I blew on them and rubbed them together.

My burns weren't so bad. There were holes in my clothes but I was wearing so many layers that the fire had barely kissed the skin. I felt my face with my good hand and found that my other eyebrow was fried. That pissed me off. Eyebrows, like toilet paper, are things you don't miss till you reach out and realize they're gone.

Tippity stopped moaning so I kicked him in the ribs to start him up again.

"Seems your recipe is a little unstable, Tippity. I think I should find myself another pharmacist."

New fury filled his eyes. Before he had a chance to speak, I put a knee on his chest and knocked the wind out of him. I stayed there while I cleaned him out; from top to bottom, like the well-trained mop-boy I was.

Around his neck he wore a silver chain. The pendant on the end had sharp edges so I snapped it off and threw it away. Cloaks are known to hold all kinds of secret pockets so I ran my fingers along every part of the lining. I didn't find any hidden compartments, just one large cavity holding a crust of stale bread.

Tippity struggled but he couldn't push me off. He wasn't in great shape and I wasn't letting him get enough air to settle himself.

His right trouser pocket was gone in the fire. In the left one, I found two of those little leather pouches, just like the one that had exploded at the drug store. I gave him the full once-over, searching for blades or hidden objects against his skin. I ran my fingers behind his neck, under his arms, all the way down to his feet. I removed his boots and shook them upside down but only a few small stones fell out.

A satchel hung over his body on a long leather strap. I cut it loose and looked inside.

It was a medical kit full of powders and colored liquid. Amari had carried something similar when she was working as a nurse.

I looked through the vials and packages, searching for anything familiar. Luckily, some of the packages had labels on them because Tippity sold his drugs to civilians (unlike Amari who only needed to prepare the medicines for herself).

I found two small vials; one black, one white. The black one had a picture of a closed eye on the label. The white one had a similar sticker but the eye was open.

"Leave my . . . things alone . . . you oaf."

Tippity was digging his nails into my leg, so I wasn't too concerned about accidently giving him the wrong gear. I opened up the black "eye closed" bottle, grabbed a chunk of Tippity's long, gray hair and lifted up his head. He thrashed around so much that I almost lost the bottle but eventually I got it up to his face.

When I lifted my knee off his chest he couldn't resist taking a deep breath.

"You moron," he spat. "You don't have any idea about anyth—"

His eyes rolled back and his head felt twice as heavy. The mixture sure was potent. I'd been planning to put it in his mouth but the fumes had done the job on their own. I held the vial at arm's length while I put the top on and tucked it back in the satchel.

I needed to tie Tippity up, but my curiosity demanded to be dealt with first. The glowing ball from the Fire Sprite was easy to find in the darkness. I stepped back along the path that we'd cleared during our fight, through broken bodies and splintered Fae, and got down close to the little red star.

It was the color of a campfire or stained-glass window and the light inside moved like it was liquid. It was only the size of a berry, but covered in barbs. Some of them were sharp, others had been snapped off, making them shorter and easier to touch. When I scooped it up, it was warm. Almost hot. I cupped the precious jewel in my hands and the heat thawed out my frozen fingers.

This was the magic from inside the Faery: pure, precious and still beating.

How much of the creature was contained in that little capsule?

Was it just the elemental power, or something more? Thought and memory, perhaps? Personality? The bodies of the Faeries were frozen but these little glowing orbs had survived. Waiting for . . . what?

I wrapped the little red gem in soft bark, then a piece of leather, and tucked it into the satchel. I fixed the strap, put the bag over my shoulder, and when the ruby was safe, I pulled one of the little pouches from my pocket.

The pouch itself was nothing special, just leather with wool padding on the inside. Nestled in the padding was another orb.

This glass globe was made by hands, not nature, and had been filled with a translucent, slightly pink liquid before it was sealed shut. The liquid was quite unremarkable. Some kind of acid, I imagined. Strong enough so that when the glass shattered and the acid touched the Faery-essence, the gem would dissolve and the magic would be released.

I put the pouches in my inner jacket pocket, away from the satchel that contained the red gem. I didn't want to blow myself up the way the Warlock had.

Tippity was still passed out. Where his trousers had been ripped open, there were burns underneath: fire and frost had hit him all at once, making a mess of the skin and probably the flesh beneath it. I would have felt sorry for him if I hadn't seen the hole in Lance Niles's head or the screaming Warlock in the block of ice or the way he'd smashed open the innocent face of the Faerie only moments before.

There were plenty of vines scattered around the church. Some were dry and fragile but others had some green in them. I cut a few from the Forest Sprites, shaved off the leaves, and wrapped them around Tippity's hands and throat. Then I tied a long rope of vine around his neck like a dog collar and waited for him to wake up.

14

The journey back to Sunder was even more painful and tedious than the way out. I was grateful that the rain had hidden my tracks, but it also turned the snow to slush and made the whole path a frustrating mess. The showers came and went, never leaving long enough for anything to dry. There was no food, no shelter, and I was sore as hell. The hand that had been hit by the blast was cramping and the top of my head was a crusted scab full of wet hair.

Then, there was Tippity.

He was a whining, bitching, indignant piece of work, stumbling along on the end of his leash. Just because it was logical that he wouldn't want to follow me, it didn't make it any less frustrating. His wounds weren't going to kill him. The blast hadn't gone deep and his skin had been cooled at the same time as it was burned, so it was uncomfortable and painful but walking wouldn't do him any damage. I told him that, when he protested, but he didn't listen. Reason didn't work on him at all. Or bargaining. So, I resorted to punching him in the balls. Sometimes I mixed it up; socking him in the guts or slapping him across the cheek to keep him on his toes, but it was the kicks to the bollocks that kept him moving.

We were both beyond exhausted but it turned out that the liquid in the white bottle (the one with the open eye) was quite the stimulant. I took a whiff, gave one to the Warlock, and it put a spring in our step for a good half-hour. Unfortunately, it also got him ranting like a street-side preacher after ten cups of coffee.

"You like this, don't you? The mud and the struggle. I can tell. You pretend to be upset about what happened but really, you're thriving. Because now this is your world. Just as simple as you are. Just as mean. Do you have any idea the path I was on? Decades of study. Of progress. I was on my way to changing the world. But your kind couldn't hack it, could you? You'd been left behind and you couldn't catch up so you stopped the game. But it will all happen again. I promise you. We will find another way to rise above. I already have. You've only seen the beginning. Before long, you'll be back at the bottom of the—"

I yanked the leash. Tippity tripped over and landed face down in the mud. It was even more satisfying than I'd imagined.

We were back at the hunter's cabin by sunset and I was sad to discover that the possum had moved out after clearing the place of spiders.

"Lie down," I said, pushing Tippity towards the hammock.

"You're giving me the good bed?"

"It'll be easier than pinning you to the floor."

I tied him to the hammock, wrapping the vines around his body as many times as I could. When he was all tucked up, I gathered pieces of cloth from around the room, shook them free of insects, and made myself a sad little bed of rags.

"Why do you care what I do to the Faeries?" asked the Warlock, all wrapped up like a homicidal sausage roll. "They're already dead, and your side has a lot more to do with that than I do."

"I'm not gonna spend my night explaining why desecrating corpses might be frowned upon. If you can't see why it's a problem, then you've got more bugs in your brain than I thought. And let's not forget about your buddy back home. Did he piss you off so much you had to blast him with ice?"

He gave a melancholy sigh, like I'd reminded him about some beautiful, long-ago summer.

"Jerome wanted to walk down the same path as I am. He was an innovator, like me. He just . . . made some mistakes."

The ice man's screaming face pushed its way back into my mind and I tried to force it out. My brain was too packed full of nightmares already.

"Go to sleep. We've got more walking to do tomorrow."

I pulled the red gem out of the satchel. It was warm, even through the wrapping.

"You don't know," said Tippity, his voice tired and weak. "You have no idea what it was like to make magic. It was what I was born for. Why I was given these fingers and this . . . feeling inside. I was made for something great but your kind took it from me before I had a chance to reach my potential." I rolled over and tried to convince myself that I didn't regret giving him the hammock. "I'm just unlocking the power that I deserve. That's why you're so angry. For a moment, you thought we were equal. But now you know you're nothing, again. Like you always were. And were always meant to be."

I didn't say anything else. It wasn't long before Tippity was snoring and I let exhaustion take me too.

When I woke the next morning, Tippity was facing the floor, hanging from the vines and the twisted hammock.

"Comfortable?" I asked.

He'd flipped himself over during the night but had been too proud to call for help. While he was dangling, I gave us both a hit of the wake-up powder, and then we got moving.

Everything felt worse. The pain of the day before had settled into my bones. Every part of my body creaked and snapped like the gears of a machine left out to rust in the rain. I was heavy and tired and Tippity was angry. From the moment I tied the collar around his neck, he was trouble.

"I can go anywhere," he said, mumbling like a madman. "But you, you're stuck in Sunder. You're gum on the street. A stain on the sidewalk. You're a smear. When this city dies you'll go down with the ship. Me and my kind, we matter everywhere."

My belly was empty and my throat was dry and all we had was rainwater to keep us going. My hands were blistered from holding the vines. The back of my head ached but that was better than when it went numb and I got all dizzy. If I passed out, I doubted that Rick would be kind enough to use his professional expertise to patch me up.

The world was against me and my body was broken but I had one last thing to push me on. Hate. I've never found a better fuel. A man might cross an ocean for love but with enough hate, he'll try to drink it. The blisters and blood only helped. I wasn't going to stop. Not with a killer on the end of my rope. A killer who cut open miracles and took out their hearts. Who used the souls of sacred creatures to blow people to pieces and ice his friends. I kept those Faery faces right in front of me. I saw them all along the path and in the trees, dried and naked and snapped open just so Rick Tippity could put their souls in his pocket.

If the hate for Tippity ever wore out, I always had myself: the stubborn soldier who sold out his mentor to impress his new friends. Hendricks trusted me enough to share his secrets and I gave them away to the army who ended the world.

I was stupid and I was proud and I'd done nothing to make up for any of it. But this guy was worse. Wasn't he? He had to be. I'd ruined the world with ignorance and accidents but he was cutting up bodies so he could blast people on purpose.

That had to be worse. Right?

We moved too slowly and night came again. The clouds smothered the moon and when we made it back to Maple Highway we had nothing to follow but the feeling of the path beneath our feet. I was dragging Tippity along in the darkness. Whenever I turned to belt him, he would try to scratch my eyes out or dig his fingers into the wound on my scalp. But he wasn't a brawler and I had more hate to hold onto, so his efforts gained him more bruises but nothing else.

We followed the road over a small hill and were moving down an incline when the Warlock made his most desperate break for freedom.

I felt the vine go slack. That usually meant that he'd moved closer, hoping to hit me while I was half asleep. I pulled on the vine and it flicked towards me, limp and loose. He'd cut through. Probably with his teeth, or maybe a stone he'd picked up during one of our previous scrambles.

I spun. Stopped. Listened.

I couldn't hear his footsteps. He was being real careful. Walking slow. I stepped backwards, ears cocked.

Would he attack me? No. Not now that he was free. I had the advantage in a tussle. He was making a run for it and I had to find him. Fast.

I took out the red orb and ripped off its cover. A faint, red shimmer blinked in the darkness and the heat kissed the cold from my fingers. I took out one of Tippity's pouches and stuffed the gem inside, beside the glass ball of acid. I raised the pouch over my head and prepared to smash it against the ground. It would make more than enough light for me to find my runaway Warlock.

Then I remembered the face. The broken Faery on the church floor. I was holding the last of her. Maybe it was nothing. But maybe it was everything.

I wouldn't do it to Amari. Of course not. So, I decided that I wouldn't do it to her.

I lowered my arm and put the pouch back in my coat.

Then, there were lights. A carriage. Somewhere behind us, over the hill. Just enough to illuminate some of the road ahead.

There! Tippity was stumbling up the road, heading straight for the city. I focused on the hate, and followed.

He'd been planning this for a while. That's why he'd been so troublesome on the last part of the road. When he slowed himself, it conserved his energy but cost more of mine to pull him along. He'd made me drag him halfway home, but I knew how to punish myself better than he did. I took hits for a living while he sat in a little room, mixing potions and muttering to himself.

I would have caught him eventually, even if he hadn't tripped on his own feet. As soon as he hit the ground, my boot landed between his legs without breaking stride. This time, he was ready for it. He grabbed my calf and wrapped himself around me, bringing me down with him.

Apparently I wasn't the only one with a belly full of hate. We rolled along the path like lovers, trading kicks, slaps and scratches instead of kisses. I couldn't risk letting him go. When his fingers dug into my face and clawed at my eyes, I held on. When he sunk his teeth into the soft flesh between my thumb and fingers, I just pushed back and choked him. This was my business, not his. Whenever he actually landed strikes, he couldn't turn them into a real advantage.

There was a rumbling in my ears. The carriage. But it was sounding way too loud. I found myself on my back with my arm around Tippity's throat and realized the lights in my eyes weren't stars.

"Out the way!" shouted a voice, and a chorus of horses neighed in agreement. The light moved left, so I rolled to the right, keeping Tippity locked in my arms. We hit the edge of the road and tumbled into scrub as the carriage corrected its course and continued on towards the city.

"Lunatics!" yelled the driver, without slowing down. I suppose he couldn't. Not with the other carriage traveling right behind him. And the one behind that. And the trailer, pulled by mules. And the unbelievable marvel that followed them all.

The last vehicle in the convoy had no horse. No mule or bison either. It was roaring like an animal but there was no animal involved. It was a truck. Automatic. Rumbling down the road, towing a metal carriage that was twice as big as my office.

We watched the caravan move past, both of our mouths gaping open. I'd never seen anything like it. Not even in the old days.

Tippity shouted after them, asking for help, but his voice was hoarse and the truck was too loud. I grabbed him by the throat and pulled tight until the bastard passed out.

15

"I'm fucking freezing!"

"That's your fault, Tippity. I gave you a nice little leash made from vine but you went and bit through it, didn't you? So, now you get this."

While he was unconscious, I'd ripped his cloak down the middle and twisted it into a replacement collar. It was shorter than his old one but that meant he was in easier slapping distance. I had him yoked tight, with the material twisted up so it wouldn't tear. When he tried to lag behind, I put him in front of me and kicked him forward till he met my pace again.

The cold helped. With his cloak off and the rip in his trousers, he actually was freezing. Judgment was waiting for him at the end of the journey but it would be better than death on the road. By the time Maple Highway turned back into Main Street, he was as relieved as I was to be back in the city.

The sun was up and it was amazing that nobody stopped me. No one even tried. I guess it was the balls of it. If I'd tried to be discreet, someone might have stepped in to see if the poor Warlock needed help. Instead, we were squabbling like siblings every step of the way. I'd kick him in the ass, he'd swear and spit, so I'd slap him in the back of the head. We looked like a couple of overly committed street performers who'd got caught up in the show.

The police department was way uptown so I went straight for the jail. I wrapped Tippity up in the cloak, pinned his arms to his sides, and kicked the front door till somebody answered.

It was a Dwarfish boy with no beard who couldn't hide the fact he was asleep on his feet.

"Uh . . . what seems to be the . . . uh . . .?"

"This is Rick Tippity, responsible for the murder of Lance Niles, an unidentified Warlock, and the desecration of untold Faery corpses."

"That's ridiculous!" screamed Tippity. "I—"

I punched Rick in the face. The cop reacted like he was the one who'd been hit, and stumbled back inside shouting, "Doris!"

A moment later, a lady Ogre joined him.

"He says he's arresting this guy for murder."

"Bullshit! This man assaulted me!" shrieked Tippity, hoping to save his skin with a convincing performance. "I have no idea what he's talking about. Please get this maniac off me and lock him up!"

Doris wasn't any more skilled in decision-making than her sleepy partner but I was tired and cold and I wanted to get it over with.

"Lock us both up," I said. "Separate cells. Then call Detective Simms and tell her Fetch Phillips found the killer." I pushed Tippity through the door and the cops politely moved aside. "And tell her to bring some coffee."

After an hour, Simms still hadn't made it downtown. Typical. Even when I do their job for them, the cops won't wake up early to help me out.

Tippity had screeched his innocence for fifteen minutes then fallen back into indignant stoicism. We both sat silently, in neighboring cells, falling in and out of sleep. I must have dozed off for a while because when my eyes snapped open, Simms was standing in front of me. Richie Kites too. My cell door was unlocked and a hot cup of coffee was pushed into my hands.

"This the pharmacist?" she asked.

"That's him. I caught him cutting open corpses in an old Faery church. Tried to blast me with fire and ice again, the same two spells that killed the victims. I don't have much more than my word and missing eyebrows. Oh, and this." I took the glowing red globe out my pocket. It was just as warm as the first time I held it. "This is what Tippity was taking out of the Fae. I guess it's evidence but just . . . make sure you take care of it. I don't know what it is. Not really. But maybe there's still something inside . . ."

"It's okay," said Simms, taking it from me with as much care as I hoped she would. "We took apart his drug store and found his lab. He has a bunch more of these, along with plenty of other evidence that matches your account. We'll take good care of this, I promise. Now, let's take you uptown so you can put it all on record."

They had a carriage waiting. A nice one. Simms even held my coffee and opened the door while I took a seat. It was better treatment than the usual boot-heels, phonebooks and lights in my face.

At the station, the hospitality continued. They brought me breakfast and more coffee. While I gave my account to the records guy, he kept saying things like "take your time" and "that's very helpful". It was goddam spooky and when it was all through, I was happy to be out of there.

They organized the coach again, and Simms joined me on my ride home.

"That was good work, Fetch. I know it didn't come easy."

"If someone turns in a couple of eyebrows – brown, fuzzy, in need of a pluck – can you push them through my letterbox?"

"There will be a reward. An official one from the city. But we'll have to hold a trial first. In the meantime—"

She held out a roll of bronze bills and, instinctively, I pushed them away.

"While I do believe the city pays you too much, I'm not going to dig into your personal salary."

She glared at me like I'd just spat in her face.

"Don't make this harder than it already is, Fetch. This money is so you can keep yourself off the streets, go to a doctor and get a warm meal. You're our prize witness against Tippity and I don't want you dying before the trial. When you get your reward, you can pay me pack. Deal?"

I took the roll.

"Deal."

The carriage stopped right outside the door to my building and I shooed Simms away when she tried to help me down.

"Call a doctor," she repeated. "This city's too dirty to go walking around with wounds like those."

"I read you loud and clear, Simms. Just let me drink a few barrels of whiskey and sleep for a year, then I'll get myself stitched up."

She glared again, but there was actual concern in her eyes. I gave her the sincerest nod I could manage without my head falling off, and she closed the door and rode away.

I looked up at number 108 Main Street, Sunder City; a gray-brick façade, spotted with barred windows and Angel doors. There was a rusty revolving entrance and a conspicuous tin chamber pot lying out front. I picked up the pan, dusted it off, and examined the dent on the side. It wouldn't take too much work to hammer it back into shape.

I pushed my way inside and each stair was a mountain. Five floors up was an eternity and if it hadn't been for the handrail, I never would have made it. My fingers could barely hold the keys. I must have stood outside for a whole minute, fumbling with them, before I realized the door to my office was already unlocked.

There were scratches on the frame where it had been forced open.

I kicked it in and called out.

"Anyone in here? Answer me now, because I'm too tired to ask any more questions before I start throwing punches."

But there was no one. Not even the ants. It was all the way I'd left it, except for one thing.

A package about the size of a brick was sitting on my desk. It was wrapped in black cloth and tied up with thick green string. The shape was curved and unusual.

There was a little envelope attached to it. Inside, all it said was: "A gift, from a friend".

I cut open the rope, unrolled the cloth, and unpacked something I'd never seen before.

It was made from cold metal and dark polished wood, screwed together with steel bolts. The metal part was a piece of pipe half an inch in diameter. It was welded to a kind of gear that didn't turn when I pushed it but looked like it would rotate if given the right kind of leverage. Sticking out from the gear was a spike. No. A small lever. Similar to the switches I'd seen on automobiles and pre-Coda magical torches. I played with the switch, gently, careful not to turn the contraption on before I knew what its purpose was. The wooden part slid smoothly into the palm of my hand, telling me just how it wanted to be held.

It was heavy, but balanced like a well-made sword. The wood in my grip was thick to offset the length of the pipe. I looked in the hollow end, wondering if something was supposed to go inside. Perhaps there was another part of it somewhere; a piece that fitted into the piping and locked in place. I searched back through the packaging for instructions but there was nothing else there.

When I lifted up the tool, and held it in the way that felt most natural, my index finger rested on the switch.

So, I turned it on.

BANG!

An explosion went off in my hand and I screamed, dropping

the machine on the floor. My wrist ached and my eardrums pounded against my brain. They must have heard the sound all the way up Main Street. I was worried I might never hear again.

The machine sat on the floor, motionless and unassuming, like it hadn't just let off the loudest sound ever made. The smallest wisp of smoke floated up from the pipe and it smelled like . . . something familiar that I couldn't quite name. A memory from somewhere far away.

I didn't want to touch the machine but there was no way I was going to leave it there on the floor, watching me and waiting to explode again.

I opened the bottom drawer of my desk, cleared out the old bottles, wrapped the machine back up in the cloth, tucked it inside, closed the drawer and locked it.

There were people out on the street. I could hear them shouting at each other, wondering what had happened. I wanted to look and see but if I poked my head out the window, I might give them a target on which to fix their curiosity.

I waited for my heartbeat to slow or my ears to stop ringing. After a minute, nothing changed so I pulled my bed down from the wall and climbed into it.

I was shaking. Not just from the shock, but because of the hundred thoughts that were slamming their way into my skull: ideas and revelations that were coming too late.

When I'd pulled the switch on the machine, just before the sound of the blast forced my eyes closed, an explosion came out the end of the pipe that pushed back my hand with a shocking amount of force.

It was bright. Just a flash, but full of yellows, oranges, blues and reds.

There was no mistaking it.

I'd made fire.

16

There were plenty of dents in the floor under my desk and even more holes in the bug-eaten rug. You might think that it would be impossible to notice a new one, but I'd spent so many days staring at the space between my feet that the fresh spot stood out like a sinkhole in the middle of Main Street.

The divot went through the rug and an inch into the floor. When I held my lighter over it, I could see something shiny at the bottom. I got out my knife and was under the desk, lying on my side, when I noticed a pair of shoes standing in the doorway.

They were pointed and elegant, holding up a couple of thin legs in charcoal tights. I stared at the legs for a while, wondering how long they'd been there and what kind of person they might be connected to. They weren't moving. Maybe they weren't connected to anyone. Maybe they were just a couple of legs, off on their own, out for a walk.

"I've come to see the *Man for Hire.*"

The voice was educated but touched by fatigue, like a classic book in need of rebinding. I popped my head over the desk.

"That's me. Sorry. Chasing termites."

"You have termites?"

"Sure. Just look at my divan?"

"I don't see any divan."

"Exactly."

I waited for a laugh. Or a smirk. I got neither.

"Please forgive me, Mr Phillips, but I recently lost my husband and pleasantries such as polite laughter are still beyond me."

She was an Elf. It was impossible to tell her age due to the fact that the Coda killed all tension in Elven skin. The ageing process that Elves avoided for so long had finally caught up with them. Her small frame was enlarged by a black fur coat and her hair was wrapped in a black scarf. She wore sunglasses, pearl earrings, and a gold wedding band.

I stood up, dusted off my knees, and moved my chair back to its place behind the desk. "Please," I said. "Have a seat."

You can tell a lot about a lady by the way she walks. Sure, her joints would be tighter than they once were and her bones would be creaking without magic, but when you've spent a century refining the way you move in the world, you don't let a bit of arthritis bring you down.

We took our seats and she smiled like I was an old friend, instead of some dirty, five-buck gumshoe with a bloody cloth wrapped around his head. I tried to offset my appearance by taking a pad and pen out of the drawer and placing them in front of me, acting all professional.

"How can I help you?"

She bit her lip and looked troubled. The hair beneath her scarf was pure white.

"My name is Carissa Steeme and my husband, Harold, went missing three months ago."

"I'm sorry to hear that, Mrs Steeme."

"Harold and I were married for almost a hundred years. Our home was in Gaila but we moved to Sunder after the Coda. It was Harold's idea."

She pulled a photograph out of her pocket and laid it on the desk between us. It was Harold and Carissa, younger and full of life. Again, it was impossible to tell their age because their bodies were full of magic. Both of them were finely dressed, like they were at some formal event, but sporting more style than your typical Elven couple.

Traditionally, the High Race draped themselves in flowing robes made of silk and satin. Carissa's outfit was cut from the same cloth but it had taken a trip through a poppy field and been dipped into a rainbow. It also showed off more skin than traditional Elvish dress.

"Mr Phillips?"

I looked up.

"Mmm?"

"My husband is the one on the right."

"Oh, yes."

He was dressed more conservatively than Carissa but still sported a few extravagant touches. His hair was dark brown. Eyes green. He had rounder features than your average Elf and his skin was olive. Carissa was quite pale, and they made a complementary couple.

"Why the old photo?"

"It's the most recent one I have. After the Coda, we weren't rushing to be in front of the camera."

I put the picture down on the desk.

"Three months since your husband went missing? Why wait so long to try and find him?"

A touch of frustration rose up in her, but she swallowed it. I liked that. Most clients who come through my door resent the fact that they might need my help. To make up for it, they make a big show of how stupid I am before deigning to offer me the job, overlooking the fact they know why they've come to talk to me and I don't. It was nice, for a change, to meet someone with restraint.

"I only waited four hours before I called the police. Harold was always responsible and he knew that I was waiting for him. He left work on the Friday and never made it home."

"What did the police say?"

"They told me to wait a few days, so I did. I called his office, his friends and his colleagues but nobody knew anything. After a week, the police decided to help but they didn't do anything I hadn't already done. After a month, I mourned him. After two months, we had a memorial. I know how this city works and I know what this world has become. Harold never dropped the habit of wearing his old jewelry. You could spot him from a mile away: nice clothes and sparkling ears, shuffling along without any meat on his bones. He was a glittering target and it wasn't a complete shock that someone would take advantage of him."

"Then why are you here?"

She leaned back in her chair, folded her hands in her lap and exhaled, long and slow, like she was breathing out a lifetime. Her eyes closed, almost as if she'd forgotten I was there. Time floated by. I felt like I was intruding in my own office. Even the building stopped creaking in respect. The world went silent, watching the old lady swim through a century of memories behind her eyes.

"A stranger came to my door," she said eventually. "Three days ago. He was a large man: bald, with dark glasses and a blond beard. Half-Ogre, I think. He wore a suit. Inexpensive. The kind you might wear when you want to look sharp but are also prepared to get dirty. He was a gangster, Mr Phillips, and he came looking for my husband to collect on an outstanding debt."

"What did you tell him?"

"The truth. That my husband wasn't a gambler. That my husband is dead. That this man had no business at my door and should kindly take his leave."

I had to stop myself smiling at the image of this sweet lady shooing away a professional gangster like he was a pigeon on her doorstep.

"And how did he respond?"

She took another long, sad exhale.

"He *smiled*, Mr Phillips. And in that smile I saw that my words were not the truth. That my husband *was* a gambler and that he owed money to men who would do terrible things to him if he didn't pay them back. Suddenly, all the little things made sense. The confused back-and-forth with his boss about where he'd been. The knowing looks from the police force when they asked about his hobbies and his friends. People have spent the last three months looking at me with pity. Not because of my husband's passing, but because they knew about something I didn't even suspect."

She squinted up her face, as if that fact made her more frustrated than the rest of the story.

"How much did he owe?"

"Ten bronze. Not a fortune, but more than I had on hand."

"What did the Half-Ogre do?"

"Nothing. That was the strangest part. He told me to forget about it and he left."

"Are you afraid that he'll come back? You want to hire me as protection?"

She laughed, and I tried not to look insulted.

"No, I don't think so. Nothing like that." Carissa Steeme reached into her bag and pulled out a roll of bronze bills wrapped up in a black ribbon. "Ten bronze. This is the money my husband owed. This is what I'm going to offer you."

Her eyes were as clear as polished crystal. That's the difference between the really old Elves and the younger ones who were robbed of their youth too soon. Their skin is the same but their eyes still hold an eternity of life.

"To do what?"

"To find out who killed my husband and make them pay. If Harold died with debts, I doubt that this was the only one. I believe some other piece of muscle in a cheap suit came after him first and I believe they gave him more than a mean smile. You're going to find out who killed Harold and make things right."

I looked at the roll of bills, all dressed up and hoping to impress. They weren't doing a bad job.

"If you're right, and some gambling house knocked off your husband for racking up a loan, then there isn't going to be anything to find. Operations like that don't stay in business leaving evidence. At least, not the kind of thing that holds up in court."

"I tried the law, remember."

She was as cool as a shot of iced liquor. I didn't know whether to be turned on or terrified. I looked down at the roll of bills, then back at those evergreen eyes.

"Mrs Steeme, I'm not a killer. Even if I was, I don't hold out hope of digging up any proof of a three-month-old murder. Guys like that don't leave bloody daggers on their bedside tables, waiting for someone to sneak in and find them. If I go knocking around the gambling houses it will put me, and you, in a lot of trouble. And for what? I can't imagine coming back with anything more than a hunch. Nobody is going to confess and you're not going to find his body in someone's basement. He's gone. You're not. Spend that money on something for yourself."

That was usually the part when people got angry. Not her. She nodded like she understood, picked up the cash, peeled off two bills and dropped them on the desk. There weren't as many of them now but they were all undressed and winking at me.

"Go get your hunch," she said. "See what your instincts tell you. Let me know what you find out and I'll take it from there."

I tried to stare her down but you couldn't win with those eyes. They didn't push back. They drew you in. She knew I was going to say yes before I did.

I snatched up the bills, threw them in my top drawer, and nodded.

"Now," she said, "what have you done to yourself?"

"Sorry?" Carissa pushed back her chair and came around behind me. "Oh, my last case got a little rough."

She unwrapped my homemade, bloody bandage and gasped.

"Mr Phillips, you have a hole in your head."

"Believe it or not, you ain't the first person to tell me that."

She sniffed. "What have you been putting on this?"

"Alcohol."

"Whiskey?"

"Yeah."

"Are you a moron?"

"It's been suggested."

Her fingers combed my hair away from the wound.

"You need to see a doctor."

"It's on my to-do list."

"Right after hunting for termites, is it?"

"And breakfast."

She was less amused than she'd been all morning. Carissa threw the bandage on the desk, walked over to the sink, turned on the tap, then pointed at the hand-towel and sneered.

"Has this place ever been cleaned?"

"Maybe. You'll have to ask the last guy who lived here."

She shook her head again, more serious than when she was trying to hire me to kill someone.

"Stay right where you are. Do not move an inch, Mr Phillips, or when I get back you're going to regret it."

I didn't even nod.

"Yes, ma'am."

She walked out the door and I heard the rhythm of her feet disappear downstairs. I did exactly as she said, not moving a muscle, other than to reach into my drawer, past the two curly bronze bills, and dip into my overflowing collection of Clayfields.

I didn't want this job. Not because it was pointless. Not because Simms told me to stay put. But because of where it was asking me to go.

The darkest corner of Sunder was the gambling district known as the Sickle. The last time I'd been there was back before the Coda, and I'd barely made it out alive.

I decided that I was going to give her back the bronze. This case wasn't going to get either of us anywhere good. If her husband got on the wrong side of a gambling house, then wherever he ended up, I didn't want to join him. I'd just come to that conclusion when Carissa came back through the door carrying a small glass bottle and a steaming pot of water.

"Well, isn't he just a darling?" she said brightly.

"Oh. You met Georgio?"

"What an incredible fellow." She put the pot down on the desk and rummaged around in the little handbag she'd left on her chair. "Just as filthy as you are but far more entertaining."

She pulled out a crisp, white handkerchief and came back behind me to deal with my wound. She dipped the cloth into the boiled water and then I felt the gentle touch of it on the top of my head. We didn't say anything while she worked. I just listened to her dip her hand into the water, wring out the cloth, and then slide it down my scalp to clear away the dried blood, dirt, and any ideas I had about refusing this lady my services. I was just starting to relax when she said . . .

"Don't flinch."

. . . and dabbed again.

"Shit!" I jerked my head forward. She'd switched out the water for rubbing alcohol while I was daydreaming.

"I told you not to flinch."

"Sorry."

The next part wasn't anywhere near as relaxing. She rubbed alcohol over everything and pulled hairs out of the cut. When she picked up the bandage, I thought she was preparing to wrap it back around my head, but she threw it in the dustbin and washed her hands in the sink.

"Stay right there, sitting up, and do not leave the house today."

"I thought I needed to see a doctor."

"I called one from downstairs. She'll be over in an hour. Don't you dare lie down and fill that wound with dirt before she arrives."

I'd spent my youth around army generals and political leaders but this lady put them all to shame.

"Uh . . . sure. Thanks."

"When the doctor leaves, go back to bed and get some rest. You can look for my husband's murderer in the morning."

I watched her age-defying body slide out into the hall and

waited thirty seconds before I went back to digging up the floor. I cut a hole around the shiny object, put the blade underneath and flicked it out onto the rug.

It was metal. Gray and burned. The fireball had propelled it out of the machine hard enough to sink it into the floor.

I rolled the misshapen ball around in my fingers. It was so *small*. Seemingly insignificant. Surely something so tiny couldn't do any real damage. Not like the magic of old, or even what Tippity had been throwing around.

I pulled out the bottom drawer and looked at the machine. It was just a piece of pipe with a wooden handle. Nothing remarkable. Nothing to worry about.

I put the projectile beside the machine and closed the drawer carefully, so as not to set it off again. Then I closed my mind on all the uncomfortable questions that were coming to the surface. Questions about Lance Niles and the Bluebird Lounge and the mysterious present.

I didn't want to think about that. I didn't have to. Because I had a new case all lined up.

Find out who killed Harold Steeme.

Simple. Better.

Even though I'd told myself that I'd never go back to the Sickle.

17

The doctor came over and patched me up properly. There was too much skin missing for stitches but she shaved a bit of my head and glued a bandage over it. Then she made some recommendations: get myself a hat to cover the wound, take a few days off, ease up on the Clayfields, quit the hooch and eat something that didn't come from the greasy diner downstairs once in a while.

I ignored it all except the bit about the hat.

East Ninth Street was luxuriously wide and paved with large, red stones instead of cement. Haberdasheries and tailors lined both sides of the street, occasionally dotted with cafés, bars and shoe stores. A lot of them were still open. Not booming, like they used to, but seemingly getting by.

There was a leather worker's window full of scabbards, dusters, belts and a wooden mannequin with a chest-strap made to hold a hidden dagger. It was impressive work, and if I ever started to take my job seriously, it would be the perfect place for a shopping spree.

Wren's Hatters was across the road. The window was full of hand-made, expertly crafted specimens but, as soon as I stepped inside, it was clear that most of his business was cheap woolen beanies, bakerboy caps and earmuffs. This time of year, in this cold new world, most folk favored warmth and affordability over style.

That was all I needed anyway; just something to cover the top of my broken head and hold in the heat. What I didn't need, at all, even remotely, was the weather-beaten, brown/blue, wide-brimmed hat on the top shelf.

The spectacled Warlock in white shirt and green waistcoat saw my eyes land on it and didn't miss a beat.

"It's rabbit," he said.

"Looks sturdy."

"Decades old but in beautiful condition."

"I don't need it."

"Of course not. Nobody *needs* it."

I looked at a pile of plain, sweat-shop beanies in a barrel.

"How much?"

"For . . .?"

"The rabbit."

He used a stepladder to pull down the hat that was taunting me. I changed my mind.

"Actually, I just need something simple to—"

He dropped it on my head and it slid down gently, resting just above the top of my ears.

"How does that feel?"

I reached up, gripped the sturdy pinch of the crown and pushed it down on my forehead. When I looked up, a mirror had materialized in the hatter's hands.

There I was.

One of the reasons I'd never been a "hat guy" was because it always felt like I was dressing up. Graham, my first adopted father, wore a hat. Tatterman, my first Sunder boss, wore a hat. I was just the boy they ordered around.

But now? The eyes in the mirror were cold and ringed with folds of dark skin. There was gray in my stubble. Scars, old and new, ran down my cheeks. It wasn't a boy's face anymore, and somehow the hat suited it.

The hatter slipped the tip of his finger in between the hat and my forehead.

"Almost your size. I'll put in some lining. Do you have a preference for what kind of fur?"

"I don't really—"

"What's this?" He put his hand on my collar and rubbed the material between his fingers, trying to guess its origin. "Is this fox?"

"Lion," I said. "A big one."

A thread of mischief sowed its way across the hatter's face.

"Come with me."

The old man took me out back to his workroom. A single cluttered desk was crammed in between shelves, racks and wooden crates, all stuffed with strips of leather and reams of colored ribbon. Offcuts and trimmings were strewn across the floor, dusty and covered in hair.

The hatter hunched down and moved from box to box, reading labels out loud to himself. He pulled open cupboards, rifled through the folded material inside, then slammed them closed. Finally, in a suede sack at the back of a closet, he found what he was looking for.

"Take a gander at this."

He brought the sack up onto the desk and opened it. Inside was a fur of familiar color. The hatter pulled out the pelt and unrolled it, revealing a terrifying face wrapped in brown hair.

There were no eyes in the lion. No teeth either. They'd probably been used as cufflinks or buttons. The boneless head was all misshapen from being rolled up for so long. Its muzzle was squashed and its lips were inside out. The mane was matted, dry and malting. The beast still had its front legs but the body went to pieces after that, disappearing into strips where the fur had been used to make hatbands and lining. The Warlock looked from the lion to the Chimera fur on my collar and nodded with approval.

"Looks like a match to me."

I kept my eyes on the cat. He was right. It was just like the Chimera I'd killed in my youth. A tenth of the size, but similar. The hollow eyes made it easier to look at than the bigger one, whose eyes had been full of pain. This one was empty all the way through.

"What do you say?" asked the hatter. "Shall we complete the set?"

With a disappointed shrug, the hatter passed the poor-boy cap over the counter. When I put it on, the saggy crown fell over my ears. It was a little too big but at least the small brim didn't cut into my vision. He reached for the mirror.

"Leave it," I said.

I pulled the hat down on my head and went out to make some mistakes.

18

It isn't smart to leave the house with a hole in your head. It isn't smart to take a case when the cops have told you to sit tight. It isn't smart to ask a loan shark what he does when poor fools fall behind on their repayments. And it's never smart to walk on down to Sickle Street.

On the south-eastern corner of the city, the Sickle was a cut in the belly of Sunder that bled down into the slums. When I'd first arrived in town, I took every paying job that was on offer, including being sent down onto the curve of the blade to pick up curious packages, deliver sealed messages, or search for a particularly troubled missing person. Never by Hendricks, though: his quaint fascination with Sunder's dark side didn't stretch that far into the shadows.

My first trip to the Sickle was for the mundane task of asking somebody a question and coming back to The Ditch with the answer. A hooded Gnome with an unconvincing smile asked me to find his friend and enquire whether he would still be coming for dinner, now that the third party was out of the picture. It sounded like an easy way to make a few bucks until the Gnome handed me a set of brass knuckles. With sober seriousness, he told me to keep them wrapped around my fist from the moment I stepped onto Sickle Street.

Despite the Gnome's intimidating instructions, the job went smoothly and I made my way back to The Ditch without needing to use my new weapon on anyone. When I got back, the Gnome was gone and the brass knuckles became my payment.

The success of that trip made me cocky. I took more trips down to the sharpest corner of the city, not realizing why people were choosing to send me. It wasn't because I was tougher or braver than their usual goons. It was because I was expendable. If I got stabbed, tied up, and thrown into the Kirra Canal, they might lose their merchandise but they wouldn't lose the trusted service of one of their more capable employees. For one-off, risky deliveries, Fetch Phillips was on the top of everyone's list.

I even started bragging about it. One night, picking up dirty glasses at The Ditch, I overheard a couple of shady characters talking about the trouble they were having finding someone called Hank.

"I know Hank," I said.

"You do, kid?"

"Yeah, I met him a few times."

"Well, ain't that something. You wouldn't know where to find him, would ya?"

"Sure. He's usually around The Afterlife Lounge. If he's not there, it shouldn't take me too long to track him down for you."

"How about that? Ain't today our lucky day?"

When I knocked off work, I led the guys down into the Sickle and through the alley that would take us to The Afterlife. There was a split second of cold understanding when I took a step forward and they didn't follow. I couldn't even turn my head in time. The blow came from the right and as I stumbled, the guy on the left pushed me to the ground. I passed out after a few kicks but when I came to, I couldn't move.

It turned out that I'd misheard the conversation. The two gentlemen worked for Hank, who wasn't happy to hear that I'd been throwing his name around town like I was his best buddy. I needed to be taught a lesson and Hank needed to make an example of those who used his name too lightly.

I'd been beaten up before. I've been beaten up plenty of times since. But this was different.

I was hung upside down from a chain in the back room of Hank's casino. First, I was just there to keep Hank entertained.

He used my body as a punching bag or my mouth as a cigar holder. But as he got bored, or called away on business, my usefulness was extended to anyone else in the room.

Hank's casino was a twenty-four-hour operation, meaning there was always someone around to mess with me in some new and twisted way. The lack of sleep became the worst part. That's what makes you crazy. That and all the blood that was building up in my head, making it feel like my eyes were about to explode from the pressure.

They might have, in time, but a couple of Hank's cronies got too carried away, seeing how far they could swing me around the room. I don't know if my head hit a wall or the chain snapped but I was dumped back on Main Street with my brains coming out my nose and the side of my head feeling way too soft.

When someone stopped to help, I had just enough life in me to ask to be taken to Amari.

I don't remember being carried through the city but I do remember getting to the gate of the Governor's mansion and the doorman trying to turn me away. He kept saying Amari wasn't there, but I wouldn't listen. Eventually, Hendricks came out of the house.

Amari was the real nurse but Hendricks knew a thing or two about medicine. He stopped the bleeding and used some kind of magic to seal up the cracks in my skull.

He didn't do much for the pain, other than ply me with alcohol. I ended up somewhere between tipsy, concussed and comatose, with my head in his lap as he recited old war stories to try to keep me awake. When I did sleep, it lasted for days and he was gone by the time I woke up. The Governor kicked me out as soon as I could walk and I had to wait months before I could thank Hendricks for saving my life.

I have a few injuries that have never gone away, like the click in my left knee and the sharp pain in my chest. They're annoying, but they make sense, and I know how to deal with them. Hank broke something inside my head and I'm still not sure if Hendricks was a good enough nurse to put it all back in the right place. It's not like I can strap it up or stretch it out. I can't even see it. But I was left with this awful feeling that something in me didn't heal right.

I hadn't been back to the Sickle since. It was the dark heart of Sunder City, twisted and dangerous but somehow vital. I thought I'd seen the last of it. Turns out it only took a kind-hearted widow with a sway in her step to make me wander back down to crazy town.

19

I came down Tar Street, eyes low and ears cocked, till it hit the intersection of Sickle and Fifth. There was music coming from somewhere around the corner. The foot traffic was sparse and everyone walked at that deliberate speed where you wanted to keep moving but couldn't afford to look like you were afraid.

Three Humans dragged a Warlock out of a bar and slammed him into a brick wall. I wondered if it was just normal Sickle business or if word had got out about Rick Tippity's murders and it was making people nervous. I walked away so I wouldn't have to think about it.

The face of the Sickle was a beaten-up block of stone called The Rushcutter, made from gray boulders and mud. It started out as a bunkhouse then evolved into an elite bar, a bordello, and finally a casino. The façade was the only piece of the original building that remained: flat-faced and intimidating like a beaten guard dog.

There wasn't a lot of traffic, in or out, but the expressions were all the same: hopeful on arrival and sweating with shame when they left.

The bouncer was tall and wiry with metal-capped teeth and a sad mustache made of too few hairs that all grew in different directions. I didn't want to linger out on the street so I pulled down my cap, put my hands in my pockets and sauntered up to the entrance.

The bouncer grabbed the brim of my hat when I tried to pass. I caught a glimpse of the thin dagger on his belt before he pulled my eyes up to his face.

"What you here for, fella?" he asked, with a voice like a school-yard bully.

"Fifteen minutes, two drinks and one big win."

He pulled open my jacket to search my belt for scabbards or steel. It was half-hearted. Insulting, actually. He waved me inside with a dismissive flick of his wrist.

It smelled like an ashtray's acid reflux. Pipes, old beer, sweaty pits and no ventilation. At least it was warm. I came through a curtained corridor into the main room. Seven dice tables were being circled by serving girls and quiet gamblers. The decor was a lot of brown pretending it was red and a lot of stains pretending they were part of the pattern. A lone piano player was hunched over an upright, tapping keys warily as if one of them might bite back.

There was a long bar on the southern wall with two servers: a one-armed male Ogre and a tattooed lady Werewolf. When the Ogre walked off with a tray of drinks, I took a seat.

"Whiskey, neat," I said, throwing out a bronze coin and turning to take in the room.

Gambling always seemed stupid to me. If winning a one-off handful of cash will change your life, then you really can't afford to be losing any. If you can afford to lose, winning won't matter so why bother at all? Everyone essentially knows this, but there are two things that make us look past the logic: alcohol and superstition.

Elves weren't typically drinkers. Hendricks was an anomaly in that way (and many others). It was only after the Coda that other members of the High Race turned to the bottle. If Harold Steeme had gone down that road, I was pretty sure Carissa would have noticed. I figured it was far more likely that he'd tried to cash in on a few years of bad luck.

Good gamblers can separate math and emotion. Bad gamblers look for ways to make them align. After the Coda, when so much was taken, folks who believed in karma could make the argument that they were owed a big return. Every bad thing that happened only brought them one step closer to the day when it would all come tumbling back.

A man like Harold might have followed that hope to the very end of the line.

I didn't know enough about him to guess which sport would tickle his fancy. The dice games being played here were all based on luck. No strategy. Just anxiety. Money was counted desperately, hidden in shaking hands. Drinks were ordered to calm nerves, not raised in celebration. There was a door beside the bar that made me shiver: one of those rooms where you come out walking funny or not at all.

"You're new here," said the server. Good. Always better to let them talk first.

"Yeah, a friend recommended this place."

"Really?"

She was right to be suspicious. Over in the corner, a woman was crying into her handbag.

"Yeah, his name was Harold Steeme. You seen him around?"

Her face stayed the same but her irises squeezed her pupils and her clawed fingers rapped against the bar. I'd already outed myself. I might as well have told her straight out that I was gonna be trouble. The world went quiet and neither of us blinked.

"No," she said finally.

I nodded, eyes always up.

"Oh well." I lifted my glass to my mouth and just before it covered my eyes, she looked over my shoulder. Shit. My glass went back down before I took the sip. "Thanks."

The one-armed Ogre was already approaching; a well-dressed, walking concussion with one clenched fist. I put a table between us to cut him off.

"Sir," he growled.

"I was just looking for a friend."

There was no point even reaching for the brass knuckles. They'd barely put a dent in his concrete head and I had a feeling there were others coming to join him.

"Sir!" He tried to grab my shoulder but I spun away. I wasn't gonna get dragged out back so they could break my bones one by one. I might risk my life ten times a day, but I still care *how* I die, and there are better places for it to happen than a homemade torture chamber behind a shitty gambling house.

I came out the door and hit the streets before the bouncer got wind of the commotion. My heart and stomach were heaving but I pushed through the pain. I ran for two blocks then I jogged for two more and eventually I found an alley that was dark and quiet where I could throw up, spit and cry.

What a goddam amateur. I'd managed to show my face, reveal my hand, kick up a stink and prove that I'm a coward in under five minutes.

The Sickle. Anywhere else I would have been fine, but I just kept flashing back to the feeling of my skull being split in two. If that happened again, I wouldn't have Hendricks around to fix me up.

I told myself that it was long ago, when I was wet behind the ears and still learning about life outside the walls. I wasn't an errand boy anymore. I'd slayed monsters, led armies, traveled the world and torn it to pieces. I'm the Man for Hire now. I get kicked in the teeth for breakfast and break my nose for lunch. I don't turn chicken just because one little street has a few bad memories.

I couldn't go back in The Rushcutter. Not ever. But I knew that every place on Sickle would have the same effect.

I needed to rig the deck in my favor. I needed something up my sleeve to strengthen my nerves and kick-start my mojo. So, I went back to my office and opened the bottom drawer. I tucked the machine into my belt and buttoned up my shirt.

I felt better already.

It was too obvious, though. If a bouncer checked my belt, I'd have some explaining to do. So, I went back to East Ninth Street, into the leather store, and asked about the chest-strap in the window that was made to hold hidden daggers. Could it be adapted? Of course it could. I showed him the machine and paid him enough not to ask any questions. We workshopped the design till it sat snug under my ribs on my left side. I checked myself out in a mirror and the sling was invisible when I wore my coat.

I felt much, much better.

The pipe dug into my side if I hunched over too much, so I stood up straight and tall like I was ready to take on the world.

Then I went across the road and bought the fucking rabbit hat.

20

I took a long walk downtown so I could meet the Sickle from the blade instead of the handle. Not a route I'd recommend unless you have a miracle strapped to your side that makes you feel invincible. With the soft padding of the lion's pelt against my head, I forgot all about the wound. I chewed a Clayfield as I came around the corner and I wasn't afraid to make eye contact.

Half-Ogre. Bald. Blond beard; that's what Mrs Steeme had said.

I approached an underdressed woman coin-first and gave her the description. She told me I might find him in Sampson's so I tipped my new hat and headed further into the curve.

I stared men down. I walked tall and didn't rush. I looked into alleys and doorways and the others turned their eyes away from mine. It was all an act, but what did that matter? Everyone was willing to play along.

Sampson's was a tall and narrow gin joint whose front was made from sheets of rusted iron. I looked the doorman square in the eye and he let me through without even checking my belt.

It was just as cold inside as out. The roof was high and the iron wasn't doing anything to keep in the heat. Five card tables were each dedicated to a different game, and the croupiers and servers were wrapped in fur (some wore coats, others had grown their own).

At the back of the room, under intentionally dim light, a round, red velvet table held prime position. Sitting on one side, chewing a toothpick, was a Half-Elf in an expensive suit. The ageing process hadn't cut through his good looks entirely like it would have if he'd been full-blooded. He had salt-and-pepper hair and so many creases in his forehead it looked like he kept it in his back pocket. On the other side of the table there was a bald Half-Ogre whose blond beard had been trimmed into three prongs. All his muscles were blown up like carnival balloons and his suit looked ready to burst.

I walked straight towards their table. Not so fast as to set the whole place on edge. Like I knew them. Like I'd been invited. They didn't notice me until I pulled an unused chair from the card table and sat down.

"Gentlemen," I said, giving my attention to the well-dressed Half-Elf who I assumed was in charge. "My friend is missing. I heard a rumor he crossed your path. How about you tell me what happened before I have to disrupt all these nice little games."

The Half-Elf's eyes went from me to his muscle, and the Half-Ogre raised a hand from his glass.

"Keep your hands on the table, big guy," I said. "Or you'll be using them to drag yourself out of here."

Both men raised their eyebrows and smiled like they were pretending to be impressed. The Ogre didn't drop his hand straight away, but turned it over, palm up and open, and gestured towards his companion.

"Please excuse me, Thomas," he said, in a voice more educated than I'd expected. "This matter does sound urgent. Here is your key. Someone will come up to your room shortly to make sure everything is in order."

"Of course," replied Thomas, taking the key from the table, standing and smoothing out his suit. "Thanks for your time, Sampson. You've really saved my neck."

When the Half-Elf was gone, I looked up at the Ogre and felt my confidence slip away.

"You're Sampson," I said.

"And you're very rude."

He picked up his glass of wine to have a sip but stopped halfway to his mouth. Then he gestured inquisitively, as if he was asking for my permission to move his hands again. That pissed me off, and some of my confidence came back.

"Harold Steeme," I said.

He took a sip and put his glass back down.

"What about him?"

"He owed you money."

"He owed a lot of people money."

Footsteps approached from behind me. Sampson looked over my shoulder and I spun around, rising from the table and reaching into my coat for the machine – until I found myself face to face with a rosy-cheeked girl holding a tray. She jumped back, startled, and the Ogre swore behind me in his upper-class accent.

I looked back and realized that I'd knocked the table, tipping Sampson's drink into his lap. People were staring and staff were on the approach, but Sampson waved them away.

"Phara, please pass me your towel."

The nervous waitress handed Sampson a cloth and he dabbed himself down.

"A normal person would leave after a display like that," he said.

"I just want to—"

"If you're going to stay, order a damn drink."

There wasn't anything else to do. I turned to the girl.

"Burnt Milkwood."

"Sure. What about you, boss?"

"I'll have the same. And bring more towels."

She strode away, and I was left standing over the increasingly unimpressed owner.

"Sit down and stop being so agitated. You're making me nervous."

I searched the room first. The security guards weren't pulling out their batons or making eyes. The card games were back in swing and it didn't feel at all like someone was waiting to sock me. So, I took a seat.

"What's your name, then?"

"Fetch Phillips."

"And Harold is your friend?"

From the tone of his voice, he already knew it was a lie.

"I've been hired by his wife to find out what happened to him."

"How strange. It was Mrs Steeme herself who told me that he'd passed away."

"And you took her word for it? With outstanding debts on the table? You would've been back the next day to break her door down if you hadn't found some proof that he was really dead."

Footsteps behind me again. I didn't jump up this time, but I turned. Phara placed two milkwoods on the velvet. Then, we all waited.

"What's the problem?" asked Sampson.

"People have a habit of slipping things into my drink. Since you're not calling over the boys to drag me into the back room . . ."

"Good grief." Sampson wiped a hand down his face till he was pulling on his beard. "Just pay the girl so we can get on with this."

"Three bronze coins," said Phara warily.

I pulled out the bits and handed them over.

"That wasn't so difficult, was it?" said Sampson, as Phara scampered away. "So, do you want to swap drinks or will you trust me when I say that there's nothing in them expect sap, liquor and spices?"

I picked mine up and took a sip. It was damn good. I told him so.

"See? Now, why would I waste my time dragging you out back, cutting you into pieces and throwing you in the canal when you're a decent paying customer? Look around, Mr Phillips."

He waved a graceful hand and I twisted to take in what he was showing me. Five tables. Four customers, each nursing warm drinks and playing minimum bets. No music. No heating.

"Do you think I can afford to rough up my patrons? Or pay goons to administer my beatings for me? We are a *business*, Mr

Phillips. A struggling one. We've resorted to renting out rooms to keep the lights on. So please refrain from stabbing any of my staff, they are all quite invaluable and I am rather fond of them."

I sighed and put my stupid hat on the table.

"I'm sorry. This part of town was . . . different last time I was here."

"I was here back then, too. Broke my fair share of arms, don't you worry about that. But a casino requires two kinds of customers: those that consider gambling to be a luxury, and those that become trapped." I watched one of the customers, on his own, drop chip after chip on a cold deck of cards. "We still catch those who have no choice, and they keep us going, but we need both to thrive."

"Which was Harold?"

He took a long sip.

"He was a gambler with a plan, to begin with. He knew where he wanted to go and he hoped the cards would get him there. That's how they all start: with a magic figure that they're aiming for and a few strict rules to keep themselves in line. Of course, if they don't reach that figure, they keep trying. If they do reach it, it feels like free money so they are tempted to try again. We catch them all eventually."

There was something familiar about the way Sampson talked. He was leading me away from my specific question to somewhere poetically vague.

"And who caught Harold?"

He sucked his whiskers and snapped his lips.

"Mrs Steeme appears to be a strong woman. She has already accepted that her husband has passed. Why would you want to disturb her mourning any more than you need to?"

"Because she paid me. I just do what I'm told."

"I see." He drained his glass. "This is too sweet for my liking. I'll talk to Phara about her recipe."

"Really? It's just to my taste."

He wiped his whiskers with the towel.

"Well, bring your manners next time and I'll show you a real cocktail. Something for polite gentlemen, like us."

He stood up and I became aware of how huge the Half-Ogre actually was. I was glad that I hadn't tried to throw my weight around. He could have twisted me into a pretzel and served me up as a snack.

"Cornucopia," he said. "Down the Rose. There's a top-floor room for high-rollers who like to mix some girls in with their game. You'll find answers there, Mr Phillips, but if it were me, I'd keep them to myself. Don't put that poor woman through any more pain."

He left and I finished my drink in one big sip. I liked the guy. Maybe I would be back. But first, I had to peel back the petals of the Rose.

21

The canal was frozen over and the sunset painted it pink, hiding reality under a layer of color like so many others who called The Rose Quarter home. The warm light of the Rose collected moths, coins and lonely hearts, offering companionship to those who could afford it. I knew all its tricks and I'd fallen through the cracks of its hospitality more than once but I'd be lying if I didn't say it called me in my sleep.

It's easy to turn up your nose at the idea of paying for someone to hold, but a touch is a touch and a kiss is a kiss. Real love can be just as fleeting but it comes with the risk of pain. Down the Rose, you get what you pay for and you know when it's going to end. For some folks, that comes as a relief.

The mobsters who ran the Sickle back in the old days would never have allowed gambling in another part of town. Apparently, those rules had softened like Sampson. Cornucopia was a two-story black-brick building right by one of the bridges that crossed the canal. It was going for a "modern" look. Rather than the flags and flowing petals of the older whorehouses, Cornucopia was plain and elegant. Instead of a bouncer, I was greeted by a bob-cut girl in a little black dress, white coat and bright red lips.

"Evening, sir. Coming to play tonight?"

"Just here to watch, if that's all right with you."

"Of course. There's no entry fee as long as you buy a drink and a girl."

"Sounds like a deal to me."

She pulled open the black door and I stepped into a round room wrapped in red velvet drapes. Six tables hosted beautiful topless dealers who handed out cards to trios of gamblers. At the back of the room there were two staff doors and a stairwell leading up.

There was even a girl who exchanged denominations. Ten coppers for a bronze coin. Ten bronze coins for a bronze leaf. Twenty bronze leaf for a silver coin, and if you were lucky enough to get twenty of them, she even had some silver leaf. I'd never managed to get my hands on one myself. There were gold versions, apparently, but I'll be damned if I knew where they were.

Things were healthier here than down the Sickle. There was laughter mixed into the anguish, and when the cash was handed over, there was a smile in the exchange. I wouldn't be surprised if the entire gambling industry moved to the Rose in a couple of years.

I wound my way up the circular staircase and arrived on the top level. The room was smaller than the one down below, with only a single table set in the center. Five of the eight seats were full and each player had a woman at their side. One guy had two. The dealer was a top-heavy woman who seemed to be Half-Ogre, Half-Elf. I heard people call them High-and-lows, but they preferred to be known as Amalgam.

She had a warrior's body draped in a glamorous black dress that suggested she didn't feel the cold like the rest of us. Her eyeliner had been applied generously and no sculptor would be able to shape more perfect lips. She was dealing and smiling and had the whole room eating out of her hands.

There were three spare chairs at the table and five more around the wall. I sat on one of the outer seats and the Amalgam batted her fake lashes my way.

"You waiting to play, honey?"

"Just watching."

"You know the rules?"

"Sure. I'll take a beer and a blonde."

That got chuckles of approval from around the room.

I'd made a better entrance than at Sampson's but I still didn't know what I was looking for. It was likely going to be the same

routine as last time: talk to the server, then the boss, and hope
my answers came in words not knuckles.

I couldn't see anyone else in charge, other than the Amalgam,
but someone must have been watching because a few minutes later
a tiny Human woman came up the stairs with an ice-cold drink.

"One bronze, handsome. Can I take your hat?"

I handed over the note. It was almost my last.

"Nah, better leave it on. It keeps my brains in place."

Her laugh was rehearsed and routine and would have sounded
the same no matter what I'd said. Then, she pushed my legs apart
and sat herself on my left thigh.

"So," she stroked my chin with a painted finger, "you just a
fan of the game?"

"That depends. What is it?"

She laughed again. There was a bit more truth in that one.

"I suppose you're here for the view, then."

"I'm actually looking for a friend." Worry flashed behind her
eyes. "Don't worry, I'm not here to make a scene. I just want a
little information, if you can spare it."

"That's not my department, Mister."

"C'mon, sugar." I don't know if it was the location or the hat,
but I could hear myself laying it on too thick. "It can't be the
craziest request you've ever had. And I promise not to get you
into trouble."

She was scared, but that was no surprise. Most girls who do a
job like this have some mean boss behind the curtain to answer to.

"How about you just enjoy the game, Mister? We'll have fun."
She stroked my other thigh. It was a cheap and transparent move
but I've been bought for less and I'll be damned if it didn't work.
I nodded. She relaxed. There was no need to spook the girl too soon.

"How long have I got with you?" I asked.

"Fifteen minutes. But then all you gotta do is buy another
drink and I'll stay around."

I sipped my beer and wished I'd ordered something warm

instead of the drink with the best alliteration. It was a hangover from my days with Hendricks. He didn't only teach me combat and culture, but did his best to impart an appreciation of poetry as well.

Compared to my old mentor, the other patrons were a disgrace. The kind of rich folk who made money look cheap. Their clothes were new and tasteless and they laughed at their own jokes without listening to each other. The dealer always kept her smile as she pushed the game forward at a healthy speed that gently drained their stacks.

The guy who had splurged on two girls was an Elf. His face was buried in the neck of one of his ladies, whispering sweet nothings, while the other lady was placing his bets. A mohawked Human with an under-bite was agitated over losing too much dough so he asked if he could change his girl to someone luckier.

The blonde put her arm around my shoulders and came in close. She smelled like sadness and vanilla.

"If this isn't fun for you," she whispered, "you can watch me instead. I'm very entertaining."

I had no doubt about that. I turned my head to her ear. It was my turn to whisper.

"Harold Steeme."

She looked confused.

"What about him?"

"What can you tell me?"

She looked back at the table. I was worried that she was trying to get the dealer's attention but then she broke out in a cheeky grin.

"Oh, you're wondering how he got the two girls? Just costs another bronze, Mister. I have a friend downstairs who would love to take the other seat. What do you say?"

I didn't understand what she meant until I looked across the table and the Elf turned his face from the two girls.

It was Harold Steeme. No doubt about it. He looked just the way he did in the photo.

Not like Carissa, who looked *similar* to the photo but with a lifetime of wrinkles on top. No. Harold looked *exactly* like his picture. Smooth. Youthful.

I could barely believe it. Harold Steeme had found a way to turn back time and make himself youthful again. To fill his body with magic. He'd done the very thing that I spent my days telling people was impossible.

I jumped up and my girl almost hit the floor. I caught her, and she giggled, grabbing my jacket to keep herself up. She put her mouth to my ear again.

"The surgeons did a good job, but he looks pretty silly, right?"

Surgeons?

Oh.

I sat back down and took a real look at the man who was supposed to have been murdered for his gambling debts.

His hair had been dyed. Not badly, but it was easy to tell when you looked long enough. It was dark brown, like in the photo, but too uniform in color. His cheeks were smooth and his lips were tight. He looked young, I guess. But now that I had had time to take it in, something was off about the whole thing.

"Harold had a big win down the Sickle a few months ago. Bought himself a whole new face. But you don't need to do that, do you, handsome? You can spend it all on me instead."

She tried to tuck her hand under my shirt. I thought of the machine and I grabbed her wrist before she touched it.

"Hey, careful, Mister."

"Sorry." I let her go. "I'm a bit jumpy. Just seen too many impossible things for one week. What happened to him?"

"He just went to some doctor who knows how to smooth out old skin." She leaned right in and kissed my neck. "But your skin is perfect, Mister. So is mine. Ain't it good to be Human? How about we go out back and you can have a taste?"

I picked up my beer and drained it.

"No, let's play."

The girl looked at me warily.

"I thought you didn't know how."

"I don't. What's your name anyway?"

"Cylandia."

"You sound like a princess."

"Maybe I am."

"Okay, Your Highness, get me up on that table."

"How much do you want to bet?"

I took the last bronze leaf from my pocket and handed it to her.

"Is this enough?"

"Not for long."

"Unless I win, right?"

Even her automated positive attitude couldn't humor me on that one. We moved ourselves to a seat at the inner circle.

"I'll deal you in on the next hand," said the Amalgam.

Good. One last chance to pay attention.

"It's called *Stracken o' Heros*," said Cylandia. "It's Gnomish."

"What does it mean?"

"Roughly, it translates to *Fuck the Legend*. Each player is dealt four face-down cards. Each round they take a card from the pile, look at it, then choose to swap it with one from their hand or discard it. When someone thinks they have the best hand on the table, they say 'I Heros,' meaning, 'I'm a Legend.' Then, the other players are each allowed to swap the position of any two cards on the table. That gives them an opportunity, if you know where the cards are, to push a bad card into the Heros' hand. Hence, Fuck the Legend."

I watched the game while she described the rules. Players took cards from the pile and exchanged them with others in their face-down hand. As the Mohawk Man called for more drinks, I realized the true nature of the game: distraction. With each round, more cards were moved across the board, out of your hand and into others'. It was a constant shifting game of memory, deduction, statistics, bluffing and luck. You had to keep track of where the cards you'd peeked at had gone, and deduce from the actions of the others what they might be holding. All the chatter was a way of interfering with the minds of the other players. Unlike some other games, where conversation was frowned upon, the boisterous energy happening at the table was part of the strategy and the appeal.

I must have looked like I was struggling to take it all in because Harold Steeme gave me a warm smile full of recently replaced teeth.

"Don't worry. We'll go slow for your first few games."

His face was close to being youthful but wasn't quite there. I found it hard to look at, like he was wearing a mask of skin, peeled from the skull of a much younger man.

"I Heros," said a slender Werewolf through cracked lips. She was the only female player at the table. Her date had unbuttoned most of her blouse and hadn't stopped kissing her neck since I'd entered. If that was supposed to distract the other players, it was working.

The other four made their final moves. They were each allowed to swap any face-down card on the table with any other. The goal was to have the lowest amount of points in your hand at the end. If the "Heros" won, they would keep the whole pot. If somebody else won, they would take fifty per cent, the dealer would take the twenty-five, and the rest would stay in the middle to raise the jackpot for the next round.

"There are two strategies with the final swap," said Cylandia, "either you can bring the lowest points into your own hand to win, or you can slam the Heros with large cards to ruin their score. Ideally, you try to do both."

Each player made their moves without hesitation, as if the choice was self-evident. Despite the drinking and canoodling, they all had a fair shake of where the good cards were at. The large man stole a card from the Werewolf and Harold stole it from him. A Gnome, who obviously didn't have a hand worth saving, pushed a card towards the Werewolf's that made her groan. A slurring Orc took a different card from Mohawk Man. Then they flipped.

The Werewolf's hand was busted by the two picture cards that had been thrust upon her. Mohawk Man and the Gnome weren't much better. At the end, Harold had the lowest score.

"Number Three challenges," said the dealer, then she flipped over a card for herself.

"Dealer plays last," said Cylandia. "Four cards in a row. If she wins, the house takes the pot. It's very rare because there isn't any strategy, but it helps keep the house in the green."

The dealer threw out an average hand of middle-range cards.

"Number Three holds."

The Amalgam split the deck into four equal pieces. Two were pushed into Harold's pile, she took one herself, and the other was left in the center to spice up the next round.

"What are the rules about talking during play?" I asked the dealer.

"Say whatever you want."

"Can my lady help me as I go?"

"Sure, but remember that the other players have ears too."

"And you might not have bought her loyalty yet," said the Werewolf with a wink. "Right, Cylandia?"

Everyone chuckled. I could see the glint in the eye of the other players, ready to take the new guy for a ride. Not the Gnome, though. He knew, like I did, that a new player is unpredictable. The usual strategy goes out the window because neither you nor they know what they're going to do next.

"Everything is worth what it says on the card," said my hopefully trustworthy partner, "picture cards are worth ten except for knights, which are one, and jesters, which are zero."

I put my mouth to Cylandia's ear.

"When you're lying, squeeze my knee when you talk."

A wicked smile curled up her perfect cheeks. She squeezed my knee twice to show she was ready. The Amalgam dealt out four cards to each player. They were placed separately, side by side, all face down.

"First," said my side-kick, "you can choose two cards to look at. This is the *glimpse*. After that, you're only allowed to look at a card when it comes off the pile."

The Werewolf and Mohawk Man were already bantering, getting back into the game of distraction. The Gnome was stoic and Harold Steeme was sipping champagne. The Orc on my right was counting his cash like he wondered where it had gone. The dealer rested her hands on the table and said, "Glimpse."

All the players lifted up their first card.

"I know your wife," I said.

Every hand froze but mine. I looked at the card on the very left. It was a picture card. I'd need to get rid of that at some point.

"Nice," said the voice in my ear as my knee received a squeeze. I put it down and picked up the one beside it.

"Whose wife?" asked the Orc. I realized that my opener had been even more effective than I'd intended. Harold wasn't the only one at the table who was keeping lies from a loved one.

"Relax, I was talking to the double-dipping Elf."

Harold barely looked at his card before he placed it back down. My second one was on the lower side.

"I don't know Gnomish," I said to my date. "Is that good?"

"Not great." Small squeeze to tell me she was lying.

Harold's girls glared at me. I guess bringing up wives wasn't polite behavior at Cornucopia. Probably put a dampener on the spending.

"Oh yeah?" said Harold. "And I know your mother." He must have hoped that I was just trying out banter. A couple of the others chuckled along. "How is she doing, son?"

"Dead."

The Werewolf groaned. Apparently I wasn't playing the distraction game right.

Knowing what card to play was easy enough. We took turns to take one from the pile, look at it, throw it back in the center or swap it with one of our own. When a card is thrown out, it is left face-up so that the next player can choose to take it, rather than draw one from the deck. The kicker is that you don't always know what you're getting rid of. If you happen to throw out a good card, the next player can pick it up, but then everybody knows where it is when it comes to the vibrant final round.

"You're dead too, aren't you, Harold?" I pulled a one-point knight from the pile and held it up to Cylandia so she could admire it.

"Hold on to that one, honey," she said without squeezing. The Gnome looked confused when I obeyed Cylandia and swapped it for the picture card I'd glimpsed at. He'd thought we were just playing opposites.

"I'm what?" Harold asked finally.

"Dead. Ground down to teeth and dirt because you got yourself in trouble with some bad guys downtown. Well, that's the story, anyway. I don't think you tried to create it – it was just some happy accident – but that's what she believes." The game went on. The other players were used to turning cards while they talked but I had more of their attention than they wanted to spare. "You know what's funny? I was hired to kill the man who killed Harold Steeme. Now, here I am without a body or murder weapon or a bad guy's confession. All I have is a question that I don't know how to answer."

The Orc threw out one of his unseen cards. An ace. I snatched it up before anyone else saw it. Mohawk Man swore as it slid into my deck without him knowing what it was.

"Maybe you can help me, Harold. Maybe you can shine some light on my predicament." The cards kept falling from nervous fingers. "Is Harold Steeme alive? Or did you kill him?"

We went around again. The Orc dropped a card on the discard pile. I took one from the stack and didn't even look at it. My eyes stayed on Harold but I tilted it enough for Cylandia to take a look. She gripped my leg like a vice.

"What are you? Some kind of private cop?" asked Harold.

"Just a guy who helps out when he can."

"Well, I'm sorry my wife dragged you into this but it's not any of your business. You probably think you're doing a good deed for a poor, helpless woman. I assure you, this is more complicated than you understand. What say we finish up here, I buy you a drink, and we can square this all out? You'll be compensated for your time and I'll even give you something extra for your silence. How does that sound?"

All eyes were on me as I swapped the unseen card in my fingers with a face-down card in front of me. I slammed that card down on the discard pile and said "I Heros!" like I'd already won the game.

Everyone chuckled. I looked down at the ace I'd recklessly thrown out.

"Shit."

Cylandia sighed.

"Why didn't you listen to me?"

"I thought I did."

Laughter bubbled out from everyone except Harold, whose tightened skin had turned sickly and pale.

"We usually go around a few more times before anybody calls it," said Mohawk Man. "We were just getting warmed up."

The Werewolf took my discarded ace. It was the right move, unless you thought I had a winning hand that needed to be sabotaged. Nobody thought that. In fact, nobody thought anything. They'd all been watching the back-and-forth between Harold and me and had missed most of the cards in play.

Because of that, they all took the ace. It was passed from one player to the next until it was the Orc's turn. He was looking at my hand, grumbling into his mouth, trying to remember where I'd put the knight that he'd thrown out two rounds earlier. But he was too drunk, and had been too taken in by my story.

"Blast," he said eventually, and succumbed to stealing the ace just like everybody else.

His nervousness put all the other players on edge as they realized they'd missed something. The Orc was the first to start flipping.

My partner bounced up and down on my leg.

"Do the honors," I told her.

The little blonde turned the cards from left to right. First, the knight that I'd taken from the Orc. Second, a three. Third, an ace.

Cylandia looked around the table. A lot of bad hands. One jester was wasted on the Werewolf whose overall score was twenty. Harold was lowest: he had two aces, a knight and a three. Six points. All eyes fell to my last card. Cylandia slipped her fingers beneath it and took a breath. Then, she spun it around.

Jester.

She cheered and grabbed my head, planting a smacker on my cheek. The Amalgam played her hand but it was all over when she turned a six as her first card. The whole pot was pushed in front of me: seven bronze-leaf bills. The Gnome was the only other player smiling. Everyone else was sour.

"Well done," growled the Werewolf. "But don't expect it to happen again."

"I won't."

I plucked one leaf out of the pile and handed it to Cylandia. I gave another to the dealer and folded up the rest inside my jacket pocket.

"Come on," said Mohawk Man. "It's bad form to leave like that. Have another go."

"Thanks, but I'm all good. I've got some news to deliver."

Harold's mouth made shapes as it searched for the right thing to say to me. I walked away before he found it.

"You sure you don't want to stay?" asked the blonde. "I can think of a few fun ways to spend those winnings."

"Sorry, darlin'. Got a job to do."

I went down the stairs and back outside. The evening crowd was building in the Rose. Even the chill air coming off the Kirra couldn't keep all the lonely hearts away.

I crossed the bridge and kept moving. Maybe Sampson and the Sickle had stopped knocking out kneecaps but that didn't mean it was completely out of fashion. My pockets were full of bronze and I'd solved the mystery in a single day but I couldn't shake the thought that something was wrong.

As I went out into the night, I could feel someone stepping on my shadow.

22

I got a few blocks away from Cornucopia, back in the guts of the inner city, and found a late-night barbershop with a working payphone. I called Carissa and it sounded like I woke her up.

"I have some news. Not what you were expecting. It would be best if I deliver it in person."

"All right. I'll come by in the morning."

Out the window of the barbershop, across the road, there was a narrow alley. Something moved in the darkness. A stray animal? No. There was a small flash of fire as somebody lit a pipe.

"I don't mean to spook you, Mrs Steeme, but certain elements are already in motion. Would you mind if I made a house call?"

"This evening?"

"I think it would be best."

She took a long time to think about it. Outside, the orange glow in the alley flared as the smoker breathed in. I pulled back from the window to hide myself behind the wall.

"I suppose that's fine," she said. "Will you be long?"

She told me her address. It was a short walk uptown to East Thirteenth.

"I'll be fifteen minutes."

I could have made it in under ten but I wanted to take a detour. When I came out of the barber's, the glow went away as whoever was watching me covered the pipe with their hand. I went west.

Somebody was following me. But who? I walk fast. Harold's skin might have been tightened up but his bones were old. There's no way he would be able to keep up with me. Maybe he'd paid some hired brute to wait downstairs. Not a bad idea when you play the high-rollers' table and want to be sure your winnings make it home.

I turned right, then left, then ran through an alley into an alcove behind a bakery. I waited without even reaching for a Clayfield. I stayed still and silent until I heard my stalker make his way down the cobblestones.

Pat. Pat, tap. Pat. Pat, tap.

He came around the corner. Slowly. Not at all like a man in pursuit.

Pat. Pat, tap.

He had a cane in one hand. A pipe in the other.

Pat. Pat, tap.

He wore black over white and his face was hidden under a bowler hat.

Tap.

He stopped right at the end of the alley where I was hiding, looked one way, then the other. He sighed, and there was a hint of laughter in it.

The light from the street barely touched him. He was only a silhouette. The outline of a character that would look at home on a liquor bottle or a packet of peanuts. Then, he reached inside his coat, pulled out a match, and put it in the end of his pipe.

He puffed, and the fire gave me a momentary flash of his face.

He appeared to be Human. Middle-aged with a thin mustache. His eyebrows, straight and severe, looked like they'd been slashed onto his face by a talented swordsman. There were bandages wrapped around his fingers and whenever the fire flared up, his mouth was always smiling.

After he'd taken a few puffs, the stranger threw the match on the ground and walked away, humming in a croaky voice.

I should have stopped him. I knew it, even then. But two worlds were trying to fit into my mind at once.

The world I wanted to live in was the one where Rick Tippity had created an alias so that he could set off a fireball an inch from

Lance Niles's nose. That was the world Simms wanted to live in too. The one she paid good money for.

But I'd stumbled into another world. One where a man in a black suit and bowler hat was walking around town. A man who perfectly fitted the description of Lance's killer but looked nothing at all like Rick Tippity.

I let him go, back into the shadows, humming some disturbingly familiar tune in time with his footsteps.

Pat. Pat, tap.

23

The whole way uptown, I stayed in alleys looking for thinly mustached men in formal suits. Every tap against the cobblestones sounded like his cane. When I found Carissa's doorstep, I knocked more urgently than I intended to.

She came to the door in a black velvet dressing gown with a leopard-print collar.

"Mr Phillips, are you all right? You look quite pale."

"Just jumping at shadows, Mrs Steeme. Can I come in?"

"Of course. Head straight down to the end of the hall. I have the fire going. I swear these post-Coda winters get worse every year."

We went into the living room and I sat on the sofa while she turned a smoldering log in the fireplace.

"I apologize for my appearance," she said. "The cold leaks into my bones and makes me tired, so I usually go down with the sun."

"I'm sorry to intrude, Mrs Steeme, but the news is rather strange. I didn't think it was a good idea for you to be alone when you found out."

"Very gallant of you." She sat on the opposite sofa and tried not to look nervous.

"I went down to the Sickle, just like you asked. I spoke to the Ogre you mentioned, and his information led me to the Rose. Are you familiar with that part of town?"

"Only by reputation. But the same corner exists in every city, under one name or another. I know how it operates."

Despite the elderly lines on her face, Carissa Steeme was street-smart. I hoped that would make things easier.

"I ended up at a new kind of card-house. One where you can

get your gambling and your girls under the same roof. A good-time place where you only go if you're happy to let money fall through your fingers. Did you and Harold put much money away, Mrs Steeme?"

She breathed heavily. "Yes. We did."

"Have you checked your finances in the last few weeks?"

Her eyes lowered, sad and embarrassed.

"Just today, after seeing you. I should have done it when I first found out about the gambling but I suppose I didn't want to accept what he'd done."

The fire coughed a spark onto the rug. She reached out and squashed it with her slipper.

"Did you ever suspect he might be lying to you?" I asked.

Her eyes shot back up.

"Harold had his vices. As do we all. I wouldn't have thought a man like you would be so quick to judge."

I tipped my head in apology and held up a hand.

"I meant nothing by it. I just hope that you might have taken precautions. Put some money aside in a place he wasn't aware of. I don't want to know where it is, I just hope you might have had that foresight."

She took a gulp of water to push down the anger that was bubbling up.

"Yes, I did. Not that I mistrusted him or suspected he would ever do anything wrong by me, but Harold was a complicated man. He had his troubles."

"Has," I coughed, like the word was a bit of phlegm stuck in my throat.

"Sorry?"

"He *has* troubles, Mrs Steeme. Your husband is still alive."

She went backwards through all the stages of grief. After ten seconds, she looked like she'd wring the neck of any man who glanced at her and I wondered whether I should be running for the door.

"You're sure about this?" she asked.

"Yes. I saw him."

"At this . . . whorehouse?"

"Yeah."

Her glass smashed against the wall. I sent my eyes to the floor.

"Apologies," she said. "Give me a moment."

She got up and went into the other room. Ten minutes later, she came back with a couple of glasses and a bottle of whiskey. She poured us each a slug.

"Does he know you saw him?"

"Yeah. Sorry. I kind of shot my mouth off."

"It's fine."

I'd never seen anybody compose themselves as quickly as she did. She sat back and sipped her drink like it had all happened a hundred years ago. The whiskey was better than I'd had in a long time. I told her so.

"It was Harold's. He was saving it for something special."

"Then I guess I'll have some more."

She laughed, and it was balanced as perfectly as the whiskey: just the right amount of darkness and light.

"There's something else," I had to say.

"Please, I don't want to hear about any other women. This has been quite enough for one night."

"No. Not that. But it's something kind of strange."

I told her about Harold's face. How some doctor had stitched him up like an old jacket. Smoothed out the wrinkles to make him a strange new version of his old self. When I was done, she didn't move. Her face was blank. She put down her glass, sat back, and was silent for a long time. Maybe a quarter of an hour.

"I guess I should get out of your hair," I said.

Carissa lay down lengthways on the sofa and kicked her feet up over the side.

"No need to rush off. I don't think I'll be sleeping tonight. Stay if you like. Enjoy the whiskey."

So, I did. I topped her up and took off my boots and got comfortable while she told me about her life and her doomed marriage and the way things were before the world fell apart. We got wasted and she got flirty and we laughed to tears over things I can't remember. I must have finally got drowsy because I opened my eyes to see her tucking a blanket around my shoulders.

"Did I fall asleep?"

"It's all right. You've had a big day, kid."

When she leaned over me her gown fell open. I kept my eyes up on hers. There was a whole world inside them, swimming in circles; memories and centuries and anger and shame and a whole other person who'd vanished from the mirror one night. Those eyes made me sad, so I closed mine, and her fingers brushed the side of my face before she went away.

24

I woke up on the sofa at the Steeme house. There was the stale taste of whiskey on my tongue and someone standing over me, mumbling angrily to themselves.

I opened my eyes. The machine was on the floor, beside my boots. I'd taken it out during the night so I wouldn't drunkenly blast a hole in myself.

"Cheap and nasty piece of shit. It's still my . . ."

It was Harold, back home for the first time with his fresh new face. He was looking down at the coffee table and shaking his head. I reached under the blanket but couldn't find my knife or my knuckles. They were still in my coat, somewhere on the floor. Harold kept muttering. He was still drunk. So was I.

". . . this is still my home."

Harold picked up the poker from the fireplace and brought it down on the empty whiskey bottle, shattering it into pieces just like his wife had done with the glass.

I sat up and Harold must have only just seen me. He raised the poker and fixed his eyes on the top of my head.

"I told you that this was none of your business."

He brought the iron down and I defended myself with my forearms. Harold's muscles hadn't been mended like his skin so the hit wasn't so hard. I pulled the weapon from his fingers and threw it across the room.

"I was just doing my job, old man. No hard feelings."

I stood up. Harold stepped back.

"Get out of my house."

"Sorry, Harold. I only take my orders from the lady."

The top of the bottle was still on the table and Harold snatched it up. He held it by the neck with the jagged edge pointed in my direction. I wasn't confident I could take it from him without opening a vein. My eyes fell to the machine. So did his.

"What is that?" he asked.

"Nothing."

"Get back."

He swung the bottle and I did as he asked. Then he moved forward till the machine was at his feet. I tried to close the distance while he was looking at it but he slashed out with the bottle again.

"I said get back."

"I am."

"Get out of my house!"

I took a big step backwards and felt the poker under my foot.

Harold reached down and picked up the machine. It was just like the first time I'd unwrapped it. No instructions needed. His fingers folded around the wooden handle and he considered its weight. Wondered at its purpose. Perhaps he even felt its power.

That was enough.

I tucked my foot under the poker and kicked it up towards my hand. It was clumsy, but I managed to catch one end of it. I whipped it around and smashed Harold's forearm. He dropped the machine back on the carpet and cried out as I kicked him in the chest. His knees buckled and he hit the ground. I stopped myself from punching him. Despite his new exterior, he was a fragile bag of bones underneath.

His hands were bleeding because he'd fallen on a piece of the broken bottle. For a little old man like him, that was enough of an injury to end the battle.

"What do you want?"

I picked up the machine. "I want you to leave."

"This is my home."

I pointed the end of the pipe right at his face.

"Not right now, it isn't. I want you to dry yourself out and come back when you're sober."

He tried to sneer but couldn't quite manage it.

"Or what? What are you going to do with that thing?"

I was hungover and sore and I'd had enough of his high-nosed, rich-boy attitude.

"I'll make your head explode, Harold. How does that sound? I'll push this button and your brand-new face will go to pieces."

He scoffed. "That's impossible."

My hand held steady. Suddenly, he wasn't so certain.

"You're right. It is impossible. The magic is all gone. Forever. So, how about I show you a little miracle?"

"That's enough."

Carissa was in the doorway with her gown wrapped tight around her and the exact expression on her face that no man wants to come home to.

I tucked the machine into its holster and tried to make myself invisible.

Harold got up. His hands were covered in blood. He was trying to put words in his mouth: something that would make some kind of sense, but he knew there wasn't any way to explain himself.

Instead, he opened his wallet and pulled out a wad of bills. His bloody fingerprints smeared the bronze leaf as he held them out to her, crumpled and pathetic.

"What are you doing?" she asked.

Harold took a step forward, arm outstretched, but Carissa made it clear that she wasn't going to take his meager offering. He was forced to drop the sticky pieces on top of the coffee table.

"I just . . . I wanted to pay you back."

"Pay me back?"

"Yes. For what I took."

I'm not a smart man. I know nothing about life and less about women, but even I wouldn't have come out with a clunker like that. You could have filled a hot air balloon with the steam coming out of her ears.

"What's in your other pocket, Harold? A hundred years? Are

you smuggling a lifetime of memories up your ass? You didn't steal money, darling. You took meaning, and dignity, and you sold them all for a painted face."

Harold kept opening his mouth, hoping the right words would come to him, but they never did. So he sat down.

"Get up, Harold," she said. "You're not staying."

"No," he replied. "I'm not."

And there was the crux of it. Some part of her had been waiting for an apology. To see him down on his knees, confessing his sins and mistakes and asking for forgiveness. She might even have given it to him.

But he wasn't here for that. He was here to pay her off. To buy her forgiveness so he could walk away in his new body guilt free.

I thought she might spit in his face. Instead, she just muttered, "Leave. Both of you."

Harold looked down at his hands. Carissa closed her eyes. I could almost hear the voice in her head, telling her to wait till he was gone before she let herself cry.

I put a hand on Harold's shoulder.

"Let's go."

He nodded. I helped him up, led him out, and did Mrs Steeme the honor of not looking back.

Outside, the sunrise hit my eyes like pepper spray. Harold covered his face, not enjoying it any more than I was.

"You want to get a drink?" he asked.

What a lunatic. A minute ago, we'd been trying to kill each other. Now he wanted to be my friend. Harold Steeme had a serious problem if he'd forget all that for a drinking buddy.

"Sure," I said. "Lead the way."

25

The only place that was open and serving alcohol was a strip-mall dive bar with stale carpet and no windows. The counter had five seats, one keg of warm beer, and a single electric light buzzing over the only other customer: an ancient Cyclops who was asleep with his head in his hands. The barkeep was an old Witch with no teeth and two missing fingers. Harold grabbed a bunch of napkins for his bleeding fingers and ordered himself a pint as if I wasn't there. I ordered my own. It tasted like it was brewed from the first bit of tap water that comes out the pipes when they haven't been used in a while.

Harold sighed. The Cyclops snored. The Witch hiccupped and I wondered if I'd finally found the worst bar in all of Sunder City.

I didn't want to talk to Harold. I hated the guy about as much as I hated myself, but it was better than listening to the symphony of bodily functions.

I took a big gulp of beer and it helped my hangover despite the taste.

"How you doing, Harold?"

He sighed again, like I hadn't heard him the first time.

"I'm confused. I don't want to go back to her but I wouldn't say I'm happy where I am. I know that I just need to wait till I get used to the new way of things, but it takes time to adjust. More time than I have left."

"Then why'd you do it?"

His drink was done. He ordered another. The Witch gave him a wink when she handed it over. His new face seemed to work for some.

"Because I only knew one woman my whole life. I was happy

with that because I thought I had an eternity ahead of me. Commitment is easy when you think you'll have more than one life to live. I don't know how you Humans ever managed it. Eighty years, if you're lucky. Thirty good ones. How do you give that all to one person?"

Harold was speaking of things outside my realm of expertise. I'd had few lovers. No relationships. But I'd sat at enough bars with similarly troubled men to fake my way through.

"You're not the first guy who wanted to screw around on his girl, Harold. That happens. But did you need to spend her savings on a new mug?"

"Maybe not. Certainly not for the girls. I'm still paying them all anyway. But it makes me feel better about it."

"But why do it in secret and let your wife think you were dead? If you hadn't lied to her, she might have been happy to see you like this again."

He licked his lips and some real emotion pushed its way through his renovated face.

"Because this wasn't about her. Sure, I'm miserable and the days are long but they're *mine*. If I was looking out at a century or two like this, then I'd worry. But I've got a decade left, tops. It's a lonely life but at least it won't last forever."

I couldn't help wondering what it would have been like to grow old with Amari. To grow at all with her. I couldn't imagine getting bored of her voice. Becoming tired of the things that had once delighted me. Hearing her tell a story so many times it made me want to pull my hair out. Knowing her morning breath and her bad moods. Seeing some part of her body that I didn't find perfect. Being disappointed by her. Embarrassed by her. Disgusted. Looking forward to a moment alone. Wondering what the touch of someone else would be like. Lying to her. Leaving her. I was furious with Harold again. He'd had everything I'd wanted and he'd thrown it all away.

"That's a selfish way to live, Harold."

"Fine. Who says we aren't supposed to be selfish? Who says we're supposed to be anything? Only a fool would look at what's happened to the world and think that there's any kind of plan. Nobody is going to care if I spend my last days cuddled up with Carissa or bouncing on top of a whore." Then he turned and looked at me like he'd only just realized I was there. "Why do you care?"

"Because despite what happened to the world, there's still right and wrong."

He snickered. "That's why you do this? Because you believe in right and wrong? I call bullshit on you, buddy. You're just keeping yourself busy with the little things because the big things are too hard to think about. Just like the rest of us." He ordered a whiskey to go with his beer. It was turning into quite the breakfast. "Besides, this is better for her. She wasn't strong enough to do it herself but once she grieves, she'll know that this was the right thing for both of us."

I turned my head away in disgust. Beside me, there was yesterday's afternoon edition of the *Sunder Star*. The headline read: "Warlock Chemist Accused of Murder."

Harold Steeme was lying to himself. It was obvious from the outside. Unmistakable. He'd written a version of events inside his head and he was holding onto them so he wouldn't have to admit what a mistake he'd made.

But he wasn't the only one.

I'd tried to distract myself with the Steeme case but now that it was over, I couldn't hide from the lie I'd been telling myself.

I'd put a man behind bars. At the time, I'd believed it was for all the right reasons. But now? Now, I had a killing machine strapped to my chest. Now a man in a black suit and a bowler hat was wandering the streets.

None of it made sense anymore, no matter how much I wanted it to.

I needed to talk to Rick Tippity.

26

Tippity wasn't where I'd left him, in his cell downtown. He wasn't up at the station either. I stopped by Richie's desk to find out what was going on.

"He's down in the Gullet."

"What's the Gullet?"

"A new prison the Mayor's been building. A special set of cells for troublesome crims."

It was the first I'd heard of it. In a city without enough food, employment or public services, paying for a new prison should have been lower on the list of priorities.

"Why the hell are we making new prisons?"

"Because bums like you are filling everybody's heads with monsters. When you and I were Shepherds, even if people weren't any safer, the Opus made people *feel* like they were safer. I remember telling you once that the way people perceive you can be just as important as the work you actually do. Now everyone thinks they're on their own, hiding from creatures that don't have names yet. The Mayor wants us to look like we're back in control."

It's true that rumors scare people more than reality. If people on the street were hearing stories about undead Vampires coming back to Sunder and biting off the heads of little girls, folks would want to know that the city had some kind of response.

Their response was the Gullet. Nothing but a dirty hole to throw strange and unpredictable criminals into. It was an old grain silo on the north-eastern side of town that had been given an unflattering makeover. They'd cut a door in the side, reinforced it with recycled steel, ripped up the floor, dug down into the clay, and built a few impenetrable cages at the bottom. It was a slap-dash effort thrown together as a publicity stunt, completed just in time for a deranged Warlock to shoot some magic from his fingers and an over-eager Man for Hire to drag him to the cops' front door.

When I arrived, Simms was out front talking to a couple of prison guards. She saw me, and there was nothing but frustration on her face. At least we didn't need to fake the animosity this time.

"I told you to stay put. You look like shit."

"Don't say that. I've been moisturizing and everything."

"Did you see a doctor?"

"Yeah."

"What did they tell you?"

"To buy a hat. Where's Tippity?"

"In the hole."

"I wanna see him."

She actually laughed. "You're kidding, right?"

"Nope. We bonded on the road. What can I say? I miss him."

She wasn't having any of my cracks but our newly formed almost-friendship stopped her from dismissing me completely. Instead, she told her subordinates to give us some space.

"Fetch, you shouldn't be here. This is a murder investigation. I'll come to you before the trial so we can talk about your testimony but I don't want you doing anything stupid that could fuck up the case."

"Like what?"

"With you, I can't even imagine. You antagonize the prisoner? Tell him something you shouldn't? Slap him around? We *have* him. Things are playing out just the way they should. Go home. Get some sleep. Wait for my call. That's what I paid you for."

I looked up at the silo. It was a mixture of metal, stone and wood supposed to look impregnable. There was one heavy door and no windows. Some jails were created for necessity. Some for punishment. This one was created as a warning.

"Simms, what if he didn't do it?"

Her mouth fell open in shock but her long fangs and black spit made it look menacing.

"You're the one who brought him in!"

"I know."

"You saw the frozen Warlock."

"I did."

"And Tippity confessed to that killing."

"In a way."

"You saw him desecrating bodies with your own eyes!"

"Yep."

"And he used the magic from those bodies to burn you, and himself. Didn't you say that?"

"I did."

"So what's the fucking issue here, Fetch?"

"Nothing. As long as he's the one who killed Lance Niles."

She spat into the mud.

"Fetch, I hired you to find Niles's killer. A killer who used magic. You brought in a Warlock with a pocketful of fireballs: the first spells we've seen in six years. Now you want to question whether we've got the right guy?"

"Not question. Just confirm. It would really help me sleep."

She was a better cop that she wanted to be. A bad cop would have sent me home. A bad cop would have held onto that nice story she had in her hands. But a good cop cares about the truth.

"Damn it, Fetch. You've got five minutes."

It wasn't as dark inside the Gullet as I thought it would be. That's because there was no roof. The top was left open, making it colder, wetter, crueler in its design.

The stairs were stone and unfinished, leading down without a rail to the eight cells in the center of the room. Six were empty.

One was still under construction. The other was home to Rick Tippity.

He was sitting on the floor, in the mud, and his previously well-maintained hair was slick and brown. His glasses were smeared to uselessness. He had a white and black beard coming in but his eyes were the same. Indignant. Superior. Patient.

A guard waited at the bottom. He had an umbrella and boots but was otherwise condemned to the same punishment as the prisoner.

"Don't get too close," he said, and I tried not to roll my eyes. Without his little leather pouches, Tippity was harmless. He looked at me over his dirty glasses with cold and unflinching hate.

"Hey, Rick. I like the new digs." I waited for him to respond but the bastard didn't even blink. "I assume they're keeping you here till the trial. The trial in which you stand accused of a whole number of awful crimes. A trial in which, along with a barrel-load of physical evidence, I've been called as the key witness against you."

His left cheek gave an involuntary twitch. I continued.

"I saw you cut open the heads of the Faeries, Rick. I—"

"They were already dead, you piece of shit."

At least he was talking.

"Let me finish. I saw you cut open the remains of those Faeries. I saw your frozen partner in the back room, trapped in a scream. I lost both my eyebrows to one of those little packs of magic you carry around with you. But I didn't see you kill anyone. You *tried* to kill me, I suppose. If you'd hit me a little harder on the top of my head, you might've succeeded. And if you'd mixed up your potion a bit better, you might have burned my face off at the beginning of this mess and saved us both a lot of hassle. But that didn't happen, did it? When the bomb exploded in your pocket, it didn't even blow your balls off. So, either the last two fireballs were considerably less powerful than the one you used to open up Lance Niles's head or things aren't adding up the way we want them to."

Tippity couldn't work out my angle. He must have thought I was preparing for the trial: working out how to trip up his defense before he made it on the stand.

"What are you asking me?"

"I'm asking you how powerful your magic really is."

He wanted to talk. We were on his favorite subject, but he knew that he needed to be careful.

"Why do you want to know?"

"Come on, Rick. You talked a big game on the way back to the city but I never saw anything to back it up. Are you really sitting in this shithole because of a little powder-puff of Faery dust? Don't tell me all those speeches were just about a little light and color." He was literally biting his tongue. "It will be a sad day for all of us if I have to go on the stand and tell them that this whole mess was just a Warlock setting off sparks."

"It depends on the source, you idiot."

Here we go.

"Excuse me?"

"There are hundreds of species of Faery, each with their own history, talents and connection to the sacred river. Sentient pieces of fire, forest and air that walked upon the world. Each one of them contained a different chemical make-up. Therefore, it makes sense, does it not, that their essence would react differently when released?"

It did. I thought about the faces spread out around the church and how Tippity had carefully selected each one, plucking out specific souls to experiment on. I felt sick again.

"Is that what happened? You used one of your bigger bangers on Lance Niles? Is that why he got cooked and I didn't?"

The sneer crept up his face like a ringworm.

"No. I didn't kill that man, you moron."

I watched him for a moment. Neither of us had anything left to say.

Goddamit.

I believed him.

I was sore and exhausted but I couldn't sleep. So, after nightfall, I picked up a lantern and went south. Back to the stadium.

Things had changed out there since that night with Warren and Linda. A whole section of the field had been barricaded off and construction equipment was scattered across the field, illuminated by electric orange lights. Maybe the Mayor was hoping to start up the games again. Nothing like a bit of sport to take your mind off the misery on the streets.

I waited a while, till I was sure that I was alone, then I ducked under the bleachers. Beneath one of the seats, I found an old training dummy: a man-shaped sack used for tackling practice. I dragged him out into the open and pushed him up against the lamppost.

I took the machine from its holster and held it up, a foot away from the sack man's head.

Then, I pressed the button.

A crack of lightning went off in my hands, echoing all the way back into town. From the end of the pipe, a curl of smoke cut the lantern-light.

There was a hole in the dummy's head. Little clouds of cotton had come out of it and were catching a ride on the wind. I lifted up the lantern to get a better look at the damage.

The hole was small at the front. Just like the gap where Lance Niles lost his front teeth. I pulled the dummy's head forward and there was a crater at the back. Just like the hole that had appeared in Lance Niles's cheek and neck. Stuffing had sprayed out in both directions, like Niles's spattered blood. The canvas was burned around the edges, just like the blackened collar and cravat.

Rick Tippity hadn't been in the Bluebird Lounge. Lance Niles had met some other guest. Someone who'd been holding the same ugly death machine that I was.

There was no magic here. Just a vile combination of nuts and bolts. A tool made from twisted metal and chemicals whose only purpose was to administer a single shot of murder. I hated the thing in my hands, and I hated the way it sang to me even more. It was a fast-acting poison. A fall without the fear. It was drowning in your sleep. A cut to the heart. It was death delivered in an instant.

I looked into the pipe. Into that elegant darkness.

I let my finger rest on the button.

Instant.

My hand was steady. My eyes were clear. Clear enough that when I looked past the pipe, I saw the little shield stamped into the metal. The tiniest of letters engraved across the finger-guard.

V. Stricken.

The machine of death had a maker. Maybe it was the same person who shot Lance Niles. Maybe it was the same person who dropped it on my desk.

At the very least, it was something to work with; a chance to set things right.

I took my finger off the button and headed back home.

The next day, I copied the manufacturer's stamp onto a piece of paper and took it around the city, asking other crafters if they recognized the mark. I went to a blacksmith first, then an armorer, but nobody knew the maker. I took it to weapons stores on both ends of town but didn't have any luck. I finally got my answer back on East Ninth Street, from a Goblin at a corner store that sold lighters, switch-blades and tobacco.

"Yeah, that's Victor. As far as I know, he's still back in the Valley. He makes good stuff but the guy's an asshole and too

damn expensive. Tell me what you want and I'll whip you up
something at a quarter of the price."

I didn't dare show him the machine itself. Flashing it around
the Steeme household had been enough of a mistake. I thanked
him for his help and jotted down the name.

Somebody had put the weapon into my care and I could only
think of three reasons: to frame me for Lance Niles's murder, to
tempt me to use it on myself or to lead me down this road of
discovery.

Whatever the reason, I only had one idea about where to get
some answers: out of Sunder to Aaron Valley in search of Victor
Stricken.

27

I was broke again. Cash poor. Though I did have a small fortune under my ass, pushing her way through the snow.

The trainer told me I'd get most of the bronze back if I returned the horse in one piece. Easier said than done in this weather, but I was given plenty of tips to help me out: don't run her too hard, keep her dry, warm her up slow and warm her down just the same, check her hooves regularly and keep to the road.

We took off her horseshoes so her hooves wouldn't snowball in the ice. I bought a rug to keep on her back when we were riding and another to add at night. The trainer trimmed her forelock and gave her a good feed and we walked her around the yard to stretch out her muscles. I lost half a day and all my savings but she was, without a doubt, the most beautiful thing I ever owned.

The trainer gave me as much advice about my own care as he did about the horse: bring food and a thermos of hot tea, take breaks, stretch, and don't fall asleep in the saddle no matter how tempting it might be.

My horse's name was Frankie. She had a thick mane and a brown and black coat that puffed out around her hooves like bellbottoms. I fed her some oats from my hand and a fresh apple and then we were off.

We'd had horses back in Weatherly but they were only used for pulling carts or plows. Never riding. That training came after I joined the Opus.

The night I enlisted, Hendricks, Amari and I celebrated by damn-near poisoning ourselves. I was allowed one day of recovery before Hendricks dragged me out of bed and shoved me on the back of a horse.

We went outside the city limits with a couple of insolent colts and Hendricks did his best to make me a rider. It didn't come naturally. The next morning, we were met by a team of Shepherds and began our journey west.

Hendricks was my friend and mentor but, first and foremost, he was a leader. On the long trek to Opus headquarters, I was given my first taste of what our new relationship would be.

He knew how to push me till I was tired but not broken. I tried not to complain, but when my ass was red and my legs cramped, protests sometimes slipped out. When that happened, he would always keep moving. Push me just a little harder. Show me that I was tougher than I thought I was. When I was silent and stoic again, he'd announce that it was time to rest.

With those gentle, almost invisible lessons, he turned me from an errand boy into a warrior. We still laughed. We still ate together by the fire. We were still friends, but the tone shifted. It had to. He was my boss. What were once recommendations were now orders. Lighthearted jokes became reprimands. Questions turned into tests and I wasn't allowed to sleep until I answered them correctly.

I understood why things had to change. By allowing me into the Opus, he was risking his reputation. Everything I did was seen as a reflection of his judgment. My failings were now *his* failings. My naïvety exposed a lack of education. My confusion slowed things down. My mistakes undermined his authority.

I'd always thought that there were no wrong answers with Hendricks. The question was always more important than the response. Not anymore. On the journey back to headquarters, I was taught facts, dates and the correct foreign words to use in certain situations so as not to set off an international incident.

But I was happy. How could I not be? We were together, out on the road, ready for adventure. For the first time in my life I felt like someone really knew me. I could have lived in that time forever.

Frankie shook her head, frizzing up her mane and sending vibrations through my arms. The clouds had cleared and there was nothing ahead but white powder and open sky. The glare off the snow gave me a headache so I kept my eyes closed and let Frankie lead the way.

It was slow going at first but, once Frankie was warmed up, she increased the pace on her own. She found a rhythm that suited her and I didn't interfere. The road was ours. The snow was only six inches deep and she kicked her way through without worry.

As the sun turned red on the horizon, Frankie slowed down to tell me that it was time to camp.

"You're right, girl. We don't wanna get caught in the dark."

I took her off the path to an empty brick building with only three walls and went about making a fire. Frankie found a place for herself out of the wind and I put another blanket on her back.

I drank weak tea, cooked some rice and curled up in my bedroll to listen to the night, but it didn't have anything to say

28

The second day of riding is always a bitch. My muscles were stiff and sore and my ass was a big red rash. We were riding straight into a cold wind that pushed tears out of my eyes and chilled my cheeks. Frankie started slow and I didn't argue with her.

The thermos was well-crafted and likely kept me alive. I boiled tea in the morning, drank my share, and filled the flask. When the contents went empty or started to freeze, we stopped by the side of the road and I built another fire, fed Frankie warmed water, refilled the flask, and headed off again.

I was headed north, on a rocky road beside a set of train tracks. The Sunder City express wasn't running anymore but it once went all the way up to the northern cliffs, through the Dwarven caves and out to the desert.

Sunder didn't have its own farms, so most food was imported from other lands. There were no farms on this part of the conti-nent. Just the memories of mining towns that rose up over a season, cut the earth for a few years, then dissolved as quickly as they appeared. Roadhouses marked our way: places to buy refresh-ments or a room for the night, but all of them empty. On the second night, Frankie and I took over one of the abandoned buildings. We lit a fire in the fireplace and Frankie lay in front of it like a bloodhound.

On the third day, our path intersected with the Edgeware Trail: a wide track that hugged the June River from the mountains all the way out to the Western Sea. As we came to the crossroads, I saw smoke up ahead.

We crossed the track, then a wooden bridge, and continued into a brown forest of underdressed pine trees. At first, the trail was scattered with dry pine needles. After fifteen minutes, it was overgrown. After an hour, it was gone and we charted our course by following the gap in the balding trees and the smell of smoke. It was metallic and unnatural, like the steel district back when it was in action.

"Smells a bit like home, huh, girl?"

Frankie huffed her disapproval but continued weaving forward until she found the edge of a cliff that looked down at Aaron Valley – the very first Goblin village.

Pre-Coda Goblins were nocturnal creatures, deathly allergic to sunlight. Over time, they created technology that would allow them to venture further out of their caves. The history of their inventions was visible in the architecture of the valley walls.

At the bottom of the valley, in an area that would have been in shadow for most of the year, there was a spattering of round clay huts. The layer above was brick and stone: round arches and flat-topped fortifications. Higher again were copper suspension bridges that stretched between the cliffs joining shining metal towers together. The next level was reminiscent of the Opus headquarters or a picture I once saw of the Wizard home of Keats, smooth glass and silver bunkers cut into the rocky walls. Each layer was specific, beautiful, and appeared to be utterly abandoned. The only sign of life was the single hut on the valley floor responsible for belching out the black smoke.

There were many ways down but they were all made from narrow walkways and rope bridges. Far too precarious for a horse.

"It's still early," I told Frankie. "There should be enough light for me to make it down the side of the cliff, ask my questions, and come back for you later. Sound good to you?"

She groaned, which I took as reluctant compliance.

I led Frankie back into the woods and tied her to one of the trees, leaving some water and the last of the oats. She wasn't impressed with where she'd found herself but I had a feeling she'd known what she was in for from the first moment she saw me.

I hadn't brought enough food. Hopefully whoever was at the bottom of the valley would have some to spare, or could at least point us in the direction of something green.

I went back to the edge of the cliff and surveyed the possible paths down. I chose one that looked like it had been reasonably maintained, off to my left, and took three steps in that direction.

Then, I was launched into the air.

My first thought was that someone had pushed me out into the chasm, but I wasn't actually falling. I was hanging upside down with my arms flailing about and my belongings dropping out of my pockets.

There was a rope around one of my feet. Looking up, the rope was suspended between two of the pine trees. The cord was already cutting into my ankle as my body swung stupidly around in the air.

Swaying between the trees, I searched for a way to take the pressure off my leg. I was too out of shape to get my hands near the knot, so I flailed out with both hands and snatched one of the trunks.

The tree had been trimmed and sanded. No branches. There weren't even any notches or grooves that I could use to hoist myself up. My grip was tentative at best and the idea of trying to get higher felt risky because if I lost connection to the tree I'd go swinging on my ankle again.

Now that my hands were taking some of the weight, my foot did feel better. The pain was being shared equally along my hamstring, back, shoulders and shaking hands.

A bell was ringing. It must have been set off when I stepped into the trap, but I'd only just settled enough to hear it.

I looked down, and noticed the outline of more traps around the ridge of the valley. Pits covered with nets and more ropes running between tree trunks. Every gap was filled with some near-invisible trick that was only made obvious from my higher vantage point.

From here, I could see all the way down into the valley floor where the door to the smoking hut was open and someone was standing in the entrance.

He watched me for a bit, then went back inside. A minute later, he came back out and climbed a path towards me.

He didn't need to rush. I wasn't going anywhere. My body was stretched out between the tree in my hands and the rope around my foot, with my belly hanging out of my clothes begging to be disemboweled. I wrapped one arm around the tree trunk so I could use my other hand to search my pockets.

My Clayfields were gone. Brass knuckles had fallen out along with the last of my coins. The machine was still in its holster under my ribs and my knife was in my belt. I took out the knife.

There was no way I could get it anywhere near my foot. If I wanted to cut myself free, I'd have to get to the line at the top of the trunk.

The wood was tough, so I couldn't just stab my way up like an ice climber. Instead, I sawed a little groove into the wood, deep enough so that when I re-sheathed my knife, I could use it to lift myself up a few more inches. Then I took the knife out again and repeated.

I was three notches up when the world glowed orange.

"That's enough of that."

It wasn't easy to look down. I'd got myself all twisted up like a fancy pastry. When I tucked my head between my shoulders, there was a Goblin standing under me. He had a tired expression, a light on his hardhat, and a crossbow.

"Drop the knife," he said.

I hesitated, hoping to steal one final moment in which I could come up with some daring escape plan.

The Goblin was having none of it. He poked the tip of the loaded crossbow into my bare belly. I dropped the knife.

"I told your friends that you lot better not come back here," said the Goblin.

"I . . . I don't have any friends."

He cocked the crossbow and I panicked. My hands came loose and I went swinging again. I slammed into the trunk on the other side and spun madly around. When the momentum slowed enough for me to see clearly, the Goblin had the crossbow pointed between my eyes.

He had green-blue skin that looked rubbery and wet. His bat-like ears were lined with copper rings, and his dark-tinted goggles hid everything behind them.

He was wrapped in fur – it looked like wolf – but his trousers only covered one leg. The other was made of metal: a complicated arrangement of cogs and pistons with an articulated claw at the bottom. The joints moved smoothly as he shifted his weight.

"I know what you're here for, and you ain't getting it."

"I don't think—"

"I warned you what would happen if any of you came back, and I pride myself on being a man of my word so—"

I'd put my hand on the holster while I was spinning. So, before the Goblin could put an arrow in my brain, I pulled out the machine and pointed it at him.

It wasn't like that time I'd pointed it at Harold Steeme. The Elf's first reaction had been one of confusion because, of course, he had no idea what the weapon was capable of. The Goblin, on the other hand, stared at it with fear, disbelief and familiarity. He knew exactly what I was pointing at him.

"I told you, I don't belong to any group," I said. "I have no idea what threats you made or who you made them to and I haven't come looking for your weapon because I already have it." He looked from me to the machine, and lowered the crossbow to his side. "Victor Stricken? I'm Fetch Phillips and I believe this machine of death belongs to you."

29

I handed over the machine. That convinced Victor, for the moment, to give me the benefit of the doubt. He cut me down and I refilled my pockets, then we went and got Frankie so we could trek down the cliffs together.

Night was falling but the light on Victor's helmet lit our way. We had to walk farther south to get to a bigger path that would accommodate the horse and I asked Victor if he wanted to jump on her back.

"That's nice of you, but no thanks. Heights and me don't mix. To tell you the truth, I'll be happy when we're back at the bottom of the valley with a roof over our heads."

"Where's everyone else?"

"Same place I bet you came from. Sunder is sucking in everyone like it's made of quicksand. We could've made this place work on our own terms. Adapted. But a couple of my kind got all excited, saying there was money to be made in the big city. They all followed each other out there and now I'm the only one left."

We walked the long way down to the bottom of the valley on dirt paths, avoiding the bridges and stairs. I thanked Victor for taking the extra time so we could bring the horse, but he shrugged it off.

"Better for me, anyway: the leg don't like stairs. Not rickety bridges much either. So it don't bother me to—" He held up a hand and we all stopped. Up ahead, on the path, the lantern light caught the outline of a large hare.

Victor pulled the machine out of his belt and held it in front of him. He closed one eye, grimaced, and pressed the button.

It clicked. But nothing happened.

Victor swore.

"I see you've been busy."

The hare ran away, but not far. Victor handed me the machine, less possessive of it than he'd been a minute ago, and pulled the crossbow from his side.

He walked ahead, which gave me a chance to check out his metal leg in action. I'd seen peg-legs before but this was a far more impressive piece of engineering. The movement was so smooth that if he'd been wearing full trousers I wouldn't have guessed that he was an amputee.

Thump.

The bolt hit its mark and Victor made a satisfied noise.

"It seems I'm able to offer you some hospitality after all."

The clay hut had a forge in the corner, an anvil, a huge wooden tub of black water and a workbench. One corner was a living space. It had a low bed and a little fireplace with a black pot hanging over it.

There were wires wrapped around everything and pieces of metal scattered across the floor. Cogs of every size were kept on poles and in wooden containers. Hinges, screws and plugs had been tucked into containers or came tumbling out of open drawers. Leaning against the walls were half-finished versions of other contraptions: more legs, more weapons and more tools whose purpose I couldn't imagine.

Victor explained that he'd made his own leg, as well as the lightweight crossbow, the trap, and, of course, the killing machine. We gave Frankie a hut of her own and put the hare in the pot while I gave Victor a brief rundown of my history: grew up in Weatherly, moved to Sunder, joined the Opus. He listened with only passing curiosity and didn't ask any questions. Then, once the stew was cooking, he dropped the killing machine onto his bench.

"I tell you, for all the trouble this thing had caused, it ain't even that complicated. Nothing compared to the other inventions I've made in my time."

"Then why hasn't anybody made one before?"

"Because everyone else is trying to replace what was already there. You can't just shove some non-magical material into an old magic contraption and hope it works. You gotta go back to the beginning and look at it like we never had magic in the first place."

Victor cracked the machine open, bending it on a hinge. He turned it upside down and banged it against the bench so that three copper cylinders dropped out. They looked like the caps of expensive pens but each of them had a black ring around the tip.

"It's simpler than the old weapons. More unstable, too. But at least I can do this on my own. I needed a Wizard's help for the old ones. Then a Fae willing to do a little enchanting." Victor removed his goggles and turned off the lamp that was hanging above us. "You ever use one?"

"A magical firearm? No. I saw others carrying them in the Opus, though."

"You know how they work?"

"Not a clue."

"Well, Wizards were able to summon energy from some far-off place to the space between their hands. But only for a moment. We Goblins found a way to *hold* it there. A tiny portal could be contained in an instrument and opened and closed with the push of a button. It was an expensive but common technique for a while. They even used it to upgrade the lamps in Sunder. They put portals in the pipes to bring the fires up from below. Much safer than running mechanical tubes down into the pits."

That was news to me. I'd always assumed that the fires had been right beneath our feet. I suppose it made sense to keep as much distance and technology between the city and the pits as possible.

"Anyway, those magical weapons could shoot out fire or ice or whatever you wanted. They had a shelf life and they were damn expensive but they worked. Of course, when the Coda happened, that all went to shite. Since then, my kind and yours and everyone else have been working on ways to make those weapons again. But it's impossible. The only way to go forward is to go right back to the start and make something new."

He went over to the corner of the room and pulled a canvas sheet off a silver chest.

"Don't do anything stupid while I'm messing round with this, all right? It's dangerous."

He opened the lid. Whatever was inside must have been delicate because the walls of the chest were thick and padded. Victor picked a silver mug up from the floor, dipped it into the box and filled it with fine, red sand. Then he closed it all up and brought the mug back to his desk.

"You know about the Ragged Plains?"

"Only that they're inhospitable."

"*Mostly* inhospitable. Well, they were, anyway. A lot of things got worse with the Coda but some things became easier to manage, like this sand from the northern desert. I took a trip up there last year, did some experiments, and came back with these babies."

He poured a small amount of the red sand into each of the copper caps. His movements were slow and deliberate, taking special care not to spill a single grain. Then he reached into the drawer of the desk and pulled out three metal balls the size of peas.

"Can I look at those?" I asked.

He handed me one of the slugs and picked another out of the drawer. I rolled it around in my hand. It was heavy for its size. Dull gray. The same as the piece of metal that was lodged in my office floor.

"Now, don't startle me or nothing while I do this. I'm coming to the delicate part."

He placed a metal ball on each of the cylinders, resting at the opening. Then he took a tiny gold hammer from his belt and gently tapped the first ball until it stuck fast in the cap. When all three were done, he replaced the hammer and turned my attention to the machine itself.

He opened the hinge right up and pointed to two metal circles, pressed up against each other.

"When you press the trigger, these two rings spin against each other, creating sparks and a shiteload of heat." He took the three full caps, slid them inside the machine and cracked it back together. "When they do that at the base of one of these caps, it sets off the desert dust and shoots a metal ball out the end. If any poor fucker is standing in front of it when it goes off – he won't be there for much longer. So, with that in mind," he pointed the hollow end of the pipe at my chest, "take yourself over to that wall."

I thought it was part of the show but Victor Stricken's scowling face was even more serious than it had been all night.

"You'll find a set of cuffs on the end of that chain. Get them round your wrist."

I did as I was told. The cuffs were connected to a thick black chain and there was already some dried blood around the rim of the manacles.

"You could have done the same thing with the crossbow," I said.

"No, I couldn't have. You might've taken your chances with the bow. But this? This is something else, ain't it, stranger? You've seen its power, just like I have. While I'm holding this, we both know you're gonna do exactly as I say."

He was right. There was no running from the machine. No chance worth taking. I'd seen how it had blown apart Lance Niles's head, ripping the life out of him before he could blink. I closed the cuffs around my wrists until they snapped shut.

"Good lad. Now, get comfortable. You're gonna tell me why you're really here and if I don't like it or I don't believe it, then I'll give you a demonstration of how my machine works, and there will be a lot more stew for me."

30

I found a way to sit against the wall that wasn't completely uncomfortable while I took Victor Stricken through my last few days: the dead body in the Bluebird Lounge, the mistaken arrest of Rick Tippity and the mysterious package containing the machine.

There was no point lying to him. If I wanted him to fill in the gaps of my story, he needed to know where they were. Besides, he was so brutally blunt in the way he spoke that I couldn't help but trust him. He held all the cards and all the chips. All I had to offer was the truth.

His face was bunched up, acting like he didn't believe anything I was saying. But he listened. He didn't interrupt. When I was done, he didn't say anything. He just passed the machine from one hand to the other and licked his lips.

Finally, he took a single key from his belt and threw it into my lap.

"That'll unlock one of them. Not the other. The stew's ready."

While we ate, he asked a couple of follow-up questions. My answers must have done something to ease his mind because after he licked the last bit of stew from his bowl, he decided to share some of his story with me.

Just like the Goblin back in Sunder had told me, Victor was a renowned inventor and an even more famous pain in the ass. Before the Coda, he was a prolific creator of magical weapons. Not magical enhancers like staffs or wands that only work in combination with the powers of the spell-caster; Victor built equipment that granted magical power to those who would otherwise be unable to wield it.

Most Goblins gave up on invention after the Coda. They'd spent their lives making ingenious creations that would never work again so they moved on to other professions and tried to forget what was lost.

Victor had a different point of view. The world had been reset and everything could be rediscovered. For an engineering genius who had already mastered so many disciplines, being able to write the rulebooks from the very beginning was a gift, like forgetting the end of your favorite story so you can read it as if for the first time.

The killing machine wasn't supposed to be so important. It was a prototype: the simplest application of how the powers of post-Coda desert dust could be harnessed. To Victor, it was a toy. It helped him hunt on his journey home from the Ragged Plains and it gave him something fun to show his fellow Goblins when he returned. It wasn't created as an end in itself. Victor was passionate about new modes of transport, automated farming, and industrial equipment that could revive the workforce. A little pellet-shooting piece of metal wasn't supposed to be anything to sing about.

But someone did sing. A few months after Victor returned to Aaron Valley, a Human arrived. The stranger knew about the machine and he wanted to pay Victor to build another one. A *lot* of other ones.

"The whole world is hungry now. Hungry for things we lost that won't come back. But this man had a mad kind of hunger in his eyes. The hunger for power. I told him that he was never going to get the weapon but that I would feed him a couple of bullets if he didn't leave me alone."

The man went away. A month later, he came back with friends.

"Luckily, I'd already put up a bunch of those traps. You stumbled into one of the nicer ones. Some of them aren't so forgiving."

I didn't prod Victor on the details. The dried blood around my wrist let me know that he wasn't a man of idle threats.

"The next person who arrived was an old friend. Another Goblin who told me she was returning from Sunder after realizing that I'd been right all along." He smiled bitterly. "I'm a smart fellow, I tell you true, but flattery works on me as well as anyone. She spent a week assisting me, always at my side. I showed her where the traps were and we even made some more. She told me that more Goblins would be coming home soon because they'd all realized that I was right. How easy it is to believe the things you most want to hear. Then, one morning, she was gone and the weapon was gone with her."

We sat in silence for a while, both thinking about the gap between our stories. How had the machine gone from a Goblin thief to being wrapped up on my desk like a gift?

"I should kill you," he said, so casually that it took me a moment to process the words.

"Uh . . . why?"

"I told you how I made this. When I did that, I already thought I'd be using it on you so I didn't worry too much. Now, I think I might've made a mistake."

He shrugged apologetically, like it was no big thing. As if he'd forgotten to water my houseplants or eaten the last piece of cake.

"I appreciate the fact you're torn up about it, Victor, but is there anything I can do to change your mind?"

He scratched his head, thinking it over.

"I'll sleep on it and tell you in the morning. Let me get you a blanket."

He got me more covers and a sack stuffed with padding to use as a pillow.

"Thanks, Vic. I have to say, out of all the people who've wanted to kill me, nobody has ever been quite so nice about it."

I slept better than I had in years. Peaceful. It's funny what a death sentence can do.

Around midnight, the screaming started.

31

I was pulled from dreamless sleep by the echoes of a man wailing somewhere up above. From the sound of his unbridled screams, he had stumbled into one of Victor's more devilish traps. His cries were full of shock and fear and disbelief. The ringing bell returned to cheer him on.

The door to the hut flew open and Victor pointed his killing machine at my face. I flinched. I don't think I'll ever become accustomed to staring that thing down.

"I thought you said you work alone."

"I do."

"So that ain't one of your friends up there?"

"I don't have friends, Victor."

"Bullshit."

"But I have been thinking. Whoever stole your toy likely didn't choose to hand it over to me. Somebody must have taken it from them."

"You think they're here to get it back?"

"More likely, having lost the original, they decided to track down the one guy who would be able to make them a new one."

Victor wanted to argue but my logic was too sound.

"Stay there. I'll go ask our visitor a few questions. He don't sound like he's in much of a state to spin a good yarn, so you better hope his story matches yours."

He tucked the machine into his belt and picked up his crossbow.

"How many were there?" I asked.

"What are you talking about?"

"How many men? The last time they came here?"

Victor sucked his teeth, already angry that I was thinking clearer than he was.

"Half a dozen. Or thereabouts. A couple of them ran off."

He'd already worked out what I was getting at.

"What are the chances that they'd come back with fewer men this time?"

Of course, there were other possibilities. Maybe some hunter had stumbled into a trap by mistake. Maybe it was a returning Goblin who hadn't got the memo about watching his feet. It didn't *have* to be an angry army coming for his secrets. Of course it didn't. But, we both knew, it probably was.

"Sit tight," he said. "I'll be back."

He marched out into the night. The screaming continued. Then, it was joined by another noise. A thumping, rumbling rhythm. First, up above. Then closer. And closer again.

BANG!

The sound of cracking beams and splintering wood.

"You bastards!" screamed Victor. Frankie was making all kinds of noises. I hoped she wasn't hurt. More rumbles and more crashes came from all sides. I had no idea what was happening.

Then, the room exploded.

A boulder came through the wall on the other side of the room, shattering wood and scattering tools. It went through the fireplace and spread hot coals everywhere. One wall collapsed. The roof followed, and I was left tied to half a house, covered in shards of broken clay.

There was no way of breaking the chain. No way of snapping the thick wooden beam it was connected to. But the clay around the beam was already cracked. I pulled back as far as the cuffs would let me, then jumped forward and rammed my shoulder into the wood. It didn't go down, but there was just enough movement to encourage me to do it again. It took three more cracks before the beam started tipping.

I tried to slow the fall but the beam was too heavy. It slammed against the ground pulling me with it, and the side of my head hit the wood so hard it could have driven in a nail.

I shook the stars from my vision, spraying specks of blood like a wet dog, trying to identify that strange sound.

It was Victor and Frankie. They were screaming.

I dragged the chain beneath the wooden beam as the hot coals set alight the debris at my feet. The attackers must have been running out of rocks because the crashes only came once every ten seconds and they were smaller but still deadly. I stood up, chain dangling from my wrists, and found Victor pinned beneath a boulder, on his back, with blood coming out of his mouth. He wasn't moving and his eyes were pointing in different directions.

The boulder wouldn't move, even when I put my whole weight against it.

Thunk.

An arrow landed in the dirt. Our attackers had turned to more conventional weapons.

I pulled at Victor's body but couldn't free him. Then, I saw the machine, still tucked into his belt. I let go of Victor and grabbed the weapon instead

Hard little hands wrapped around my wrist. He was awake.

"Did you do this?"

When he talked, red spittle hit my face.

"No. I swear."

He grabbed my collar. Pulled my face in so tight I feared that he was going to use his last ounce of strength to bite off my nose.

"Destroy it. Don't let them have it. Don't tell them anything."

SMASH!

Another hut exploded right beside us.

"PROMISE ME!" he coughed. "Before I shoot you myself!"

I nodded and he let me go.

I looked back at the boulder with his one real leg pinned beneath it. Victor looked like he was ten breaths from oblivion and I couldn't see any way to help.

Frankie screamed again, so I left Vic in the dirt to go find her. The fire was spreading and kicking up smoke. Frankie was tied to the remains of a broken weapons rack, freaked out but uninjured. I unharnessed her and hopped on top. There was no time for the saddle. I put the machine in its place beside my ribs, right where it belonged.

Thunk. Thunk.

More arrows. All too wide. Too inaccurate. Knocked about by wind and distance.

I kicked Frankie's sides and we took off south, between boulders and broken huts. We left the Goblin to die in the dirt and I didn't feel good about it but there was nothing I could do. As we weaved between the huts and the towers, arrows landed uselessly in the dirt and a bitter kind of pride burned in my chest.

They couldn't hit me from up there. Not with those weapons. They needed the machine.

But they couldn't have it.

I had it.

Frankie carried me out of the valley and we left them all behind.

32

We were in a bad way. Our blankets had been left behind, along with the saddle and the thermos that had saved our lives on the way out. Everything was back in Aaron Valley under piles of broken clay.

I was shivering. Even Frankie was shivering. The air was full of mist that made everything wet and undefined. The world had lost its edges like we'd all been wiped with turpentine.

I had trouble keeping my bearings and there was no way to tell what time it was. Wild animal sounds came from all directions. We plodded on, miserable and hurting.

Then, Frankie stopped.

The world went quiet. No bird calls. No wind. Just Frankie's breath. She sniffed the air and made a noise like a growling dog.

"What is it, girl?"

Her eyes were locked ahead and her body went tense between my legs. Fear passed through her body into mine. Then, I heard it.

Hooves. Thundering against the path. Closer and closer.

Somebody was charging on horseback, through the mist, right in our direction.

I couldn't see them through the fog. They wouldn't be able to see us. I kicked Frankie to move off the path but she was petrified in place.

"Hey!" I screamed into the white. "Hey, look out!"

The hooves kept coming. Just as fast. Faster. Then I saw it.

The shadow of a horse. No rider. Thundering through the haze.

Frankie reared back on her hind legs and I had to dig my hands into her mane to keep from tumbling over. She lashed out at the air with her front legs but the display did nothing to slow down the incoming steed. It charged through Frankie's wild limbs and sunk its teeth into the flesh under her neck.

The wild horse bit down hard and didn't let go. I could see our attacker's deformed face up close. Its eyes were clouded over with insanity and the flesh of its muzzle was punctured with pieces of shining stone. A jagged, broken rock punctured its forehead like a crystal third-eye.

It was a Unicorn.

A horse with a horn of pure magic sprouting from its forehead that some stories claimed was a piece of the river itself.

Well, it seemed that the storytellers were right.

The horn of pure magic had frozen, just like the sacred river, and created a cluster of sharp crystals that cut through its skin. One purple dagger of dark stone sprouted from under its eye socket and the wound was surrounded by old scabs and dead flesh. From the way the horse was acting, I guessed that the crystal had also grown back inside the animal's brain.

The beast clenched its teeth, full of blood and foam. Despite the horror, I felt myself wanting to reach out and comfort it. The Coda had made so many monsters. So much pain. But it had never been captured as perfectly as this.

This was one of the sacred wonders of the world. A rarely seen symbol of how beautiful life could be, sent mad by a piece of corrupted magic cutting into its mind. The Coda had infected the whole world, but never had I seen a more sorry and terrifying victim.

Frankie screamed and stumbled to her feet. She landed a few hits with her flailing hooves but the Unicorn was unstoppable. It drove the jagged point of its horn forward and cut Frankie across her face.

I scrambled away as blood and hooves filled the air. The beast bit into Frankie's side. She squealed, spun around and kicked out with her hind legs. The Unicorn avoided the attack, which at least created some much-needed space between them.

Blood dripped off both their faces, though I feared most of it came from my horse. They circled each other, breathing deep and limping. Frankie was exhausted, weak, and already badly wounded.

The Unicorn charged again and I rolled out the way. Frankie tried to keep her distance, spinning and kicking out with her back legs, but the Unicorn had no sense of self-preservation. Their heads smashed together. Mouths searched for ears or bits of soft flesh, both beasts wailing in anger and pain.

I fumbled the machine from its holster and held it up with frozen, shaking fingers. The fighters' heads were locked close, rolling over each other, slick with blood and spittle.

Then Frankie broke free. The Unicorn reared up on its hind legs and I had a chance at a clear shot. My finger hovered over the switch.

It was a Unicorn. The first I'd ever seen.

Frankie got up on her haunches to strike out with her front hooves. There was a cracking sound as she made connection, slamming the rabid animal right on its skull, but the beast shrugged off the hit like it was nothing.

Then, my horse came down and the Unicorn launched itself up. Their bodies met in midair and the splintered, broken horn of the beast stabbed deep into Frankie's neck.

Frankie's scream came out as a wet gurgle, unable to rip her throat from the Unicorn's horn. Her wide eyes found mine. She was begging me to save her.

I fired.

The two animals dropped to the ground.

The Unicorn died quickly. Frankie died slow. I put my hands in her mane and petted her until she was as cold as everything else in this broken, empty world.

33

All the best memories have music.

In Sunder, space was expensive. Those at the top had grand houses and gardens, while those at the bottom were crammed together like sticky candies left at the bottom of the tin. That was why the night at Prim Hall felt so strange: Sunder City's most important persons were all squeezed in together, shoulder to shoulder, in tiny seats around a small stage.

For some reason, I was there too.

At the end of the row, Baxter Thatch had one ass cheek on the seat and the other dangling into the aisle. The woman sitting behind them was visibly frustrated by the size of the Demon but was trying not to show it.

To Baxter's left, there were two empty seats, then me, then Amari.

I was wearing a bow tie, and I looked ridiculous. Amari was wearing a gown, and looked like a queen. It was sewn from sheer silk and skeleton leaves and I spent the whole night struggling not to stare.

On the other side of Amari, Governor Lark grumbled about the size of his seat and its comfort and just about everything.

"I thought you brought him here to butter him up," I whispered to Amari.

"Just wait." Her lips touched my ear as she whispered back. "It will all change when they start playing."

There was movement down below as the stage flooded with musicians. Dozens of them, all dressed in suits as ridiculous as mine.

The chairs creaked painfully as Baxter leaned over and said, "Where the hell is Hendricks?"

The only empty seats in the whole place were the two on our row. Before I could shrug, the doors at the back of the auditorium were flung open and the High Chancellor stumbled in. He was sweaty, drunk, and laughing loudly. A beautiful Warlock scholar followed behind him in a similar state of intoxication. Hendricks and I had met the young man at a bar the previous night. I'd found him fairly boring but he'd approached Hendricks flattery-first so it was impossible to get rid of him.

The latecomers skipped down the stairs and Baxter stood up to let them in.

"Just in time," Baxter mumbled. Hendricks gave them a kiss on the cheek and slid along the row to my side.

The hush of the room descended into a powerful silence.

"Fetch, you remember Liam."

"Hi," said Liam, reaching over Hendricks and holding out a hand.

"Shh," said Amari. "It's starting."

So as not to irritate her, I turned my attention to the stage. Hendricks thought I was just refusing to greet his friend.

"Don't be jealous, boy."

"I'm not," I said out of the corner of my mouth. "I'm trying to be quiet."

"Ohhhh, of course." I could hear his smile without even looking at him. "This is why I had to bring Liam along. You're going to spend all night making googly eyes at your "

I elbowed him in the ribs and he squealed. Every head in the room turned in frustration and we both had to stifle our laughs.

Amari reached out, took my hand, and held it, resting on her knee. That shut me right up. Hendricks gave a knowing chuckle but I'd left him far behind.

Amari and I were still in our early days (in truth, it was early days till the end). This was right back at the beginning when I was just the tour guide who occasionally got invited to the big kids' table. This was the most physical contact we'd ever had. I knew that she'd only taken my hand to shut me up but it still warmed me like the afternoon sun.

Then came the music.

I'd never seen so many instruments. Certainly not in one place and never all playing the same song. How many were there? A hundred? Violins and cellos and trumpets and drums and twisted pieces I'd never seen before. Listening to them all, working together, I realized why I'd never seen some of those instruments out on the street – they just wouldn't work on their own.

Back in Weatherly, there were small bands that only ever played anthems and hymns. Sunder was full of traveling bards and bar-room crooners, but it was hard enough for them to make money on their own, let alone split their profits with other players. I'd never imagined that anyone would dedicate themselves to an instrument that would only ever be featured as part of some extravagant collective. Only here, in this impossible collection of perfectly timed players, did they have a place.

At the end of the front row of musicians, there was a young girl with some kind of horn resting on her lap. As far as I could tell, she was the only player who hadn't done anything since the music started. She just sat there, staring at the floor, doing nothing.

I turned to ask Amari why the woman wasn't playing but her eyes were closed and she had a far-away smile on her face.

Then the strings dropped away. Then the cymbals and the chimes, and a new sound rose up from the center of the room. It sounded like the saddest voice in the world. I was reminded of a grieving woman I'd heard down by the riverbank, keening at the funeral for her plague-taken son.

It was the young girl and her horn. So slow. So sad.

The whole audience sat perfectly silent. All those folks who spent their days being so damn important didn't dare shift in their seats as that heartbreaking, lone cry washed over us all.

Amari squeezed my hand. I watched her breathe in, deep, like she was drinking in the music. I squeezed it back and she slid her fingers through mine and we held each other tight till the end. When the music stopped and the crowd stood up to cheer, she let go so that she could applaud too.

I missed her hand immediately, like it was something of mine she'd taken away. The feeling of a newly missing tooth or too-short haircut.

I clapped along with the crowd but all I could think about was the feeling of her skin against mine and wondering if I'd ever be able to touch her again.

34

I needed to get up. I needed to keep moving.

But why?

Why shouldn't I just lie down with my horse and go to sleep? I had no friends waiting for my return. No lover. Not even a fish that needed feeding. I was ready to accept that the world would be a lot better if I just listened to my aching body and never moved again.

But I turned my brain over one last time, and an answer finally dropped out. One that surprised me.

Rick Tippity.

He hadn't killed Niles, I was sure of that now, but I'd told Simms that he had. Also, I could no longer ignore the fact that he'd never truly confessed to killing his partner. It was more likely that the ice man got frozen through an experiment gone wrong. Tippity had tried to explain that to me but I'd been too committed to making him fit into my story.

I hated the guy, sure, but I didn't want to be responsible for sending him to the hangman.

I focused on his stupid, beady little face, and somehow it was enough reason to stand up. Enough reason to at least *try* to survive the journey home.

I took the only supplies we had left – matches, knife and a single blanket – then, I did something horrible.

Please know that I spent a long time standing in the cold, contemplating whether it was worth it. I went through the journey home a dozen times in my mind, doing the sums on how long it would take, before finally admitting to myself that it was unavoidable.

I cut a slab of meat from Frankie's shoulder.

I know. But it would take days to get back to Sunder and it was unlikely that I'd find any food on the way. Besides, I'd spent every cent on that horse and it didn't seem right to let good meat go to waste.

Then, just because I was already past the point of decency, I also cut the horn from the Unicorn's head. I stomped off the main section with the heel of my boot, and then pried as much of it as I could from its skull. The jagged edges cut my fingers and all our blood mixed together: Frankie, me, and the legendary beast.

I'd managed to acquire the very thing that Warren was looking for, but he mustn't have known what the Unicorns had become. The shards were dull and cloudy. They didn't look magical. They were nothing like the glowing orbs that Tippity had taken from the Fae bodies. Nevertheless, I wrapped the pieces up in leather and put them in my pocket. It was as stupid as carrying around a broken whiskey bottle and I was already anticipating the moment when I'd reach in for a Clayfield and slice myself open. But it was too late for me to worry about being stupid.

Having added a few more terrible deeds to my name, I started the long walk home.

That night, I found a storage house with an underground cellar and was able to get some rest away from the elements. The mist was still there when I woke the following morning. I stayed on the road but I always felt lost. I considered doubling back or waiting for the sky to clear so I could tell which way the sun was setting but I feared that if I stopped moving forward I'd die on the spot. Finally, I passed the shack where Frankie and I had stayed on the way out, which let me know that I was going in the right direction. Without it, I might have lost my mind.

At night I'd cook strips of horse meat on the fire. They were the saddest meals of my life, though I wouldn't have lived long without them.

For the first couple of days, I was expecting someone to follow me. I kept one ear cocked, and was constantly turning to look back the way I'd come. After days of silence, I had to assume that they hadn't brought horses and so believed they couldn't catch me. Also, if they'd only come to get Victor, and hadn't known that I'd be there, they'd have no idea that the machine was with me. To them, I was just some stranger caught up in their mess.

One morning, at dawn, I was curled up under a bit of old canvas asking my blood if it felt like flowing that day, when I heard the sound of an engine. At first, I thought I might have misjudged my distance from Sunder and was hearing sounds of the city on the breeze. But it got louder. Closer. I peered out from under the cloth to see a shining piece of the future drive by.

It was an automobile. But not one of those pre-Coda machines that puffed black smoke and rattled like a sack full of jackhammers. It was sleek and smooth with orange lights at the front and dark windows that hid the driver.

It must be owned by the same folks as that truck that had almost flattened me and Tippity on our way back from the woods. If they were the same people who were pushing boulders down the valley, then I'd need to watch myself. I kept to the side of the road after that, ready to jump into the bushes if another car came rumbling in my direction.

More days passed as I shuffled along the trail. I slept in a hollow tree and an old wagon and an abandoned inn but I never woke up feeling refreshed or renewed. It was one long walk. A punishment for my mistakes. It was painful. It felt futile. But the whole time, I had a machine at my side that could have ended it all.

Somehow, that made it okay. Because I had a way to stop it if I really wanted to. Each step was a choice. It was my decision. With that strange, destructive mindset, it took me six days to get back to Sunder.

I shuffled up Main Street, one foot in front of the other, and saw that Georgio wasn't in his café. I had no idea what time it was. Not even what day of the week. The revolving door attacked me with my reflection. There was blood and dirt all over my face, cut with lines of tears. I looked like a corpse that had been re-animated by a Necromancer of questionable skills.

Somebody had gone into the building while I was away and made all the stairs different sizes. I stopped trying to stand upright and crawled up the last flight of steps on all fours.

I pushed open my office door with the top of my head, slid inside, and collapsed on the floor.

I looked up at my bed, unable to convince myself that it would be worth the effort to climb into it. Then it moved.

Two police-issue boots hit the floor beside my face.

"Oh, golly. Mister, are you all right?"

I growled a bit of spit out of my lips. The boots went over to my desk and somebody picked up the phone.

"Detective? He's back . . . I . . . I don't think so."

The boots returned to my side and the owner of them got down on his haunches and looked into my face like it was a flat tire.

"Sir. Detective Simms wants you to accompany me to the police station. We have to get you ready for the trial."

"Hgadnatdsalizz . . ."

I closed my eyes. His boots squeaked against the floorboards as he went back to the desk.

"Detective, you better come down here."

While he was busy with the phone, I reached into my coat, pulled the machine out of the harness, and pushed it under my bed.

35

This is more like it.

The *friendly* version of Simms was getting weird. After more than a week away from home, it felt good to be back somewhere familiar: like at the end of the Detective's steel-capped toes.

She got a few kicks in and called me a bunch of names and tried to get me up but I just kept laughing like an idiot because I couldn't make my body do what I wanted it to, even when I bothered to try.

A couple of heavies dragged me out of there. They'd done it before, so they had practice handling the banisters and stairs with me in their arms.

At the station, they cut the manacles from my bleeding wrists. I was force-fed coffee and then I got the fire hose. The shock of the water slapped a bit of life back into me. Someone went out and bought a second-hand suit that was too big for my body but cleaner than anything they could find at my place.

Someone cut my hair, which I thought was hilarious. A nurse shoved some medicine down my throat that had a similar effect to that wake-up powder Tippity had been carrying. Not quite as good, but it did open my eyes.

I was a prize-show pooch being prepared by a team of groomers. I kept trying to get the thoughts from my head out onto my lips but they wouldn't come. Not in the right order and not making any sense. Simms pulled back my eyelids and examined them.

"Get me a quart of whiskey and a pack of Clayfields."

"Heavies," I muttered.

She slapped me hard. Someone ran off to get the order.

"I told you to sit tight, Phillips. I asked you not to leave your apartment, and you went and left the city. For over *a week*. You missed your turn in the witness box but, lucky for you, I've convinced the judge to let you speak before she makes her verdict. Let's be very clear about one thing: *you will not screw me on this*."

She wasn't just angry. She was worried. More stressed than I'd ever seen her.

"Simms, I don't think I can—"

She slapped me again.

"You're going to go up there and you're going to tell it to the judge just like you told it to me and then I'm going to let you go to bed, all right?"

I tried to shake my head but someone had replaced it with an overflowing fishbowl.

She slapped me again.

"All right?"

I was staring out of my eyes from five miles away. I must have looked like I'd nodded because when the Clayfields and the whiskey came, she gave them to me. I'll say this for Simms, she sure knows how to administer the right kind of medicine. It gave me just enough strength to stand on my own two feet.

We crossed the road from the station to the courthouse and I told myself that it would be better this way. I'd be able to make my explanation to the judge and Simms at the same time and get the whole thing cleared up in one go. Simms wasn't going to like it no matter how it came out, but at least I'd only have to say it once.

We were just about to enter the courthouse when I realized that the building was rumbling.

I asked Simms what the noise was.

"The crowd."

Shit.

36

It was worse than I'd expected. Way worse.

I'd only ever been to court to assist in small, semantic cases of lost-and-found property or weighing in on an argument of who-hit-who-first. When that happened, there was never any audience. Every person in the room was involved in the case.

That's what I'd thought I was walking into. But, this? This was theatre.

There were a hundred people. Maybe more. By missing my appointed day, I'd turned it into a double-feature: key witness and judgment all in one morning.

Some of the crowd were seated. Plenty were standing. They were all talking over each other, getting louder by the second.

The judge was a skinny Werewolf seated in a wooden box. Impatience was written on her face as clearly as a billboard.

Simms and her team of obedient errand boys led me down the aisle to the front of the room and a chair that had been shaped for intentional discomfort. Simms pulled the Clayfield from my lips.

"Can you string a sentence together?" she asked.

"I'm sorry," I said.

"Good enough for me."

She went over to the judge and negotiated the order of events.

The crowd were from all walks of life. All manner of dress. All species, races and ages. A bunch were there on business: notepads and pencils at the ready. Somebody was sketching me. That was weird. I took out another Clayfield and chewed it, getting ready to piss all over Simms's perfect little party.

They brought Tippity in from the back. He looked like I felt: broken down, starved and tired but all dressed up in a stupid

second-hand suit and tie. His long gray mane had been cut short
and it made him look pathetic. I didn't feel too bad about that.
He might not have done what they were accusing him of, but
the guy was still an asshole.

Simms came over and put a hand on my shoulder, like we were
back on the same team, then the judge called for everyone to be
quiet.

"Just tell it to me like you did the first time," said Simms.

"You're going to question me yourself?"

"Of course."

Great.

The noise dulled to a loud murmur. Tippity tried to kill me
with his eyes. Simms stared at the floor. The judge gave a raspy
cough and I got ready to make everybody's day a whole lot more
interesting.

They went through some official statements and ceremonial
things that I didn't pay any attention to. I stood up when everyone
else did. When they sat down again, I followed. I repeated some
words and nodded my head and agreed to things I barely heard.
Finally, Simms took the stage.

"The witness, Mr Fetch Phillips, is a *Man for Hire*. I will not
lie to the court and say that I have always approved of his methods
or his manner or many of the things he has done, but I will tell
you this: Fetch Phillips is a simple man. He speaks plain. He
speaks true. And I believe he will tell you the truth today."

Simms stood at my side and faced the crowd, to give the
impression that we were speaking with one voice.

"Mr Phillips, when did you first learn about the murder of
Lance Niles?"

"When I met him. There was something about the hole in his
head that tipped me off."

I got some chuckles. Simms didn't mind. She still thought we
were a double act.

"Mr Phillips is sometimes hired by members of the public to

investigate rumors of returning magic." I almost butted in to correct her, but she was on a roll and I didn't want to throw off her rhythm. "For that reason, I invited him up to the crime scene to see if any of his cases could shed light on the murder. They could not. But Mr Phillips began investigating on his own because he believed that solving this case might produce a reward. Isn't that right?"

I liked this side of her. She had a good little performance going. I wished I wasn't about to send it all to hell.

"Sure."

"And where did your investigation lead you?"

"Well, I looked into the different spells that once made fire. I wondered if maybe there was some kind of magic that, while not being *the same*, might still have some dormant, residual energy. The power of Warlocks and Witches seemed most likely, so I asked around about who might know such things. When I heard about Tippity's pharmacy, I went over there for a chat."

"And what did he tell you?"

"Nothing. He threw a fireball in my face."

I got a couple of gasps. Simms was smiling. She asked about the rest of the story and I told it to her just how it came out. The frozen body and the trip out to the church and watching Rick rip open the heads of the long-dead Fae. It was everything Simms wanted me to say and the crowd were eating it up.

"So, there you have it. This man, Rick Tippity, defiled the bodies of sacred Faeries to extract their magical essence. He harnessed that essence to create terrible weapons, then he used those weapons to freeze his associate Jerome Lees, attack Fetch Phillips and murder Lance Niles."

"Well . . . maybe not."

Every head in the room turned to look at me. All except Simms.

She really, really, really, really didn't want to ask me a follow-up question but it was hanging there, in the middle of the court, all lit up and shiny with everybody staring at it. She didn't have a choice.

Simms reluctantly pushed the words onto her forked tongue. "What . . . what do you mean?"

"I mean I'm alive. So is Tippity. I had one of his gift bags go off right in my face. He had one blow up next to his nuts. But I've still got all my gorgeous features and he's still standing. What does that tell you?"

"It tells me that the potion he used on Lance Niles was stronger than what he used on you."

"Come on. All Tippity can do is make a little flash of fire. You saw the body, Detective. Whatever killed Lance Niles smashed out two teeth but left the rest in place. It ripped through his cheek but didn't burn his lips. Whatever did that, it was some real, new kind of power." I couldn't look at Simms anymore. I felt too bad about embarrassing her in front of all her friends. I looked at Rick instead. "What Tippity did? It was nothing. A shadow of things that were once great but we all know have been gone for years. The last breath of something better and brighter than all of us. He should still be locked up for being a sad little pain in the ass but he's no killer. Look at that ferret-faced idiot. He dreams of ever being that interesting."

Simms was shaking.

"But, Jerome. His partner—"

"Iced himself in an experiment gone wrong, from what I can gather. I'm starting to think that if I hadn't barged in on Tippity and accused him of this Niles murder, he would have made a similar mistake, burned his pharmacy down with him inside it, and saved us all a lot of bother."

Things went a bit mad after that. Simms asked for a moment with the judge and they got into an argument. Tippity got up and tried to make a speech but it was all muddled because he wanted people to know that he didn't kill Niles but kept proclaiming that he could have if he'd wanted to. The crowd were laughing and jeering and talking amongst themselves.

Except for one man.

He was a couple of rows from the front, wearing a wide-brimmed hat and a thick black coat. There was something wrong with his face. It was like he'd sustained an injury but the doctor who patched him up had been coming down from a three-day bender. He was watching me. Only me. And there was something familiar about him. His smile was split like a crack in the sidewalk. Maybe he just reminded me of the Unicorn: a majestic face that had been changed by something unnatural. Then he stood up, dusted off his coat and picked up his cane.

I knew where I'd seen him before.

It was in the alley after leaving the card game. I'd thought that Harold Steeme was following me but it turned out to be this man with a bowler hat and a pipe. He'd changed his headwear but the face, cane and coat were the same.

He moved out of the crowd, towards the exit. I wanted to scream out, *There he is! That's the real killer!* But the room had already fallen to pieces and I would have sounded ridiculous.

I sat there, stunned, as he weaved his way out of the courthouse.

A minute later, Simms came over with her hands curled into fists. She couldn't even look me in the eye.

"Get the fuck out of here, Phillips. Get the fuck out."

I did, knowing that it wouldn't be long before her lackeys picked me up again and I'd have to go explain myself.

Outside the courthouse, I searched the crowd for hats and canes but there was no sign of the well-dressed man with the scarred face. I left the babbling horde behind but found another when I came onto Main Street. Some kind of hubbub had brought everyone out into the cold. A few blocks from my front door, I saw the first construction workers. They were wearing matching coveralls that had *NC* written across the back. They'd opened up one of the old fire lamps and were messing around with the mechanisms inside. Further down the road, one of the lamps had been taken down completely.

Pedestrians asked each other what was happening and found

no answers. The workers responded with things like "just doing my job" or obvious statements like "we're taking down the lamps".

Then two red horns rose up from the rabble. Baxter Thatch stood on a bench and addressed the crowd with a voice like a warm hug.

"Ladies and Gentlemen, I apologize for the inconvenience as we make some changes to the streetlights throughout the city. Over the next few weeks, we will be refitting the lamps so that they can benefit from a new kind of energy that will soon be coming from the Niles Company Power Plant. That's right, everyone. By the end of winter, the lights of Main Street will be burning once again!"

Baxter said it like they were expecting us to cheer, but it was too soon. We all needed a moment to understand what was being said. To decide whether we believed it. We were all sucked inside ourselves – thrown back to a place that was part glorious past, part painful present and part unknown, brightening future.

Main Street would have lights again. The city would have real power. That was good news. Maybe the first good thing that had happened since the world went dark.

Baxter shook hands and slapped backs, and finally the folks around me let themselves laugh and hug each other.

A little hope. A bit of change. Progress.

Suddenly, the day didn't look so bad. It was a good day to be better. A good day to take the machine out of town and destroy it, just like Victor had asked me to do. A good reason to quit my silly game and go do something real that didn't require my name on the door. Maybe put on a pair of Niles Company coveralls, slide in with those workers, and build something. Something real. Something that would actually help.

But I didn't. Of course I didn't. I went back to my office and got into bed. I slept, and the next time I went out of the house, I still had the machine strapped to my side.

I didn't go to the Niles Company and ask for work. I didn't need to.

The Niles Company soon came looking for me.

37

"What the hell are you talking about?"

"Dragons!" he said.

I wanted to punch him.

"I know you said Dragons. I just don't understand *why* you said Dragons."

I was trying to keep my cool but the wind was blowing a particularly cold southerly, I hadn't had a proper meal in weeks, and now some toothless Dwarf had dragged me out west on a job that didn't make any sense.

"I heard one," he said.

"No, you didn't."

"I did!"

"Where?"

"Here!"

He pointed to the silos all around him. This part of town was full of storage houses where businesses would keep produce and materials in bulk. There weren't many homes or shops and there certainly weren't any Dragons either.

"I was right here," he continued, pointing between his feet, "and I heard it roar. Twice!"

"And what do you want me to do about it?"

"Well, I thought you might like that information."

I breathed all the air out of my lungs and rubbed my face.

"Why would you think that?"

"Because that's what you do, right? That's what they said at the courthouse. You investigate bits of magic that ain't buggered off yet."

He wasn't the first client to come at me with that idea.

Though it was usually phrased more elegantly. In the two weeks since the trial, I'd been fending off all kinds of desperate, hopeless souls.

"You just thought I'd find this useful, did you?"

"Well, I imagined it might be worth something."

He rubbed his fingers together and raised his eyebrows in a gesture that couldn't have been more preposterous.

"You're kidding. You drag me out in this weather to show me imaginary Dragons and you want *me* to pay *you* for the privilege?"

He had a little grumble about it, then he said, "Fine. I'll sell this information to the other one, then."

"The other what?"

"Investigator. The lady one."

"Sir, do you ever say anything that makes any kind of sense?"

"Here."

He pulled a newspaper clipping out of his pocket and thrust it into my hand like a shiv into my belly.

I couldn't believe what I was reading.

Linda Rosemary – Magical Investigator.
Unlocking What Was Lost.

So that was her next grift: ripping off the most desperate citizens by selling them back their own lost hope. I put the clipping in my pocket.

"Hey, I need that!"

"No you don't. You have enough bullshit of your own without buying more. I'm going home."

I left him with his invisible Dragon and went back east. I was freezing. Simms still hadn't returned my coat so I was making do with a second-hand, moth-eaten trench over the top of an old wool suit.

Main Street looked strange without the lampposts. Apparently they'd been taken away so the Niles Company could convert them to fit the new power supply. Those workers in coveralls were all around town, renovating buildings and ripping up the road. I passed a group of them pushing carts full of rubble and a couple on Main Street coming out of the sewers.

As I approached number 108, I got a tingling feeling on the back of my neck. On the other side of the street, an Ogre in a dark suit was hunched over a payphone. His wild head of hair and chest-length beard had both been combed with the utmost precision.

He was watching me as he spoke into the receiver, not bothering to hide the fact that he was staring. When you're the size of an ox-cart, I suppose subtlety would be a waste of time.

My attention was stolen by a puttering sound. I turned to see a big black automobile roll down the road. It was that shiny, fully covered number I'd seen on the road back from Aaron Valley, with white-rimmed wheels and dark windows. It was even more impressive up close. A real upgrade from the first crates that coughed their way into the city a decade ago.

I wanted to run. I had the terrible feeling that this car had been following me all the way from the valley, but I just froze, praying that it would pass me by.

It didn't. The sleek black carriage pulled up on the curb right where I was standing and a short Half-Elf with thin green eyes looked at me from the driver's seat.

"Get in, Mr Phillips," she said. "Somebody wants to have a little chat."

She had the bored voice of someone who usually finds themselves to be the smartest person in the room.

"Tell *somebody* that they can come by my office whenever they want. I've got a new policy: during winter, I don't go anywhere until I get paid."

The Ogre was already at my side. He didn't need to threaten me or put a hand on my shoulder. When you're that size, every breath is a warning. On the collar of his jacket there was a little gold button, etched with the letters "NC".

I was more curious about the Niles Company than I was about seeing the Ogre pull my intestines out through my nose, so I got in the damn car.

38

I might not know every square inch of Sunder, but I know most of it. When we turned left onto Sixteenth Street and I saw the big house for the first time, I was sure it hadn't been there at the beginning of the year. It put both the Mayor's house and the Governor's mansion to shame: sprawling, decadent and unbelievably busy.

There were two more Ogres at the gate, half the size of the one crammed into the seat beside me but both wearing the same charcoal suits. They pulled open the copper gates and we drove in, winding our way down the long driveway. The gardens on either side were full of workers in coveralls digging trenches and planting trees.

The house itself was all wood, which further set it apart from most Sunder City architecture. It already had three stories and it looked like a fourth was on the way. There was a balcony on the second level that wrapped all the way around the building and the windows were the largest I'd ever seen in this city.

We pulled up at the front of the house and more monkey-suited attendants came out to open my door. They were putting on a performance but I couldn't tell who the audience was supposed to be. Not me, I knew that much. I was just being delivered. Dropped at the doorstep like the morning paper.

A butler opened the front doors and I stepped into a room as big as most Sunder City buildings. The floor was checkered with black-and-white tiles and there were two identical staircases that led up to a landing with a carved white banister. Standing behind the banister, there was a man that I'd never seen before.

He was Human. About fifty. One of those guys for whom age had been a gift not a burden. There was a touch of gray above his ears and his laugh-lines only made him look more interesting. He wore a light brown suit and had the masculine air of someone who knew how everything worked.

"The famous Fetch Phillips," he said with a deep, reasonable voice that would make a limerick sound like gospel. "My name is Thurston Niles. Thank you for accepting my invitation."

"It seemed a better choice than being dragged in by my heels. I wouldn't want to scratch the woodwork."

He smiled politely. Nothing to prove. No reason to do any more than was absolutely necessary.

"Cyran is a sweetheart, really. He can't help the way he looks but having him around certainly makes things move more efficiently. Please, come on up."

I glanced between the two stupid staircases.

"Which one should I take? Is it some kind of test?"

The second smile was more real than the first.

"My architect has a thing for symmetry, but you're right, it's superfluous. Climb up the curtains for all I care. I'll pour you a drink."

He went out through a doorway behind him and I took the left staircase up to a long hallway that broke off into a multitude of rooms.

"Third on the right," came the confident voice, and I followed its directions to the only room in the place that looked finished: thick black-and-red carpet, a variety of leather chairs, wooden side-tables, and a full-length bar that filled one wall. The fire was roaring and the windows were covered with heavy velvet curtains.

"I hear you're not too picky about what you drink," said my host, handing me a crystal tumbler of amber liquid, "but I am. This is a hundred-year-old Dwarven whiskey. If we opened the curtains, it would be the first time it ever saw sunshine. It has a mossy quality but I think you'll like it. Take a seat."

We took the two armchairs closest to the fire and he gave me a moment to sample the whiskey.

Goddam. It was like drinking rainwater from the roots of an old tree, but smooth and even a little salty.

"You certainly know how to start a meeting, Mr Niles."

He raised his glass.

"Call me Thurston. This whiskey was discovered by my brother, Lance, on one of his expeditions across the continent. Lance was a people-person with an enquiring mind and a generosity of spirit. He could walk into any city in the world, find the most important person, be invited into their home at lunch and be their best friend and business partner by dinner time. My task was to come in afterwards, once everyone was already on-side, and handle the actual *business* of whatever caper my brother had concocted. Sometimes they were sound investments, often not, but in the last five years we've made changes all across Archetellos that have improved the lives of many."

"You've also made a lot of money."

"Of course. I hear you have a certain romance for living life on the lower rung. Well, that's fine with me, but if we're going to be friends you should know that making a profit is the last thing I will ever apologize for."

"Is that why I'm here? You need a friend?"

"I need you to find the man who killed my brother." He went back to the bar and refilled both our glasses. "I arrived in town after the trial. Lance, as usual, had taken the lead on this project. After talking to the police and visiting the morgue, I knew immediately that you were very wrong and then very right about what happened. If you hadn't corrected yourself at the courthouse, we might be having a different conversation right now."

If I wasn't paying attention, I might have missed the threat buried under his hospitable demeanor.

"Then I'm glad I got my story straight."

"As am I. It means that, together, we can work to bring the

real murderer to justice. You can start by telling me everything you know."

I gave him the same version of events that I'd told them at the trial. From the Bluebird Lounge to the pharmacy to the forest. I explained that after bringing Tippity back, I had time to digest all that had happened and realized that things didn't match up.

"And then you left town, correct?"

He had asked around.

"An unrelated case. It was supposed to be a small trip but it spiraled unexpectedly out of control. It tends to happen in my line of work."

He looked at me over his glass. He knew I was lying. I'd failed the test. He was going to get that behemoth of an Ogre to break my bones one by one. I was about to jump up and run when he said, "I want to hire you."

Breathe.

"You have an army of people at your disposal. What do you need me for?"

"You know this city better than any of my men, and you've proved that you value the truth."

"I already went looking for your brother's killer. I didn't do much good."

"True. But now you have me to help you out."

Both our drinks were empty but he didn't refill them.

"We are here to build a power-plant and bring industry back to the city. We're going to fire up the lights and fill the factories. To accomplish this, we're hiring the most forward-thinking engineers we can find. When Lance arrived in Sunder, he was vocal about the opportunities our company was offering and spent his nights courting talented candidates with experience in technological invention. One such candidate was named Mr Deamar."

Thurston opened a small leather-bound pocket-book and put it down on the table between us. It was a diary. On the day of the murder "Deamar, Bluebird Lounge, 8 p.m." was scrawled onto the page. Thurston pulled another piece of paper from his pocket. "I found this on Lance's desk. Take a look."

Mr Niles,
   I have been informed of your plans for Sunder City and humbly offer my services. In the days since the Coda, I have spent every waking moment researching ways to not only return this world to its former glory, but to go beyond what was possible in the magical age. I am delighted to hear of another like-minded entrepreneur and believe that you and I should meet in person at your earliest convenience.
   To whet your appetite, I will tell you that I have spent the last year traveling to the Keats University on Mizunrum and I have information regarding the Wizards there that I am sure you would find most interesting.
   Congratulations on all your recent successes and I look forward to our meeting.
   Your Friend,
   Mr Deamar

I looked at the word "Friend" over and over. I couldn't be sure, but it seemed like a match for the card that had come with the machine. *A gift, from a friend.*

I now had a name for the strange man with scars on his face. Deamar had killed Lance Niles with the machine, dropped it at my door, and was now following me around the streets. But why?

I put the letter down on the coffee table.

"The return address for the letter was the Hotel Larone," said Thurston. "Mr Deamar stayed there for five nights. After the murder, he returned to take his things and has not been seen since."

"If you knew this, then why let us carry on with the whole Rick Tippity production?"

"I told you, I only arrived in town after the trial had taken place.

My employees know how delicate my company's work is. They made a show of assisting the police while working to delay the true investigation till my arrival. In that regard, your whole Tippity adventure helped us immensely. Of course, as soon as I arrived in town and saw my brother's body, I knew that the explanation was ridiculous."

"How did you know that?"

"Because I know what it was that killed my brother."

I breathed in sharply and felt the metal of the machine press against my ribs.

That's why I'd seen the same sleek automobile out on the road. It was Thurston's men who'd come for Victor. The ones who'd dropped boulders and arrows as I made my escape. Instead of destroying the weapon like I said I would, I'd brought it right into the lair of the man who was doing everything he could to find it.

"You do?" I asked, hoping that Thurston didn't notice I was unseasonably sweaty.

"Yes."

He's screwing with me. He knows the machine is right there in front of him. Why didn't I destroy it? Why did I insist on carrying it around?

I tried to play dumb.

"What kind of magic was it?"

He scoffed. "No magic. Just science. A prototype tool that Lance had acquired on his way to Sunder. As far as I can tell, Lance showed the prototype to this Deamar fellow, who murdered him with it and then fled with the weapon in his possession."

And then delivered it to me.

"What do you think the motive was?" I asked.

"I have no idea. Maybe this Deamar works for a competitor. Maybe he's crazy. Maybe it was an accident and he just panicked. I don't know. But I do know that he is impossible to find. Nobody has heard of him, other than the few people he encountered at the hotel. They describe him the same way as those at the Bluebird Lounge: Human, thin mustache, black suit, bowler hat, cane."

I didn't need the description. I'd seen Deamar twice already. I couldn't tell Niles that, though. I couldn't tell him a lot of things.

"Look, Thurston, I'm sorry about what happened to you brother but as far as continuing the investigation myself, I don't think it's a good idea. I've already crossed the cops on this one by taking Tippity off their suspect list."

"Which was the right thing to do."

"I suppose. Then there's the fact that I have something of a code. I don't work for Humans. It's nothing personal, just one of my quirks. I'll give you any information I have, but I think you should find yourself another investigator."

Thurston leaned forward. The guy gave nothing away. I couldn't tell a damn thing that was going on in his head.

On the table beside him, there was a little bell. He picked it up and rang it, then he finally filled our glasses again. Moments later, the big Ogre entered the room, his bespoke suit straining at the seams.

I tried to mentally prepare for the beating. It wasn't easy. A single punch would likely send me to the cemetery.

"Cyran," said Niles, "please give Mr Phillips ten bronze bills."

Cyran reached into his pocket and pulled out a roll of bronze. He counted off ten and held them out to me. I didn't take them.

"Mr Niles, I just told you that—"

"Cyran, repeat after me: Mr Phillips, I would like to employ your services as a *Man for Hire*. Here are ten bronze bills. Please find the man who murdered Lance Niles."

Like a three-hundred-pound parrot, the Ogre did as he was told. I had no choice but to go along with it. If I refused, I didn't know what would happen next. Maybe the brute would turn me upside down and shake me till I took the job. The worst part of that would be if the machine fell out onto the floor and I had to try to explain how the murder weapon I was supposed to search for was already hidden under my jacket.

I took the bills.

"Thank you, Fetch," said Thurston Niles.

"Thank you, Fetch," said the Ogre.

Thurston dismissed Cyran with a smile.

"You really should reconsider your stance on working for Humans," he said. "You might think it makes you seem honorable but it only looks naïve."

"I don't care how it makes me look. It's just how I like to work."

"You haven't traveled much since the Coda, have you?"

"Not far, no."

He smiled to himself in a way that made me feel uncomfortable.

"If you had, you might not be so quick to turn up your nose at your own kind. Things have changed out there, and men like us need to stick together."

We had another drink and I pried all the facts I could from my new client. There wasn't much to go on. Partly because Thurston wasn't sharing the whole story and partly because Deamar was some kind of ghost. Niles hadn't been able to find any record of him outside of his stay at the Hotel Larone and his visit to the Bluebird Lounge. I had two more sightings to add to my list but they still didn't paint much of a picture.

"You think Deamar has got some sort of vendetta against you?" I asked.

"Perhaps. Though I'm not sure why?"

"Is there anything else we can pin on him? Other attacks?"

His face lit up like I'd thrown him a surprise party.

"I like the way you think! A month ago, when Lance was first traveling down here, one of our trucks was hijacked on the road. We assumed it was bandits but something never felt right to me. Too many valuables left behind. Instead, the thief stole documents. Just some itineraries and logbooks. They tried to tell me that, since it was winter, the thieves would take anything they could burn in a fire but I think you're right. I think this Deamar fellow has been screwing with me for longer than I realized." He threw back a whole glass of whiskey and nodded like we'd already solved the puzzle. "What do you plan to do next?"

There wasn't much to go on. A handful of sightings around town and a month-old hijack that might not even be connected.

"I'll work the truck angle first. Any witnesses?"

"No. But Yael, the driver who picked you up, was first on the scene. She might be able to give you something."

"Maybe I should head out there and see it for myself."

"A patch of empty road? It happened a month ago."

"But why that spot? Was your truck targeted on purpose or do bandits camp out in that area? It might help us prove if it's really connected to the case or not."

He looked at the floor and nodded in a satisfied way.

"Talk to Yael, then come back in the morning. I'll give you a carriage and some directions and you can see if there's anything out there." We stood up and shook hands. "A pleasure to finally meet you, Fetch. I like the way your mind works." He brought up his other hand and enclosed mine in his grasp. For a moment, his tough exterior cracked. "Please, don't let my brother down."

39

The same duo of thugs drove me home: Yael, the Half-Elf, with her hands on the wheel, and Cyran, the Ogre, crammed in the back beside me.

Yael made no effort to hide the fact that she resented being told she had to talk to me.

"So," I said, tiptoeing into the conversation like it was a live bear trap. "You were the first one to find the hijacked truck?"

"Yes."

I waited for her to go on. She didn't.

"What do you think happened?"

There was a mirror hanging from the roof right near the windscreen. In it, I could see her eyes. It looked like she might quit her job right then, step out the car, and never come back.

"Somebody put spikes on the road. Driver wouldn't have seen them because there was a blind spot on the corner. Slashed all four tires. When the driver got out, she was shot in the chest with an arrow. Another in the head. Some equipment was stolen from the back of the truck. Documents too."

"What kind of equipment?"

"That's classified."

"I'm working for Thurston now too."

"So you say."

Her eyes were locked on me through the mirror.

"Okay, I'm coming back in the morning. Talk with your boss and see if you're allowed to tell me anything else. And do me a favor: draw up the scene to the best of your recollection – where you found the driver, direction of the vehicle. Stuff like that."

She huffed, like I'd asked her to help me move house.

"Sure."

"Thanks, Yael. You're a real hero."

I stepped out of the car right where they'd picked me up and as soon as I closed the door, they were off.

"Holy Moly!" Georgio was standing at the door of his café with a grin that stretched out to touch his ears. "What a ride, Fetch! Are you a big-money guy now?"

Georgio's constant enthusiasm was equal amounts endearing and infuriating.

"Just another troublesome client, George. The only difference it'll make is the quality of the knife they put in me when we're done."

I went inside and sat at my desk and tried to evaluate what kind of mess I was in. Why had Deamar delivered the murder weapon to my door? Was it just because I was already on the murder case or was there some connection I was missing?

Maybe I'd find my answers out on the road.

The road.

I thought back to my last trip outside the city. My blisters hadn't healed and I still looked gaunt from the days without food. If it wasn't Deamar who hijacked the truck, and there were bandits out there, then my transport could be destroyed the same way. If that happened, I didn't think I could handle another week-long crawl back to Sunder City. Not on my own.

I needed some back-up.

Thurston had paid me handsomely. So much so, that I'd be able to pay for a little company. But I needed more than someone to talk to. A tracker would be good. Someone who could handle the snow. Tough, but smart. And someone who would keep their mouth shut if we found something important.

Oh no.

I took the newspaper clipping out of my pocket and flattened
it out on my desk.

Linda Rosemary – Magical Investigator.
Unlocking What Was Lost.

40

The office of *Linda Rosemary – Magical Investigator* was over on
Five Shadows Square. It got its name back in the pre-Coda because
if you stood in the middle of the square at night, the five fire
towers around the edge would illuminate you from every side.
The businesses around the edge were a mixture of boutique
jewelers, tailors and wine bars. I couldn't imagine what kind of
ruse Linda had pulled to get herself a piece of prime real estate
so quickly.

She'd taken over an old florist and the signs on the window
advertised a range of products that hadn't been seen in years:
ever-blooming bouquets and purse-protector fly-traps. Still, it was
less of a lie than what Miss Rosemary was actually selling.

A bell over the door jangled as I entered. Linda Rosemary –
Magical Investigator was seated at her desk, across from an
emotional Reptilian woman. Linda looked at me like we'd never
met before, and addressed me with the same lack of familiarity.
It wasn't the first time someone had wanted to pretend they didn't
know me while in the presence of others.

"Sorry, sir, do you have an appointment?"

"No."

"Have a seat if you must. We're almost done."

I did as I was told. The old-lady-lizard had her head wrapped
in a shawl. She'd been crying. Linda pulled a handkerchief from
the pocket of her noticeably unblemished new coat. She'd swapped
her beret for a black fedora that was pinned into her dreadlocked
hair.

"Sorry, Ms Tate. Please continue."

Ms Tate dabbed her eyes with the handkerchief.

"That's all of it really. I wasn't so worried about my appearance but the pain is getting worse. Especially in the cold. Where the scales are gone my . . . flesh is so raw. I talked to the doctor but he just told me to cover it up. That's fine for my body but I have to work. I just thought, maybe you knew of some way . . ."

She trailed off. Because how could you finish that sentence? *Some way to bring the magic back?* How could a Werecat in a fedora help her more than a doctor?

It was the same problem I'd seen Simms deal with for six years, and she hadn't found any way to help herself other than to cover up her skin with as much clothing as possible. But Linda nodded like she had everything under control.

"I understand," she said. "And I have some ideas about where to ask around. It might take a while and I'm not promising anything, but I'll do my best to find a way to help."

I laughed out loud. I didn't mean to. Bitterness pushed it out. Linda looked over but the serpent kept her head down.

I kept quiet after that. Linda finished with her customer, helped her out the door then punched me in the shoulder.

"What kind of an asshole are you?"

"Sorry. I didn't mean to ruin your grift."

She punched me again.

"Come over to my desk, Mr Phillips. I like to be comfortable when I'm being insulted."

We moved to the middle of the room and it was a topsy-turvy version of our last encounter. Last time, she'd had the last word and the upper hand. It was my turn to even the score.

Linda put her feet up on the desk. Her chair was nicer than mine. Everything about her office was nicer than mine. I tried to convince myself that it was because I was actually trying to help people and she was running a con.

"You're really going to take her money?" I asked.

"If I can help her."

"You can't help her."

"How do you know?"

"The same way you do. Because the magic is gone. It doesn't matter how much bullshit and false hope you dangle in front of her, that ain't going to change."

She took that in, not letting herself get rattled.

"Listen. I haven't always conducted myself in ways that I'm proud of. Our first meeting was regrettable. I was desperate. I was lost. I was still working out how to survive in this strange city. So do not think that you know me, Mr Phillips. In fact, you don't understand anything."

"You're repeating yourself, Miss Rosemary. You said the same thing last time."

"And you still aren't listening. You look at us, the ones who once had magic in our hearts, and you think you know what we're going through. But you have no idea what we *feel*. You think that our power was snuffed out? Like a candle? No." She hammered on her chest, biting out her words. "It's still in here. I can feel it."

"I'm sorry. I—"

"Shut up! Just because you cannot see it, it doesn't mean it isn't there. This is my body and these are my people. You can roll your eyes and laugh as much as you like but I will work to make myself, and anyone who comes to me, whole again."

There was no response to that. I nodded as politely as I could, then I dared to try to change the subject.

"Great office."

"Thanks."

"Mustn't have come cheap."

"No." She took a deep breath and finally relaxed a little. "I found some traveling merchants who paid big money for the Unicorn horn. As long as they don't come back this way, it should be fine."

I was thankful for an excuse to laugh.

"So, what are you doing here, Phillips? Just come to steal my decorating ideas?"

"I need to leave town. Another case. I'm hesitant to go on my own."

"I thought that was your whole MO."

"Yeah, I'm even surprising myself. I'll be leaving on a carriage first thing in the morning and, if you're available, I'd like to hire your services."

For an extortionate fee and mostly her own amusement, she agreed to come along. Her next client arrived: a Cyclops who was losing his vision. As I left, she was already soothing him with her soft, optimistic voice. I tried to tell myself that the gesture was important, even if her business was boloney. I didn't quite believe it, but I was happy to argue with myself all the way home.

41

"I thought you said we were taking a carriage."

"We are. Sort of."

I'd headed back to the Niles compound early, expecting to find a horse and carriage being prepared for me. Instead, there was an automobile waiting in the driveway. Cyran gave me the basics on how to get it going. It was a simpler model than the one Yael had been driving but it was still a more comfortable ride than a saddle-less horse or swollen feet. The fuel was the same kind of oil that Mortales shipped in from out of town to run the power plant. Cyran showed me how to open up the front of the vehicle and to pour it into the motor at regular intervals.

I'd stalled it a dozen times on the way over and put a big scrape down the side, but I was starting to get the hang of it.

Linda looked it over like it might bite.

"How far are we going?"

"Apparently only a couple of hours, so we should be back by nightfall if you ever get in the car."

She gave me one of her trademark withering stares, squeezed into her seat and pulled a big bag onto her lap.

"What's that smell?" I asked.

"Fresh bread. Some sardines . . ."

"You packed us lunch? I knew I asked the right woman."

"Who said it was for you?"

I put the car in gear. Stalled it, twice. After twenty minutes we were on the open road.

I was fucking freezing. Yael's car had a windscreen and a roof. This one had none of that. I tried not to make a big deal about it because Linda just put her sunglasses on and stared into the screaming wind like it was a summer breeze.

There was a trunk at the back of the car with a canister full of fuel. Every half an hour, I had to stop and fill it up. We were going south, and the flat peak of Sheertop Mountain could be seen in the distance.

"Isn't that where the prison is?" asked Linda.

"Yeah. Right at the base. The walls were pure magic, though, so there's not much of it left."

"You've seen it?"

"Yeah, I was there when it all came down."

She turned around in her seat and looked at me.

"Why?"

Oof. I'd said too much. Some people knew my history but Linda was new in town so I guess she hadn't heard anything too juicy.

"Just a silly mistake. Check Yael's paper for me, we can't be far away."

Fifteen minutes later we crossed a creek that Yael had referenced in her notes. A mile after that, the road curved around a rock formation and Linda told me to pull over.

"This should be the place." The pile of rocks was on the right side of the road. On the left, there was an overgrown field. The asphalt road curved around the rocks, which is what helped the hijackers keep an element of surprise. "How about some lunch?"

Linda used a switchblade to slice the bread.

"That hasn't been in anyone's belly, has it?" I asked.

"Yeah, but I've cleaned it since."

We covered the bread with sardines and pickled chilies, leaned against the car and ate in silence. Our heads turned in all directions, taking in the landscape and playing out possible scenarios. Still chewing, I kicked away some of the wet debris that lay thick across the road.

"You seen many roads like this up your way?" I asked.

"Never. All our roads are dirt or stone. This must be a southern thing."

"A Sunder thing, I think. And only recently. There's no real need for it unless you plan to drive vehicles like this one. Whoever is making these cars must have something to do with laying the roads too."

"That has your boss written all over it, right?"

"Yeah. Maybe."

There were tire marks across the asphalt. Something that looked like a burn where, I imagined, the metal spikes were dragged against the road.

"Let's look at that picture."

Yael's drawing of the crime scene was half-assed but it told us a few key things. After hitting the spikes, the truck had spun around so that it was perpendicular to the road. The driver was found on the left of the truck, which put her on the northern side, facing down the highway towards Sunder.

Another drawing highlighted the injuries. Two arrows: one straight into her chest, the other all the way through her skull and coming out the other side.

"Where was the truck coming from?" asked Linda.

"South. That's all they'd tell me."

"What was it carrying?"

"They wouldn't say."

Her eyebrows told me I was an idiot.

"You sure they actually want you solving this mystery?"

"They want me to find Deamar. We just need to work out whether this hit was him or someone else."

"Okay. Act it out."

"What?"

"Step out of your invisible truck. Show me how it happened."

I shrugged. "Sure."

I took the drawing over to the skid marks. There were four

black lines. The ones that finished farther north would be the front wheels, which would be right under the driver's seat.

"So," I said. "The truck spun around like this."

"Do the sound effects."

"Shut up. Then the driver gets out this side."

"And she's shot in the chest."

"And the head."

"But the chest first."

"How do you know?"

"Look at your drawing, Fetch. If it's accurate, then the arrow in the head went in much deeper. More power. Most likely, the chest hit took her down from a distance then the other one finished her off from up close."

I'd picked the right partner.

"Okay, so she steps out and is hit in the chest."

"But she's not found by the door, is she?"

"No."

"So, she wasn't shot immediately. Where was she going?"

"Probably to check the tires or the cargo."

"Show me."

I walked along the side of my invisible truck.

"First of all," said Linda, "we can cancel out half the landscape. The truck is blocking everything to the south. Now, if the shooter was directly north, they would have hit the driver in the side."

"Unless the driver was walking away from the truck."

"Why?"

"Uh . . . to admire the view?"

"Unlikely. My guess is that the shot came from the east or west. Face west for me."

I did. I was looking at the rock formation.

"You think the attacker was hiding behind there?"

"Not unless he's an idiot. It's too close. What if they spotted the spikes and came searching? You can look in there if you want, but I don't think so." She stepped back off the road. "Look east."

I followed my orders and walked back alongside my imaginary truck, as if I was returning to the driver's seat. Linda was right in front of me.

"On this angle, I can see straight down the road to the south. If I was camping out, waiting to see how my trap would affect an incoming car, I'd be somewhere," she turned around, "in this direction."

It was a wet, overgrown field of brown grass and puddles.

"I hope you brought your good boots," I said.

"Don't worry about me, city-slicker. You watch your own feet."

Linda marched off into the mud.

We walked through the grass, side by side, about ten meters apart. The plan was to get past the point where an arrow could be fired from, spread out from each other, go back to the road, spread out again, and repeat till we stumbled upon . . . something.

"What are we looking for?" I called out. "An armchair and a telescope?"

"Maybe. If I was going to lie in wait for a car to come up this road, I'd want to be somewhere comfortable, well-hidden and out of the elements. It would be impossible to know exactly when a certain truck would arrive, so I'd want to feel safe."

We went beyond the point where even a specialist Elven archer would be able to hit a target, and separated ourselves. I counted out the distance, turned and walked back towards the road.

"You said you saw this Deamar guy?"

"Yeah, twice."

"And he looked Human?"

"As far as I could tell. That's what the witnesses say, too."

"You know what it means, don't you?"

"What?"

"Deamar."

I started to wish I hadn't brought someone who liked making me feel so stupid.

"No," I conceded.

"I guess you wouldn't. It comes from one of those old stories that even most magic folk have forgotten, so I wouldn't expect it to spread to your kind." She lifted up a pile of weeds but didn't find anything interesting. "At the beginning of creation, a piece of the river stepped out onto the surface of the world so that she could be a guardian to all the creatures. Deamar was her first son. He defied his mother by declaring war against the Humans. His desire was to wipe their entire species from the planet. To protect the Humans, the Creator banished Deamar to a dark place, under Archetellos, using the power of the river to keep him locked away."

"You think an ancient angry teenager is hobbling around Sunder City killing businessmen?"

"No. But whatever Mr Deamar is planning, choosing a name like that makes his intentions clear to those of us who know what it means."

My foot hit something hard and hollow. I kicked away the dead grass and found a floor beneath my feet.

"Hey! Come here."

I peeled away more of the foliage. There had been a hut here once. The roof and walls were gone. The furniture too. But maybe . . .

I stomped against the floor and heard the hollow sound again.

Linda arrived as I pulled back the hatch to the basement.

42

It was a single room dug into the dirt, with walls of rotten wood. There was a bedroll on the floor beside a bow and a couple of arrows. Some discarded cloth in the corner. Animal bones. Someone had been camping here for a while.

"What do we know about Deamar?" asked Linda.

"Next to nothing. That he's Human. That he murdered Lance Niles, stole a weapon, and is wandering around town creeping me out."

"So, he could be the kind of guy who would live underground in a field waiting to kill a truck driver?"

"I have no reason to rule it out."

The basement was mostly waterproof but some moisture had slipped in. It smelled like wet clothes and mold. I kicked over the bedroll but didn't find anything.

Linda was looking at the bow.

"Mean anything to you?" I asked.

"Not really. Simply made. No markings. It's more of an Elvish design than Human, but they're fairly interchangeable these days. Not sure why he would have left it here."

"If he was on his way to Sunder, it would make sense for him to swap his long-range weapon for a fancy suit and tie."

"What did he look like?" Linda used the end of the bow to search through the old cloth.

"Hard to say. He moved like he was old but his face was youthful. Kind of. There were scars on his cheeks, like he'd had an accident."

Linda bent down.

"And you're sure he was Human?"

"Well, that's what they said at the Bluebird, and he looked Human to me."

She lifted up something from the pile of clothes and held it up to the light.

"I didn't think there were too many Humans in the Opus."

No there weren't. Just one.

Linda was holding up a blue coat. It looked just like one I'd left back at the police station. It didn't have fur, like I'd added onto mine, and it still had all the official insignia, but otherwise it was exactly the same.

An Opus uniform.

I took it from her. The material was wet and broken down, which made me kind of angry. Even though I'd betrayed the Opus more than anyone in history, I still didn't like to see the uniform disrespected.

I looked up at Linda and she asked the question I didn't dare to.

"Was Deamar a Shepherd?"

43

While I drove back, Linda went through the pockets of the coat, finding scraps of notes that confirmed the fact that the hijacker and Deamar were the same man. They were all written in the same fancy handwriting and they referenced Lance and Thurston Niles alongside dates and locations that Linda assumed were transport routes. I was still obsessed with the jacket.

"Maybe he found it. Maybe he stole it. Maybe he took it off someone he killed."

She pulled out another note.

"Does this address ring any bells?" she asked, hinting that it most certainly would. "One hundred and eight, Main Street?"

Deamar *had* known about me before he entered the city. I'd been hoping that he only brought me into it after Simms put me on the case: a killer meeting with the man he thought was coming after him. But this was something else.

I didn't feel like talking much after that. Partly because we had to yell over the sound of the wind and the motor, but also because there wasn't much else to say. We'd linked the hijacking to Deamar just like we'd wanted. It was a job well done, I suppose, but what we'd discovered made me feel queasy.

I dropped Linda back at Five Shadows Square and handed her a couple of bronze.

"Now, isn't that a better way to make a buck than lying to little old ladies?"

She flashed her canines at me.

"You don't learn anything, do you?"

"I've fallen out of the habit."

She stood there, chewing her lip, deciding whether she should say something else. I tried to leave before she made up her mind.

"Thanks, Linda. If you hadn't come with me, I'd still be out there searching in the wrong direction for—"

"So, you were in the Opus?"

"Yeah."

"And you said that you were in Sheertop, right?"

"For a bit."

She gave me a good look up and down. I was being weighed on a set of scales and I could tell that Linda didn't like the outcome. She didn't even say goodbye. Just nodded, like it all suddenly made sense, pocketed her bronze and walked away.

Fine. Thanks for the memories, Linda Rosemary.

I'd gotten used to the automobile and I wasn't ready to give it back, so I took it up Twelfth Street to the police station and parked it right out front, just to piss them off. I went in looking for Richie but he'd already finished work so I swung by Dunkley's and found him at the counter.

Dunkley's was a cop bar. Not exclusively, but once the pigs decided it was their favorite spot, anyone with any sense went somewhere else. There were a few stools by the window, otherwise it was standing room only. I guess cops did enough sitting during office hours.

I dropped Deamar's jacket beside Richie's glass and asked the bartender to bring me whatever the sergeant was having.

"You want me to do your laundry now?" he grunted.

"I found one of your killer's hideouts. He left this behind."

Richie inspected the collar of the uniform and checked the badge.

"Eyewitness said our killer was Human. You're the only Human who ever wore one of these. Is this your way of confessing?"

My drink arrived and I took a sip. I should have known better than to follow Richie's taste, it was Orcish cider served lukewarm.

"Why you showing it to me?" he asked.

"I thought you and Simms would want to take a look at it. See if you can find anything useful."

"I don't think Simms wants anything from you."

Shit. Richie Kites was always such a stone slab of monotony, even on his good days, that I only just noticed he was giving me the cold shoulder.

"Kites, are you pissed at me too? You know I didn't plan to screw you guys around."

"But you did. That was our one chance to keep control of this case. After the trial went to shit, the Mayor stepped in and took it off our hands. If Simms sees you in here, she'll lock you up just for looking at her."

It wasn't worth explaining myself. He'd get over it in a week or two. He always did.

"Fine. I didn't want that shithouse cider anyway."

I reached for the coat but Richie dropped a hand across it first.

"I'll take a look," he said. "But since Simms is off the case, which means I'm off the case, which means you're off the case, I don't know what good it's going to do."

I didn't dare tell him that I was working for Niles now. I took his advice and got out of there quick in case Detective Simms decided to drop by for a drink. From the way Richie was talking, it sounded like she'd need one.

I dumped the car back at the Niles house. It was still early evening. Turns out you can get a lot done in a day if you travel by automobile instead of blistered feet.

I told Yael what I'd found. Not about the coat or that my name was on the paper, just that Deamar had been the hijacker. She told me that she'd pass the information onto Thurston and he'd call me with further instructions.

I walked back to the famous 108 Main Street and climbed the

stairs to the fifth floor. The door to my office was still broken. I wasn't worried about anyone coming in while I was away (I didn't own anything worth stealing) but I would need to get it fixed if I didn't find Deamar soon. If he was determined to mess with me, I couldn't have him coming by while I was asleep.

But someone had already let themselves in.

The Angel door was wide open and a figure stood in the door-frame, silhouetted against the twilight. It was a body that liked being seen that way. She waited a moment before she turned and made her big reveal.

My mouth opened slowly over a whole minute as I tried to make sense of what I was seeing.

There was a beautiful woman standing in my office. She had vibrant blonde hair, full cheeks and familiar eyes. I'd seen her face once before, in an old photo, standing next to a young Harold Steeme, back before the Coda had stolen their youth.

Now Carissa had stolen it back.

She closed the Angel door, shutting out the sound of the street, and stared at me with those green, pinprick-pupil eyes. I don't know how long we waited without speaking but I missed my cue a million times. Eventually she just swore.

"You're really not going to say anything?"

I tried, but only the beginnings of stammered syllables came out.

"Well, uh . . ."

"Screw it." She marched around the desk and walked right up until we were inches apart. I was only slightly taller than she was. Looking into those peepers from right up close, I still couldn't work out what she wanted. So, she helped me.

Mrs Steeme ran one smooth-fingered hand around my neck, onto the back of my head, and pulled my mouth down to hers. Her lips were timid but grew with confidence as I finally snapped out of my shock and played along. Her other hand wrapped around my waist and her tongue moved in to massage mine. My trench coat fell to the floor. When her hands went around my body, they got caught on the leather strap that held the machine. She pulled back.

"What is that thing?"

"Nothing. Sorry. I'm looking after it for someone."

She went to take it from the holster and I stopped her hand.

"Best you don't touch it." I removed the whole sling, pulling it over my head.

"Is it dangerous? You pointed it at Harold like you could hurt him with it."

"I was just drunk." I stuffed the machine back into the bottom drawer. "Mrs Steeme, I'm not sure what's going on here."

She came closer again.

"Just tell me I'm beautiful."

She was. It was undeniable. But there was something strange about it all. Everything was in the right place: symmetrical, polished and free of imperfections, but it was all too perfect. If that was possible.

"You are beautiful. Really." I meant it, but no words have ever felt so phony coming out of my mouth. "I'm just not sure who you think I am. I'm not the kind of guy you want to get involved with. I—"

She put a delicate hand against my chest.

"Mr Phillips, with all due respect, this has *nothing* to do with you."

I leaned down and kissed her and her body curled into mine.

44

I was used to surprises. Mostly they came in the form of cheap uppercuts or unexpected bills for things that I did while I was blackout drunk.

This was an entirely different experience.

I was on my back. She was on her side with her arm across my chest. Her leg was over mine and her head was tucked into the nape of my neck.

I noticed that my shoulder was wet.

"Carissa? Are you okay?"

She sniffed. "It's just strange. After a hundred years of only kissing one mouth. One body. It's . . ."

"I'm sorry."

"No. Don't be." Her fingers ran over my skin. "It's just different."

We were quiet for a while. I felt the skin on her arm. The scars, not quite healed, against her ribs. Her breath on my ear.

"How about you?" she asked.

"What about me?"

"Who was the last person you held?"

I suddenly noticed how naked I was. And cold. I pulled up the covers.

"It was a long time ago."

"You don't have to say that."

"It was. Six years."

"Oh."

It wasn't six. It was eight. But six made sense. Everyone knows when the Coda happened. Six is romantic. But eight? Eight is just strange.

Still, I was surprised when she said, "Tell me about it."

"Sorry?"

"Tell me."

"About what?"

"The last time."

Her hand was flat on my chest, over the part that always hurt. She rubbed the muscle between my ribs like she knew. Women have that thing, don't they? They know where the pain is.

"I was on the coast. Alone. I wrote to her and asked her to visit. She did."

"You weren't together?"

"No."

"But you loved her."

"Yes."

"Always?"

"Always."

She pulled her body tight onto mine.

"In Lipha, where Harold and I come from, men and women are more equal than they are here. There would never be a club like the one where you found him. Never so many men in power."

"Do you think that's why Harold wanted to come here?"

She took a long, sad sigh.

"Perhaps. I'd had other lovers when I was young, but when it came time to get married, I entered into it with all my heart. I thought Harold did too. We fell for each other. Every year, I found new ways to love him. What happened when she arrived?"

She changed the conversation so quickly, I'm surprised we didn't both get whiplash.

"It was everything I'd wanted. More of her than I ever thought I'd have. We walked on the sand and watched the ocean. She kissed me. I kissed her back. We went back to the hotel and it was . . . everything. But I couldn't hold onto it. I kept trying to stop time . . . to make her stay because I knew she wouldn't. If

I could have just enjoyed it and been good to her . . . just been thankful for the time she was willing to give me, then maybe it would have been okay."

She brought her fingers to my hairline. Stroked my forehead.

"And then the Coda?"

"No."

"No?"

"No. She left."

"Why?"

"Because she didn't love me. For her it was . . . it was just a holiday."

"She said that?"

"No. She said she had to work."

"And did she?"

"Yes."

"Then why do you think she didn't love you?"

"Because she didn't ask me to go with her. Or try to stay. And . . . why would she?"

My chest was sore again.

"What did she do?"

I took a big breath.

"Nothing. She packed her bags and while she was in the shower, I just got out of there."

Her hands traced my body. My cheek. My jawline. My throat. Down my arm. My waist. Her fingers were cool against my skin. Had it really been eight years?

"So, you were the one who left," she said.

"I guess so."

I wrapped her up in my arms, she wrapped me in hers. I looked at her face from an inch away. The morning light kicked its way through the window and danced on her shoulders. Her hair had a chemical perfume, from the fresh dye. The surgeon hadn't been able to smooth her skin everywhere. The older Carissa Steeme was still visible on her ears and eyelids. I ran

my hand over her face, feeling her nose and lips and the line
of her chin.

"Why did you do this?" I asked her.

I was worried I'd offended her, but she just needed a moment
to gather her thoughts.

"Harold and I were a team. During all our time together, I
never kept score or worried about who was getting the most
out of our relationship. I didn't get jealous. I didn't think about
what I might be missing while we were together. But after
seeing him and accepting what he'd done, I just felt so fucking
angry. I . . . I try to think about what kind of life I want now
but it's all tied up with him. I can't live alone as an old woman
if he's out there . . . doing whatever he's doing. I know it's
petty . . ."

Her nails scraped my back.

"Why do you think Harold did it?" I asked.

"Because all men are fools. You think women care about things
like looks and clothes and all that crap, but I'll tell you the truth.
Only one thing really matters. Authenticity. Those of us that, for
some daft reason, are interested in men, we get thrown into this
awful waiting game. Like some insufferable party. All the guys
and gals standing around, passing the time until a man finally
grows up and gets over his shit. You can be fat or bald or broke,
it really doesn't matter to most of us as long as you're authentically
yourself. As soon as that happens, I promise you, a good woman
will find you and take you home. The world is full of women
just tapping their toes until the boys grow up. That's what's so
infuriating about Harold and all the other idiots like him. They
forget themselves. They get out of the party, but then they find
too many wrinkles or gray hairs so they panic and run back, but
now they're more out of place than they ever were. You saw him.
He looks ridiculous. But who am I to talk? I've followed the
fucker back in."

I turned her head to mine.

"Well, as one of the dumb boys who might never get out, I'm glad you came back for a visit."

She laughed. She had a beautiful laugh.

"Thank you."

She rolled on top of me, we closed our eyes, and used each other's bodies to push the sadness from our minds.

45

I woke to the smell of coffee.

Carissa was sitting at my desk, in my chair, with my trousers on her lap. The bed creaked as I sat up.

"This isn't your only pair, is it?"

She put a hand down the leg and waved at me through the hole in the knees.

"I have others. Somewhere."

"Good. I'll take these home to stitch them up." She came over to the bed. "I've left you coffee and a paper. I'm sure you can't sleep the entire day away."

"I've been known to try."

She kissed me on my forehead.

"Thank you, Mr Phillips."

I put a hand around her body, rekindling the memories of the night before.

"You are beautiful," I said. "Right now, and every time I've ever seen you."

That got me a kiss on the lips.

I waited till she was gone before I slid out of the sheets and wrapped my coat around me. On my desk there was a steaming cup of Georgio's coffee and the morning edition of the *Sunder Star*. I never bought my own, just flipped through the stained and torn copy downstairs. I sat back in my chair, sipped the brew, and wondered why it had never become part of my routine.

My answer came quickly. The front page alone irritated me so much I had to stand up and pace around the room.

There had been a retrial of Rick Tippity's case. Somehow, he'd been convicted. Everything I'd said during the trial had been scratched from the record. The theory of him using Faery bodies to fry Lance Niles had been sold a second time and the judge had ordered him to stay in the Gullet forever.

That wasn't even the worst part.

The article went on to say that the Mayor was already putting new laws in place: placing restrictions on unstable magical practices and any old-world craft that had become unpredictable. You could smell the bullshit of bureaucracy coming off the page. Somebody was using this case to turn the gears of Sunder in the wrong direction and I'd helped grease the wheels.

I called the Police Department.

"Detective Simms please."

"Who's speaking?"

"Her neighbor. The cat's looking really bad this time. It's coming out both ends."

The receptionist relayed the information and I heard Simms scream out, "Hang it up!"

"Tell her I want my coat back too!"

The line went dead. I threw back the rest of the coffee, swearing at myself and Simms and the whole stinking city. I was so caught up kicking the furniture that I didn't notice two tons of Half-Orc stuffed into a police uniform come through the door.

"Just because we stopped beating you up, doesn't mean you've gotta do it to yourself."

Richie came in without waiting for an invitation and sat down in the clients' chair. I threw the newspaper in his lap.

"What kind of game are you and Simms playing?"

He glanced at the front page and didn't seem to like it any more than I did.

"You want to change the story, Fetch? Tell us who really did it."

"I would if I knew."

He chewed his bottom lip.

"Would you?"

"Of course."

He chewed some more, squinting, like some answer was written across my face but he couldn't make it out.

"Did *you* do it?" he asked.

My eyes went so wide, my lashes scraped the cobwebs off the ceiling.

"I'm the only person left who cares that you convicted the wrong guy!"

"Exactly."

"Exactly? What kind of plan is that? Commit a murder, frame someone else, then single-handedly fuck up the case when they try to convict him? What kind of criminal mastermind do you take me for?"

Richie shrugged, like he wasn't being completely absurd.

"I'd never pretend to understand how your mind works," he said, "but I wouldn't put it past you to frame someone, then get all guilty so you sabotage the whole thing. It's not like you haven't switched sides before."

That part I couldn't argue with, but the rest was still nonsense.

"No, Richie, I didn't kill Lance Niles."

He nodded. Maybe he just needed to hear it. He was about to say something when his eyes caught a little scrap of cardboard in front of him. He flipped it over.

A gift, from a friend.

He raised an eyebrow.

I pointed to the rabbit hat hanging on the hat-stand.

"A gift from a client."

"A friend?"

I shrugged.

"They're nervous about anyone knowing that we work together. I'd say they were overly paranoid but as I have cops coming by unannounced, going through scraps of paper on my desk, I suppose they were right."

Now Richie shrugged. I'd batted away his suspicion for the moment.

"Fine. You didn't kill Lance Niles. But there is something strange about this whole thing. We're looking for a man with scars on his face," he pointed a thick finger, indicating the lines left by Linda Rosemary, "in a suit and hat," he gestured to the rabbit hide on my head. "A Human who might have been a Shepherd," point, point, "that commits an unheard of crime that nobody seems to understand except for," point, "you."

Now that he mentioned it, I could understand his suspicions. If he knew that I had the one-of-a-kind weapon responsible for the murder in my bottom drawer, he'd have no choice but to throw me in the Gullet and let Tippity go. Still, I can't say I wasn't hurt by the accusation. "Really, Rich? You think I did this?"

"No. But I'm worried that other people might. What if someone is trying to set you up?"

I went over it all in my head but it didn't seem right. Surely Deamar would have worn his Opus outfit when he committed the murder if that was the goal.

"I don't think so," I said.

"Well, either it was you or someone trying to frame you, or . . ."

"Or it's a coincidence."

Richie leaned back in his chair, and I swear I heard it give a muffled scream.

"No," he said, "this is no coincidence. There's something weird about this one, and I'm worried that you're gonna do that thing you do and get yourself in trouble."

"What thing do I do?"

"That *thing* where you half-ass a case until it's too late. You get all messed up in it, piss everyone off, but don't follow it through and the rest of us end up picking up the pieces. This city is changing, Fetch. You're not gonna get away with making your old mistakes anymore."

I felt myself getting shitty with him. That often happens when someone sees more of you than you want them to.

"Thanks for the warning, Rich, but I'm not scared of Niles or

Simms or whoever else is getting sick of me. But thanks for coming down here to threaten me personally. That's a nice touch."

"You're not listening!" he snarled. "I'm not threatening you. I'm scared that someone is trying to hurt you and you're too stupid to see it. So either put your whole ass on this case and sort it out or step away. Tippity didn't do it? Fine. But if you're gonna go up against all this," he threw the newspaper back in my face, "then you'd better start acting a lot smarter than you have been. You're a Shepherd, Fetch. We both were. So either act like one and do the job properly or put your head down before someone cuts it off."

He stood up and the chair breathed a sigh of relief. He didn't say goodbye. I didn't thank him. I should have. He was right. There was something strange about this case. Something off about the whole goddam thing.

I flicked the scrap of cardboard in my fingers, looking at that fine handwriting.

I needed to find Lance Niles's killer. The real one. Then I could give some closure to his grieving brother, free the wrongly convicted (but still annoying) prisoner, and push back against whatever screwball plan somebody was pushing in the papers.

It was time to find Mr Deamar.

46

As I got dressed, a little voice reminded me that I needed to destroy the machine. But what about Tippity? If I got rid of the real murder weapon, finding Deamar wouldn't do much of anything. I had to hold onto it for just a little longer.

But I wasn't going to carry it around anymore. Too many close calls. So I left it wrapped up in my bottom drawer and tried to ignore the empty space under my left arm where it had become so accustomed to sitting.

The Hotel Larone was the obvious place to start. That's where Deamar was staying when he sent the letter to Lance Niles. I went over there and buttered up the staff with bronze but I didn't discover anything new. The room had been rented out several times since Deamar had stayed there. He'd left no belongings behind and the staff had already mentioned everything they knew to Thurston Niles: he was Human, well spoken, well dressed and left the night of the murder.

The busboy told me he thought there was something not-quite-right about his face, like he had an injury and it hadn't healed properly. Everything I was being told I'd already seen myself. I'd heard his cane against the cobblestones and seen his crooked smile wrapped around his pipe. I'd seen his round ears, short fingers and black suit. I'd seen his bowler hat and the wide-brimmed one he'd swapped it for.

Well, I suppose that was something.

I went over to East Ninth Street, back to the hatters where I'd bought my over-priced bonnet. The old man looked worried when he first saw me, dreading that I'd come to ask for a refund. He

was relieved when I brought up Mr Deamar, and delighted that
he remembered him.

"Yes. He's been in here twice now. Strange fellow. Couldn't
quite place the accent but he was very well spoken. Or, what's
the word? Worldly. Especially for a Human. No offense."

"Did he tell you anything about himself? Where he'd come
from or where he was staying?"

"I don't think so. He just enjoyed marveling at my wares. He
was full of flattery and he bought two pieces. The good stuff.
Told me that he enjoyed indulging in the finer things."

I handed him a card.

"If he comes back again, make sure you give me a call."

I was chasing a ghost around a dead city with nothing to go on
but a name. As the cold wind blew hard between the buildings,
I decided to go back to where it all began.

The Bluebird Lounge was quieter than last time, no crowded
cops hanging around, hoping to steal a look at the gory miracle.
It was weird thinking back to that first day, and how excited we'd
all been. We'd thought something incredible had happened. But
it wasn't incredible. It was an ordinary kind of awful. Mundane
in its brutality. Predictable in its cruelty. The machine was just
like everything else in this new world: cold, lifeless and made
with death in mind.

I pulled out a stool at the main bar. The only soul around was
the short, middle-aged bartender.

"Are you a member?" he asked.

"No. But it's blowing pure ice out there and I need something
to warm my blood. Can you bend the rules for few minutes?"

The words wouldn't have worked on their own but a couple
of coins won him over.

"Sure. What are you having?"

"Burnt milkwood. Plenty sweet."

He went to work. I waited long enough to make the conversation sound spontaneous.

"Good thing they caught that killer, right? Didn't it happen in here?"

He gave me a look I'd seen before: when someone has a lot to say but they've been told to keep it to themselves. If I'd been in a nice suit or looked like I'd come from out of town, he never would have opened up to me. But I was average. Unthreatening. Unintelligent. An everyman. The kind of person you think you can talk to because it will all be washed away by beer before the end of the night.

"That's not the guy," he said, like he'd already told me a hundred times. "I was here. I saw the killer. Hell, I even *served* him. He was a Human. Well, he looked like one. Didn't have long fingers like a Warlock, that's for sure. We're supposed to keep an eye out for things like that. And the guy looked completely different. Different to *anyone*, actually. I told the cops. I told them twice. But here we are with some poor chemist getting thrown in the Gullet for eternity."

I let him stew on his frustration for a few seconds while he mixed up my drink.

"What do you mean, he looked different?"

"Just, unnatural. Like he was . . . like he was wearing a mask that didn't quite fit. But it wasn't a mask. It was his skin but it . . . it wasn't. Sorry, that doesn't really make sense."

But it did make sense. Maybe not to him, but to someone who'd seen Mr and Mrs Steeme up close after their recent transformations.

Of course, with Deamar, the effect was completely different. Carissa Steeme had been buffed and polished like a gold statue. Deamar was . . . broken. Twisted. And yet there was something about them that fitted together.

The barman dropped the drink in front of me but he didn't let go. His hand stayed on the glass and he bit his lip like he was searching for some vital memory in his head.

"Funny," he muttered finally.

"What is?"

He stepped back and looked at the cocktail like he was wondering where it had come from.

"We don't make many of these. It's not a popular drink with our kind of clientele. The last time I mixed one up was a couple of weeks ago." He chuckled, but it was in confusion, not humor. "It was that night. With the Niles guy. This is what the killer was drinking."

It took every bit of my strength to force a bemused, relaxed smile.

"Yeah," I said. "That is funny."

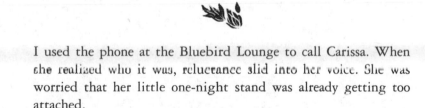

I used the phone at the Bluebird Lounge to call Carissa. When she realized who it was, reluctance slid into her voice. She was worried that her little one-night stand was already getting too attached.

"Is there a problem, Mr Phillips?"

"Not at all. I was just wondering if you could give me the contact for this . . . this doctor?"

A long pause. I was bringing up all kinds of things she didn't want to talk about. Some things are fine in bed, at night, but you're supposed to keep them tucked away during daylight hours.

"What are you trying to do, Fetch?"

"Nothing that will come back to you, I promise. It's for a friend. He needs help and I just want to make some inquiries. I'm sorry to ask."

Another long break of silence. Then a sigh.

"All right. The surgeons' names are Dr Exina and Dr Loq.

Their clinic is down on West Fifth near the corner of Titus. Way past Swestum and the Rose but . . . you shouldn't go down there."

"I only want to ask them some questions."

"I know. Just be careful."

"Of a couple of doctors?"

"Yes, Fetch. They're Succubae."

47

Everything on the far west of the city was hushed. Behind every curtained window in every unmaintained building on every potholed street, the folks inside were living lives that they wanted to keep secret. The eyes that peeked through windows or out from under hoods were equal parts fear and aggression, ready to lean all the way in one direction depending on who they saw outside.

The surgery was in a cellar underneath one of those stores that sold whatever goods they'd managed to "acquire" that month: handbags, scarves, gardening tools. No cohesion to the products other than the fact that they were going cheap.

The stairs led down to a red door with three different locks and a small plaque that read "Dr E and Dr L" above a little silver buzzer. In a part of town this full of crime, the fact that nobody had pried off the buzzer or plaque to fleece the metal was a sign that the owners were either well-respected members of the neighborhood or far too dangerous to screw with. I pressed the buzzer and waited. I hadn't called ahead. Sometimes it's best to go in cold. Most folks find it easier to hang up a phone than slam a door in your face.

A panel slid open in the door. I looked into it and a bright light shone right in my eyes. I pulled down the brim of my hat but I'd already been blinded.

"What's your business?" came a male voice from the other side of the door. It was deadpan. Almost bored. Not a voice you try to sweet-talk and not a voice you tell the truth.

"I'd like to talk to the doctors. Somebody recommended them to me and . . . well, it's kind of personal but I'd really like their help."

I let his imagination fill in the rest with whatever condition came to mind. He undid the locks, one after the other, and opened the door.

When I saw him, I worked very, very hard not to let my face explode in surprise.

He was a Dwarf. I think. You don't usually see Dwarves completely shaved from head to toe. Or with fangs. Or wearing silk. He even had little white horns stuck above his eyebrows. The skin around them was still red. They must have been new.

"Come this way," he said.

The hall was full of scented candles but they couldn't hide the sharp chemical sting underneath. It didn't feel like a surgery: it sat somewhere between a brothel and a morgue. The concrete walls were painted red and the floors were tile, but there was velvet furniture, mica lampshades, and strips of soft fabric draped over any surface that would hold them. The attempt was admirable but like all of the doctors' work, the effect was imperfect.

We passed a dainty little waiting area and the Dwarf directed me into a dark room with nothing in it but a mattress on the floor. I couldn't picture Carissa going along with this journey but, as I'd already found out, a woman scorned is liable to act a little recklessly.

"Wait here," said the Dwarf.

"For what? Someone to take my clothes off?"

He shrugged.

"Probably."

He walked away and I thought there must be nothing in the world that would surprise that guy. He should have my job. Someone could come in claiming that the last piece of magic was trapped under their right tooth and he'd just shrug, say *probably*, and go and get the pliers.

I'll say this for the surgeons, they keep the place warm. I took off my trench coat, laid it beside the mattress, and wondered if I'd made a mistake by not bringing the machine.

No. There had been too many close calls and its existence wasn't a secret anymore. Thurston Niles knew what it was and he probably wasn't the only one.

When my hosts stepped into the doorway, my mind jumped through a few hoops very quickly.

It was clear that the surgeons had turned their knives on themselves, but not with the same intention they had when working on Carissa. With her, they'd just smoothed out her skin and stolen a few years. The work they'd performed on themselves was more in line with what they'd done to the Dwarf. Each woman was a walking assortment of odds-and-ends. A medley of other creatures' body parts added to their own skin.

"Greetings. I'm Dr Exina. This is my partner, Dr Loq."

Exina's hair was black on one side, blonde on the other, and it ran down her back between two short wings of naked bone that poked through special holes cut in her sheer gown. A line of reptilian scales started just under her left eye and went all the way down her cheek. Her bottom lip was too full for her face. It was borrowed. Half of her body had belonged to someone else at some time. Maybe they were offcuts from patients. Maybe they'd been taken by more nefarious means. I was hoping that no part of my ill-maintained form would interest them.

Exina's outfit wouldn't be acceptable in any real medical practice. Her neckline was low and open, good for catching glances, gazes and fools.

Loq had short red feline hair and a forked tongue that she flicked out over her teeth. Not a real Reptilian tongue, though. Hers had been sliced in two. Her gown plunged even further than Exina's generous neckline and revealed a Cyclops' eye on her sternum that lolled around in its socket like it was drunk. If she'd ever had breasts, she didn't have them now. Maybe her partner had them grafted to her lower back for lumbar support.

Exina scanned me with her shadowed eyes. Loq pushed the

duel tips of her tongue onto her lips and sucked them. I felt like the first course at a fancy dinner.

They sat on either side of me. Exina's two-tone hair on my left. Loq's red pixie-cut on my right. They both leaned in close.

Then, Exina laughed.

"I can usually guess," she said. "But I honestly have no idea what you're here for. You're a bit thick from drink, maybe. A few scars. Too many nights without sleep. But a guy like you doesn't worry about things like that. Is it something more," she put a hand on my thigh – upper, *upper* thigh, "delicate?"

Each of her fingernails was a different color. It looked like paint, but it wasn't. Each claw had been taken from a different creature. Nails and talons, sharpened down to the same size. One looked like stone. Another like obsidian.

"Delicate, yes. But a bit higher."

Exina smiled. "I thought so."

"No. Higher than that."

I rolled up my sleeve and revealed the four tattoos wrapped around my forearm. The girls weren't exactly impressed, but not quite disgusted either. Somewhere in between.

"The Human Army and the Opus?" said Exina. "That's got to be a first."

"First and last," I said.

She pointed to my prisoner's stamp.

"You've done time. But what's the other?"

"Weatherly," Loq butted in. Exina, who I doubted was ever surprised by anything, actually looked shocked.

"My, my. You are far more interesting than you first look. And you want us to . . .?"

"Get rid of them. Maybe. I haven't decided yet but I just wanted to know if it was possible. My friend told me about you so I thought I might as well come and ask."

"Who's your friend?" asked Loq, as her hand went onto my other thigh, equally ambiguous in its intention.

I had a choice. I could give them one name, and continue the ruse, or I could throw out the name of the person I really wanted to know about. If they knew *that* name, then I'd have my answer. If they didn't, then they'd know I was lying and there was a very good chance they'd rip my balls off and use them as earrings.

"Harold Steeme," I said, taking the easy option. "Not so much a friend, really. We play cards sometimes. You did fine work on him. If only you could clean up his personality the same way as his skin."

That warmed them both up. Perhaps Harold hadn't been the most charming customer during their time together.

"It can be done," said Exina. One of her polished nails flicked open the top button of my shirt. "But I don't like the idea of taking away your history like that. It's part of you."

Another button.

"Isn't that what you do?"

Exina pouted.

"We work our patients' outsides to better reflect their insides. We show the world who you really are." She reached over and stroked Loq's hair. "This sweet thing was adopted by Werecats when she was young. This is her sister's hair. Now, she is always with family."

Loq put her hand on Exina's face and her thumb stroked the line of scales down her cheek.

"My darling's first love was a Reptilian warrior. He died defending her honor. Now, this part of him is part of her."

They kissed each other. It was a hell of a thing.

"And the tongue?" I asked.

"Well," said Loq, "there were other things that my darling missed about her love. So, this was . . . a gift."

They both giggled, leaned into each other, and knocked me down on my back. *Really, Carissa? You followed your husband's trail down here?* She had more gumption than I'd given her credit for.

"It's just so boring," said Exina, cutting the third button from my shirt so that it went flying across the room. "To get rid of something so unique. So *you*. Why don't we do something really special? Haven't you ever wanted a tail? Just a little one?"

"Or tits?" asked Loq, giggling.

Exina took her hand past upper-thigh, right to the top floor. "What about a Centaur cock? We have some on ice."

"You could have two!" squealed her partner.

Loq cackled and crawled up my body to put her tongue on the bare skin of Exina's neck. Exina turned to kiss her, apparently the idea of the double-dong had captured their imaginations.

"I might need to think about this. Thanks for the ideas."

They'd stopped listening. Exina's hand was in my shirt, on my chest. My thoughts weren't coming clearly because blood was in all the wrong places, so I made a completely unprovoked, clumsy attempt to get back on the case.

"Has anybody ever asked you to . . . to change their race? Or their species? Is that . . . is that a thing?"

Exina's hand slid over my collar bones, her rainbow of nails scratching my skin.

"Why do you ask?" she purred.

"Well, I just—" Her hand closed around my throat. She wasn't even looking at me. Her face was pressed against Loq's. I thought it was part of the game until she gripped so tight I could no longer breathe.

"Why are you really here?" growled Dr Exina.

Her body was pressed onto mine. Loq's too. They had me pinned. The world was going dark and her nails had drawn blood.

Then, Loq was laughing again.

"My darling," she said to Exina, holding up my left arm, "Army and Opus? One of a kind? I think I know why he's here."

It took a moment, but Exina laughed too, and her fingers unfurled from my neck.

"Wow," she said. "You're right, my love. And *he* wouldn't be too happy if we harmed his little pet."

They stroked my hair and smirked in a way that was condescending, all-knowing and with just a touch of pity.

"Get out, boy," said Loq. "We only work on grown-ups."

I got up, and they were back on top of each other before I made it to the door. The Dwarf was waiting.

"Found what you wanted?" he asked.

I had nothing to say. No wit. No snide remark. I exited the building and the Dwarf shut me out. I heard all three locks snap closed. If you ask me, they were on the wrong side of the door.

48

Pet.

No.

I spent the long walk home sending white noise into my mind, trying not to think about the only thing I could possibly think about. Deamar had always looked familiar. Right from the moment when I first saw his face in the alley.

No.

Maybe I just wanted it to be him. Maybe I was seeing connections that weren't there.

But did I really want it to be him?

I wanted him to be alive. Of course. But could I handle seeing him face to face?

He was my mentor. My one true friend. But I broke his trust and fled. Never apologized or tried to contact him again. I was a coward. That was why he'd sent me the machine. It was a test. To see if I would take responsibility for what I'd done.

There was only one punishment fit for the man who'd broken the world. I'd known that for six years. I'd wrestled with it. And finally, I'd been handed the perfect tool for the job.

I still hadn't fixed the lock on my door. Add it to the list of things that will never get done. My failures. My mistakes. I went behind my desk and was about to bend down but—

There was a package on my desk. Another one.

My heart seized up. What would it be this time? Another never-before-seen killing machine?

There was no note from Deamar this time. No fancy handwriting. I unwrapped the package and saw . . . my trousers. Stitched up by Carissa's caring hand.

I collapsed into my chair and shared a laugh with the laundry.

Harold, you piece of shit. What kind of chump would throw away a woman like that? I leaned down to open the bottom drawer.

The machine was gone.

No.

I'd been living in that office for six years and nobody had ever stolen from me. It was the last place anybody would go looking for valuables. Somebody must have known it was there.

I looked from the empty drawer to the patched-up trousers and wished it didn't all make so much sense. She'd seen me waving it around. She'd seen where I'd hidden it. She'd been in my office only hours ago.

The phone rang.

No.

"This is Fetch."

"Hi. It's Linda."

"Oh, thank God. I thought it might be Simms or something."

"Why would you think that?"

"No reason."

"Because Simms just called me."

No.

"Why?" I asked.

"I've become a consultant. She calls me in on any cases that look magical."

Please, no.

"Well, I'm glad things are working out for you."

"Yeah. Apparently somebody got blasted the same way as Lance Niles. I thought you might want to know."

Please, please, no.

"Well, thanks for telling me, Linda."

"Of course. Just don't mention it to Simms."

"I won't."

"You haven't cracked the case already, have you? It would score me some points with the city if I could work this out for them."

Yes.

"No."

"Let me know if you do. Or if you need any more help. You're a pain in the ass, Phillips, but we don't make the worst team. Speak soon."

"Wait. Linda?"

"Yeah?"

"Out of interest, who was it that got killed?"

No. No. No.

"Nobody important. Just an Elven gambler named Harold Steeme."

49

Carissa didn't answer her phone but I went to her house anyway. I didn't have any better ideas. I rang the bell. No response. I was about to knock hard on the door but stopped myself.

I looked over my shoulder, back down the street. Had I just heard voices? The cops? If they hadn't come already they'd be here soon. Was Carissa down at the station confessing to everything? Telling them who'd found her husband and where she'd got the weapon? Had she already cooked me to a crisp?

I wiped the moisture off the glass panel in the door. I couldn't make out details, but there was a light flickering inside: a few candles or a burning fireplace.

The cops wouldn't drag her out but leave something smoldering, would they?

I took off my hat, put it up against the glass and punched it. The rabbit hide protected my hand. At least it was good for something. I reached in, opened the lock, and let myself inside.

"Carissa?"

I checked every room along the hall. Nothing. In the lounge, the fire was roaring, the candles were lit and there was a half-drunk glass of whiskey on the table.

"Huh?"

A voice from down the hall. I followed it and found Carissa in her bedroom, half-undressed and fully loaded. Her body was splayed out on the bed like a broken doll. Legs open. Eyes closed. The machine on the floor at her feet. You couldn't have asked for a clearer picture of the crime.

"Goddam it. Get up."

She was a dead weight just like her husband, but she was awake. That was something.

"Harold, let me sleep."

"Oh honey, I ain't Harold. Harold is gone, remember?"

She laughed, and the smile looked strange on her artificially straightened cheeks.

"Pop," she said.

"Yeah, pop. You popped him good. And I bet you weren't careful about it, were you? Did anybody see what you did?" I couldn't get a clear response but I had a fair idea of the answer. If you plan a murder properly, you're smart about what you do next. You don't go home and get drunk with the weapon at the foot of your bed. "Get dressed. They'll be here soon."

I sat her up, adjusted her clothes, and added some more. It was cold out and she wouldn't be coming home for a while.

"We need to pack a bag. You gonna help me?"

She fell back onto the bed and gurgled, so I searched through the cupboards myself. I dragged a suitcase out from under her bed and threw in the first clothes I could find.

"Carissa!" I gave her a good shake and her eyes opened properly for the first time.

"Mr Phillips? Have you come to keep me out of trouble?"

"Sister, you are trouble. And try as I might, I can't keep a thing out of itself. Let's go."

I dropped a pair of boots into her lap and went to the bathroom to grab what I assumed were a woman's essentials. My experience in such things is limited but Carissa wasn't being any help so she'd have to deal with whatever I dug out for her. I closed the suitcase and picked up the machine. I hadn't brought the harness so all I could do was tuck it into my belt the way Victor had and hope I didn't accidentally castrate myself.

Carissa was useless. She had her handbag beside her but had barely managed to slip her boots over her feet. I bent down to tie her laces and heard voices at the front door.

"Mrs Steeme, is everything all right?"

Shit.

"Is there a back exit?" I asked.

Carissa put her arms around my neck. Oblivious, or maybe just resigned to her fate.

"It's my life now," she said, and leaned forward to kiss me. I ducked out the way and threw her over one shoulder.

"Remind me to cash that kiss in later." I took the suitcase in my free hand and spun out of the room.

I found a back door through the kitchen. When I ran for it, the suitcase knocked over a broom that clattered to the ground.

"Whoever is in here," called the cops, "get on your knees! We're coming in!"

I lumbered through the backyard and kicked open a gate that took us onto a neighborhood park. Everything hurt. If Carissa could feel anything, I'm sure I was hurting her too. She might have looked like a young woman but the work was only skin deep. By the morning, she'd be a bundle of bruises, but, if I kept running, she might at least be free.

So, I kept running.

50

Two blocks past the park, I put Carissa down. The action had slapped a bit of life back into her but she still needed help to walk in a straight line.

We stumbled through backstreets till we arrived at the stables. The trainer wasn't impressed that we'd woken him up, or that I had a drunk woman on my arm instead of his horse.

"You were supposed to bring Frankie back," he said. "I may be going blind but I still know the difference between a filly and a tipsy Elf."

"I need a carriage out of town. Tonight. Do you know someone?"

He took a breath that seemed to last an hour. "I've got one myself, and an able horse."

"I thought you said you were going blind."

"I can see clear enough to spy the lack of other drivers lining up behind you. Where are you going?"

I turned to Carissa. Her mind had crawled from comatose to merely intoxicated.

"Carissa, where's your family?"

"Dead."

"All of them?"

She racked her brain like a rusty gumball machine. Finally something dropped out.

"My cousin. Back in Lipha."

I turned back to the driver.

"Do you know it?"

"On the coast between Mira and Skiros. A couple of days' ride, if the weather doesn't slow us down. Then I have to get back here, of course."

"What will it cost?"

We negotiated a price that reflected the fact that I wasn't in any position to negotiate. I handed over the last of the cash that Thurston Niles had given me. We poured Carissa into the carriage and wrapped her up in blankets.

"I won't be able to leave for a couple of hours," he said. "Gotta prep the horse and shut up shop. You want to hang around? I'll make some tea."

If Linda had thought to call me about this, Simms wouldn't be far behind. They might come asking for information. I may even need an alibi.

"No thanks," I said. "I got some things to do." Like making sure I didn't get caught on the street carrying a recently fired murder weapon.

I took a peek into Carissa's handbag. She had enough cash to keep her going for a couple of days till she found her cousin. It wasn't an ideal plan but she hadn't given me much time to make it. Carissa hadn't just killed her husband; she'd blown him apart with a one-of-a-kind weapon that had also murdered the brother of the most powerful man in the city. They wouldn't just lock her up, she'd fill so many newspapers with her story that they might as well feed her into the printing press.

I put my head into the carriage. She was lying across the seat, curled up and asleep.

I'm not great at goodbyes, so I was glad I didn't have to give one.

I stopped on Main Street, worried that cops might already be watching my place and taking notes. I'd been asking around about Harold Steeme. I'd been seen in a bar with him. Shit, Georgio had seen Carissa come down to buy coffee. Twice. Simms had kicked my ass for less, and she was more pissed at me than she'd ever been.

What if they were already inside waiting for me? If they dragged me uptown with the weapon in my belt, I was toast. I needed to hide it. Hell, I should *destroy* it. That's what Victor had asked me to do.

But Victor hadn't given it to me. Not the first time. Deamar had dropped it on my desk and I still didn't know why.

Mr Deamar.

Was it really possible?

I slunk into the shadows and stayed away from Main Street, taking backroads all the way to the Gilded Cemetery.

The graveyard was reserved for unfortunate Elves who got stuck in Sunder during their last days. Sunder wasn't that popular with the Elvish population before the Coda, so the grounds had never been overly busy, but there was one Elf of distinction who had always been fascinated by what the fire city had to offer.

Governor Lark had commissioned the crypt in honor of his friend. In honor of my friend. A beautifully crafted mausoleum placed at the heart of the city to signify that High Chancellor Eliah Hendricks always had a home in Sunder.

I entered the crypt and lit one of the torches on the wall. It didn't look like anyone had been inside since I chased a group of teenagers out of there last autumn. At the back of the room, there was a specially made stone coffin with Eliah's name carved into it in Elvish.

I'd always taken it for granted that Hendricks had died in the Coda like millions of others. I never asked whether his body had been brought back or whether it had been stuffed into this stone block. I'd always been too scared to have my fears confirmed.

Now, I was terrified of an entirely different outcome.

I put my palms on the lid and the dust moved under my fingers. The wind came through the archway and blew the burning torch till it roared. I pushed with the heels of my hands and the lid shifted, opening the coffin.

And it was empty.

Of course it was.

But that didn't mean anything at all, did it? Who would have brought his body back here anyway? He could have died anywhere. Probably on his way to take back the mountaintop.

This just meant that I had a safe place to keep the machine for a while.

I took it out of my belt and dropped it into the empty space that had been made for my old friend. Then I pulled the lid back to its original place.

Tap.

Someone else was in the cemetery.

Tap.

A cane against the cobblestones.

Tap.

Coming straight for the Hendricks' Crypt.

Tap.

Made for my friend.

Pat, tap.

Back at The Ditch with laughter and light.

Pat, tap.

Streets at sundown. With stories and song.

Pat, tap.

The mansion.

Pat, tap.

The second mark.

Pat. Pat, tap.

Leaving town on horseback.

Pat. Pat, tap.

That terrible night and my stupid ideas.

Pat. Pat, tap.

Goodbyes. Empty, unworthy goodbyes.

Pat. Pat, tap.

Pat. Pat, tap.

Pat. Pat, tap.

Deamar stepped into the light.

Black suit, cane, hat, and a body that had been worked over by the Succubae surgeons. I looked past his scarred face and fell into his familiar green eyes.

"Hello, Eliah," I said. "It's been too long."

His old, contagious smile pushed through his new, unnatural face and he spread out his arms as if to hold the whole world.

"My dear boy," said Hendricks. "It's been an eternity."

Emotion surged in my chest, stealing my breath and filling my eyes with tears. I wiped them away just in time to see Hendricks swing his cane at my head.

51

It was an attack six years in the making. Eight, probably. Maybe even more. As the bone handle of Hendricks' cane glistened in the torchlight, I realized that I'd been waiting for it just as much as he had.

I'd taken a lot of hits since becoming a Man for Hire. A lot of hits from a lot of people, waiting for the one I deserved. And here it was. Some divine retribution delivered by a specter of judgment who had just stepped out of the past.

Maybe there was some justice in the world after all.

The handle of the cane came down on my brow just above my left eye, breaking the skin and splattering blood across the cold stone floor.

Hendricks grabbed both ends of the cane like he was going to snap it over his leg, and yelled out.

"FUCK!"

There was a tormented look of pain on his face, unlike anything I'd ever seen before.

He shouted again, and the walls of the crypt shouted back at him. His hands were white-knuckle tight around the wood of the cane and he curled himself over it as if a great spasm was shooting up his body. I stood there, stupidly, mouth hanging open and blood dripping down my face, waiting for some kind of hint about what I should do next.

He looked at me the way you might look at a stillborn puppy. Like I was a tragedy. A hopeless, nonsensical bit of cruelty that couldn't be explained.

He swung again. Backhanded. I took it just like I had before.

The back of the handle cracked me across the cheek but there was less effort in it this time. Less medicine.

"Do you know how many different pictures I've painted of you in my head?" His eyes seemed incapable of looking at me for any length of time. Instead, he examined the smear of the blood that tipped a sharp corner of his cane. "The Human spy who used me. The piece of pure evil I mistook for a good man. The traitor. I convinced myself that you must have planned it all along. That you were some kind of mastermind. But then I see you here and . . . what are you? You're nothing. Nothing more than what you were when I first met you. Despite all that I tried to teach you. All we trusted you with. You're just . . ." He shrugged, like it wasn't even worth giving it a word.

"I'm sorry."

The next hit had some force in it again. It came up under my chin and knocked my teeth together so that they bit my tongue.

"Who do you work for?" Hendricks buried his eyes six feet deep into mine.

"What?"

"Who do you work for?"

"I . . . nobody. I just—"

He put the base of the cane against my chest and pushed me back against the coffin.

"I was just starting to think that I could forgive you. That you'd made a series of stupid mistakes and were trying to be better. But now you're with *them* again. Siding with your own kind."

Niles. I'd taken his money to find Deamar. And Hendricks had seen me. After everything that had happened, he'd come back to Sunder to find me working with the Humans. Against him. Again.

"I didn't know it was you. I thought . . ." I wiped my face, smearing the blood. "I got talked into it. It was just a job."

Hendricks shook his head and I watched the worst of the anger drain out of him. His expression was back to one I recognized: the slightly bemused, condescending stare of a teacher who has just heard me say something profoundly stupid.

"You still think, after everything that happened, that what you do doesn't matter? That because you take your orders from someone else, that you're no longer accountable for your actions? Nothing is just a *job*, Fetch. Especially now. Not at a time like this. And not for a man like that."

"I know. But he didn't give me much of a choice."

He jabbed the end of the cane between my ribs.

"You always have a choice. Beware of anyone who tries to make you forget that. They are only seeking to serve themselves."

We weren't in the crypt anymore. We were back at The Ditch. By a campfire on the road. In the garden of the Governor's mansion with cigars at sunset.

Oh, how I missed this! Maybe more than anything else. The Coda had taken a lot of things that would never come back, but my mentor was here. I felt like I could finally see through the darkness.

The words bubbled out before I could think of them.

"I'll work for you, Eliah. If you'll let me."

Despite himself, he smiled. Then he remembered himself and looked me over, suspicious, like he thought I might lead him into a trap.

"You don't even know why I'm here, boy."

"Leaving the Opus was the worst mistake I ever made. I can't fix what was done but if you're here to make things better, I'll do everything I can to help."

He seemed almost disappointed. Like he'd been looking forward to beating my head in, and I'd taken all the fun out of it.

"Please," I said.

The war inside his head wasn't over. Not even close. But I hoped that he would look away from it for long enough to give me a chance.

The tip of his cane came off my chest and tapped back against the floor.

"I'd be lying if I said you wouldn't be of use. My body is rather limited these days. But you can't work for Niles if you're working for me."

"I was never really working for him anyway. Only enough to justify taking his cash."

"That's a start. Soon we'll be taking a lot more than that."

He wiped my blood from his cane and the sweat from his brow. Then he shook his head and chuckled.

"You're not giving me much of an option, are you?"

"Nope."

"Either I let you tag along," his smile dropped like a guillotine, "or I kill you."

His eyes were still familiar, more familiar than the rest of that stitched-up face, but they were different too. I couldn't put my finger on what it was, but there was something different inside that deep, endless green.

"See," he said. "There's always a choice." He tapped the cane twice against the floor, like a drill sergeant calling his troops to attention. "Now, let's get ourselves a drink."

52

Where do you take a friend who was once the leader of the greatest organization in the world but is now the city's most wanted murderer? The Ditch was too risky. Even with Hendricks' new face, the two of us together could spark somebody's memory. Hendricks' appearance was unrecognizable but his voice, though strained and raspy, still contained that inimitable essence of wonder. He'd shaved off the mustache and changed his hat but anybody who had heard Deamar's description might still be suspicious, so that ruled out the Bluebird Lounge or anywhere that collected cops like the Runaway or Dunkley's. I suggested that we find some dive bar down the bad end of town but Hendricks had other plans. He ducked into a liquor store and came out with a bottle of port wrapped in a brown paper bag. He took a swig and looked around.

"Which way is north?" he asked. I pointed him in the right direction. "Follow me, my boy. I need to show you something."

He hobbled up the road, his cane tapping away on the cobblestones. After another long sip, he handed me the bottle.

"Why *this* whole thing?" he asked, waving a hand in my direction but keeping his eyes ahead.

"Why what?"

"This whole 'hired muscle' routine. What's it all about?"

"I uh . . ." I'd been throwing out snappy half-answers to that question for years but none of those quips would work on Hendricks. "I knew I needed to help but I didn't know how. This made sense. At the time."

He was suitably unimpressed.

"I think we can do better than that."

We walked and drank and Eliah unraveled his last six years

with that unrivaled eloquence. He'd been traveling from the Opus headquarters to Agotsu when the Coda happened.

"I only survived because I was given more medical attention than anybody else in the caravan. Opus medics kept me alive and delivered me to a Warlock village in the shadows of the Agotsun cliffs. My boy, I have never known such pain. It was an arduous process of rehabilitation just to be able to move again. And for what? Just so I could reenter the world as an old man. I cannot tell you how tempting it was to let go. The only thing that kept me going was a sense of duty. The belief that it was my obligation to find out what had happened and set things right."

Hendricks finally made it to the top of Agotsu, a year too late to fight the battle. A year too late to stop the massacre. A year too late to fix the worst mistake in history.

"It was supposed to be the most sacred place on the planet. When I arrived, it was a construction site. It seems that as soon as the massacre was over, the Human Army cleared out the bodies and brought in their machines. Mining equipment. Weapons of defense. But after the deed was done, they just walked away. No soul left alive. No monument. Just waste."

Filled with anger and a thirst for revenge, Hendricks set off for the closest Human city: Weatherly. On the way, he set traps for Human travelers and sabotaged vehicles so that he could investigate what they were up to.

"The Human Army hasn't gone anywhere. They just call themselves *Mortales* and act like they're only interested in building appliances and helping people get back on their feet. But it's the same brains behind it. The same black hearts. They have no shame capitalizing on the tragedy that they created. Profiting from our pain. Even now, Mortales works with other organizations to claim as much land, wealth and culture as they can. They know they need to move fast, before the magical species get back on their feet."

"You . . . you think that can happen?"

He seemed confused at my question, then annoyed, then patronizingly amused.

"Oh, not like that. The magic as we knew it is gone. But mark my words, Fetch Phillips, this is not over. The Humans know that. That's why they are moving so swiftly. If we don't stop them now, we will never have a chance to fight back. We will lose this world once and for all and we will have handed it over like it was nothing."

I took a healthy drink of the sweet wine and found that I was excited. Hendricks was already speaking to me like I was back on his side. Of course, neither of us could forget that I was a key player in the event that won the war for his enemy. That would be impossible. But he was at least contemplating the idea of letting me return to his ranks.

I realized, with some surprise, that I wanted nothing more.

"For the past five years I have been waging a one-man war against Mortales and its allies. I have hijacked vehicles coming out of Weatherly, followed convoys to new camps and stolen reams of correspondence. Mortales is not a lone company. Weatherly is not the isolated city they would have you believe. The Niles Company is not a just a couple of brothers with a mind for business. It is a network. It is an attempt at occupation. This is an invasion that has been hiding in the shadows since the Coda, preparing to make its move, and Sunder City will be the final battleground.

We passed a construction site where someone had started building a house but given up halfway. A bunch of Gnomes had started a fire on the bare foundations, burning something that emitted black, toxic-smelling smoke.

"Why here?" I asked.

"This place has a gravity to it. It always did, even in the old days, but now it's something else. In every other part of the continent, crops are failing and families are falling apart. That's because they relied completely on the natural world. This place? It had already shaken hands with the darkness. It had Human machines. Human ideas. It's almost as if Sunder knew what was coming."

He smacked his cane against the ground, like he was scolding the city itself. "Now, every sad village and struggling country town knows that Sunder City could bring them their salvation. Whether we like it or not, we are standing in the center of the new world. Whoever controls this city holds the future in their hands."

I thought about all the places Hendricks had taken me. Kingdoms where they trained the strongest warriors. Castles with wealth beyond belief. Libraries of untold wisdom. Surely these mean streets weren't the best of what was left.

Hendricks must have seen my doubt because he went on, deadly serious, as if our lives depended on my understanding.

"The real war is coming and we will not clash with swords and spells this time but with industry. With economy. Right now, the Humans have the lead. If nobody steps in to challenge them, the leaders of this city will decide the fate of Archetellos unopposed."

I couldn't help remembering what Linda had told me about the origin of Hendricks' stolen name. Deamar. The first creature who declared war against humankind.

"So, you came here to . . .?"

"To stop this *Niles Company* for good. The citizens of Sunder may be cheering them now, believing that they're just here to bring jobs and toasters and automobiles, but a ruse is being pulled. I don't know what it is. Not yet. But this city is far too willing to close its eyes to the truth. I am here to open them up."

I was conscious of each breath. Each moment. I was fully awake for the first time in years and it was all because of Hendricks. He was magnetic. Inspiring. Terrifying. The dark thoughts that slowed down my days vanished whenever he opened his mouth.

I did my best to ignore the hint of desperation in his voice. To not look too closely at his bloodshot eyes or focus on the way his fingers were shaking. The hardest thing to get used to was his eyes. There was something strange about them. Something more subtle than the obvious changes made to his now-unfamiliar face.

"Why the disguise?" I asked.

"Oh, this?" Hendricks gestured to his malformed mask like it was some bit of jewelry he'd snapped up on sale. "I'd seen those surgeons work wonders on other Elves, stretched the centuries from their faces and created a façade of youth, so I went looking for the same. It turns out that hundreds of years of indulgence and hard-drinking will rise to the surface when the magic stops holding them down. My skin was like old parchment. When they tried to pull it tight, it tore. I'd been hoping to come out of that clinic looking vibrant and handsome again. Instead, they could barely keep me together. They did what they could and I came out like this. But it's not so bad. At least I've got my fucking eyebrows."

He wasn't such a monstrosity. Most Lycum had come out of the Coda far worse. Everything was still in the right place but his lip was cut with scar tissue. One eyelid looked a little lazy. His cheeks were smooth but they didn't look natural. Too shiny. Still, it wasn't really that bad unless you remembered the man he'd been before.

High Chancellor Eliah Hendricks had glowed. From his copper hair to his perfect teeth to the tips of his dancing fingers, it was like an artist had painted him into existence. Now, his hair was short and gray, his lips were dry, and his ears . . . well, the sharp Elven points had been completely lopped off.

"But why do you look like a Human?"

He did a little wave. A quirk of his. It was a circular swirl with his right hand that had a habit of knocking over tray tables or accidently starting fights with people sitting too close. Its meaning was something like, *Well, why not?*

"Because I wanted to walk among my enemies," he said. "It worked. I knew enough about Lance Niles to tempt him into a meeting and with these ears and this face, he trusted me as one of his own. So much so, that he handed me the secret I'd been looking for."

"The machine."

Hendricks chuckled.

"Is that what you call it? In some correspondence I acquired, Mortales referred to it as a *pistol*. Lance showed it to me, thinking that I was some great engineer. He hoped that I would unlock its secrets. Instead, I used it to kill him."

The spectrum of Hendricks' personality had always been spread wide. He was a warm-hearted, idealistic dreamer. Sometimes. Other times, he was the most cold-blooded rationalist I'd ever met.

"Why?"

"Because he disgusted me. Lance Niles believed in the mask that I was wearing, so he took off his own mask and showed me his true self. If a man like that takes control of this city, he will soon be making his fortune in murder. I saw the sickness of this city in the heart of that two-faced con-artist and before I knew what I'd done, his brains were on the back wall."

He gave another of his carefree flourishes, like that last part of the story was inconsequential. The killer I'd been searching for was confessing his crimes to my face but he was playing it off like it was nothing: a side-note to another story that was far more important. Maybe it was, but I was struggling to merge these two men into one: my dear old friend and the murderous Mr Deamar.

"Was it really that easy?"

That slowed him down a little. I always felt good when I asked Hendricks a question that he didn't have a locked-and-loaded answer for. He licked the wine from his lips and thought it over.

"Disturbingly easy. Does that surprise you? You've touched the pistol. Nobody needs to show you how to hold it or the way to make it work. It is the most elegantly designed piece of evil I have ever seen. From the moment you pick it up, you *want* to use it, don't you think? It's almost impossible not to."

I felt some relief, hearing him talk about it. Until that moment, the burden of the machine had been mine alone. Even Victor didn't see it the same way. Finally, I could talk to someone else about its unique, addictive power.

"Is that why you gave it to me? So you wouldn't be tempted to use it again?"

"I suppose. And other reasons."

"Like what?"

He shrugged. "To see what would happen."

Hendricks laughed. Wide and high like I had just asked the silliest thing in the world. Try as I might, I couldn't join him.

"What happens now?" I asked. "Lance is gone."

"Yes, but his brother isn't. From what I understand, the same darkness runs through him."

Thurston Niles hadn't seemed so evil to me. Not at the time. But Hendricks was making me realize how asleep I'd been. How I'd only looked at the things that other people wanted me to see. Because there hadn't been any reason to go any deeper. We were all just holding on, waiting to see what would die next. Now, all of a sudden, the blood of the world was bright red and beating again.

"Hendricks, where are we going?"

We'd walked past the Mayor's home, his gardens and the House of Ministers, and were climbing up a small hill with the grand name of Mt Ramanak. Ramanak separated the city from the forest beyond: a protected park known as Brisak Reserve.

When they first built Sunder, Brisak wasn't much more than swamp. Over time, the Ministers introduced all kinds of trees and shrubs to the landscape and created a haven of exotic plants and animals. Lovers would walk up to the waterfall. Witches could explore its nooks and crannies to pick rare ingredients. It was a little piece of nature tucked into the backbone of the metropolis.

Of course, most of the flora had at least some magical component so the whole place took a mean hit from the Coda. We'd all been hoping that the natural world would find a way to fight back and fill the area with non-magic plants sometime soon.

Hendricks was breathing heavily.

"Eliah, we can go back. Do this another time."

"No. You need to see this."

He slowed but he didn't stop. The bottle was empty so he threw it by the side of the path. Finally, we crested the hill just as dawn pushed away the stars. There should have been enough morning light to illuminate the reserve, but I couldn't see a piece of it.

That's because Brisak Reserve was gone.

The whole area had been cleared of trees and covered with cement. At the bottom of the hill there was a building as big as anything else in Sunder. Huge metal walls with workers moving in and out.

How had they done it without the fire pits?

Nobody had constructed anything like this. Not since the Coda. Not in Sunder, but likely not anywhere. We might renovate old, out-of-date businesses or give a city block a fresh coat of paint but we weren't building new factories from the ground up. The last time I'd seen anything like it was Amari's doomed hospital and even that was minuscule compared to whatever was happening down below.

Trucks drove down the hill and unloaded supplies. Carriages dropped crates at the door and laborers came out to collect them. The workflow wasn't only smooth, it was being done with a certain amount of enthusiasm.

"It's incredible," I said. Hendricks made a disproving noise in the back of his throat.

"From what I can gather, this power plant is the most crucial part of their operation. They've been employing hundreds of workers to keep it going night and day."

His tone was all condemnation, but it was exactly the kind of thing that Sunderites had been praying for.

"Isn't that a good thing?"

"Don't confuse business with altruism, boy. Lance Niles was in town a long time before he announced what his plans were. The company purchased a sizable amount of the city before anyone knew what was happening. The government and the citizens, desperate for profit, sold their assets for next to nothing. Now, if this power plant actually gets going, all those businesses will be functional again."

"Eliah, that sounds like progress."

Hendricks spun around to face me, his stranger's face grimacing as he pointed a fingertip into my forehead.

"Didn't I teach you to be smarter than this? To question everything? Think! I didn't spend all those hours testing you just so you would believe whatever anybody tells you."

"I know. I'm sorry."

"Nothing is what it seems," he said, turning my attention back to the bustling power plant below. "The Niles brothers have greased the palms and slapped the backs of every Minister in town so nobody will look at what the company is actually doing. That responsibility has been left to me." He put a hand on my shoulder. "Left to *us*, if you have it in you to do what's right."

I don't believe in second chances. I don't believe you can undo what was done. But if I didn't believe I still had it in me to do something good, I would have jumped out the Angel door a long time ago.

"Tell me what we need to do," I said.

He nodded. It wasn't much, but it was enough.

"First, we need to find out how the Niles Company are creating their power. When we know that, we can decide what happens next."

"How do we do that?"

He smiled, finally, and it almost made him look like his old self.

"We need to get inside that building."

I must not have hidden my shock because he let out a cheeky laugh. When I heard it, all uncertainty vanished from my mind. We were a team again. Off on a quest to uncover the inner workings of the Niles Company, and nothing could have made me happier. He laughed again and patted me on the back.

"Come on, Mr *Man for Hire*. Let's have ourselves an adventure."

53

To my relief, Hendricks' plan required further preparation. Once we'd gone back down the hill to the top of Main Street, he suggested that we should both catch up on some sleep.

"You can stay upstairs at mine, if you like," I offered. "It's not that big but we can work something out."

"Thank you, darling, but I have a place. Get some rest and I'll come for you later in the day."

He walked off into the dawn light and I couldn't help but wonder where he might be staying. How many other people had he contacted? How high had I been on his list of old friends?

I got back to my office and my head was on the pillow for less than a minute before someone knocked on the open door.

"Are you going to come quietly or do I need to get the big boys?" Simms looked like she'd had even less sleep than me.

"You look tired, Detective. How about you hop in, we both have a nap, and deal with whatever you need when we wake up?"

She threw a near-freezing glass of water on my face.

"You. Me. Station. Now."

No carriage this time. But there was no interrogation room or phonebook either, so I counted myself lucky. She brought me into her office, closed the door, and collapsed in her chair like her bones had vanished from her body.

"What a mess," she said. "What a screw-balled, stupid, cock-eyed, mangy, puddle of piss. This Niles case is a sham and it's all my fault."

"Don't beat yourself up, Simms. Could have happened to anyone."
She threw a folder of papers at my head.

"It's my fault because I was dumb enough to bring you in on it."

There was a knock on the door. It was the timid cop who had
found me on the floor of my office after I returned from Aaron
Valley. He put two cups of bad police-station coffee on the desk.

"Thank you, Bath," said Simms.

"No problem, Detective."

Bath left. Simms didn't even blow on her coffee before she took
a sip.

"How did you know it wasn't Tippity?"

Ugh. I'd had weeks to think of a good answer to that one but
I hadn't come up with anything convincing.

"Do you trust the Niles Company?" I asked.

"Do you want me to jump over the desk and slap you? Don't
change the subject."

"I'm not. I knew it wasn't Tippity the same way you did.
Because, just like everybody else, you know that there isn't any
magic left. Nothing that powerful. Not anymore. Whatever killed
Lance Niles, it was something else." I shrugged. "Maybe some
kind of machine."

"You know more than you're saying, Fetch."

"So do you."

"I'm supposed to know more. I'm the fucking police. You were
meant to be working for me."

"I did exactly what you asked me to do, I just got it wrong.
We all got wrapped up in the idea that Tippity had unlocked
something special. But he hasn't. *Of course*, he hasn't. I'm sorry it
took so long for me to come to my senses but this murder has
nothing to do with magic. So why don't we forget the *how* and
look at the *why*? Does anybody really know what the Niles
Company is up to?"

"You can't fill me up with crumbs, Fetch. Who killed Lance
Niles? Who killed Harold Steeme? How did they do it?"

"Who's Harold Steeme?"

If Simms wasn't so tired, that question might have got me killed.

"Harold Steeme is the gambler who got killed last night outside a little club called Cornucopia where, a few weeks ago, some lippy gumshoe came in and gave him shit about leaving his wife."

"Right. Sorry. I meant to say, *Harold Steeme is dead?*"

"Who killed him, Fetch?"

"You think I know that?"

"Yes!"

"Well, I don't."

I held my gaze to her narrow, golden eyes, shrugging like an idiot.

"I don't believe you," she said. "I don't believe a single bullshit thing coming out of your mouth. Give me something to go on or I'll lock you up till this thing is over."

Something was strange. She was pissed – that wasn't anything new – but it was different. She was frustrated and irritable instead of wheeling out her tired, hard-ass routine.

"Why *haven't* you locked me up?" I asked.

"Keep this up and I will."

"Come on, Simms. You don't usually beat around the bush like this. If you really thought I was keeping things from you, you'd have me tied up in interrogation. What's got into you? Don't get a kick from seeing me in cuffs anymore?"

"I *know* you're keeping things from me."

"Then what's the deal? I saw the story in the paper. You've dropped Tippity in the Gullet for a crime you know he didn't do. The Mayor is using that story to crack down on anyone that tries to revive the magic, even in little ways. This isn't how you do things, Simms."

"I'm *not* doing this."

"Then who is?"

She did her best to hold it in, but something finally snapped.

"Thurston Niles. The brother. He's buying up the whole city.

Some of it with cash. Some of it with handshakes and smiles. I can't move an inch in this case without one of his partners closing in around me. You say Tippity didn't do this? Sure. Well, whoever *did* do it killed Harold Steeme last night."

"Don't be so sure about that."

Her eyes went wide.

"See! You know something!"

"I don't! I'm just bouncing around some ideas."

"If only you could see what a terrible liar you are, it would save us both a lot of embarrassment. Are you really going to let Tippity rot in jail rather than open your mouth?"

"You saw what he did to those bodies. Tippity is a creep."

"But he's not a murderer. Right? Isn't that what you told the judge? And while he's locked up, the real killer walks free. Isn't your conscience heavy enough without adding this to the load?"

But what was the alternative? Hand over Hendricks? How would that fit into my tightly packed closet of skeletons?

"I don't know who did it," I said, even less convincing than the last time. "If I did, I'd tell you. That's what you paid me for."

I didn't need to convince her. She'd showed me her hand when she told me that Thurston had handicapped her on the case. The Niles Company wanted to pin the crime on Tippity because it was a neater story than Deamar. With everyone looking the other way, they hoped to quietly take care of the real killer in the shadows. Even if Simms arrested me, her superiors wouldn't want to hear anything about it.

"You had your chance, Fetch. Now stay away from every part of this. The Bluebird Lounge, the prison and the Niles Company."

"That's gonna be difficult."

She bit her lip so she wouldn't scream.

"Why?"

"Because Thurston Niles hired me to find his brother's killer."

If she'd spontaneously combusted, I wouldn't have been surprised.

"Since when?"

"Couple of days ago."

"You should have told me."

"I just did."

"I thought you didn't work for Humans."

"He got me on a technicality. As you said, Thurston is a guy who gets what he wants."

She rubbed her temples. "You got one of those painkillers?"

I threw her a Clayfield and she stirred it around in her coffee.

"Nice trick," I said. "Never tried that one."

"Fetch, this case is a pile of shit and you're walking it all over my carpet. Give me something solid, right now, or I'll throw you in the Gullet with Tippity."

"On what grounds?"

"Whatever grounds I want. You have a long history of crimes that I can pull into the light if I want you out of my way."

Another time in my life, I might have let her. But my old buddy was back from the dead and asking for my help. I needed to throw somebody under the bus so Simms would let me out. If it had to be someone, it might as well be the woman who was on a carriage out of Sunder City jurisdiction.

"A couple of weeks ago, a woman came to my office. She wanted me to find out who killed her husband. The husband was a gambler who'd disappeared without a trace. So, I went looking and found the husband who was alive and well, with a smooth new face. When I told the wife what had happened, she was emotional, of course, but took it better than I'd expected. That was the last I heard about it until last night."

I didn't need to fill in the blanks. Simms was way ahead of me.

"So you *do* know who the killer is."

"I can take a guess. All I know is what you know. What *everyone* knows. Some guy got blasted through the face. Now, an old-lady-Elf *might* have killed her husband in the same way. There are no spell-casters left and, even if there were, this is not a spell-casting world.

Maybe you're not looking for a killer, Simms. Maybe you're looking for a weapon. But go back to where this started. With a stranger in town trying to buy this city for himself. I'm not the problem here. I might have walked this shit onto your carpet but we should be working together to see who dropped it in the first place."

My speech was as thin as cigarette paper and just as likely to go up in smoke, but it gave her something to chew on besides the Clayfield.

"Thurston hired you?"

"Yep."

"Is he getting his money's worth?"

I stirred a Clayfield in my coffee and took a sip. It wasn't half bad.

"Between you and me, it's not his best investment."

Simms put her elbows on the desk and her head in her hands.

"I have nobody left," she said. "The whole department is kissing the ass of this Niles guy and I don't know who to talk to. I don't believe you've said one honest thing to me since you walked in here but I'm not convinced you're my enemy either. Not yet, anyway. I'll let you go. If you decide that you want to help me, you know where I am. But if I have even the faintest hunch that you're going to screw me over more than you have already, I'll lock you up with Tippity, and you'll be begging to be on my side again."

I just nodded. After years of making the same mistake, I'd finally learned when to shut myself up.

54

When I opened my eyes, Hendricks was sitting at my desk, holding one of Tippity's glass balls up to the light.

I really needed to get that lock fixed.

"What's this?" he asked, shaking the bauble to watch the pink-tinted liquid splash around inside.

"Careful, it's acid or something. Tippity used it to unlock the Fae magic."

"How extraordinary."

"If you say so."

"Do you mind if I keep one?" Without waiting for an answer, he popped the ball back in its pouch and then put it in his pocket.

"So, what's the plan?" I asked.

"The plan, my dear boy, is a little old-fashioned espionage. When Lance Niles came to town, the power plant was his first project. Workers are already up there, punching their timecards night and day. I've made some enquiries but I can't find out what's actually happening inside."

"So, how do we get in?"

"I'm glad you asked. It will be impossible for me to pass myself off as an employee of the company but there is a good chance you can slip into the plant during a shift change and find out what they're up to."

Not my favorite idea.

"The Niles Company knows who I am," I said, "and Tippity's trial put my face in the papers. I'm not as incognito as I used to be."

"That's why we're off to see the Succubae," he joked. At least, I thought he was joking.

"I don't think we have time for me to heal from surgery."
Hendricks smiled like his old self, all rascally and full of cheek.
"They do have other skills."

55

"Gentlemen, what a lovely surprise."

Exina kissed Hendricks on the lips like an estranged lover. Perhaps they were. Or maybe just like-minded, uninhibited creatures who'd cut their teeth on better times.

Hendricks gave her a brief rundown of the plan as Exina led us down the hall and into the surgery where Loq was waiting. The room still had candles and silk curtains but there were also racks of sharp instruments and drains in the floor that were stained with rust or blood.

When Exina told me to sit down on the metal patient's chair, she noticed that I was shaking.

"Oh, darling, don't worry. We won't do anything permanent."

"Not yet," said Loq. "But I know you'll be back."

Hendricks and the surgeons stood around me, scratching their chins.

"Elf?" suggested Hendricks.

"We'd have to source too much skin," said Loq.

"I'm thinking Lycum," said Exina. "After the Coda, every member of their species ended up with a different percentage of animal and Human. If we make a couple of significant changes, nobody will ask any questions."

The group agreed. I was still deciding whether I should run away.

"I'm going to be a Werewolf?" I asked.

Exina turned to Loq.

"Take a look in the icebox, my love. See what we have left over."

Were*cat* was the final decision.

The Succubae made preparations while Hendricks went out and got some wine. As soon as he left, they strapped me into the chair. Loq said that it was because they didn't want me disturbing their work by moving around too much but I'm pretty sure it was just so they could screw with me.

Exina focused on the teeth first. She hollowed out two feline fangs so they would fit over my real canines. Loq gave me a haircut and dyed a ginger streak into my fringe. I hated it, which only made them love it more.

"I'd love to change one of your eyes," said Exina, "but we don't really have time. Let's give you a patch and let them wonder what lies underneath."

"I'm surprised," said Hendricks, returning with a healthy collection of beverages. "I didn't think you had it in you to leave anything to the imagination."

Exina slapped him and gave him a kiss.

My eyebrows had barely grown back so it was easy to cover them with ginger fur taken from some previous patient.

"Have we got any whiskers?" asked Exina. They checked with the Dwarf, who found a few discarded in the trash and attached them to my stubble. "They look a little sad but that's the fashion these days. What else?"

"Claws, of course," said Hendricks, with a devilish grin.

"Just the left hand," I said. "If things go south, I'll need my right in working order."

They attached sharp black nails to the top of my own.

"They're canine," said Loq, "but I've filed them down so nobody will tell the difference unless they get up close, so don't try to scratch anybody's eyes out."

They didn't let me look in a mirror till it was all done. I hate to admit it, but the work was impressive. Subtle enough to be believable and I didn't look at all like myself. They'd used glue to pull my skin in a few strange ways that changed the shape of my face and made it look like the Coda had made its mark but been merciful.

"Almost there," said Hendricks, as he produced a Niles Company uniform from his bag.

"Where did this come from?" I asked.

"The laundry room of the Hotel Larone. I've been hatching a version of this plan for some time."

They stuck a pair of socks in the back of my underwear to make it look like the stump of a tail.

"Just don't let it fall too low, boy, or it will look like something else entirely."

Loq put a beanie on my head and pulled it down tight so that only the ginger hair poked out the front. I looked unrecognizable, even to myself.

"Well, what do we call him?" asked Hendricks.

"He's your pet," smirked Loq.

They were having way too much fun.

"I had a cat once," said Exina.

"What was his name?" asked Hendricks.

"Montgomery Fiztwitch."

Hendricks nodded. "Monty for short."

56

We walked along the path at the top of Mt Ramanak and found
a patch of trees that hadn't been cleared. Lying back between the
thick roots of an oak, Hendricks and I could see the factory's front
gate while the foliage left us sufficiently disguised. Our plan was
to wait for the shift change so I could slip in with the new group
of workers.

"Drink?" asked Hendricks.

"Sure." I reached into my jacket and pulled out a silver flask.
When I held it out to Hendricks, he already had an identical one
in his hand. We both laughed.

"Don't say I never taught you anything." He took a healthy
swig. "What have you got?"

"Whiskey."

"I've got rum. Give me a taste."

We swapped flasks and both had a drink.

"Yours is better," he said. "You won this round, Fetch *Phillips*."
He let my name hang out in the air like a kite in the breeze.
"When did you take back that name?"

"On the day I moved into my office. The painter asked me
what I wanted written on my window and it just came out. I was
Martin Phillips when I was born. Martin Kane in Weatherly. Then
just Fetch. Shepherd Fetch, for a while. Private Fetch after that.
Then, when it was all over and I needed a new name for this new
world, it felt right to be Phillips again."

He chewed on it for a bit and washed it down with whiskey.

"Did you remember that name? From your youth?"

"No. I read it in some documents when the Human Army were
trying to recruit me." I wasn't really ready to go down this road

but I didn't know how to turn myself around. "It was a report of what happened in Elan County. They named me as the only survivor. I definitely don't feel like a Martin anymore, but Phillips seems to fit."

Hendricks looked over. His lips trembled as if they were shuffling through the hundred different ways to respond.

The Human Army had told me that Hendricks was responsible for what had happened to my family, the Phillipses, back in Elan. He'd let a Chimera go free, despite many warnings, and the monster had wiped out my whole village. It was hearing that information that had convinced me to leave the Opus.

Now that time had passed, I understood that his mistake had come from him trying to do the right thing. I couldn't yet believe that of mine.

It would have been the perfect moment to clear the air of everything that had happened. To begin the impossible task of trying to move on. To apologize. But the moment passed. I felt it drift away, like when you look out the window at a sunny day but by the time you put your shoes on the clouds have already rolled in.

Hendricks just nodded and said, "Yes, boy. I believe the name fits you very well."

There was a whistle from down below.

"That's the first bell," said Hendricks. "A ten-minute warning. The second bell means shift change. You ready?"

"I wish I knew what I was walking into."

"The Niles Company is hiring so many new people, you won't be the only one in over your head. Keep interaction to a minimum but if you must talk to the others, then let them know it's your first day."

The glue was already itching.

"What exactly am I looking for?"

"Any information on how their operation works. What is their fuel source? How much energy can they produce? What are they using it for? Things like that."

They weren't the kind of questions a laborer asks on his first day, but I got the idea. Hendricks straightened my whiskers, patted my shoulder, and Monty went out into the cold.

57

Up close, the power plant looked even bigger. It was a great metal mountain with tiny windows and one gigantic monster of a door. I joined the crowd that had formed outside. The other workers were all races, all sizes, all with that distant look of men whose bodies have always been more valuable than their minds. We funneled through the door, shoulder to shoulder, and I tried to peek through the crowd to see what my first test would be.

Claustrophobia, apparently. I was in a hallway with a hundred other brutes, fighting our way to a few women with clipboards waiting up ahead. Each worker gave them a surname and a five-digit number and stepped past. I was already panicking, expecting to stumble at the first hurdle, but then I saw that the women were writing the numbers down, not checking them off a list. That meant that it was less about security and more about people getting paid. I followed suit.

"Fiztwitch. Three, two, seven, eight, one."

She wrote it down and didn't even look up. I waited for a response but someone just shoved me in the back to move me on.

The room we stepped into was a quarter of the entire building but still enormous. The walls and roof were all made of metal panels and the high ceilings were fitted with many chimneys to filter out the smoky air. There were benches all around, and doors leading off into other rooms, but I couldn't make sense of any of it. The majority of workers were heading to the east wall so I followed a brawny Ogre who looked like he knew the routine. He grabbed a pair of safety goggles from a rack so I did the same, then we picked up a couple of paper-wrapped bundles from a long table.

I opened up the package and found a buttered bread roll with a fried egg inside. The Ogre shoved his into his mouth and made a few satisfied noises.

"The only job I've ever 'ad where they give you breakfast," he mumbled. "I reckon I'll work here till the day I die."

I nodded. Smiling wasn't easy with all the glue on my face, so Montgomery Fiztwitch wasn't going to be one for socializing.

After they'd grabbed their egg sandwiches, the workers all stood around and waited for the shift to change. On the other side of the room, a bunch of employees were opening crates and moving the contents into carts and trolleys. I couldn't see what any of the pieces were, but they clanged like heavy metal when they were dropped on top of each other. Then they were pushed through a set of doors to the north.

A horn blew loud and shrill and the change of shifts was underway. Half of the new workers went through a door on the western wall but I followed the group that went north into another huge room that was filled with lines of long, narrow tables.

I'd seen half the building now. I could glimpse a little more of it through the open doors to the east. I still couldn't tell what this place was all about, but one thing was clear: it was no power plant.

It was some kind of factory. Because it was so new, the change-over didn't happen smoothly. Everyone was doing their best to swap stations without injuring themselves or the people around them. The mass confusion helped me fit in, but it made it impossible to tell what work was being done.

The group from the last shift had dropped their tools and nobody had picked them up yet. The trolleys full of metal sat at one end of the line and empty wooden crates waited at the other. I walked beside one of the tables, pretending that I had a place to go. The half-finished pieces told a story. It was an assembly line. Cylinders of wood were being screwed into pieces of metal piping. I walked on and—

BANG.

The commotion came from behind another door, off to the side. Someone was screaming. I left the assembly room and followed the noise into a smaller area that shimmered like a rusty swimming pool. The whole place was full of copper sheeting. Huge squares of metal leaned against the walls, smaller panels were stacked in piles, and tiny strips covered the dozens of workstations that were spread out around the room.

A group had formed around a young Werewolf lying on the floor. He was screaming something awful, with his hands over his eyes.

A door opened behind the group. Heads turned and voices hushed. Even the screamer dropped his volume. Someone with authority had entered the room.

"Let's have a look at him," said a voice, full of boredom and false sympathy. It was a Human man in one of those charcoal suits that people in the Niles Company liked to wear. There wasn't too much else to say about him. He had that close-shaven, new-haircut look that professional people have, as if they asked the barber to trim their personality down to the bone. "You two, grab a stretcher from the corner and get him to the medical bay."

Two Lycum carried the kid past me, and the room went eerily quiet. The concerned crowd went to their stations so I found an empty desk and sat down.

There was a small strip of copper in front of me, along with a lead box and a series of tools. They seemed familiar, but I couldn't remember where I'd seen them before: tiny scissors, little gold hammer, strange measuring spoon.

Only a couple of folks had got to work. Most were still in shock about what had happened, perhaps wondering if they were going to be the next one to lose an eye.

The man in the suit spoke again.

"You want to say something?"

I couldn't see who he was talking to. Whoever it was, they were shorter than the workstations.

"I warned you," said the short person's voice. He moved around the outside of the room and I could only see the tips of his ears. The charcoal suit followed, always staying just a step behind. "This stuff ain't to be played with. You gotta be gentle every step of the way. One spark can lose you a finger or your life."

The voice came around the room until it passed through the aisle ahead of me.

It was Victor Stricken.

His metal leg was gone and the other one was lifeless. He was in a wheelchair now, being pushed around by the man in the charcoal suit, and he looked even more unhappy than before.

"Do not rush this work. Each casing must be identical. Otherwise, it will not fit into the firearm."

I looked down at the copper sheet and realized where I'd seen the tools before: in Victor's home out in Aaron Valley when he'd filled the caps with desert dust and loaded the machine.

The machine: a cylinder of wood with a metal pipe. That's what they were assembling in the other room.

I watched Victor's ears move down the aisle as he lectured everyone on the best way to make the ammunition without blowing their faces off. I'd felt guilty about not destroying the weapon. I thought it was the inventor's dying wish. But now, here he was, making more of them. Thousands more.

"What you're making will soon be the deadliest weapon in this world. But one that feels so safe, people will keep it in their belts or tucked under their pillows. It's your job to make sure that this power only escapes when the one who is wielding it wishes it to. Do not take this responsibility lightly."

Victor and the man behind him turned on the spot to look back at the room. The obedient workers picked up their tools. Soon, the air was filled with the sound of snipping and tapping as the copper was shaped into little caps.

I opened the lead box. Sure enough, it was full of red dust. I'd seen the damage a spoonful of this stuff could do. There was enough powder on my table to kill a dozen men. In this room, enough to wipe out a village. In this city? Who knew?

Victor was wheeled out of the room into a narrow hallway. A minute later, the man in the charcoal suit came back out and went off in the direction they'd taken the injured Werewolf. Once he was gone, I got up and went down the hall. A few eyes glanced at me but I didn't care. If you look like you know where you're going, people rarely speak up. Especially those who have just been reminded how disposable they are.

The hall had doors on both sides, leading into offices. I looked in each of them, all empty, until I came to the last doorway and heard Victor Stricken give the kind of sigh that you only do when you're alone: exhausted and broken and just a hair away from tears. I went into his room and closed the door.

"You're a long way from home, Vic."

His raised his head and I got my first good look of him. I hoped that my Werecat mask hid most of my expression.

Two of his teeth were missing and half his face was paralyzed. He still wore his wolf pelts but the wheelchair was a sad replacement for his mechanical leg. All his earrings were gone and the holes where they'd been were torn through. They'd been taken out by force. I put his story together without him needing to tell it.

He didn't recognize me. Maybe it was the disguise. Or maybe the torture had rattled his wits.

"You asked me to destroy the first pistol, Vic. Why the hell are you making more?"

That jogged his memory. He chuckled when he realized who I was, but I've heard more happiness in a funeral march.

"Hello, stranger. What are you all dressed up for?"

"Oh, you know what it's like. You start out trimming your beard, get carried away, next thing you know you're chasing mice and shitting in a sandbox. What the hell happened to you?"

Rather than answer, he looked down at his hands and I saw

for the first time that they were strapped to the arms of the wheelchair.

"What do you think happened? They dragged me out of the valley and tortured me till I told them how to make these things. Then the bastards gave me a choice. Either leave me there, legless, or come back to Sunder and work for them." He was drooling a bit. Still getting used to his missing teeth. "At the time, it didn't seem like much of a choice. I guess your ideals can only carry you so far when they don't have legs to help them." Then he shook his head. "I thought I was stronger than this."

"Shit, Vic. Nobody would blame you."

"You really believe that?"

I wanted to. I knew a little something about siding with the enemy.

Vic twisted around in his chair, pulling against his straps.

"Get me the fuck out of this thing."

I reached down and tried to untie the knots that were holding him in place.

"What's it all for?" I asked.

"All what?"

"The factory. The machines."

"For profit, of course. To begin with. But you don't start making weapons unless you're getting ready for war. Now, hurry the fuck up."

The fake nails on my left hand were making it impossible. Then Vic starting thrashing around, shaking his whole body so that he almost tipped over. I grabbed his chair and steadied him.

"Untie me, for fuck's sake!" He shouted. I hoped the workshop was loud enough to smother his voice or we'd soon have company.

"Vic, be careful."

I grabbed my knife from my belt and cut him loose. He ripped his arms free, stretched them out, and gave a shattered grin.

"Ooh, that's better."

He wheeled himself out of the room and all I could do was chase after him.

"Vic, how are they doing this?" He went back up the hall then spun himself into a doorway on our left. I went in after him. "Sunder hasn't had real power since the Coda. They must be smelting and forging to make these parts. Where are they getting the fuel?"

We were in someone's office. Vic went behind the desk and opened up all the drawers, searching for something.

"The same place they always have," he said. "Same as it was from the start."

"What do you mean?"

"Ahhhh."

He found what he was looking for and lifted it up to his chest. A machine. One of the new mass-produced ones made right under this roof. He held it to his chest and stroked it like it was a treasured family pet. All his fingernails were missing.

"Victor, let's get out of here."

He pulled off his goggles and looked at me with vacant eyes. Whatever piece of him was here, it was only an echo of the surly Goblin who'd shared his stew.

Footsteps came down the hall. They went past our room to the one where Victor was supposed to be waiting.

"Victor?" said the voice. Not worried. Just annoyed.

The Goblin gave another one of those gruesome smiles.

"Like my da always used to say," he spun the gear of the machine so it rattled like a carnival game, "today's as good a day as any to stop being a prick."

The footsteps came back. Stopped at our doorway.

There was nowhere to run.

"What the hell happened, Victor?" The voice of the charcoal suit stepped right up beside me. "You've blinded one of our workers. Maybe killed him." He hadn't noticed that Victor's hands were out of their restraints. He hadn't noticed what they were holding. He turned to me. "What are you doing here?" It was impossible to tell what he was thinking. His face and voice were inscrutably uniform. "Who the hell are you?"

I've never seen so such happen at once.

An explosion of sound rebounded off the walls of the tiny room. I went deaf. All I could hear was a piercing, ringing sound, like someone had tapped a tuning fork against my eardrums.

At the same time, a spray of blood and brain matter shot out of the head of the man standing next to me. It painted the ceiling and the walls and everywhere I looked. My body was in shock. I felt the urge to burst into tears.

Victor was holding up the machine. The telltale wisp of smoke floated up in front of his face. His lips were moving but I couldn't hear him. He mouthed the words again.

Go.

I do as he says.

I stumble out of the room, back into the hallway. The floor is slippery from the spray of blood. I turn. Eyes are on me. More men in suits at the end of the hall. They look at me, accusingly. I step forward. They're yelling. One comes right for me. Their faces open in fear. Another explosion from behind me. The suit drops to his knees with his hands on his chest. Everybody is running. I'm running. I trip over. Still deaf. Disoriented. Someone stands on my fingers. I get up. A hand grabs my shoulder. Someone else trying to flee? No. It's another suit. He punches me in the face. He's wearing rings and they cut me up. I punch him back. Harder. I break away and let myself get carried by the crowd. We go out the way we came in. Through the ammunition room and the assembly room and past the breakfast table into the outside world. Some workers stop here. Others scramble up the hill. I follow them.

I hate running. I'm not made for it. The old pain in my chest hates it even more.

By the time I got to the top of Mt Ramanak, I was dealing with a dozen different kinds of pain. I went down the first familiar street, found a tavern, went straight to the bathroom and cleaned my face of blood and whiskers and ginger eyebrows. I flushed the eyepatch and threw away the stupid stump of a tail. I ripped off the top half of the uniform. Nothing but a white shirt underneath, so I was going to freeze, but it was better than being spotted by anyone from the factory.

It wasn't perfect but, at a glance, I wasn't the same man who'd come running in. I left the tavern and went west – cold as hell and with blood still pouring from my forehead.

Machines.

A whole factory of pistols and powder-filled shells. I'd thought mine was special. Not anymore. The Niles Company were ready to make them as common as house keys.

We'd all been waiting for something new. Finally, it had arrived. The future was here and it was mind-blowing.

Just ask the guy in the charcoal suit.

58

It was warm inside the surgery. My shirt was off and the two Succubae were on either side, stitching up the cuts on my face. I'd come in heaving and bleeding, making a spectacle of myself and ranting about Victor Stricken's explosive outburst, but things had calmed down. I was sitting on the mattress and Hendricks was at a nearby table with maps and papers spread out in front of him.

I'd managed to wheeze out most of the story. Hendricks was pleased with what I'd brought back but disgusted by what the Niles Company was doing.

The surgeons sewed up my forehead where the guy had punched me, then I laid back and they stroked my hair and Hendricks congratulated me on a job well done.

It felt good. Better than stumbling up my stairs to crawl into bed alone and bloody most nights of the week.

The Dwarf came in with warmed whiskey mixed with honey and herbs and I sat up to sip it. Exina took the dirty surgical equipment away but Loq stayed with me on the low bed.

In the old days, I would have been wary about getting too close to a Succubae. But as we were in a post-Coda world, I let myself relax when she curled up on my chest. It felt better than medicine and almost managed to push out the memories of the suit's exploding head.

"This is fantastic progress," said Hendricks, "but it only gives us a piece of the puzzle. You're sure that they weren't making the actual pieces of the weapons there?"

"From what I gathered, they were just putting them together. The pieces were being delivered from somewhere else. Wooden handles and metal pipes. Copper sheets for the ammunition. Desert dust. All kinds of things."

"It's the metal I'm most interested in. To smelt that, they'll need more energy than they can get from the Sunder City grid."

"Maybe they're bringing them in from out of town. I saw plenty of trucks on the road."

"Perhaps at first, but they're talking about putting the lights back on Main Street. They must have some energy supply hidden in this city that we don't know about. They're buying up every business they can get their hands on: blacksmiths, mills, whole residential blocks. They've even bought the stadium. It's clear that they've got more planned for this city than just building weapons."

"The stadium?"

Hendricks examined one of his stolen maps.

"East of Main Street, just south of the archway. Isn't that what it is?"

"It is now." I excused myself from Loq's arms and went over to the desk. "But it used to be the first fire pit. Weren't you the one that told me that?"

He rubbed his forehead. "Oh, yes. You're right. I'd quite forgotten."

"I asked the Goblin where the factory was getting its power. He said it was the same as at the start."

Hendricks looked at the spot on the map where the stadium stood.

"You think he means the first pit?"

Weeks ago, when I'd been out there with Warren, the stadium was abandoned. When I went back to test the machine on the dummy, someone had been tearing up the earth.

"Some kind of construction is happening out there," I said.

"But the fires went out as soon as the Coda hit."

"I know, but . . ." I thought back to the Faerie in the church. They'd been cold and dead for six long years but when Tippity tore them apart, a final piece of magic was still alive inside them.

"There might still be something down there," I said.

"Like what?"

"Like with the Fae. The magic is gone but their bodies still hold a piece of their spirit."

"You think the fires might have also left something behind? A shadow of their power?"

"And the Niles Company is digging it out."

Hendricks laughed and jumped up, slapping me on the back. "This is good, boy. Very good. We have our next target. Well done, well done!"

That was the moment to stop the world. What else could I want? A job well done. A puzzle solved. A warm drink. A beautiful woman on the bed and a good friend at my side. Let time stop turning. Throw an anchor around the sun. Board up the windows so no more life gets in.

We did stop. We locked the doors and drank in celebration of a successful mission. Hendricks and Exina disappeared into another room; it appeared that I was right about those two having some history. Loq didn't seem to mind that he'd taken her partner away. I supposed a Succubae would be the last kind of creature to be squeamish about such things. She stayed with me on the mattress and did her best to make me forget about tortured Goblins and walls sprayed with blood.

I'm glad that we stopped. Just for a moment.

Before the horrors came tumbling in.

59

We slept through the middle of the day and made our plans for the night. An hour before sunset, Hendricks and I headed downtown. The ladies had patched me up pretty well and the Dwarf had even done my laundry. We had a good feed. A little wine. The air was cold but for the first time all winter, I liked the feel of it.

We were in the bad part of town but that didn't stop us from taking in the sights. Laughter tumbled out of bars and drunk lovers spilled onto the streets. We passed delicate piano music coming from an open window and kids on the corner throwing snowballs.

I'd been walking these streets for most of my adult life. Every single day since the Coda. But that night, they felt different. I felt different.

I'd been searching for something when I first went with Hendricks into the Opus. But I hadn't found it. So I went looking for it with the army, which proved to be a mistake. I even waited for it after I wrote *Man for Hire* on my window. I don't know what to call it but it doesn't come with a uniform and it doesn't come with a cause and it certainly doesn't come when you're out on your own just trying to keep your mind busy so you don't do yourself too much damage. Maybe it's a feeling that you can't have in real time. Only in retrospect. In memories.

"Why did you let me join the Opus?" I asked.

I was surprised that the question came out. Most thoughts never made the brave journey from my brain to my tongue. I suppose my guard was down. For the first time in a long time, I wasn't watching everything I said.

Hendricks didn't seem so surprised by the question.

"What do you mean?"

"Well, no Human had ever been in the Opus before. So, why me?"

"Why do you think?"

Goddam Hendricks. Loved nothing more than turning a question back on itself.

"I don't know."

"Come on! What do you think it was? Your unmatched strength? That dazzling intellect? Your famous wit?"

I already regretted saying anything.

"Well, someone told me that it was about creating an alliance. Showing the Humans that we could work together . . . or something."

"Interesting." He nodded thoughtfully, like the idea had only just occurred to him. "Eventually, I suppose I saw the value in that. But that's not why it happened. Not really. Do you want to know why I really enlisted you in the Opus?"

He stopped. I stopped too.

"Yes," I said.

He stared into me with those centuries-old, pale green eyes.

"Because you asked. And, because you were my friend, I accepted your request. That's it." He must have seen that I'd been hoping for something more. "Everything that has happened to you has been your doing. You chose to leave Weatherly. You chose to join the Opus. You chose to leave us and sign up with the army. These are the facts. If you're looking for some greater meaning behind anything that happened, there's only one place to look."

He started walking again. His cane happily clicking against the road.

"I've still never met another one," he said.

"Another what?"

"Weatherite. Or Weatherian? See, you're so rare out here that we don't even have a name for you."

"You think there might be others who got out of Weatherly."

"There must be. I've just never met one. I always wanted to. Especially after meeting you."

I didn't know whether to be flattered or brace myself for the incoming insult.

"Why?"

"Because you're a strange one, Master Fetch, but I don't know how much of that strangeness is you and how much of it is because of where you grew up. I have nobody to compare you to. I am supposed to be the world's greatest diplomat. I know all the Dwarven handshakes and what words to avoid in front of each species of Lycum, but with you, there was never any way of knowing what might set you off."

I didn't like thinking of myself as being from Weatherly. When I was there, I already felt like an outsider. But I can't deny the fact that it had an influence on me.

"What makes me so strange?"

Another one of his secret smiles that would never be fully explained.

"The way that so many things seem to shock you. I thought it would wear off in time. Don't you remember how Amari used to play with you? It was so easy for her to stir you up." It was the first time he had mentioned her name, and the sound of it stopped the conversation dead.

I felt like Hendricks was waiting for a response, but I couldn't really remember what we'd been talking about. We fell into a silence that carried us all the way to the southern end of the city.

The stadium came into sight sooner than I'd expected. It was buzzing with the same electric lights as last time but now there were many, many more. The whole place had transformed into a bustling building site. Canvas tents, crates of equipment and uniformed workers filled the space.

We slid into a dark alley to watch the site, unseen. I chewed a Clayfield and Hendricks smoked his pipe.

"You're right, boy. This is some operation."

"Even bigger than the last time I was here. What do you think they're up to?"

"I don't know yet. Maybe Montgomery Fiztwitch can find out."

"I . . . I really didn't want to try that trick again."

Luckily, Hendricks laughed.

"No, no. This is far busier than the factory. More protected. You might get in but I doubt you'll be able to get out. We need more information. Let's follow one of the workers away from the sight, ambush and interrogate them."

I couldn't help grinning at the idea. It was ridiculous. But I'd been doing a lot of ridiculous things recently and this time I'd have my mentor at my side.

"We must wait for the right candidate," said Hendricks. "We need someone slow. Someone alone."

It wasn't like the factory, where huge groups of workers changed shifts at once. Here, people were always coming and going. Eventually, a Gnome with a limp exited the gates and peeled away from the pack, moving to the north-west.

"Here we go," said Hendricks, putting a hand on my shoulder. "Let's keep our distance as long as we can. Don't be afraid to leave me behind if he should pick up the pace. I'm not as sprightly as I once was."

"Then what? We follow him home?"

"Hopefully not. He might have a family or be living in some crowded apartment. We jump him in an alley and pretend it's a mugging. Try to let the information come out as if by accident. We don't want his employers knowing what we're up to."

It was madness. I was about to stalk a defenseless Gnome on his way back from work, but it was worth it because I was doing it with Hendricks: a man who could make a cup of tea feel like an adventure. I had to stop myself giggling with excitement as we prowled through the streets, watching our mark, ready to put on a show.

There were many reasons why Hendricks picked our target. For one, he had short legs and a limp so Eliah's old bones could keep up. He also walked alone, so we wouldn't have to wait for him to part ways with any colleagues. It was also because he was heading west.

There were *some* nice areas on the western half of the city but they were all in the neighborhoods closest to Main Street. Our friend was walking right out towards the city limits. If the Gnome lived out in that part of town, we would have plenty of time to ambush him on the empty streets along the way.

It couldn't have been any easier. The Gnome even had a cold, so after Hendricks' leg cramped and we had to slow down, a sneezing fit from our target put us back on his trail.

Fifteen minutes into our journey, the Gnome took a shortcut through a narrow alley between two warehouses and we were given the perfect chance to make our move.

"Quick," said Hendricks. "Run around the building and block him in on the other side. I'll keep following."

I did as I was told but, hoping to shave a bit of time off my trip, I cut through the warehouse instead. The space seemed abandoned but it hadn't been cleaned out. Only a small amount of light came through the holes in the roof so, a few steps in, I banged my shins against a piece of forgotten machinery. It hurt like hell but I found it kind of funny. It was all so stupid. I smashed into a trash pile and tripped over a bit of old pipe that went skittering into a stack of tin cans. I couldn't have made more noise if I'd tried to.

The Gnome was so slow that when I came out the other side, I still had time to button my coat, pull up the collar so that it covered my mouth, and yank my hat down over my eyes. I took out my knife and got myself into character. Then, I turned the corner.

The Gnome stopped. He was already on edge because he'd heard me clanging around inside the warehouse. Hendricks had been walking without the cane to keep himself quiet but he used it to catch up to us. The Gnome looked between us, eyes wide with fear.

"Please," he said, "I have nothing."

He was shaking. That kind of sucked the fun out of it. Luckily, Hendricks took the lead.

"That's not what I hear. Word around town is that the Niles Company pays real good."

He was putting on a stupid, gruff voice. It was a good thing that my collar covered my smile.

"No!" protested the Gnome. "Not to me. I'm just a digger."

"A digger?" Hendricks gave me a wink, like we'd discovered something important. "Don't lie to me, little man; why are you digging up the stadium?"

His bottom lip trembled but he couldn't find his voice.

"Answer him," I threatened. "Or we'll . . . we'll . . . hang you upside and . . . shake you till the money comes out."

The Gnome was looking at me so he didn't see Hendricks laugh. I wasn't quite selling the dialogue.

"I just . . ." blubbered our poor victim, ". . . just do what they tell me. I only started today. I haven't even been paid yet."

"I don't believe you," said Hendricks, getting his character back under control and closing in. "Where's the money?"

"I don't have any money!" he screamed.

I looked up at Hendricks, hoping for a hint as to what our next play would be. While my gaze was high, the Gnome kicked me in the shin, right in the spot that I'd already bruised while running through the warehouse.

"Dammit!"

He kicked the cane out from under Hendricks who fell onto his side. I made a grab for the Gnome but he slipped through my arms. I mean, he *really* slipped. He was wet or slimy or something. I stumbled past him and tripped over Hendricks who was still wheezing on the floor.

Our victim disappeared around the corner.

"Eliah, are you okay?"

"Just a little bruised, my boy."

I held out a hand to help him up and Hendricks broke into hysterical laughter. So did I. It was ridiculous. Tears ran down my cheeks as Hendricks finally grabbed my hand for support.

"Ugh. What is that?" He wiped his fingers on his coat. "Did you slip in something?"

"It was the little guy. He was . . . slick."

Hendricks looked at the inside of my sleeves where the Gnome had slipped through my grasp. I'd been tainted by something translucent, thick and sticky. Hendricks wiped off some of it and held it up to his face.

"Is it some kind of gel?" I asked.

"Sort of." He smelled it, then he thought for a while. "Hold out your lighter."

Hendricks wiped his hand across my arms and chest, collecting as much slime as he could find. I held out my lighter, flicked it on, and Hendricks put his hand a few inches above the flame.

"Hold it steady," he said.

Hendricks dropped his hand right into the fire and held it there.

"It's fireproof," I said.

Hendricks whistled in celebration.

"Of course it is. It's Dragon saliva." Hendricks moved his finger around in the flame. "But where in the world would the Niles Company get that?"

60

It felt like someone was playing a joke on me. We were back at the spot where the toothless Dwarf had told me about Dragons, looking for exactly the thing that I'd told him wasn't there. This time, I was the believer and Hendricks was the cynic.

"Fetch, when was the last time you saw a Dragon?"

"The night of the Coda."

"Exactly. Niles must have found an existing stockpile of saliva from the pre-Coda days."

"I know. But it's worth taking a look, right?"

We did look. We walked around the storage units and the silos for an hour. Sometimes we tapped the sides of them or pried open rusted doors to peer in at the always-uninteresting empty spaces. The sun went down and the night grew cold and our flasks went empty. I apologized to Hendricks that I'd wasted his time.

"No, no. It's an idea and it might still bear some fruit."

I felt like he was humoring me but I pushed on.

We split up and walked around for another half an hour until I heard Hendricks calling out my name. When I found him, he was holding a dull glassy object shaped like a large toenail.

"Dragon scale," said Hendricks.

"You're sure?"

"No. They used to be colorful, even when they weren't on the creature's body. Reflective and vibrant. Strong enough to make into armor. This is," he snapped off a corner, "brittle, like dry bone. But the shape is right, so maybe . . ."

We looked around. It was too quiet. Too dark. It was the last place you'd expect to find some legendary beast.

"The Dwarf said he heard a Dragon," said Hendricks. "Well,

let's go back to that exact spot and wait a little longer. Maybe we'll hear the same thing he did."

On our way, Hendricks pointed to a metal drum discarded on the path.

"Bring that with us."

I placed the drum at our starting point and Hendricks handed me a bronze bill.

"Get some more of that whiskey and something to eat. Maybe soup. Soup would be good. I'll get a fire started while you're gone."

I took the cash and left him to scrounge for firewood. When I returned, I had a large bottle of booze and two tins of chicken soup. Hendricks was sitting next to the bucket, smoking his pipe and staring into the flames.

I sat down, handed him his dinner, and cracked open the whiskey. It was strong and peaty and even the fumes warmed me up. I took a swig and Hendricks did the same.

The fire crackled.

"Where did you find all this wood?" I asked.

"Broken off from old crates or pulled from piles of garbage. I wouldn't breathe too deeply, boy. Some of it looked a little toxic." The soup was hot and we sipped it carefully from the tins. The fire was bright. There were no other lights around, just stars and a sliver of moon. We could have been anywhere. Back out on the wild road to Gaila or camping up in the Groves. I could imagine our horses tied beside us or a whole team of Shepherds waiting over the next hill. It was nice to imagine those things, instead of the reality. Instead of High Chancellor Eliah Hendricks, leader of the Opus, crouched around a pile of burning garbage in the dirtiest city in the world.

He washed his soup down with whiskey and examined the bottle.

"You're probably thinking I should slow down on this, after what happened?"

After *what* happened? Was he talking about that night? The last time I'd seen him before the Coda?

"What do you mean?"

"Look at me, Fetch. I did *everything*. For hundreds of years I ate, I drank, I fucked and I danced my way through this world. I put my body through hell because I knew it could take it. But now, without the magic to hold back the smoke and the poison, my history is coming back to haunt me. Now that the magic is gone, I'm being dragged away before my time."

"Maybe not. There are other doctors. There might still be a way to turn things back."

"I thought you didn't believe in such things, Mr Man for Hire." I couldn't pin down his tone. "All I'm saying is, this can't be helping, but I'll be damned if I'm going to slow down now. If this is the end, I'm going to dance my way towards it, just as I always have. With whiskey and wine and tobacco and honey and song."

He tilted his head back and bellowed out a few notes to warm himself up. His voice was rougher than it used to be, but still sweet, and he belted out the beginning of a Dwarven drinking song that we used to sing on the road.

We'd first heard it in a country tavern and it had become our favorite tune for many months. Whenever the days felt too long or the ride too tough, one of us would strike it up. We started out with the traditional lyrics but were soon inventing our own verses.

"Oh, Vera is a woman with a head of hair.
That is more impressive, way down there.
Look up her skirt and you'll get a scare.
What a lovely lady is Vera."

Nothing summed up Hendricks quite like the fact that he could speak a dozen languages, play untold instruments, sing like a Siren, and *this* was his favorite song.

I had a hit of whiskey to knock back my ever-present embarrassment and took the next round.

"Oh, Penny is woman with skin so green,
Like making love to a lima bean,
Not just a date, she's a fine cuisine!
What a lovely lady is Penny."

Hendricks cackled and pitched up his voice to an even louder volume.

"Oh, Fetch is a boy who loves to brood,
Takes ten strong men just to lift his mood,
He might cheer up if he ever got screeeeeeeeeeewed!"

His high voice vibrated in the air and I joined him in the final line.

"Ohhhh, what a lovely boy is Fetch!"

Our laughter echoed off the brick walls of the warehouses. Pigeons scattered from the roofs. Hendricks had his eyes turned up to the night sky and the firelight reshaped his face back to the one I remembered. Flawless, full of mischief, free from fear or worry. I couldn't believe that I was here with him. Not just because he'd practically come back from the dead, but because I still couldn't understand why, out of all the people in the world, he'd want to waste time with me.

I'd always felt that way. Even before all the bad things happened. I especially felt it now. I couldn't say that to him. Of course not. So I just said, "I missed this."

He turned his eyes from the stars.

"Me too, boy."

We sipped our soup. A million unfinished thoughts filled my

head. All the things I'd never shared over six long years because I didn't think I had anyone around me who would bother to listen.

"It's just . . ." I wished, not for the first time, that I had Hendricks' talent with words.

"It's nice to be with someone who actually knows me."

Hendricks looked over the fire and I couldn't work out what he was thinking.

"Let me tell you something."

He put down his tin of soup and wiped his hands on his trousers. Then, he leaned over and tapped a finger on my temple.

"This mess, in here, is all you." He tapped his own head. "And this whirlwind of madness is all me. We have our long talks and our secrets, years of adventure by each other's side, but try as we might," he put his whole hand across my face and squeezed it like he was trying to crack my skull, "we can never break through. I will never get inside your head and you will never really know what is happening in mine. That is our curse, boy. Each and every one of us." He took his hand away and his eyes glowed bright green. "We are all alone."

Then the Dragon roared.

61

We both jumped up.

"You heard that?" I asked.

"I'm old, not deaf, boy. This way."

We left the fire and went in the direction of the sound. Buildings rattled in the breeze but otherwise the night was silent again. Nothing seemed out of the ordinary. They were the same broken-down storage houses we'd been searching all day. Hendricks tapped a stone against the metal wall of a silo and sang as loudly as he could manage.

"Oh, Kelly is a boy with feet so big . . ."

The echo of his voice reverberated around us.

"He quakes the earth when he does a jig—"

"GROARRR."

The sound had come from a little shack attached to the side of one of the old factories. It was a foreman's office with no windows and one great padlock on the door.

"You know how to open one of these locks?" asked Hendricks.

"Sure. But why bother?"

The wooden shack was old, so I kicked the wall beside the door and a whole plank came loose. I punched out another plank and looked inside.

"There are stairs going underground." I kicked out a few more planks till the hole was big enough to climb through. "Come on. Careful of the nails."

We both flicked our lighters on. Dust covered everything inside the office but the floor was full of footprints that went through a hatch and down a set of steep metal stairs.

I led the way down into a narrow tunnel that appeared to have been built recently: the dirt under our feet was powdery and unpacked and our feet kicked up clouds that sent Hendricks into a fit of coughing. The dust only cleared when we stepped out of the tunnel into a huge room.

Pre-Coda, magical machinery covered the stone floor: the kind of equipment that would have been used to flatten the swamp into the city's foundations and carve out the canal. It was all Dwarven technology that had become outdated over the decades or just wasn't needed once the job was done. There was probably a larger entrance somewhere else: this one must have been added so that someone could enter and exit without being seen.

"Fetch, listen."

All I could hear was dripping water. Then . . . breathing. A rasping, deep rumble that came from the shadows at the other end of the room.

I gave Hendricks a look that asked him if he thought this was such a neat idea. He shrugged, which made both of us laugh, and we walked on.

The room kept going. Our lighters barely illuminated our path and the closer we got to the breathing, the stranger it sounded. A grating, scraping wheeze.

When the darkness squealed with fear, I jumped back. Hendricks stood strong with a look in his eye that I'd only seen a few times before.

Most of the time, Hendricks made his way through the world with an unflinching air of grace and relaxation as if he were hosting a glamorous party wherever he went. The more dire the situation, the more easy-going he became. His warm demeanor could turn the tide of tense diplomatic talks, send swords back to their sheaths and part crowds who were ready to riot. Other leaders would bluster where Hendricks would laugh and sing and play the fool.

But every now and again, the world would cut too deep.

Hendricks knew what we were going to find before the light hit the Dragon's eyes.

It was a traditional Dragon: one created from the body of a flying lizard up in the Ragged Plains. The Dragon's head was the size of the Sunder City streetcar but it looked small because of what had been done to it.

There were two rough stumps where its wings had been hacked off. Whoever had done it, their work was a far cry from the careful hands of the Succubae. The cuts were uneven, and sharp bone stuck out from the creature's back. Even with its wings, the Dragon wouldn't have been going anywhere. Chains were wrapped around its whole body, pinning it to the floor.

The scales were the same as the one we'd found outside: colorless, dull and flaking. Many were missing and the flesh underneath was scabbed over and rotten.

The Dragon's mouth was open. Once upon a time, that would have been a signal for us to run away or else be turned into soot. It wasn't open in anger, though. It wasn't even open by choice. There was a contraption jammed between the Dragon's blunted teeth, full of springs, wrenching the jaw apart like a reverse beartrap. There were tubes in its mouth, running inside the gums and then out over its lips into a metal vat.

"What are they doing to it?" I asked.

"Milking her saliva in the cruelest way possible."

Her claws had been removed and her arms were strapped down. I couldn't see her tail. Perhaps the surgeon had taken that too.

It reminded me of a boy back in Weatherly who'd caught a lizard in his garden and wanted to keep it as a pet. Of course, the lizard had other ideas. So, when the boy brought it out of its box, he always held it too tight. Then somebody told him that if you pulled off the tail it would grow a new one.

The tail didn't come off easy so the boy got a knife. The whole thing made me feel sick, but I didn't want to miss out on seeing the tail grow back so I stayed around to watch.

The tail didn't grow back. It turned out to be a different kind of lizard. It did stop trying to escape, though.

Hendricks stepped up to the Dragon and put his hand on the side of her face. She didn't try to pull away. Dragons are smart. She knew that Hendricks wasn't the one who'd put her there.

Eliah put his forehead against the creature, rubbed her scales and closed his eyes. The Dragon's eyes closed too.

Hendricks wept. Not loud, but his chest heaved and his cheeks glistened as his hands reached out and found one of the screws that held the metal mouthpiece in place. He turned it, pulled it out, and then he searched for another. I went to the other side and did the same.

The screws came out bloody but the wounds were so old that it didn't seem to hurt the beast in any significant way. Her pain threshold had been tested far beyond anything I could fathom. She carefully closed her jaws and groaned. Hendricks kept a hand on the side of her head.

"What do we do now?" I asked. "Take off the chains and walk her down Main Street?"

Hendricks wiped his cheeks with his sleeve.

"I don't know how they're keeping her alive or what they're feeding her, but it isn't natural. There is nothing else left for us to do."

Hendricks took out his knife. So did I. Hendricks went to his side and I went to mine. The flesh underneath the Dragon's neck was already soft and wet. The knife went in easily and the Dragon didn't fight us. We slid our blades down, across her throat, until our knuckles touched. Then, together, we both pushed up. The Dragon's final breath rolled over our fists, hot and full of relief.

We pulled out our knives and stood beside the body of a miraculous beast that had been reduced to nothing but a shameful slab of rotten meat.

I dared to look at Hendricks. I could almost see the blood coursing through his body, full of hate and anger. His hand was shaking.

Then, the faintest of sounds from the east. The clanging of metal against metal.

Hendricks cleaned his knife on his clothes, put it away, turned in the direction of the noise and started walking.

62

I could smell sulfur. Old smoke. Maybe I was right. Maybe there was something down here that the Niles Company had stumbled upon. Some element in the rock, or a sediment left over from the old days that they were using for power.

We were in another tunnel, sloping downward. Hendricks was full of energy, charging ahead on his cane.

"What are these pipes?" I asked.

Running along the roof above us were six nickel tubes, each the diameter of a dinner plate."

"They used to bring the fire up to the surface. The bursts that Fintack Ro saw in the swamps were just small pockets of gas compared to the larger pits underneath. To harness the full power, the founders had to dig down, deep into the earth, and install these pipes."

At the end of the tunnel we came to a metal cage that was the size off my office. There were chains on all four corners that went up to the roof and down through the floor. The clanging sound was coming from beneath us.

"What the hell did they keep in there?"

Hendricks went right up to the cage and pulled open a door that was cut into the front.

"It's an elevator," he said. "Old Gnomish technology."

Hendricks went inside. I stepped up to the edge and looked down. The floor was made from the same wire mesh as the walls so I could see down into the deep chasm below.

"No way," I said.

Hendricks slammed his cane against the floor and the whole thing rattled like it was going to break apart.

"Gnomes don't mess around, boy. They've been making these things for hundreds of years. It's safer to walk on than Main Street."

Nobody else could have made me do it. Amari, maybe, but that's it. I put a foot out on the swaying cage and stepped inside without letting go of the walls. Hendricks cackled.

"If only your clients could see you now. It would probably put you out of business."

I was already regretting eating such a big dinner. There was a barrel in the corner of the box and I grabbed it for support. Hendricks pulled the door closed.

"Ready, boy?"

"Absolutely not."

"Good. Here we go."

He flicked a lever above the door that released a catch on a large cog. There were gears all around the roof that started to turn, feeding the chains through their teeth. We were descending at a steady pace down into the depths.

"How long will this take?"

"No idea. Just sit back and enjoy the ride."

That was an impossible suggestion. I gripped the barrel tight, for no logical reason other than giving me the false illusion that I still had some control. Hendricks rested on the ground with his cane across his lap.

The cage moved slowly, which I didn't mind, but my heart was going a million beats a minute and all my bodily functions prepared to throw me a surprise party. I needed a distraction.

"What are we going to do when we get down there?" I asked.

"Depends."

"On what?"

"On what they're doing."

His eyes were closed. The cage jangled down for another minute.

"We should talk to Baxter," I said. "They might be able to help."

"Perhaps."

More minutes dropped by as we went further into the dark. The cogs screeched and the chains clanked along, sometimes catching on the teeth. Whenever that happened, it momentarily tipped us slightly sideways, then shook us back to normal. I wanted to scream. Hendricks just smiled to himself, eyes shut, like an experienced sailor cruising through a storm.

The longer he stayed silent and the further down we went, the busier my mind became: filling up with self-conscious madness and all those questions I'd wanted to ask every day of every year that we'd spent apart. They rolled through my mind, one after the other, like the faces of passengers in a train window. Eventually, my shaking nerves and the clank of the chains became too much and I let some part of the madness tumble out of my mind onto my tongue.

"Did you see Amari?"

Why did it suddenly seem so quiet?

"Only once more after you left," he said finally. "I was having some trouble in the Farra Glades, her home, and called on her assistance. It's a shame you weren't there with us. You would have loved it. She would have loved to have you there. It was one of her rare trips away. After the funding for her hospital came through, she mostly stayed in Sunder."

"You never saw her back here?"

"No. Isn't it funny, though? You spent so many years pining for her, moaning into your whiskey whenever she was away. Then, just when she was about to move to Sunder for good, you took off on a horse and left her behind. But I think she understood why you left."

Did she? I wasn't sure *I* fully understood why I left.

"In what way?"

"I told her what happened when you were young. With the Chimera, I mean. She agreed that it was a misguided and foolish impulse but she empathized with it nonetheless." His eyes were still closed and the only thing that moved was his scarred mouth, pulled up in an impish grin. "You Humans have such little time to grow up, so you rush it. Too much to prove. Too determined to become something important. It's why we never got around to bringing your kind into the Opus. You just couldn't see the world the same way as the rest of us."

"Well, we're all in the same boat now, aren't we?"

It came out bitter, because it was. I didn't like anybody telling me that I was just like the rest of my kind. Even Hendricks.

He opened his eyes. The smile didn't fade; it just became more condescending.

"Where is she?" he asked.

I stalled. He saw it.

"Amari," he specified needlessly.

"Lark's mansion. In the main hall. I own the building."

I said it like I was proud. That was a mistake. He had to stop himself from laughing.

"Oh, Fetch, you haven't changed." He tilted his head to the side. "I'd like to see her."

He said it like he was asking permission. Like I should respond. But I couldn't. Nobody had been in there. Not *anyone*.

But Hendricks had known her longer than I had. He'd introduced us, after all. There was a good chance that, to her, their relationship was far more important than ours.

So why didn't I want to take him there? Did I still just want her all to myself? Yes. I didn't like it but I couldn't pretend it wasn't true. It was more than that, though. After seeing how he'd scoffed at the fact that I'd bought the mansion, I was afraid of what he would say when he saw what I'd done.

Crack!

The chain snagged on the cog and shook the cage even harder than before. The barrel almost tipped over and I had to wrap my arms around it to keep it upright.

"Shit!"

The look on my face sent Hendricks into hysterics. The barrel rocked back and forth and something wet spilled out from under the lid. When things were stable again, I looked inside.

It was three-quarters full of the thick, syrupy Dragon spit.

"Is it just me," asked Hendricks, "or are things getting rather toasty?"

Finally, the elevator came to a stop and Hendricks stood up. He was right, it had gotten hot. And bright. I pulled open the gate, put my feet on solid ground and took a few deep breaths to settle my stomach.

"Come on, boy. There's light up ahead."

The clanging was louder now. Closer. We walked forward. The nickel pipes had followed us down and were still running along the roof.

"What are these bumps about?" I asked. Every now and again, the metal bulged out like something was stuck inside.

"Fans. They propelled the fire up at a constant rate, pushing it straight into the forges and factories that first shaped this city. They got things moving but they weren't always reliable. That's why Sunder switched to Wizardry a few decades later."

"Victor Stricken told me about that. Said they used portals to send the fire up to the surface."

"Yes. Far more efficient. By the time the Coda happened, all these pipes had been shut off and the fire was transferred entirely by magic."

I reached up and touched one. It was scolding hot. I whipped my fingers back before they burned, but the tips were already tingling.

"Eliah."

But he was stepping out of the tunnel into a dome-shaped room with exits in all directions. Pipes everywhere. All of them emanating with heat.

"What is this place?" I asked.

"Some maintenance area from back in the early days, I imagine.

Look, here . . ." Hendricks pulled a piece of canvas off a pile of metal barrels. Each container was filled with some kind of propeller. "This is one of the fans from the first system. I suppose they kept replacement parts along the path so they could be swapped out when needed. See what I mean about magic making it easier? A skilled Wizard would be able to make all kinds of changes to the energy flow without setting a single foot underground."

He kept going, but I couldn't help feeling like something about the fans didn't match up with the story.

"Eliah, these look brand new."

He couldn't hear me over the clanging. It was almost deafening now, coming from the exit that was responsible for all the flickering light. I caught up with Hendricks as he stepped into a huge room with a high ceiling and metal paths cut into the stone floor. There was another elevator on the far wall with its door hanging open.

I walked onto one of the metal paths and felt a hot breeze under my chin. There were holes in the floor. The paths were constructed from a metal mesh, like honeycomb. I looked down between my feet to a long drop that went into— *Impossible.*

I fell to my knees.

Impossible.

"Eliah." I was shaking. "Eliah, look!"

He walked over, stood beside me, and gasped.

I laughed like a madman. Cried at the same time, unable to comprehend the beauty of what I was witnessing. An unbelievable, heavenly miracle.

Impossible.

The raging flames of the Sunder City fire pits were burning beneath our feet.

63

I was down on all fours feeling the hot metal under my fingers and the rising wind on my face. Beneath us, a burning, bottomless pit of endless flames stretched out in all directions. On the rocky walls of the chasm, molten lava spewed out of chutes and set alight streams of natural gas that went up like flocks of orange birds taking flight.

Every gust of hot air that went past my face was like a wish being granted; flying off to save the life of someone up above.

All those cold homes and empty kitchens were going to be full again.

It was over.

"They did it," I said.

"Did what?"

"They brought the fires back."

Hendricks scoffed. "Unlikely, boy. It seems to me that the fires never went out."

The idea pushed its way into my thick skull like a blunt knife through a cold block of cheese.

"The Coda killed the fires."

"Apparently not. It just killed the sorcery that brought them to the surface."

Of course. The mechanical fans had been replaced long ago by magical technology. By the time the Coda happened, the lamps, factories, and the whole damn city was plugged into portals, not pipes. When the river froze and the Wizards lost their power, the channels closed up and the flames were trapped below.

"But . . . but somebody must have known."

"Who would think to come and look? We lost everything in

an instant. Friends. Families. The Fae. With all of that gone for good, why would we expect the fires to be any different?"

He was right. Nobody questioned it because it made too much sense. Ancient Elves died on the streets. Dragons crashed from the sky. Most folks were learning to live in a world where their own bodies didn't work properly, so what would compel anyone to go check if the fires beneath the city might be the exception? They'd been here the whole time, roaring beneath the streets until somebody bothered to look.

Something had caught Hendricks' eye. He walked away while I kept blabbering.

"The Niles Company must have found out somehow. That's why they're here. That's how they're building again. They're already using it."

"Yes. They've been covering their workers in Dragon spit so that they can go down, close to the flames. They've been using this power without telling anyone else it exists." Hendricks' hand was hovering over one of the pipes. He wrapped his sleeve around his palm and put it against the metal. A split-second later, he pulled it back. "Hot."

It was all going to happen just like Thurston said it would. The lights and jobs. Heating in every home. Sunder City was alive again.

I wanted to scream. To throw my hat in the air like a fool on the stage. I had a grin that threatened to rip my cheeks to pieces.

But why did Hendricks look so angry?

"Eliah, this is good news."

He tapped his knuckles against the pipe.

"For who? The Niles Company has convinced everyone that this energy belongs to them. You've seen how they operate. You know what their intentions are. Would you hand them all of this power just so you can fill your fireplace again?"

"No. Of course not. So, we do it just like you said. We expose them. We go to Baxter, get a camera down here and put photos in the papers. People will—"

"People won't care. Not if their houses are warm and the trains are running. Not if they can buy automobiles and flashy new firearms. Nobody will give that up willingly. Not here." He bent down and put his hands around a pickax and tried to lift it. "We have to stop them. Destroy them. Now." He was straining to get it off the ground. "Help me, boy."

I took the pickax from his hands.

"What are we doing?"

"We're beginning our work. We know how they are getting their power. We know what they are using it for. Now, it's time to stop them."

"But . . ."

"Destroy the pipe."

"Hendricks . . ."

"They can't have many of these operational yet. Putting a hole in this will slow things down considerably."

"But they're turning the lights back on."

"They're making weapons. Everything else is just a side-effect. A way to pay you off. These fires don't belong to them. This city doesn't belong to them but they will own it if we don't do something. This is the Human Army with a new face. This is Mortales. These are the people that ruined everything. They waged war against all that was good in the world and now you will let them claim their prize? When Niles has been buried, the fires will still be here. You can have your future, boy, but only then."

I raised the pickax.

"I . . . I don't think—"

"Do it, Fetch. Because I cannot."

"I . . ."

"Come on! Why do you think I'm here? Why do you think *you're* here?"

"Maybe we . . ."

My mind is always too slow. Sluggish. It jams like a cheap

motor under the slightest amount of pressure. I stood, frozen, searching for a way to reason with him, or a way to convince myself that he was right, but my head was full of aches and white noise.

"Fetch, whose side do you want to be on this time? Theirs or mine?"

The pickax arced through the air. It was a strain to lift but once I'd got it over my head, the weight took over and brought it down hard on the top of the pipe. As soon as the sharp point pierced the nickel, Hendricks and I were blown backwards as a stream of roaring fire erupted from the point of impact.

The pressure peeled back the metal, widening the hole, and fire shot all the way up to the roof where it spread out like liquid and pushed smoke and ash around us. Hendricks was back on his feet before I was.

"We best be going now, boy."

I scrambled up and went back the way we came, but there were voices ahead of us: shouting at each other, alerted by the noise.

"This way!" called Hendricks, on his way to the elevator. I followed behind, breathing air that was hot and full of smoke.

We stepped into the hanging cage. It was just like the last one and made me feel just as sick.

"Close the door and pull the chain," ordered Hendricks, and I obeyed. I was back to taking orders. Easier that way. No need to think or weigh up my options, just nod and oblige. I dragged the door shut and grabbed a length of chain. When I yanked on it, the whole cage dropped.

"Shit. Wrong way."

Gravity had taken control, and the cage rumbled down. I pulled back on the chain so hard that it took the skin off the palms of my hands. Hendricks jammed his cane into the mechanism and finally brought it to a stop.

"You all right?" he asked.

"Yeah."

"Good. Up, please."

I switched to a second chain and gave it a heave. We climbed back up again. The room that we had just left returned at eye level but now there was someone waiting for us.

It was a Human man in charcoal trousers. Another of Niles's interchangeable cronies. White shirt. No jacket or tie. In his hands, he held one of the mass-produced machines.

"Stop!" he said. I yanked the chain again. We rose past him as he lifted his arm.

Pop.

I saw a flash of fire and a cloud of smoke, then the wall glided up in front of him and we continued upwards. I wrenched the chain as hard as I could to take us up to the surface.

"Looks like the new pistols have already been issued to Thurston's men," I said to Hendricks. He didn't respond. When I looked over, he was lying on the floor of the cage.

"No!" I let go of the chain. We stopped but didn't descend. I rolled Hendricks over and he was moaning. That was something. He was the first person I'd known who hadn't turned to dead meat as soon as the machine had hit them.

"Dammit, Eliah; are you all right?"

"Positively not."

There was a hole in the shoulder of his jacket. I pulled it open and blood was already soaking his shirt.

These fucking bullets. At least with bolts and arrows, they plug the wound until you pull them out.

"Does it look as bad as it feels?" he asked.

"How bad does it feel?"

"Fucking awful."

"Then yeah, it looks as bad as it feels."

I took off my coat, removed my shirt, and wrapped it around his shoulder. The blood seeped through it immediately. I put a Clayfield in his mouth.

"Bite down on that."

He did as he was told. I'd run out of ideas so I took his hand and squeezed it. He squeezed it back. Then I let go of my friend, grabbed the chain, and pulled on it with everything I had until we came up into the light.

64

I pushed open the elevator door and looked around at a completely unfamiliar room. It was a storage house. There were crates everywhere: metal boxes piled on top of each other, right up to the roof. The walls were concrete. The floor too.

I helped Hendricks out of the cage and laid him down on the floor. The wound was still bleeding heavily. He'd need medical attention soon. His body had been through too much. He was already shivering and his skin was sweaty and pale.

I tried to work out what part of town we were in, but the trip underground had thrown off my sense of direction.

"Do something to that elevator first," said Hendricks. "We don't want them using it to come up after us."

I gave him two more Clayfields and then used a nearby crowbar to jam the cage door open so that it wouldn't be able to descend.

"Maybe there's something here to plug you up."

I went over to one of the big metal crates. Even the lid took two hands to lift. Once I looked inside, I understood why.

"Shit."

"What is it?" groaned Hendricks.

"This is full of desert dust." What I'd seen in the factory was nothing. There was enough in this crate to fill hundreds of bullets. I looked around the room and saw a hundred more crates just like this one. "There's enough explosives here to wipe Sunder off the map. We should get out of here."

Hendricks only moaned in response. I picked him up in both arms, grabbed his cane, and awkwardly marched the length of the warehouse looking for any kind of escape. I just needed to get back on the streets. To get my bearings. Then . . . then what?

There was a square door on the far wall, almost as tall as the building. I put my back against it and pushed but it hardly moved at all. Maybe it was barred on the other side. A cool breeze blew through the gap, teasing freedom.

Then I saw a smaller door, off to the side. It was already ajar. Perfect. I ran over and kicked it open.

But this door didn't go to freedom. It went into an office. Standing inside the office were three men in charcoal suits and one man wearing brown.

"Mr Phillips?" It was Thurston Niles. He had the most confused expression on his face and a cigar dangling from his mouth.

One of the other men was reaching inside the jacket of his charcoal suit. There was a strange pocket sewn into the lining from which the butt of a pistol was poking out. I wished that my machine wasn't still hidden away in Hendricks' coffin.

I racked my mind for a good excuse. There was nowhere to run. We were trapped.

Thurston's eyes fell on Hendricks.

"Is that Deamar?"

I looked down. Yes, I suppose it was.

"Yeah." I stepped into the room. There was a table by the window with nothing on it but papers so I dumped Hendricks' limp body on top. "I chased him into the tunnels beneath the city. No idea what he was planning." Hendricks gargled up a mean groan, playing the perfect villain. "I hit him in the shoulder and he's lost a lot of blood. I could have let him die down there but I thought you'd want him for questioning."

I looked back at the room of hard, clean-cut faces. The charcoal suits were still itching to grab their hidden weapons but Thurston threw up his hands in celebration.

"Well done, man! I knew I could trust you. Yes, quite right. Let's make sure the bastard doesn't die before we find out who he works for."

The expressions of the other suits didn't change but they put their hands back at their sides.

"I should get him to the medical center, then," I said. "I don't know how long he'll last."

"No, no, no." Thurston patted me on the shoulder like a proud uncle. "We'll call one of my doctors down here to get him all fixed up."

Hendricks rolled his head over. He was still awake.

"Are you sure?" I said. "I can get him to the medical center real quick."

"My doctors are the best, Mr Phillips. If you want to know how to put a man together, the best practice is to take a man apart." My mind was filled with thoughts of Victor Stricken. Missing fingernails. Missing teeth. Ragged rips in his ears.

Thurston turned back to his trio of followers.

"Call Anderson. Get him down here quick and tell him to bring his tools."

The tallest of the suits reached for the phone, but it was already ringing.

They must not get many calls because it put all of them on edge. It put me on edge too. Tall Boy picked up the telephone like it was some delicate ornament, and slowly lifted the receiver.

None of us said anything while he listened. There was nothing to read on that infuriatingly blank face.

"Yes," he said, "we have the intruder here. Along with the man who apprehended him."

The call was coming from down below. My story was going to turn to ash in two more seconds, so I only had one second to take the upper hand.

I punched Thurston Niles right in his throat. He made a choking sound, and I gave him another crack on the nose. I didn't have time to confirm that he was taken out, because the trigger-happy trio were making their move. Unlucky for them, their weapons were tucked into their jackets while Hendricks' cane was already in my hand.

I cracked the first one on the side of his face, just like Eliah had done to me during our reunion. It brought his head down to kicking height and I didn't waste the opportunity. I used him like a football and he crumpled to the floor.

The tall one still had the phone in his hands, so I went for the other. I rushed him, shoulder first, and drove him into the wall. There was a satisfying *crack* as his head bounced off the bricks, and I followed it up with an elbow to the face that turned his legs to noodles.

Tall Boy dropped the phone and backed away to the far corner of the room, finally fumbling the pistol out of its hiding place. I wouldn't be able to reach him in time, and from that distance he'd have to be cross-eyed not to hit me. I raised the cane, ready to throw it, but aware that it wouldn't do any good compared to the power of the killing machine. Then I heard:

"DROP IT!"

Tall Boy and I turned. It was Hendricks. Not quite as passed out as he'd appeared to be. He was sitting on the edge of the table with Thurston Niles pinned between his legs. Thurston's nose was an overflowing waterfall of blood. His jacket was open and Hendricks was holding the pistol that had recently been tucked inside.

Now, it was tucked into the temple of the most powerful man in town.

"I said drop it," growled Hendricks, "unless you all want to be out of a job."

The tall man took a second to think about it. It was a second too long for Hendricks, who lifted the gun from Thurston and pointed it at Tall Boy instead.

The same ear-shattering explosion. The same puff of smoke. Tall Boy's chest coughed out a gush of blood and he fell back against the wall. He put his hands over the hole in his chest like he could use them to keep the life in. But judging from the abstract painting on the wall behind him, the hole in his back was even bigger.

I took the guns from the two remaining suits and told them not to try anything. They didn't look like they would but it seemed like the right thing to say in that kind of situation.

Hendricks had his pistol pointed back at Thurston's head. For some reason, Thurston was smiling.

The blood was dripping over his mouth, staining the front of that fine-looking suit. Hendricks was holding him by his salt-and-pepper hair, but he looked happier than I'd ever seen him.

"Well done, Mr Phillips. I knew I was right about you." He licked the blood from his wet lips. "I was starting to feel disappointed in this city. It turns out there are some fighters here after all."

Hendricks wrenched his head back. That only made him smile more.

"We need an automobile. You have one here?"

"In fact, we do. Good thinking, Mr Phillips. Follow me."

He got up, not needing to be told to keep his hands in the air. I had a gun in each hand, and I pointed them to the men on the floor.

"Stand up, both of you."

I only had to ask nicely and they did as they were told. Hendricks had already shown what would happen if they didn't.

We all filed out to the main room and Thurston approached a metal bar on the wall.

"Wait!" I shouted. He turned back, all innocent.

"This is just the mechanism for the door, Mr Phillips. A little something we brought over from one of our factories in Braid. May I?"

I looked to Hendricks for confirmation but he barely had the energy to stay on his feet.

"Do it," I said.

Thurston pulled the lever and the whole place shook with the rattling of chains. The huge door peeled open, letting cool air and morning light flood in.

"There you are, Mr Phillips. Your automobile."

I'd been expecting something like the little car that Linda and I took out on the road. Maybe even a flashy number like the one Yael got to drive. But no. The entire driveway of the warehouse was filled with one big truck. It might have been the very same one that almost squished me and Tippity that night.

It was the size of a small building. Too wide for most Sunder City streets. A dream getaway vehicle it was not, but it was all we had.

"Get over there," I ordered Thurston and his pack of bleeding suits, directing them to a position on the outside wall so Hendricks could keep his pistol aimed at them from the passenger window. "Get in."

Hendricks clambered up into the cabin. It looked like there wasn't an ounce of blood left in his body. Once he was inside, he pointed his gun out the window back to Thurston and his men, while I ran around the truck and got behind the wheel.

"You know how to drive?" asked Hendricks.

"I had some recent practice." I looked for the switch that was supposed to fire it up, but it wasn't there. I flicked a bunch of other levers, but nothing brought the truck to life. "Not in anything like this, though."

"Grab the handle under the wheel and pull it towards you," shouted Thurston, being frustratingly helpful. I did what he said, and the vehicle shook itself awake like a bear in spring. I put my foot down on the pedal and the truck lurched a few feet forward. We were good to go.

"You ready?"

Hendricks had his gun resting on the windowsill of the truck. He was chewing his lip, with his eyes still locked on Thurston's smiling and bloody face.

"Just give me one second," he said. Breathing out so he could
steady himself for the shot.

I didn't give him his second. I put my foot to the floor and
the truck bounced out onto the road. Hendricks spun around in
fury but I didn't have time to worry about it. I was behind the
wheel of a machine that was just as dangerous as a firearm but
ten times as hard to control.

"Get to the surgery," said Hendricks, as the truck bounced over
the gutter.

"I'll try, but I don't even know where we are."

I searched desperately for street signs, taking out letterboxes
and lampposts on the way. When I tried to take a turn too tight,
the truck skidded to a stop. Out the window I could see the
painted wall of the Sunder City printing press. We were down at
the bottom end of Riley Street.

"We're too far east," I said, scraping the side of the truck along
the wall to get back on the road.

"Let's go to yours, then."

"Too risky. How about The Ditch?"

The tires hit the gutter, almost tipping us over, and Hendricks
groaned in pain.

"I thought you'd never fucking ask."

65

I ping-ponged the truck up Riley Street, crashing through sandwich boards and grinding against walls in a shower of splinters and sparks. Hendricks had his hand pressed against his wound.

"Take Sixth," he said.

"The Ditch is on Eighth."

"Might give us away if we leave the truck parked out front."

"Fine. Sixth."

When we got to the corner, I tried to turn us left but we were going too fast. The front of the truck bounced onto the sidewalk and launched us straight into the side of a corner store.

It wasn't like being punched. When somebody punches you, you're the stationary object. This was like being inside a fist as it hits someone else. The sudden stop pushed all my bones into each other and my nose hit the wheel so hard that blood immediately covered my chest.

Hendricks bounced off the dashboard as the broken windscreen rained down on his head, then he crumpled back down in front of his seat.

"Hendricks?"

No response.

I stepped out on Sixth Street. It was early. Still damn-near freezing. Nobody was out on the street yet, but I knew they'd be coming. I wrenched open Hendricks' door. He was out cold with new cuts on his face from all the broken glass. I picked him up in my arms, carried him down the street like a bride, and turned into a narrow alley. I had stabbing pains up my arms. Sticky blood on my breath.

Shit.

I'd left the pistols back in the truck. I was pretty sure Hendricks had dropped his. I spun around, tempted to go back for them, but it was way too risky. I gritted my teeth and kept running.

We came up to Seventh. I peered out, hoping there weren't any witnesses. Nobody but a paper boy on the corner looking back down Riley in the direction of the truck.

I crossed the street and stumbled, almost losing my balance, into the safety of a muddy lane I knew like the back of my hand. I'd spent hours out there, in the early days, emptying mop buckets and taking out the trash. The smell hadn't changed at all.

I kicked at the back door of The Ditch until Boris came to the door.

First, he was angry. Then concerned. He hadn't lived in Sunder before the Coda so he'd never had the pleasure of meeting Hendricks in his heyday. It didn't matter, though. Boris had a kind heart and he could see that we needed help.

"My friend is hurt and people are trying to kill us. Can we hide here? Just for a while?"

Boris didn't even stop to think about it. He took Hendricks from my arms and brought us in from the cold.

66

Boris carried Hendricks into the kitchen and put him down on a sack of flour. He was still breathing, and the cuts on his head weren't so bad. Boris handed me some bandages, then signaled for me to wait.

One of the reasons I was so fond of The Ditch was that it was never strict about closing time. As long as there was one sorry soul that wanted to nurse his drink instead of going home alone, the bar was happy to stay open.

Boris broke tradition by going into the main room to clear out the last of the customers while we waited out back. The shirt that I'd wrapped around Hendricks' shoulder was loose and wet. I took it off him, cleaned up the wound as much as I could, then covered it with fresh bandages. It didn't take long for blood to mark the cloth.

"Where are we?"

His eyes fluttered open.

"The Ditch. As soon as Boris gets everyone out, I'll call the surgeons to come stitch you up."

He pulled the bandage from his side to inspect the wound.

"Nothing serious. Just a bit of skin and muscle. I'll be fine."

He tried to get up.

"Eliah, stay still. You need to rest."

He didn't fight me so I handed him my last Clayfield as a reward. When Boris came back, and signaled that the coast was clear, I went into the main room and used the payphone to call the surgery.

The Dwarf answered.

"Hendricks has been injured. He's got a nasty hole in his

shoulder and he's bleeding like hell. Tell the ladies to come to
The Ditch on the corner of Eighth and Main."

He assured me that the Succubae would be on their way within
the hour.

When I turned back around, Boris was behind the bar holding
a bottle of tarix sap.

"That ain't really the priority, Boris."

He pointed back at the kitchen and shrugged in a way that
said, *It's not my idea.*

I suppose that made sense.

Before I'd even closed all the blinds, Hendricks stumbled out
to join us. He was scraping himself along the wall, heading for
one of the booths.

"Are you trying to kill yourself?" I asked.

"Of course not. That's your thing. Where's my drink?"

He collapsed onto a bench and propped himself up against a
pillar. Boris placed two cocktails on the table in front of him.

"Come on, boy. You can't sew me up just by looking serious."

I took the seat opposite. We picked up our drinks and tapped
them together.

It was like some kind of cruel joke. How long had I been
dreaming of a night like this? To be back at The Ditch
with Hendricks, enjoying cocktails and conversation. It was
everything I'd wanted. Almost. He wasn't supposed to have a
new face and a hole in his shoulder that was dripping blood
onto the floor.

"Exina and Loq are on their way," I said.

"Good. I just hope the skin on my shoulder holds stitches
better than my face did."

I'd been worrying about the same thing. An injury like this
would have been nothing back in the day, but his new body had
been struggling even before he'd sprung a leak.

"You got any Clayfields behind there?" I asked Boris. The
Banshee pulled out a pack from behind the bar and dropped them

in the middle of the table. He went out to the kitchen and Hendricks and I each plucked a twig from the pack.

"They'll be coming for us," I said.

"That's why we need to move on them first."

I almost laughed. He was in pieces. I didn't know which of my injuries was hurting the most. We were the sorriest pair of rebels that had ever been seen, and he wanted to go on the attack.

"And do what?"

Hendricks leaned forward, rested his elbows on the table, and took a big sip of his milkwood.

"Take it all down." There was no glint in his eye. No irony. He was dead-set serious. "I told you that I traveled all across the continent. I know what life is like since the Coda. It isn't all lost. Not by a long shot. But it will be if we don't fight for this world. The real world. The *old* world." His eyes drifted in and out of focus but his voice strengthened with every word. "I was wrong about this place. Wrong to defend it. To feed it. It's poison. Just like this!" He slapped his cocktail off the table and the glass shattered on the floor. "When my body was strong, the poison didn't matter. I could contain it. A little whiskey and tobacco was nothing compared to the centuries inside my soul. But now? Well, look at me, boy. I'm an inch away from oblivion."

"You just need rest. Let's get out of the city. When you're better we can—"

"We don't have time! The whole world is just as sick as I am, and this city is the poison. We could contain Sunder when we were strong. But without the magic, this place is bleeding us out. It drags farmers away from the land. Doctors from their communities. It makes us forget the things we need to protect. Our traditions. Our connections. Out there, away from this place, there is a world that is waiting to be reborn but it will only happen if we stay out there and fight for it. We *will* find a way to move forward, I promise you, but not while Sunder City stands."

I didn't know where to look. I couldn't believe what he was

saying. I thought that he just wanted to stop the Niles Company. To make sure that the city stayed in the hands of its people. But this?

"Sunder is the easy option," he spat. "The short-term solution. If it continues to suck at the spirit of Archetellos, it will be our end. We must destroy it, Fetch. You and I. That is our duty. That is how we will make up for everything we've done to this world. For all our mistakes. It is the most important job we will ever do."

His eyes were full of determination. Clear. Unwavering. Certain about the task ahead. He didn't just want to stop Sunder from falling into the Niles Company's control. He wanted to destroy it completely. Main Street and The Ditch and the House of Ministers and the Governor's mansion. I didn't even know how to fit that idea into my head. It was madness.

Hendricks looked into my eyes. Reading me. Daring me. I stared back, but I couldn't pretend to agree with him. All I felt was fear and uncertainty. I watched him watch me. I saw the disappointment. Even worse, I saw his frustrated lack of surprise.

"What about Baxter?" I asked. "We tell them what the Niles Company is up to. We make sure the city takes control of the fires and we use them to . . . to do whatever you think needs doing. This city doesn't have to be a poison. If we do things right, we can . . ."

He was shaking his head. Chuckling.

"For someone who expects so little of himself, you have so much faith in other people. All creatures, Humans especially, have a crippling inability to see past their immediate needs. We all have our ideals. Our beliefs about what we stand for. Our *code*. But when the bowl of food is placed in front of us, we act like the animals we really are."

"I don't think you really mean that."

"Why would you expect everyone else to be better than you? You've been carrying around your killing machine, haven't you?

You told me that you were asked to destroy it. You didn't. Because of that, people died. Now what do you think happens when they start selling those things on every corner? At first, when people see what they are, they'll be disgusted by them. Rightfully so. Who wants to keep something like that in their house? With their children? But then your neighbor buys one. You see them stuffed into belts when you're out on the street. You no longer feel safe. Not until you have one of your own. They'll be buying them straight off the production line, I promise you. Then what does this place become? What does this world become when every single one of us is preparing to go to war with each other? How will we claw our way back from that?"

I had no answer. I didn't argue. I couldn't. I was sure he was right but I couldn't believe that destroying the city was the only way forward.

"Eliah, I've been here for six years. I know it looks bad but there are good people here, and if we—"

"You're just saying that because you wouldn't know what to do without this place. You have a frustrating inability to look past your own feelings. You always have. Made rash, dangerous choices because you wanted to follow a girl, or had your feelings hurt, or thought that somebody wanted to fuck you. But all you've ever cared about is looking like a *man*, and that's what this place gives you. Who will you be without it? I have no idea. It doesn't matter. I'm giving you a chance, for once in your life, to do the thing that's better for everyone else."

I had nothing to say. I couldn't argue. But I couldn't agree with him either.

Then he gave a horrible, all-knowing laugh.

"I was wrong," he said.

"About what?"

"That thing I said when we were out by the fire." He reached over and tapped a finger against my temple. "It turns out, I know exactly what's going on in your head."

He lay back in the booth and closed his eyes. After a few minutes, he was snoring. I sat and stared at him till the surgeons arrived.

"Will he be okay?" I asked.

"His skin doesn't like stitches but we'll make it work," said Exina. "Was it that machine you were talking about? The one they're making down at that factory?"

I nodded and left Hendricks in their care while I went out to walk in the shadows, keeping my head down and my coat wrapped around my bare and bloody chest. I needed new clothes but I couldn't go home. I needed help. I needed someone to talk to. Most of all, I needed to convince Hendricks that the soul of Sunder City could be saved.

I just needed to convince myself first.

67

The back door to the Steeme household was unlocked. Very little had changed inside. The detectives were likely expecting Carissa to return home at some point, unaware that she was already out in Lipha, hopefully sitting with her cousin somewhere on the coast.

Harold was smaller than I was but I found a shirt of his that fit me. I took new trousers and a black jacket and laid them out on the bed. I hung the holster on the doorknob and took a shower. The water between my feet was dark red: full of dirt and dried blood. When I toweled myself off, I found untold new sore spots and it was an impossible task to work out where each cut or bruise had come from.

"Well, this is a new one."

Linda Rosemary was standing in the doorway of the bathroom with her switchblade in her hand. I wrapped the towel around my waist.

"What are you doing here?" I asked.

"Waiting for a murderer to return. Or an accomplice. Which one did I catch?"

"Give me a minute to get dressed and I'll explain."

"No."

"What?"

"You can get dressed but I'm not going anywhere. I don't trust you not to jump out the window in your birthday suit."

"Fine. My clothes are out there."

We went back into the bedroom. Linda stood against the wall with her eyes on the floor, not leaving me alone but not making it any weirder than it needed to be. I finished drying myself off.

"Simms put you up to this?" I asked.

"Yep."

"Well, it's a waste of time. Carissa Steeme hopped a carriage out of town. She's not coming back."

"How do you know that?"

"I'm the one who sent her away."

"What?" She turned in shock, realized that I hadn't got my trousers on yet, and looked away in similar alarm. "You're not even going to try and lie to me?"

"No."

"Why?"

"Because it's not important."

"It is to me. I want Simms on my side. I need to find some regular work before this city eats me whole."

"There won't be a city to work in if I don't decide what to do next."

I got my pants and shirt on and she stopped averting her eyes.

"You found your saboteur?"

"Yeah."

"Who was it?"

I still hadn't worked her out. There were too many sides of Linda Rosemary to see them all at once. I took a gamble.

"Eliah Hendricks."

She struggled to swallow that one. I didn't blame her.

"The High Chancellor?"

"Yeah. He's an old friend."

"Bullshit."

"I know. It's never made much sense to me either."

"Where is he?"

"Why? You wanna meet him?"

Another gamble, but I was beginning to see my next move. Hendricks had been alone for too long. Of course he could see why shutting this whole city down might be a good idea, and I'd never been good at changing his mind about anything. But what if we had a new group of smart minds? Like the old days, when we'd sit in the garden of the Governor's mansion and discuss the best ways to live and serve and rule. Linda. Baxter. Hendricks. Me, to a lesser extent. I was sure that if I gave Eliah his sounding board and his drinking buddies and a bit of philosophy to chew on, we would be able to find a way out of this, together.

"The Ditch," I said. "It's a bar on Eighth and Main. It'll look like it's closed but if you say that I sent you, they'll let you in."

"But why?"

"Because the fires are still burning beneath this city and the Niles Company are trying to control that power for themselves. We need to find a way to stop them that doesn't involve tearing all of Sunder to pieces."

"That's an option?"

"For some people."

"Shit."

"Yeah."

"But where are you going?"

"To find some friends. I'll meet you there soon."

"Wait. How do I know you're not just trying to get me off your back?"

"You don't. But it's worth the risk, right? You let me go but you have a chance to meet High Chancellor Eliah Hendricks. Didn't you come here looking for a miracle?"

68

I didn't know where Baxter lived so I had to wait for them to arrive at one of their many jobs. With everything that was going on, I guessed that they were more likely to go to the House of Ministers than the Museum. I hunkered down in the entrance of Prim Hall where I'd have a good view of Baxter's approach.

Sitting next to me was a scruffy little pickpocket. I explained what I wanted him to do and he only needed to hear it once. While we waited for Baxter to arrive, he didn't say anything at all. He was the perfect employee.

When Baxter's inimitable silhouette came around the corner I gave the kid the signal. He was fast enough to cut Baxter off before they turned up the hill.

There might have been easier ways to do this but they would all give Baxter time alone to notify someone else. I was on the run; Thurston's men would be looking for me, the Police Department too. I wish I trusted Baxter more. I wish I could trust anyone. But I'd screwed over too many people to earn any kind of allegiance.

The kid delivered the message and Baxter looked up at me, too far away for me to read their expression. They said something to the kid then took an admirably short amount of time to make a decision and come my way.

The kid ran back, ahead of Baxter, and when I handed him his coins he paused. It was like he wanted to say something but wasn't sure if he should. I thought he might be weighing up whether to ask for more money.

"Sorry, it's all I got."

The kid shook his head and ran away. It seemed like I couldn't make anybody happy today.

Before Baxter reached me, I went inside.

Prim Hall had closed with the Coda. Maybe not officially, but nobody had booked a concert there since.

The first row of seats had been ripped up and burned in the middle of the room. The black crater that it left behind was filled with garbage, right in the spot where that perfect horn player had once been sitting. I leaned against a wall and Baxter came in, shaking the snow from their coat.

"For heaven's sake, Fetch. I can't be seen with you. Thurston has all but put a price on your head."

"How are things with the new Niles brother? His plans sure have put a spring in your step. You were one downhearted little Demon the last time I saw you."

"Yes. It's an exciting time," they said, with no hint of actual excitement. "Soon the fires will be back in every home and the city will be alive again."

"And you think we have the Niles Company to thank for that?"

"Who else?"

Baxter was a tough cookie. Trying to read their face was like guessing the emotional state of a roofing tile.

"Baxter, the fires are still burning beneath the city. They always have been. Niles is just bringing them up to the surface and stamping his brand on it. They're selling our own power back to us so they can use the . . ." Baxter dropped their head and I trailed off.

"How did you find out?"

Damn it.

I knew Niles couldn't be doing it all on his own but I never thought Baxter would be the one selling out.

"Really, Bax? You're handing the whole city over to this guy? We could have captured the fires ourselves."

"No, we couldn't! We had nothing, Fetch. Even if we'd known it was still there, which we didn't, we'd lost the technology. I couldn't get five men to fill potholes last year, now we have hundreds of workers fitting pipes, building new businesses and going home to their families with food, wages and a purpose. This is everything I set out to achieve, far more than I'd hoped for, and nobody else could have made it happen."

Baxter had always been morbidly sincere. One of Amari's favorite games was trying to get them to tell a joke. Even when they were trying to be happy, the words always seemed severe. Now, Baxter was speaking of dreams being fulfilled and there was something desperate about them. Their hands were clenched into fists and their mouth was locked in a sharp-toothed smile.

I thought about what Hendricks had just been saying: how I'd attached my identity to this city so strongly that I couldn't fathom leaving it behind. I had a feeling he would have similar things to say about our demonic friend.

"If that's true, then why not tell everybody what's going on? Why all the lies?"

Baxter shrugged. "Because Niles wanted it that way. And until I meet someone else who can bring trucks and tools into the city, someone who knows how to refit the pipes and get the fires to the surface, I have no problem giving him what he wants."

"That's how we do business in this city now? Bend to whoever writes the check?"

Baxter look like they'd been slapped.

"That's how it's always been! What the hell's wrong with you, Fetch? Have you forgotten where we are? That's what Sunder City is. That's why it survived. Because whoever pushes the hardest gets to the top. We have a future. Finally. Why the fuck does it matter to you how we get there?"

I opened my mouth but no answer came out. Why *did* it matter to me? I tried to replay Hendricks' voice in my head. To let his words convince me, again, that all of this was wrong.

"I went into the factory," I said. "The one they built on the bones of Brisak Reserve. You know what they're making in there?"

"Yes."

"And that sounds like a good idea to you?"

"What other choice is there, Fetch? Are you going to get out there and build some homes? Are you going to pay the wages? It's not the perfect deal but we had nothing to offer. Sunder City was dying. Now it's not. Don't you see what that means? You, more than anyone, should be on your knees thanking Niles for what he's done. He's the first man I've met that actually has the potential to fix your fucking mess."

That was a deeper cut than I expected from Baxter but I couldn't fault them for it. In truth, I had trouble faulting anything they said. We all wanted to move forward and this was the only real proposal we'd seen so far. If the magic wasn't coming back, then this was the only way to go. Better than trying to claw backwards like Edmund Rye had attempted to do. Or Harold Steeme and his stolen youth. Or . . .

"Baxter, there's something you should know—"

A door opened on the western wall. I spun around. Thurston Niles was standing behind me.

He'd changed his suit but his nose was still red and swollen and there were dark bruises under both his eyes. Despite all this, he seemed happy to see me.

"Hello, Fetch. How's the case coming along?"

There was a small shadow with a sorry expression tucked into the doorway behind Niles. It was my quiet little pickpocket, waiting for his second payment. That's what Baxter must have said to him before coming over – promised a few more coins if he told Thurston that I was here.

"Hey, Niles." I backed away from both of them, down the stairs towards the performance area. "Thanks for lending me your ride. You can pick it up on Sixth Street, outside the convenience store on the corner. Well, a little bit inside the store too. You might wanna check those brakes."

"You lied to me."

"I didn't want to be left out. You've been lying to everyone in town. So has Baxter. I wanted to get in on the action."

I'd been careless, but not so careless that I hadn't come into the hall first and scoped it out.

"It's time we had a little talk, Mr Phillips."

"I wish I could, Niles, but I've still got a few things to wrap up."

I jumped off the last step and onto the stage. There was one exit left – the place where I'd seen the musicians come from all those years ago. I was heading for the door but Cyran the Ogre opened it first.

I put my shoulder into his chest – and bounced back. It was like hitting a refrigerator full of lead. He socked me with a cast-iron fist and I went down like a drunk baby deer.

But I wasn't going to be taken that easy. He tried to grab me but I rolled away from his thick fingers. He ripped the cheap jacket from my back but I slipped out of the sleeves and got to my feet. I ran faster than I'd ever run before, ignoring that old pain in my chest. Cyran was tough but he was slow and I lost him around the next corner when I jumped over a fence and ran through the grounds of an abandoned marketplace.

I ran all the way back to The Ditch, taking the secret alleys and backstreets I'd been mapping most of my life. I charged through the back door, into the bar, but Boris was the only one left. He gave me a shrug that said, *They're gone.*

69

Boris gave me the details as best as he could. The surgeons had patched Hendricks up, then Linda had arrived and the three women took him away. They'd left no message for me so I called the surgery. The Dwarf answered and put Exina on the line.

"He's not here."

"But you just brought him back."

"I know, but we couldn't keep him still. He went off with that feline friend of yours."

"Where?"

"I don't know and I don't want to know."

She had a clipped, frustrated tone to her voice that I hadn't heard before.

"Should I come over? We can put our heads together and—"

"No. We have a business to run and I can't afford to get caught up in your little games anymore. If you want to pay for our services, then come with money. Otherwise stay away."

She hung up.

I listened to the dial tone and wondered whether she was telling the truth or not. Maybe she really was fed up with being dragged into our plans unwittingly. Maybe she overhead what Hendricks' endgame was and realized that it was time to opt out. Or, perhaps, Hendricks had asked her to lie for him. Maybe they were all there: Eliah, Linda and the Succubae, all hatching their next plan without me. Either way, I was on my own. Again. As always.

I started to feel a little mad, like I wanted to break things.

I called Linda's office. Nobody answered but I headed over there anyway. It was a desperate move but Boris wanted to reopen the bar and I had nowhere else to go.

When I got to Five Shadows Square, it was dark inside the old florist. The door was locked and there was no sign of anyone.

I couldn't go home. I couldn't go to the cops. Carissa was gone and Hendricks had vanished along with Linda. The surgeons didn't want to see me and Baxter had already tried to hand me over to their boss. I had no place to go and the streets weren't safe. A cop or charcoal suit could cross my path at any moment.

I was wheezing but I couldn't tell whether it was from physical pain or panic. Hendricks had abandoned me. As soon as he saw that I was doubting his plan, he'd cut me loose.

I thought he'd come back because we were friends. Because he missed me. Maybe it wasn't that at all. Maybe he just knew I was an obedient bit of muscle that he could order around, now that his own body was falling apart.

As soon as Linda had come to his side, he'd swapped us out. I felt like throwing a brick through her window.

The sky was dark. Hailstones hammered against tin roofs as I stood under the awning and tried to imagine any place in the city where I might be welcome. I dreamed of a nice hotel room with a warm shower but my only cash was leftover change, and Sunder despised charity. Besides, I was a wanted man. Any smart business owner would turn me over to one of the interested parties in exchange for a reward.

I needed somewhere cheap. A place where folks didn't make a habit of working with the police. A dark end of a dark street that didn't want to draw attention to itself.

Someplace like the Sickle.

I slunk my way down side streets swearing under my breath and kicking hailstones along the path. I was furious that I'd been left behind. Heartbroken. All I'd wanted was a chance to change Hendricks' mind.

Things had been good again. For a few days. That man in this city. Now he was off with someone else putting together a plan to steal Sunder's future and I was left out in the cold. I was pumped full of adrenaline and emotion and angst. I'd been uninvited from the party. Kicked out from the cool kids. I kept trying to bring my brain back to the things that mattered, like what Hendricks had planned for the city and whether it was right, but my heart kept dragging me back to wondering why my friend didn't want me around.

Sickle Street was quiet. Not peaceful. Never peaceful here. There was a hushed, patient tension like all the menace was just waiting for the clouds to clear. I wasn't afraid of it anymore. I was part of it. Just another drop of poison in the bottle.

Sampson's tin casino looked shabby, even compared to its neighbors. It was the last place anyone would come looking, as long as I could convince them to let me stay.

"Woah." The doorman put out an arm to block my path. "How many have you had, buster?"

"None."

"Really?"

"That's why I'm here. I'll be a lot calmer when I have something to cool my blood."

He wrinkled up his nose.

"You're not going to be any trouble, are you?"

I took a deep breath to get myself under control.

"No. I will not. I just need to get out of the cold. Please."

I wish that I was faking the vulnerability but, in truth, if he'd said no, I might have broken into tears.

"All right. Get inside."

It wasn't much warmer but it was out of the wind and rain. There were fewer customers than last time. Sampson was counting receipts at his usual table and he didn't notice me till I was standing at his side.

"Can I sit down?"

He looked as tired as I felt.

"Are you going to behave yourself?"

"Why do people keep asking me that?"

"Are you?"

"Yes. I promise."

"Then sit down."

I couldn't hide my relief as I crumpled in front of him.

"What can I get you, Mr Phillips?"

"Well . . . I'm a little short on cash."

"Then get out."

"Please. Here . . ." I unloaded my pockets onto the table, dropping out a mess of money like a kid at the school canteen. One bronze coin and a scattering of copper. "I need somewhere to stay. People are after me."

"You can barely afford a cocktail but you're asking for a drink, a room and secrecy?"

"I'd be in your debt."

"You don't want that, Mr Phillips."

"You can call on my services whenever you need."

"I've seen how you conduct your services and they don't look like they're worth much to me. Besides, from the way you're talking, I'd be surprised if you survive the week."

I couldn't argue with him. If I was in his shoes, I'd have kicked me out already.

"Just a night or two. Please. I'll be clean and quiet. I don't need anything else. Just a place to sleep and gather my thoughts."

"This is a business, Mr Phillips. One that is struggling enough already without resorting to being paid in bad promises and bullshit."

I almost slammed the table, but I stopped myself. If I'd done that, it would have all been over. I swallowed my anger and looked him dead in the eye without blinking.

"One day, you're going to have one of those jobs. When something needs doing and nobody wants to do it. Something too dangerous. Too dark. Too risky to use your own men. That's when you call me. Whatever it is, I'll get it done."

He stroked the center strand of his goatee.

"Does anyone know you're here?"

"Only the people in this room."

He threw a key across the table.

"Then get out of sight. Now."

70

The room was worth what I'd paid for it: a single crunchy mattress covered with a torn sheet and a scratchy wool blanket. No carpet, a three-legged armchair in the corner, and one small porthole of a window that looked out at a brick wall.

It was safer than being on the streets but I felt anxious from the moment I closed the door. Like I was missing something. Missing everything.

I lay on the bed and closed my eyes. I was beyond exhausted but it took me hours of turning in the bedclothes and begging for relief before sleep mercifully let me rest.

We stumbled into her hotel room. Both drunk. Laughing. I craved her lips every second they weren't on mine. She closed the door, opened a bottle of wine and poured two glasses.

"Is this . . . the bed?" I asked.

It was a basket full of leaves that took up a third of the room.

"It's a Fae cot. That's what I sleep in when I'm at home. It's hard to get a good one in Sunder because there aren't enough leaves to keep it fresh. It feels so good to be in a proper bed again."

She jumped backwards onto the cot and the leaves engulfed her in an explosion of green and brown. It smelled like we were standing in the center of a forest after it rained. I looked down at Amari, her dress caught up around her thighs, her smile giddy and her hair all wild instead of tied up tight on the back of her head.

I leaned over her and my knees sunk down, either side of her body. I put an arm through the leaves and around her back. I could only look into her eyes for a moment. It was all too real. She laughed, put a hand on my cheeks and brought my mouth to hers.

The leaves shifted as we moved. Around us and over us. Clothes got lost in the foliage. It felt like we were sinking into the earth. In a cocoon. We wrapped around each other. Her limbs like vines. The tips of her fingers, soft like petals then firm like stone. Her breath in my mouth, mossy and sweet. Lips running across me like a waterfall. We rolled over each other, panting beneath a sea of green.

Then her skin grew firm under my fingers. Her breath quickened and she gripped me, nails in my back, tight around my body, then . . . she froze.

I couldn't move. I didn't dare. With only the dim moonlight coming through the window, I could barely make out her face. She was a statue. Wood-grain covered her closed eyelids. Her legs, wrapped around my waist, were immovable. My heavy panting was the only sound in the room. For just a handful of strange seconds, she was nothing more than a solid wooden sculpture. I didn't dare move. Scared that if I shifted, I would break off a piece of her (or myself).

Then, she was back.

Her body melted underneath me. The softness of her skin returned and she sighed over my shoulder. I was laughing, in shock and relief.

"Sorry," she said. "That happens sometimes."

I kissed her. It was a good kiss. Our last kiss.

The last good thing I've done.

71

There were no clocks in my room. No view of the sky. I had no idea of the time when I woke up. I didn't even know what day it was. Had I slept for five minutes or five months?

I looked out my door into the hallway. Deathly silent. No sign of life, just a folded towel. I took it and went walking. Every other door was closed. I found a dead end. Turned around. Went back the other way and finally found the door marked *WC*. Inside was one big room with a toilet and showerhead so close to each other that you could use them simultaneously if you were particularly pushed for time.

That wasn't me. I had all the time in the world. My friends were in hiding. They didn't need me anymore. There was nothing for me to do but wait around for my enemies to find me instead.

I washed myself off and put the same filthy clothes back on, then went down the hall into the main room of Sampson's. There was no music. No customers. The place was closed and all the employees were gathered around the bar. It reminded me of the old days at The Ditch: a special ritual for hospitality staff who don't make enough money to drink anywhere else so the workplace becomes their local.

Phara, the waitress that had served me the milkwood on my first trip, was there with her arms wrapped around the doorman. A couple of dice-dealing Dwarves and a hefty Human security guard were perched on stools and a Werecat dishwasher was leaning against the wall. They were all huddled around a little silver radio, listening so intently that they didn't notice me sidle up to them, take a glass, and fill it with a double shot from the closest bottle. All their attention was locked firmly on the voice in the silver box.

". . . is still unexplained. The police department has not yet made an official statement, but eye witnesses say it happened over a matter of seconds. Only one injury so far: a young member of the police force who was standing outside the site is in a critical condition."

"What happened?" I asked.

The dishwasher was the only one who turned his head.

"Who are you?"

"A guest. What happened?"

"Somebody let that Warlock freak free," said the doorman. "Tippy."

"Tippity? How did they do that? Wasn't he in the Gullet?"

"Yeah," said Phara, "but they used some kind of spell."

Oh, great. Back to this again. If people weren't already freaking out about dangerous spell-casters mucking around with new magic, this would push them over the edge.

I wondered if it was disinformation put out by the Niles Company: a way to keep everyone afraid of Magum so they could sell more pistols.

"What was it? More little flashes of fire?"

"No," said the dishwasher, refilling his glass. "Apparently a whole tree grew right out of the ground. It destroyed the walls of the Gullet and let Tippity climb to safety. Sounds crazy."

"Sounds incredible," said Phara.

"Probably some accomplice," said the doorman. "Who knows how many of them are out there?"

I'd stopped listening. My ears were ringing. The floor felt like liquid under my feet.

Tippity didn't have any accomplices. He was a loner, like me. The police had seized everything from his pharmacy. They'd taken all his Faery hearts and they'd taken all those little orbs he'd made; the glass globes of acid that were needed to set the magic free.

All except one.

When I'd woken up to find Hendricks in my office, he had an orb in his hands. He was holding it up to the light and splashing the acid around inside. He'd asked if he could borrow it. I'd let him.

And then a tree had grown out of the ground.

I ran straight out the door and onto the street.

72

The gate was wrenched open. There were marks in the mud on the steps. Lock broken off. Door kicked in. Porch littered with splinters.

Nobody was supposed to come here. Nobody but me.

I stepped inside and there were two sets of footprints on the floor. The ones marked in blood were my own: left by my bare, bleeding feet on the night I first came back after the Coda. The others were fresh and dirty, made by the man who was supposed to be my friend. I followed them across the floor, keeping my eyes down till I reached the place where my love was waiting.

A groan escaped my lips as I raised my head.

Amari.

Her body was where it had always been but the ground around her was scattered with sawdust and curls of papery bark. Her arms were still wrapped around her waist. Her fingers, so delicate. Her breast. Her shoulders. Her neck—

I screamed as I absorbed the full horror of what Hendricks had done.

Her face was gone. Cracked open. I could see right through to the back of her head. Everything inside was shattered. Snapped. Destroyed. One of her ears was still there but the other was in pieces on the floor. Where were her lips? Her little nose? Those cheeks? Where had she gone?

I knelt among the debris and ran my fingers through her remains. I picked up the largest piece. An eye stared back at me. Her eye.

No. No. God, no.

I wrapped my arms around her. My head pressed against the

sharp corners of what was left of her skull. Tears dropped from my cheeks into the hollow of her neck. Her hair crunched between my fingers like autumn leaves and pieces of her skin snapped off in my shaking fingers. She crumbled under my touch and I crushed her body into a million tiny pieces. All empty. All cold. She dissolved into dust and with every breath, I blew another piece of her away.

I was alone.

She'd been gone for six years but I'd kept her body safe. Just in case. I'd been right to do it, too, because some piece of her had remained. A glowing heart full of power. Full of life. Until Hendricks had turned it into a weapon so he could free Rick Tippity from his cell.

I found Amari's cheek on the floor and put it to mine. It was rough and cold but it still felt good to touch her.

Pat. Pat, tap.

I looked up at the shadow on the second-floor balcony and roared.

"HOW COULD YOU DO THIS TO HER?"

The shadow shook its head.

"How could *I* do this? What about what you did to her, boy? Kept her here, like this, for so long. Pinned together and dressed up like a little doll. Don't you have any respect for—"

"I was keeping her safe!"

"You were keeping her for YOU! Because it was the only way you could ever have her. I knew you were weak but I never imagined you could be so cruel. Especially to her."

"I was protecting her! In case it came back."

There was another shadow beside the first.

"But it's never coming back," said Linda. "You told me that so many times, Fetch. Why were you saving her for a day that would never come?"

"I . . . I . . ."

Hendricks leaned over the railing.

"What were you thinking, boy? That she'd come back to life, in her broken body full of cracks and nails and bits of glue, and thank you for doing this to her? Finally run away with you?" His words landed on me like dropped knives. "In all this time, with all the things you've done, how is it possible that you still haven't grown up?"

"But . . . but Tippity found the light inside them. Inside her. We could have used that to—"

"She was dead," said a third shadow. "They all were. I told you that over and over but you didn't listen. You just wanted me to be the bad guy so you could be the hero." Tippity's glasses shimmered in the dark. "The Fae are gone. I just borrowed the last spark of what was left. There was nothing alive in her or in any of them. You blamed me for moving forward while you were here, cuddling a corpse."

She was all over me. Splinters on my clothes and dust on the palms of my hands. So dry. So fragile. All gone.

"Boy, we can't go back in time. We can't bring the past into the present, no matter how much we want to. But we can make a new future. I still want to do that with you. If you're ready."

My cheeks were hot. My chest sore. My hands reached for weapons but I had no machine. Just a knife. I drew it without thinking. I'd been doing everything without thinking for so long, why should I start now?

"I told you," said Tippity.

Hendricks lowered his head.

"Yes, I suppose you did."

Something dropped from above. Then, the sound of broken glass. A little white bottle had landed at my feet. The smell reminded me of that wake-up powder that Tippity and I had used to get back from the church, but it must have been the other kind because when the fumes hit my nose, my legs buckled out from under me and my head hit the floor.

73

The drugs wore off slowly. I was in jail. Downtown. Nothing in my cell but a cold stone bench. I couldn't move but I could feel. I could think. I could remember.

I could also overhear what the cops were saying about me. Apparently I'd been dropped on their doorstep and when Simms heard about it, she gave firm instructions to keep me locked up until she was ready to deal with me herself.

In a way, I was happy to be taken out of it all. To be locked up where I couldn't do any more damage. The real world was too confusing. Too hard to navigate. Too easy to screw up.

After a while, when I could roll my head to the side, I saw that I had neighbors: three grim-looking Mages sitting in the opposite cell. After a few hours, I gained enough control of my tongue and lips to turn my slurring into speech.

"What are you fffolks in fffor?"

They told me they'd been locked up for three nights as part of Sunder City's crackdown on unapproved magical practices.

"We were just experimenting," said the shortest of the trio. The other two had taken an instant dislike to me and refused to contribute anything more than a grunt.

"What kind of experiments?" I had neither the ability nor the inclination to get up.

"Lightning bugs. It used to be an old Mage trick. We'd tap into the bit of electricity in the beetles and use it to light candles or entertain children. When we heard what Tippity was doing with the Fae, we thought about other places where a piece of magic might be hidden. Jim here mentioned the bugs so we thought about crushing them up and seeing if we could do something interesting with the lights."

"Is that possible?"

"Probably not. It was just an idea. We were catching a bunch of them up in what's left of Brisak Reserve when these guys in suits asked us what we were doing. When we told them, they called the cops who put us in here."

So, Thurston and the police were working together to enact this Tippity-inspired attack on illegal magic. A few days earlier, thoughts like that might have pissed me off. But I'd burned myself out on bigger fights since then. I shrugged myself back to sleep.

Another day sidled past my window without acknowledging me. In the morning, the nervous cop came in. The one who'd picked me off the floor of my place and then dropped into Simms's office while I was at the station. He approached my cell and handed me the worst cup of coffee I'd ever tasted.

"Simms told you to do this, didn't she?"

"I've been told not to tell you anything about anything, sir."

"I'm your prisoner, kid. Best stop calling me *sir* or it'll damage your fearsome reputation."

"Yes . . . uh, yes."

He was a real ballbuster, this one. A carrot-topped broomstick with a resilient smile.

"What was your name again?"

"I've been told not to tell you anything about anything, sir."

"I don't think they mean your name, kid."

He thought about it for a good ten seconds.

"Corporal Bath, Si . . . Corporal Bath."

"Nice to meet you, Corporal Bath. Any news on where Tippity has got to? Do the cops know who broke him out?"

"I've been told not to tell you—"

"I know you have! Well, fuck off then, Bath. See you tomorrow. I eagerly await my next weak cup of piss."

He left me there. The talkative Mage stopped talking too. The world outside was quiet. All I could hear was the occasional sound of construction as another piece of Niles-funded architecture came into existence.

I wondered what Hendricks was doing with Linda and Tippity. Had they all agreed to his plan? Were they working to take down Niles, as well as the whole damned city?

Hendricks had been using the Governor's mansion as a base. I wondered if they were still there. I could tell Corporal Bath about it and see what happened, but then I'd be putting my nose in it again, which is just what I'd decided I wasn't going to do.

I kept thinking about putting the hole in that pipe and how much it would have slowed the Niles Company down. Maybe not at all. Maybe a lot. Maybe all that happened was that some innocent citizen would be kept in darkness because of what I did. A house would be left cold. A business broken. When I started to feel bad, I reminded myself that none of it would matter soon because my old friend was planning to bring the whole thing down.

Hendricks already had a plan, I was sure of that. He was never one to talk big without being able to back it up. Somehow, he already knew how he was going to tear this city to the ground.

But it wasn't my business anymore. I'd been left out. Whatever they did, it was up to them, and I'd just have to wait and see.

At sundown, a cockroach crawled across the floor, onto my foot and up my leg. I tried to kick it off but he clung on and crawled higher.

I took off my hat and slapped the sucker.

BANG!

I jumped up. In the next room, where the cops were, a scream turned into a muzzled cry. The Mages all jumped to their feet. Smoke and dust blew into the jail, along with Linda Rosemary.

She was carrying her switchblade in one hand and a set of keys in the other. She'd come for me. Hendricks must have changed his mind.

"Linda, what's happening. Are you—"

She turned to face the Mages.

"Gentlemen, I'm here on behalf of Rick Tippity. We have declared war against Sunder City and need soldiers who are willing to fight for our cause. We believe you've been wrongfully imprisoned by a private company: an enemy who has taken control of this city and its people. I am setting you free. You are under no obligation to join us but, if you do, we are ready to empower you. We have weapons waiting for you to wield, allies in need of your assistance and a world ready to be saved." She turned the key and the door swung open. "Gentlemen, the choice is yours."

They didn't even need to think about it. They exited the cell and shook her hand one by one. She handed the short one a piece of paper.

"Here's the address. Get there as soon as you can. I have one more piece of business to complete here first."

The Mages rushed out. Linda finally faced me. She had that glassy look in her eyes as she put the key in the lock.

"Linda, I—"

"What's it going to be?"

The key was in her hand, in the lock, but she hadn't turned it. Not yet.

"Are you really going ahead with this?" I asked.

"With what?"

She was fucking with me: enjoying having all the power.

"Look, I was fine with stopping the Niles Company but—"

"Were you?"

She caught me off guard. Until then, I'd fooled myself into thinking that I'd agreed with some of Hendricks' plan. That the Niles Company needed to be stopped, no matter how much they were helping people, but destroying the city was a step too far.

But I'd been here too long. Alongside the sick and the injured.

The ones who could never find work. The broken families with no hope. Maybe Hendricks was right. Maybe I didn't know how to look at the big picture. Maybe I didn't want to. Maybe I wanted to look up close at all the ugly details.

"No," I admitted. "Not really. I've seen too many people struggle too much."

"You've seen the people here. That's it. You don't know what it's like in the rest of the world."

"You're right. I don't. But I can't help you destroy this city. It's madness."

"This city is madness. You can't see that because you're part of it. I almost let it take me too, until Hendricks reminded me that there's another way. Without Sunder, the rest of the world will have a chance."

"But we can work within it. We can make it better."

"Do you know what I received the other day? A letter from the city telling me to stop the work I was doing because it promoted illegal behavior. They said that it was dangerous. They told me the same shit you told me the first time I met you, but now they've made it law. I understand why you want to hold onto this place. It feeds you and you feed it. But I'm ready to watch it burn."

She said it so straight. So clear. It almost hid the uncertainty underneath.

"Linda, we can find another way. There is—"

"He told me about you. *All* about you."

Shit.

"I . . . I'm sorry. I—"

"I get it. You needed to kill the monster that killed your family. It was personal. Right? More important than politics or morals. I don't blame you for that. I really don't." She pulled the key out of the lock. "But because of what you did, *my* family died. You're my Chimera, Fetch Phillips. I won't kill you, but I don't have to let you out of your cage."

Then, she left.

74

A while later, Bath came back. His face was all scratched up after his introduction to Linda Rosemary. He looked around at the state of the room, made some notes, and left. I went back to sleep.

"Curious," said a voice from beyond the bars. I sat up to see the square jaw and unflinching stare of Thurston Niles. "They left you behind. I didn't expect that."

I didn't bother to stand.

"Yep."

"How's that job coming along? The one where you were supposed to find my brother's killer. The one I paid you in advance for."

"I told you, I don't work for Humans."

"You don't work for anyone. Simms and Thatch have cut you loose. Your rebel buddies don't want you tagging along either. What happened? It was just starting to get exciting."

Thurston was used to being untouchable. I'd already seen how folks would fawn over him without question just because he liked to throw his money around. Maybe that's why he was so impressed that I'd dared to break his nose.

"The last time I offered you friendship, you scoffed at it," he said. "Perhaps you've taken the time to reconsider."

He'd seemed so benign when we'd met at his house: a grieving brother picking up the pieces. Now, I could see what Hendricks was so afraid of. Thurston wore his ego like a gold breastplate. His air of superiority reeked like cheap perfume.

No. This man should never be given the reins to my city. But I'd screwed up any chance to stop him.

"I'm fine on my own, thanks. It's safe in here. Better than

being out on the streets when everyone starts carrying your pistols on their belt."

He snickered.

"You have a point, but at least they'll be prepared if more radicals like Deamar show up." He stepped right up to the bars. "What's his plan?"

I shrugged. "I don't know."

"Yes, you do. Why would you run around killing Dragons and breaking into factories if you didn't?"

"Maybe that's why I went with him; to find out what his plan was."

"Maybe you're full of shit."

"Maybe you've been feeding it to me."

"Enough. I like you, Mr Phillips. I've always said so. But my time is precious. Tell me what Deamar wants and we can start working together. For real, this time. No more lies."

I couldn't help but smile.

A Human wanted me to betray the head of the Opus and side with them. *Again.*

It was the most impossible thing I'd ever heard. He could pull out my teeth and cut off my toes but there was no way in the world that I would let it happen. That mistake had been hammered into my head like a steel beam. Every single day for six years, I'd been regretting one thing, and Thurston thought he could get me to make the exact same mistake by *asking nicely?* It was the funniest fucking thing I'd ever heard.

"That's gonna be a no from me, Niles. Thanks for stopping by."

A different kind of man would have got angry. Not Niles. Anger, guilt, rent and taxes were for other people to worry about.

"If you change your mind and want to contact me," he said, "I'll let the Corporal know that he should put you through."

"Don't spend your nights sitting by the phone on my account, Thurston. There are plenty of other fish in the sea."

He gave a little laugh.

"If only you knew how small your pond really is, Mr Phillips, it might make you reconsider your attitude to your own kind. Whether you want to acknowledge it or not, Humans have owned this city from long before you ever saw my face. You are a Human. One of the most Human men I've ever met. Maybe one day, you'll take a walk outside Sunder and see what life is like without men like me around to keep you safe."

He left, and I decided right then and there that, despite his warnings, my time in Sunder was through. I'd had enough. I'd done enough. A war was about to be fought here and I had no interest in seeing either side come out on top.

Some mistakes you can't make twice. I could never hand over information about Hendricks to a man like Thurston Niles. No matter what the stakes were. Eliah was yoked with a similar history himself. When I was just a child, he'd protected a monster that went on to kill my family. When he heard stories about me, years later, he'd sought me out. He took care of me and taught me. Then *I* went wild. I turned against him. I became his new monster. But he let me go, and that mistake was even bigger than the first one.

Sunder was his monster now: a wild, self-serving beast, the likes of which the world had never seen. Of course he had to stop it. History had showed him what happens if he lets creatures like us go free.

And why would I stand in his way? I was done with Sunder. Without Amari, what was the point? If the cops ever let me out, I'd go home, grab my meager possessions and leave town. Hendricks could flatten it to the ground or Thurston could turn it into his fortress, it wasn't my fight. Not anymore. I closed my eyes on all of it.

The next morning, the explosions started.

75

The first one went off around sunrise, then there were two others throughout the day. Voices came and went, talking excitedly in the next room. I couldn't hear what they were saying but cops all speak at the same pitch when they're scared: trying to hide their panic by deepening their voices and raising the volume.

I closed my eyes and tried to enjoy the fact that it was no longer any of my business.

"Thurston was expecting you to call by now. I can't tell if he's impressed or pissed that you haven't."

Simms was standing outside my cell.

"So, you're in his pocket now too, Detective. It must be getting crowded in there."

"No. I'm really not." Simms stepped right up the bars. "I don't like what he's doing to this city but I know how to pick my battles. Tippity and Rosemary are wreaking havoc: sabotage, arson, theft. We need to stop them. Now. I'll worry about Thurston later."

"Nice try, Simms, but I know how this works. You convince me to blab to you, then you blab to Thurston, right? Is he out there right now, listening in?"

"No." She took a key out of her pocket, put it in the lock, and turned it. "I know you well enough to know that you won't tell me anything, so I'm not asking."

She handed me my coat: the fur-lined Opus uniform that I hadn't seen in weeks. It felt good to have it back over my shoulders.

"You came all the way down here to set me free?"

"I was coming down here to recruit the guards on duty, but I found it in my heart to let you out at the same time. Don't make me regret it."

"Recruit them for what?"

"The battle. Cops are dying out there, Fetch. We need every officer working together. Any help we can get. I don't know what to do and I don't know who I can trust."

I'd never seen her like this. She actually looked scared. What could be happening that would make her so terrified?

Another huge explosion went off in the distance. I could smell smoke. People were shouting.

"Simms, what the hell is happening?"

76

We came out onto the street and the burning smell got stronger. Black towers of smoke spiraled up to the clouds. Simms, Bath and I were the only ones outside. The Detective barked her orders to the Corporal.

"Take the eastern route to the station and grab any officers on Grove, Tar and near the Piazza. I'm swinging west. We meet in half an hour."

Bath nodded and obediently jogged away.

"Somehow Tippity got more of that Fae stuff," said Simms. "They've got themselves a whole arsenal of elemental spells."

Hendricks had used Amari's power to free Tippity because, at the time, it was all he'd had. One Fae soul and one glass orb. But he'd used them to free the man who would be able to make more. Tippity must have taken Hendricks back to the church. Maybe Linda too. All of them together, harvesting the power of every Fae body they could find.

It was freezing outside the jail. I put my hands in my pockets, then pulled them out fast. One of my fingers was bleeding. I reached back in and carefully pulled out the leather package that contained the shattered pieces of Unicorn horn.

"It all kicked off a couple of hours ago," Simms continued. "Those Mages have become Deamar's soldiers, but they're not the only ones. More followers have joined his cause. We don't know how many of them are out there or what they're planning but they're targeting any place where the Niles Company does business."

I walked up the street, away from Simms. Away from it all.

"Come on, Fetch! Help us! You shouldn't be out here on your own!"

I didn't look back. It wasn't my battle. It wasn't my city. Not anymore.

There was just one last errand I needed to do first.

I turned off Eleventh Street on Parro Avenue and saw that the whole area was deserted. The playground was always packed with kids from afternoon to sundown, but everyone was hidden away inside. Then, two figures stumbled out from behind a hedge. It was a couple of teenagers. A boy and a girl. They had debris in their hair and dirt all over their clothes. She was crying. He looked more lost than anyone I'd ever seen.

They must have been bystanders caught too close to one of Tippity's spells. The young man looked at me like he wanted my help but I had nothing to offer them. Not even any good advice. I was about to walk on when a door opened across the street and two pale faces peered out.

"Get in here!"

It looked like a mother and daughter. Satyrs, I think.

"It's not safe!" said the eldest. The couple held each other's hands as they ran for cover, thankful, at the very least, for someone to tell them what to do.

They went inside, but the youngest kept looking at me.

"Come on!"

She waved her hand, beckoning me in.

"Izzy," chided the mother, under her breath. She was obviously a better judge of character than her daughter. But Izzy gave her one of those looks that only bold little girls can give and the mother reluctantly kept the door open.

"Are you coming?" she asked me.

I just stood there. For a moment, I thought that snow was falling again, but it was ash. Drifting in from some fire a few streets away.

"No," I said. "But thank you."

I kept on walking.

77

Warren had given me his home address months ago and I still had it in my wallet. It was a cute little terrace house on the north-east side of the city, a couple of blocks away from Sir William Kingsley Drive. I knocked on the door and a Gnomish woman answered.

"Sorry to disturb you. Is Warren around?"

She was a pudgy little thing. A brown apron was wrapped around her waist and she made one of those expressions that you can only pull off when you have cheeks like ripe tomatoes: neither a smile nor a frown, just a way of pulling your entire face into itself.

"No, he is not," she said. "I am afraid he has passed away."

What?

You ever suddenly, shockingly, find yourself in the present moment? Drop right in to right now? And all it does is highlight the fact that you spend every other moment somewhere else.

There I was. Standing on a porch outside of a red-brick terrace house that I'd been invited to many times. I'd never been there before. Not once. There was a woman in front of me. She was dressed in black. This was Warren's wife. He'd mentioned his wife to me. Many times. I'd never met her. Never even asked about her. And here she was.

"I'm sorry," I said, and I turned and walked back down the steps.

"Are you Fetch?"

She had a warm voice. You know how, when you're a kid, in every group of friends there's one Mum who's the best? Well, this woman would always be that Mum.

"Yes."

I looked back and she made another one of those expressions, right on the midpoint between a smile and a cry.

"I have been trying to call you," she said.

"Oh. Sorry." Afternoon sunlight was hitting the roof and melting the snow. Water dripped down between us like a beaded curtain. "Why?"

"Because we wanted you at the funeral. With all his other friends. I am so sorry you missed it."

I tried to think of something to say but it all sounded so obvious. That I was sorry? Of course I was sorry. That I would have been there? Of course I would have been there.

Wouldn't I?

"Do you want to come inside?" she asked.

"Yes. Yes please."

It was cozy. There weren't many rooms in the house but they were all dressed with an attention to detail. I was sitting in a green, doily-draped armchair that cuddled me like a drunk aunt. My host's name was Hildra and she sat on a gnarled wooden chair that didn't match any other furniture in the room. We were surrounded by handmade picture frames filled with paintings of babies, and little porcelain figures in the shapes of cats and cottages.

You could have sculpted Hildra out of apples: all cheeks, eyes, chins, chest and tummy. The black scarf of mourning wrapped around her head only accentuated the roundness of her face. Even her frown was a kind of smile.

We were each holding a little crystal glass of her homemade brandy and she was staring at me in a way that made me uncomfortable.

"When did he . . . when did it happen?"

"Last week. It was his heart, in the end. Working too hard to keep his body going. You know Warren, he was never one to slow down." Did I know Warren? I guess so. A little. "I tried calling your office but you never picked up. I sent you a telegram too."

"I'm sorry. I haven't been home in a while. Got myself into some trouble."

"Warren said that about you. Always up to mischief. He said that the first time he saw you, you were being slapped around by a Cyclops and it only got worse after that."

She was right. The next time I was shot by a crossbow. The time after that, Warren found me tied up in a chair in my office.

"Warren saved my skin a few times," I said.

"Well then, you had best be more careful from now on." I took a sip of my brandy. Hildra threw hers back and grabbed the bottle. "Don't bother savoring this stuff. I make it in the backyard, for heaven's sake. Drink up."

I took the shot and she filled our glasses.

"Have you heard about what the Niles Company is doing?" I asked. "How they're opening up a new power plant?"

"Oh, I have heard the rumors. I will believe it when I see it."

"I've already seen it. Looks like we'll have fires again. Enough energy to get that ceramic factory working, I bet. Do you still own it?"

She nodded.

"Someone from that company came to his funeral and tried to buy up all his businesses. I will not insult you by repeating what I said to him."

"Good. Hold onto it."

"You really think they will do what they are saying?"

"They've got a better shot than I ever would've imagined."

The only problem was Hendricks. And Linda and Tippity and those Mages and whoever else they'd talked into joining their side. Would they be any kind of match for Thurston's pistols? I didn't want to be around to find out, and I didn't want Hildra to be around either.

"You should get out of town for a while. There are some folks who hate the Niles Company even more than you do, and they're kicking up a fuss. The whole city is in danger. Lay low for a while and come back when it's over."

She gave me another one of those unreadable smile/frowns.

"Mr Phillips, this is my home. This is *our* home. Even if I wanted to leave, I am older than my husband. My body is just as sick as his was. I will be in this city till the end."

I took the bundle of leather out of my pocket and put it on the table next to the bottle of brandy.

"I came here because I wanted to bring this to your husband. I'm sorry I was too late."

"What is it?"

She unwrapped the package, revealing the dull purple shards of glass.

"Unicorn horn. I know it seems ridiculous and I don't know if it will do you any good, but it was Warren's idea, not mine. Apparently Rick Tippity thought he could make it into some kind of healing potion. Give it a go, if you want. I hope it helps."

Hildia sat back. She looked shocked for the first time. So quiet. Not even smiling. Her little Cupid's bow of a mouth was hanging open.

I prepared myself for the onslaught. Waited for her to scream. To ask me why I hadn't brought it to her weeks ago when there was still time to save her husband. To give him a chance. I was ready to be berated. I deserved it.

Then, she started laughing. Not just laughing. Howling. Whooping and wheezing, with tears streaming down her cheeks. Pointing at me and slapping her fat thighs with her hands. I just sat there, pale-faced, wondering where I'd missed the joke.

"He knew it! He KNEW IT!" Laughter shook her body like a carriage on a rocky road. "Warren said it all along. You ARE looking for magic." She pointed a chubby finger right in my face. "Look how serious you're trying to be. You are just like he said you were. So grim. Always frowning. But really," she prodded me in the chest, "you are a dreamer." Her laugh turned into a cough and she had to wash it down with more brandy.

"Look, Hildra, I just knew he was looking for it. I'm not saying that I think it'll do anything but—"

She snorted, and I thought brandy was about to come out of her nose.

"You are so grumpy! Why does it make you angry if I think that you are looking for magic?"

"Because I'm not looking for magic."

"WELL, WHY NOT?" The laughter stopped. The porcelain figures rattled on the shelves "What else are you going to do, Mr Fetch Phillips? Keep half-assing your way around town, pretending to try to make things better?"

"Look, I don't know what Warren told you about me."

"He told me enough. You think you want to die? My husband did not have a choice. But right till the end, he never stopped working to make my life better. His friends' lives better. And he was sick. You are not."

"That means I'm supposed to try to do something ridiculous?"

"You think it is ridiculous to fight for something better? You don't know how ridiculous you look right now. Walking around all long-faced, like the world is on your back, and all that time you've been carrying a miracle in your pocket." She took a small shard from the pile and put it on the table, then she wrapped up the rest in the leather bundle. "Maybe this is nothing but glass. Maybe the magic is gone and everybody in the world will soon be dead. But what if there is a way to change it and you don't try because you are worried about looking stupid?"

"There are better men then me to try and do that."

"Of course there are. Perhaps you can help them. Or maybe you try and you fail and it does not make any difference to anyone. So what?" She held out the leather-wrapped bundle. "I am going to take my piece of this and see what can be done for me. You

keep the rest. Warren would not have wasted it if he was alive.
Tell me you won't waste it either."

I put the bundle back in my pocket.

"I won't."

I reached out for my brandy but Hildra pulled it away.

"Did you not just tell me to leave town because something
bad is going to happen?"

I swallowed. "Yes."

"Can you do something about it?"

"I don't know."

"Can you try?"

"Well . . . yes."

"Then why the hell wouldn't you?"

Fifteen minutes later, I was back in the Gilded Cemetery. I crossed
the grounds, entered the crypt and pushed back the lid of the
coffin.

It was still there. My machine. With one last canister of dust
waiting to be fired.

I put the pistol in its holster and marched off to war.

78

The day disappeared and another winter night rolled in and smothered the city. The air was full of smoke that carried panicked voices from one street to the next. Eyes peered out from behind curtains wondering whether it was safest to stay inside or be out in the elements where they could get answers about what was going on.

The police station was surrounded: timid-looking street cops, status-loving detectives and one ham-faced captain crumbling under the pressure. I climbed the steps, catching snippets of conversation. Business owners were demanding protection. Community leaders were gathering information to take back to their neighborhoods. It was nothing compared to the chaos inside.

I came through the doors just ahead of an errand boy who had returned with a report. A bunch of senior officers gathered around him to get an update on the state of things around the city. None of the news sounded good: a broken building here, an out-of-control fire there. Small teams were dispatched to assist civilians or to gather more precise information. There seemed to be no real understanding of what was happening and no idea of how to get things under control.

I wasn't the only one who thought so. One of the charcoal suits was screaming at Simms, demanding that police be sent to protect a particularly valuable Niles Company asset. I was trying to get her attention when a heavy hand grabbed me by the shoulder and spun me around.

"You bastard!"

I tried to back away. Usually, when people grabbed me and called me a bastard, a fist was soon to follow. But the arms went

around my back and pulled me in close, giving me a full inha-
lation of Sergeant Richie Kites's famous bad breath.

"Somebody just blew up the jail. I thought you were still in
it. How did you get out?"

"Early release for good behavior."

"Bullshit."

"Simms let me out."

"I liked your first answer better."

I gestured over to the charcoal suit that was screaming at
Simms.

"Why are the Niles Company goons coming to you for help?
Don't they have enough weapons of their own?"

"What weapons?"

"The factory up in Brisak Reserve is full of killing machines.
Hundreds of them."

"That must be why Tippity targeted it first. The whole building
is covered with ice."

"Shit."

"Yeah."

That would even the odds. Some of the Niles men were carrying
pistols already, but nobody knew how many followers Hendricks
had been able to recruit.

"What else have they done?" I asked.

"Destroyed a few buildings. Killed a couple of workers. Not
sure what their plan is, other than tearing things apart."

"From the way Hendricks was talking, that *is* their plan." I
got a strange look from Richie and realized that it was time to
fill him in on a few things. "I'll try and tell it to you quick."

We got out of earshot of the other cops and I did my best to
cram as much information into a couple of minutes. Richie and
I had met when we were Shepherds together. He knew Hendricks.
Knew who he used to be, anyway. But he'd been in Sunder since
the Coda and needed less convincing than me to decide which
side to fight on.

"But even if he wants to, how can he destroy a whole city?" he asked. "You said yourself that those Faery spells don't pack enough punch."

"I don't know. I just know he's going to try."

Simms broke away from the suit and came over to us.

"Sounds like the fight is moving downtown."

"To the stadium," I said.

"How did you know that?"

"Because Niles has a huge operation there. He's taken over the tunnels that lead down to the fire pits."

"Why?"

It still sounded ridiculous.

"Because the fires are still there. Always have been. Niles wants to claim the energy and sell it back to us. Tippity will do whatever he can to stop him, including bringing the whole city to its knees." I saw the questions line up inside their minds but we didn't have time for me to answer them. "If they've taken the fight to the stadium, we need to get down there. But we need a way to stand up against Tippity's magic, and police batons aren't going to cut it."

"We don't have anything else," said Richie.

"Actually, you do. Where did you put all the stuff you confiscated from Tippity's pharmacy?"

Simms looked dubious as hell. I didn't blame her.

"Out back."

"Take me there now."

The evidence room was an outlaw's dream. Row upon row of illegal contraband: barbed crossbow bolts and poison arrows, drawers full of blades and blackjacks, a cupboard full of counterfeit currency and boxes of secret documents just begging to be used as blackmail.

Tippity's possessions had been pushed into the corner between a portable cannon and an anatomically correct Centaur sex doll. Simms took the lids off three wooden crates.

"This is most of it. The Fae bodies went to the morgue and some of the more potent medicines went . . . missing on the way back."

Inside, there were a few familiar objects: glass vessels of unlabeled liquid, petri dishes, soaps, eye-droppers and gloves.

"Oh, the . . . things aren't here either," said Simms. "The orbs from inside the Fae. Like that one you gave me. We buried them. I'm sorry, you said to look after them and—"

"No. That's good. I wouldn't use them anyway."

I moved through the boxes till I found what I was looking for: a sturdy container full of tiny glass balls, each of them filled with a dash of pink liquid.

I held one of them up to the light.

"Isn't that just acid?" asked Richie. "I thought you needed something from the Fae to make it work."

"Yeah, but I have something else." I searched through the crates but I couldn't find any of Tippity's little pouches. "We just need to try a little experiment."

"An experiment? Fetch, I've got officers in real danger out there right now. I don't have time to be messing around."

I kicked off my boot and took off my sock. After my unwashed days in prison, it even smelled bad to me. I couldn't imagine how it must have smelled to Richie and Simms. They stepped back as I dropped the orb inside.

Then I took the leather bundle out of my pocket, laid it on the floor and unfurled it. The dull shards of Unicorn glass didn't look too impressive.

"What's that?" asked Richie.

I picked up a piece the size of a pea. It seemed too small, so I took one that was the size and shape of an almond, slid it into the sock beside the orb and stood up with the sock dangling from my clenched fist.

"Shouldn't we go outside?" said Richie.

"We don't have time for this!" growled Simms.

That sounded like my cue.

I hurled the sweaty sock at a couple of suits of armor hanging on the far wall. The sock hit the metal with a soft and unimpressive sound, and fell to the floor. As it hit the ground, I heard the orb smash.

Nothing.

"Shit." I kicked the crate. "I thought—"

WHOOOMP.

My first thought was that Richie had punched me. It was like he'd planted one of his fat fists in the center of my chest. But I wasn't the only one falling backwards. All three of us went flying into the air as the sock transformed into a pulsing purple void. Savage wind blew back my hair and burned my eyes. My ears crackled like full of foam. Every part of my body was vibrating, but it wasn't painful. It was strangely pleasant. Like being underwater without worrying about ever being able to breathe.

I couldn't stand up. I couldn't move at all. Gravity pushed me down and the ground felt like it was gripping my back. My chest, for the first time in years, didn't hurt at all. I was happy to lie there, perfectly still, for as long as anyone would let me.

Did seconds go by, or minutes? It didn't matter. At some point, the void faded away and I rolled my head to see Simms and Richie blinking themselves out of a similar daze.

Simms took a nice, deep breath and found her voice first.

"Richie, get as many pairs of socks as you can find."

79

Richie was in no state to gather the supplies himself, but the explosion alerted a whole bunch of corporals who came in and took orders from the Reptilian detective who was lying on the floor. They helped Simms, Richie and me into the mess hall and sat us down on an old couch while we tried to wipe the dozy smiles off our faces. It was like I'd chewed a whole pack of Clayfields after a pint of night-time tea and a good lay.

This wasn't like being hit by one of Tippity's spells, where some essential element smacked you in the face. This was like something drained all the effort out of your body and turned you into a cloud.

I rolled my head to the side. Richie was grinning like a circus clown.

"Did you say *Unicorn?*" he asked.

"Yeah. Found one on the road from Aaron Valley."

"And you cracked open its head like one of those Faeries?"

"No. This is . . . different."

"How?"

Luckily, Simms jumped in to save me. Her sibilance was even more pronounced than usual.

"The story goes that when the horses ate the apples from the sacred tree, a piece of pure magic attached itself to their minds. This isn't like the Faeries at all. This is more like unlocking a piece of the river itself."

Richie rolled his head back and his eyes went wide.

"Shiiiiiit," he said. And we all laughed.

It took twenty minutes for the effect to wear off. Then, slowly, that uncomfortable pain in my chest came back and we remembered that there was a war to fight. We helped each other to our feet, filled ourselves with bad cop-shop coffee, and soon the adrenaline was back in our blood.

It was a still, windless night and I was in an army again. Last time, it had been a band of Humans heading off to screw up the world. Now, I was side by side with the Sunder City police force: Ogres, Dwarves, Gnomes, Reptilia and more, all with colorful socks dangling from our fingers. Each sock contained one of Tippity's orbs of acid beside a sprinkling of Unicorn horn. We tested the amount once more before we left, and decided that a pinch was plenty.

I had the machine against my ribs, and my knife and knuckles in my hands. Simms had a crossbow. Richie had his fists. The civilians were all inside, hiding away while we marched south towards the sound of explosions.

We passed an area that was on fire. The body of a Gnome dressed in Niles Company uniform was smoldering on the road.

"Put him out," Simms said to a young cop who was relieved to have a reason to stay behind. The next anomaly in our path was a Human policeman, running towards us. He wasn't getting far, though. His whole body was surrounded by a layer of ice that was thickest at the bottom, like it had grown up from the earth, then blossomed out of his skin in sharp spikes. Another couple of cops peeled off from the pack to see what they could do to help.

The electric lights of the stadium came into view and the battlefield opened up before us. Workers were scrambling for cover behind machinery and piles of dirt, as a recently conjured fireball ripped through a pallet of wooden planks.

"Take down any agitators fighting on Tippity's side," ordered Simms. "That's anyone using magic that isn't one of us. The Niles Company isn't outside the law, either. Keep your eyes open. Remember everything that happens. There will be arrests and there will be a reckoning. We are not losing the city tonight!"

We fanned out around the stadium that wasn't really a stadium anymore. The bleachers were still there but the rest of the field had become a construction site. Mostly, it was messy piles of wood and mounds of excavated dirt, but dotted throughout the grounds were illuminated tents. The tents were built over holes in the earth that must have been the tunnels that led down below.

NC employees stood around those tents en masse. So, that was the game. Hendricks and his troops were trying to get under the city while those working for Niles were trying to keep them out. Our job was to subdue the lot of them.

I moved to the right with a half-dozen of Sunder City's finest. A few meters ahead, two Mages crossed our path.

The straw-haired cop at my side looked up at me like I was supposed to be giving him orders.

I nodded emphatically (which was all that I could think to do) and the cop took it as encouragement.

"Stop right there!" he yelled. "This is the police!"

The Mages turned, saw our squad, and something close to glee ran up their faces. They were excited to have a chance to put their new skill to use. They reached into their cloaks.

"I said stop!"

One of the other cops wasn't going to wait. She pelted her orange sock and it hit a Mage in the chest. The orb cracked on impact and before it hit the ground, the whole thing exploded into purple light. Well, not light, exactly. The opposite of light, but the opposite of dark too. And not really purple either. There was the idea of purple in there somewhere, but also yellow and fear and starshine. But not real stars, more like the stars you see when you get hit on the head.

One of the Mages hit the ground with an audible thump. The other was flung into the side of a big wooden crate. He stuck there, like he was covered with glue. They were both still alive, just pressed down with magical gravity and lulled into a non-violent state.

Carefully, the cops crept forward and put the Mages in cuffs while I kept moving. There were flashes of colored light shooting up in the air, and explosions rattling all around. I kept myself up against pallets of bricks and timber, catching glimpses of the agitators that moved around us. They weren't the only ones. Niles Company workers were ready to defend their new workplace with metal bars, shovels, and whatever offcuts could be turned into weapons.

I snuck under the bleachers and looked for an opening that would lead me down. Peering out from between the seats, I watched a clash between workers, cops and rebels that was too messy to tell who was winning. I moved past, hoping to skirt around the minions and find the leaders instead.

Footsteps. I heard them just in time. When I spun around, a Dwarf with a clawed hammer was swinging at my head. All the cops were in uniform but I was back in my modified Opus coat. To him, I must have looked like another one of Eliah's mad followers. I raised my hands and backed away, hoping I'd have a chance to explain that I wasn't here to hurt him. Then there was a flash of fire from a battle beside us, and the light caught both our faces.

"You fookin' arse!"

It was the steel worker Dwarf from The Ditch. Clangor. The one who took it real personal that I'd got him kicked out of his riverside home. It no longer mattered that I didn't want to fight him, because he'd been waiting for an excuse to hurt me for months.

"I knew you were an evil piece of shite."

He kept swinging and I stepped back, protecting the sock in my hand even more than my body.

I'd fought plenty of people in my time, but they were mostly folks my size. It's not easy to avoid attacks when they all come so low. The hammer connected with my hip and I stumbled back into more of those training dummies, like the one that I'd used to test the machine. I held one of the sacks between me and my attacker and the weapon lodged in the stuffing. I pushed the dummy into the Dwarf's face so that he lost his balance and landed on his back, then I kicked the hammer from his hand and pinned him with my knee.

"You arse!"

He didn't have a chance of moving me but I felt no satisfaction in winning the fight. His pride was so hurt, I felt more like giving him a hug than gloating. But there was no time for that. I jumped up and kept moving, knowing that his little legs were too slow to follow me.

When I came out into the open, the first thing I saw was Richie dragging a Mage through the wet grass, struggling to get the cuffs on him. It was good to see Kites in action again. The brute had been behind a desk too long. The mage was swatting at him but I could tell the old Shepherd was enjoying himself.

Behind him, a figure stepped out from the shadows. He'd cleaned himself up, but you'd need a lifetime of scrubbing to wipe that smug look off his face. Rick Tippity threw one of his pouches in a long arc, right to where Richie was standing. I ran towards it. Desperately. Hopelessly.

"Richie! Look out!"

He turned to face me, and the incoming projectile shattered on the ground behind him. Fire burst out of it, but not like the last time. This wasn't the little eyebrow-burning flash I'd seen before. It was a cyclone: an unruly, twisting spiral with flames that fanned out in all directions and burned up into the night sky.

Richie was blown towards me and landed face down in the dirt. The flames kept roaring behind him, shooting out from the place where the pouch had landed. It was so fierce that I couldn't run to him without stepping into the heat myself.

Richie crawled forward. His uniform was burning.

As soon as he was far enough from the source, I ran in and grabbed his arms. Flames licked my face, but only in flashes. The spell was finally subsiding. I dragged Richie back behind a parked truck and used a piece of canvas to pat out the embers on his shoulders and ass. Parts of his clothes had burned right through to the skin but we wouldn't know how bad it was till he got to the medical center.

"I thought you said it was just light and color," he grunted.

"Tippity must have updated his recipe."

I wasn't sure how. He said that different Fae would produce different levels of power, but this seemed like something else entirely.

I looked back at the smoldering patch of burned grass, trying to guess how Tippity had upgraded his power, when I noticed that all the canvas was flapping in the wind. There hadn't even been a breeze a minute ago but now it was blowing a gale. I took a deep breath, and the smoggy Sunder air now smelled fresh as a mountaintop.

Air Sprite. There hadn't just been a fire orb inside that pouch: an Air Sprite's essence had been put in there too. With the magical wind fanning the flames, Tippity had significantly upgraded his firepower. I wondered if that was his idea or Eliah's.

"Stay here," I told Richie. "I'll take care of the Warlock and we'll get you some help."

He grunted. "Shut your face, Fetch. I'm not done yet."

"Half your ass is hanging out!"

"That's only a problem for whoever's behind me."

We jumped up. Richie chased after another mad Dwarf and I ran towards the spot where Tippity had poked his head.

I came around the corner and found him facing the other way, approaching a couple of young cops who were timidly telling him to stand down. But he was high on power and had a dozen leather pouches hanging from his belt.

I wrapped the brass around my knuckles. The ground was damp. He wouldn't hear me. Just a couple of ribs and he'd be done for. Tippity loved to dish it out but he still hadn't learned to take the pain.

I cocked my elbow, lowered my stance, and was breaking into a sprint when the world went white.

CRACK!

Thunder rolled out around me. I was crackling. I couldn't unclench my fist or my teeth. My eyes were closed but everything was so bright. Red flashes lit up the capillaries in my eyelids. I felt the ground hit my knees and then my shoulder, and then the side of my head.

A Lightning Sprite. Tippity had diversified. Another rare creature gone to nothing just so he could feel a little magic again.

But Tippity hadn't made that attack. Someone else had been behind me. Someone who was laughing up a storm as mighty as the spell they'd just thrown at my back.

I forced my eyes open but there were so many spots in my vision I couldn't make anything out. My whole nervous system was vibrating and my bones were chattering against my joints.

Then, a voice.

"I warned you, young man! Look at me now!"

Wentworth.

My droopy nosed, drunken Wizard friend from The Ditch was reclaiming the magic that had eluded him since the Coda. His manic laughter rained down from above. I blinked the sparks from my eyes and saw that he was standing up on the same lantern that I'd been hiding in when Warren and I first met Linda.

I sat up but I couldn't even uncurl my fingers. Wentworth hollered a murderous scream and held more pouches up over his head.

"Do you feel that? We're back where we belong!"

BANG!

The unmistakable sound of a pistol and the unmistakable sight of a lead bullet going through Wentworth's brain. A glistening spray of blood filled the night sky as he fell backwards off the pole.

He dropped slowly, as if his old body was made from dry grass and cotton. When he hit the ground, it was a different story. I don't know how many pouches he had on him but they all went off at once. The lightning hadn't left my body, but I had just enough control to roll over and turn my back on the explosion. It hit me like the head of a bucking bull. Wind, lightning, fire, ice and whatever the hell else Wentworth had stuffed into his britches all went up in a big kaboom.

The Niles Company asshole in the charcoal suit who was responsible for the shot barely had time to smile before he was tackled by Simms who rolled him onto his stomach and put the cuffs on him.

I couldn't tell if I was cold or hot. I didn't know whether I'd saved myself or if my back had been incinerated or frozen or turned into toadstools. Tippity and his followers were crawling under the bleachers, throwing out pouches to give them some space. Feet rushed all around me: the boots of coppers and mineworkers stomping through the old stadium grounds. I eased myself up to standing and reached trembling fingers around my back. It was sooty and damaged but no blood. My coat had saved me.

I felt like I was getting up from a year-long nap in the sun. I was rattled to my bones. Cooked from the inside out. But I moved along with everyone else. I had to. Because I wanted to be the one to take Tippity down myself.

The men in NC uniforms around me were charging forward. Maybe they were all hoping for the same thing I was. To take down the criminal who I'd made public enemy number one. But there were so many of them. Tippity had chosen the busiest Niles Company location for his battle. Of course he had. He wanted to make a statement. He wanted to show everyone how powerful he was.

But Tippity wasn't the real villain, was he?

I stopped.

What was being accomplished here, other than Tippity's show of power? Sabotage, of course. If the war was just against the

Niles Company then this would make sense. But Hendricks had bigger plans, and he wasn't anywhere to be seen.

This was a distraction. A decoy to keep us fighting each other while he went for something bigger.

But what?

The warehouse in Brisak Reserve was covered in ice, and stealing more pistols didn't seem like Eliah's style. Not now. He needed to do real damage.

The kind of damage you can do with a storage house full of explosive desert dust.

Shit.

Pouches of every magical combination came flying out from the cracks in the bleachers. Charcoal suits fired back with their machines. Workers threw bricks and tools. Simms, having subdued Wentworth's killer, was making her way around the stadium, looking for a way to get under the seats without being set on fire.

Some feeling had come back into my fists and all they wanted to do was punch Tippity's lights out. That would feel good. It would be easy, compared to the alternative. But this wasn't my fight. Not really. My fight was with my old friend.

I turned away from the fireworks, faced the shadows, and ran.

80

Hundreds of crates of exploding desert dust, each containing enough power to blow up a city block. Forget Tippity's spells, they were nothing compared to what Niles had been hiding in his warehouse. Last time Hendricks was there, he'd just been shot and was close to passing out, but that wouldn't have stopped him from seeing the potential prize we'd stumbled upon.

Those heavy doors had been wrenched open by force, all bent back and twisted up on their hinges, but it was quieter here than at the stadium. No cops. No suits standing guard.

I'd lost my knife but I still had my knuckles. I kept low, stretching my jaw and my joints to release the tension brought in by the electric shock. I heard a woman's voice but I couldn't make out what she was saying. I stood just outside, listened, and heard metal moving against metal: they were closing the elevator door. I ran inside.

Hendricks was in the cage, surrounded by crates. Linda Rosemary was beside him.

My old friend's eyes met mine. There was none of that joyful familiarity now. Not even frustration or disappointment. Just boredom, or something like it. He said something to Linda. I couldn't hear what it was from the other end of the warehouse, but she stepped out of the elevator and closed the door behind her.

Hendricks pulled the chain and the cage lowered out of sight, leaving Linda behind to stop me following him. Her gloves were off, literally, and it turned out that not all of the animal had left her when the magic did. Both of her arms were covered with mottled black hair. Her nails looked longer without the gloves on and were still as sharp as they'd ever been.

I walked to the center of the room. She waited where she was.
"You should have stayed in your cell," she said.
"And wait for the ground to crumble beneath my feet? How much dust did Hendricks take down there?"
"Enough."
She took her first step towards me and kept coming.
"Linda, this isn't right."
"Don't you dare tell me what's right, Soldier." She was halfway across the room. "You're the one that wants to hand over the world to the people who fucked it up."
She slapped me across the face. That might sound like mercy, but a fist would have kept her nails off my skin. A split-second after she whacked me, I heard the wet sound of my blood hitting the floor.
I didn't hit back.
"This time," she said, "a bunch of men on a mountain will not be the ones who decide what happens to me."
She came up under my chin on the next one. That was a rude surprise that knocked my teeth together. I had a sandy feeling in my mouth where a corner of a tooth crumbled away
"You're right." I spat the grit from my tongue. "It wasn't fair. You had no say in what happened to you. So why do the same to the people of this city?"
She didn't want to listen. She wanted me to fight back. But I didn't even defend myself.
"You don't understand!" She closed her furry fist and hit me in my left eye, snapping my head back. There were those stars again. "You don't understand a fucking thing."
"I know." I abandoned my brass knuckles and they clanged against the floor. She noticed the gesture, and it only seemed to make her angrier. "I know I don't . . . I can't, because it didn't hurt me." She kicked me in the chest and I dropped to my knees. "I don't know how to look at this from a distance. So, you tell me what to do."

She raised her hand up high, took a full swing, and brought it down across my face. One of her claws caught my lip, tugged on it for a moment, then pulled straight through, leaving a bloody gash. I drooled a red river onto my chest.

"Linda," my voice was all fucked up from having two bottom lips, "you're smart. Smarter than me. You've seen this city from the outside. You know what it is. But what if we can be better?" She used her left hand for the next hit. It wasn't any easier to take; the Cat was ambidextrous. "We got the fires back. Do you know what that means to people? What it can do?"

She kicked me in the face. More blood on the floor. More sand in my mouth.

"It will give power to the men who shouldn't have it." Was she crying? Was I? "It will stop the rest of the world from finding a way forward. *This* cannot be our new world."

"Then let's find a better one. Tippity's throwing spells out there! The cops are fighting back with bits of Unicorn horn! Doesn't that sound like a new story to you?"

She kicked me in the guts. I tasted bile. Lucky I hadn't eaten anything in days.

"Linda, what if there's a chance?"

"A chance for what?"

It was still so hard to say it. I pushed myself up onto my feet and tried to stop dribbling.

"For the magic to come back."

She looked disgusted, but it stopped her attacks.

"The first day I met you, you told me that it was hopeless."

"And you told me I was wrong. That you could feel it, inside you, waiting to find a way out. I didn't believe you because I don't have it inside me. I don't feel it. But I've seen it. Those fires are still here, right under our feet. Like they always were. Just like you said. So, what else is still here? If you let me stop this, I promise you, I will spend every day searching to find out."

I saw her think about kicking me back down, but she didn't.

"Why you?" she asked.

I shrugged. "Because I can. Because I should. Because I'm telling you I will. I'm not much, but I'm a man of my word."

She glanced back at the cage. Then she leaned over and looked me in my eyes.

"Why do I believe you?"

"Because I mean it, and you know it's possible. But if we bring it all back, and you let these people die here tonight, you'll never forgive yourself. Trust me. Better to regret the things you didn't kill, than regret the things you did."

I saw it die in her. Whatever story she'd told herself to go along with what was happening, it faded away. She unclenched her fists and suddenly looked so tired.

"He won't send the elevator back up," she said. "We'll have to find another way."

I was shaking. My legs were like raw sausages.

"You go find another way down. Be careful, there's a war going on out there."

I stumbled towards the empty cage.

"You're just going to wait here while I do all the work?"

One foot in front of the other, Fetch. Ignore the drops of blood and the way your vision is closing over as your eyelid swells up.

"You might not make it in time," I slurred. "Hendricks knows that Tippity's distraction won't last all night. He'll work fast. I gotta get down there now."

I shook the metal wall of the elevator shaft. It was wire mesh. The holes were just big enough for four fingers or the toe of a boot. When I looked down, a hot wind hit my face and a drop of blood fell down into the endless dark.

"You're going to climb?" she asked.

"Yeah."

I grabbed the thick wire inside the elevator shaft, swung my body around and put my toes in the holes. My fingers were already hurting and it felt like my boots would slip at any moment.

Linda's look didn't inspire confidence.

"Are you sure?" she asked.

I nodded.

"Today's as good a day as any to stop being a prick."

She marched on out and I climbed down into the pits.

81

After a couple of minutes, the fear kicked in.

The darkness from below rose up and covered me. Soon, I couldn't see anything at all. Keeping hold of the wire with my hands was a tough enough job but finding my footholds was even harder. Whenever I found a rhythm, my toes would slip from the edge and I would catch myself on my tired fingers, cutting them on the cage.

Time lost all meaning. Pain followed suit. Life threatened to join them.

The fall would be enough. It was a longer drop than the five measly floors out the Angel door. My fingers were bloody and gnarled but refused to let go. My hands held on. My feet found their place. I waited for them to make a mistake, but they never did. I kept going, further down into the dark.

The air grew hotter as I descended. Sweat mixed into the blood. The world turned orange then red. Finally, my foot reached out for the next bit of wire and hit a flat surface. I was right down on the bottom floor, standing on the roof of the elevator. It was made from more wire mesh, allowing me to see inside. All the crates were still there but they were open and some of them were near empty.

I got on my knees and searched for some way to pull back the mesh and fit myself through. My fingers were useless. My sight was fuzzy. I couldn't even close my mouth because my lips were cut and my jaw was swollen.

If a thimbleful of dust could fire a piece of metal through someone's skull, how much would it take to shatter the city's foundations? Was Hendricks hoping to bring Main Street right down on our heads?

My fingers were too fucked to pry back the metal. So, I jumped. Over and over. I smashed my feet down on the roof of the elevator, time and time again. It made a racket, but I wasn't aiming to sneak up on Hendricks. I just needed to get down there. To see him. To speak to him.

The mesh snapped away from the edge, piece by piece. My body dropped lower with each jump, and then the whole thing caved in. I fell through the ceiling and the broken wire tried to slice me into strips. My jacket copped most of it but I lost some more of my scalp. More scars. If I ever go bald, my head is gonna look like a topographical map.

Damn, it was hot. I got to my feet and stepped out of the cage. The floor was red rock and the world was roaring. There was a tunnel up ahead. I went through it. A few steps around the corner, and there they were. The pits. Great glowing valleys spewing light as if the core of the planet was throwing itself an unending celebration.

The wide path ahead of me split off into a spider's web of naturally formed bridges and outcrops that had been reinforced with steel handrails and steps. I went up to the edge and looked down at the burning abyss.

How impossible it must have seemed to some, way back at the beginning, that the power of those fires could be contained. That by putting a few brains together, they could tame that unruly, godlike energy and use it for everyday things like heating living rooms and toasting bread or making tiny figurines to put up on your mantelpiece. Such ambition. Such hubris. Such a ridiculous thing to happen.

Humans could never have done it on their own. It took all those magical minds working as one. If Sunder fell apart now, we wouldn't be able to put it back together. Not like it was. It was our messy little miracle and I knew that I couldn't let it die.

The fires didn't give off any smoke but the steam and the haze made everything blurry. No wonder the workers covered themselves in Dragon spit before they came down here.

There were mighty columns everywhere: rocky towers that balanced the city on their shoulders. I couldn't see Hendricks but I guessed that he wouldn't stray too far from his supplies in the elevator. I leaned against one of the columns for support and my foot slid over the sandy ground.

No. Not sandy. Dusty.

I was standing in a pile of explosives.

"Oh, Fetch is a boy with a troubled heart,
The things he loves always fall apart."

Hendricks was standing on the path. He held a sack in one hand, weighed down with the same substance that was under my feet. In his other hand, he had a little leather pouch.

"Doesn't know when to stop, 'cause he'll never start."

He was so pale. The scars on his face stood out from his skin like insects crawling over his face. His eyes looked black.

"Eliah. Please."

"Oh, what a lovely boy is Fetch."

The pouch came at me. I jumped back and thought I'd dodged the blast, but I wasn't the real target. The pouch landed right where my feet had been and cracked open. The flames hit the dust, sizzled and exploded. I was thrown backwards, right towards the edge of the cliff.

I rolled over, sliding on the rock. My broken fingernails scraped against the floor until my feet were off the edge. Then my waist. I dug in with bloody fingers, screaming, as the hot air kicked my ass.

I stopped sliding, just in time.

Just in time to see the column crack in two.

The base of the pillar crumbled away and the whole thing came to pieces, dropping onto the path and tumbling over the edge. Where the column had joined the ceiling, there was now a gaping hole.

Water rushed in. Who knows where it came from: city pipes or the Kirra Canal? A muddy stream poured onto the path, rushed over the side, and fell into the fires. Steam sizzled up, turning everything white. I pulled myself back onto the ledge, breathing in the wet and heavy air. I couldn't see Hendricks anymore. I couldn't see much of anything. Maybe he'd crushed himself. Maybe it was all over.

I climbed over the rubble, sore and stumbling. Everything was slippery. Hot and angry. I was sweating. Bloody. Tired.

A shadow through the haze. I moved through the steam, came out the other side, and glimpsed the true scope of where we were.

Without the first column blocking my view, I could see the great clock face of the underground cavern. Each hour was a bridge, and between each bridge there was another endless pit. Hendricks was standing beside a mighty pillar at the very center. The column was even bigger than the one that had just come down. Bigger than of all of them. Two nickel pipes stretched up on either side of him, going right through the roof.

He dropped the sack of dust at his feet, beside two more sacks of the same size. I'd just seen what one small scattering could do to a column of rock. This pile would bring the whole place down on our heads.

"Oh, Fetch is a boy with half a brain,
Lives his life in the eye of a hurricane."

He pulled a pouch from his pocket, but he fumbled it. The glass orb slipped out from the leather and dropped onto the floor. Acid sizzled on the pile of dust. Not enough to light it up. Not yet.

"He'll fuck up the world, then he'll do it again."

Hendricks' shaking fingers dipped into the pouch and pulled out the glowing red globe of a Fire Sprite. I pulled the machine from its holster.

"Oh, what a lovely boy . . . You're not really going to shoot me, are you?"

The red light pulsed in his hand. Fumes sizzled up from the floor where acid and desert dust begged to be ignited. I looked into Hendricks' eyes and everything suddenly seemed so clear.

"Yeah, Eliah, I am. Unless you put that down. Carefully. Right now."

I was waiting for him to laugh at me. Or to drop the orb. Or to say that I was bluffing.

He didn't.

"Yes, boy. I believe you will."

Those eyes. There had always been a hint of mischief in them. A hidden secret. But above all, they had always been full of compassion. For the woman asking for change. For the teenager who talked too much. For his enemies. For his students. For anyone. As much as Hendricks loved to talk, he rarely had to. You could learn about life just by seeing yourself reflected back in that deep, electric green.

Not anymore. Now, those eyes just looked lifeless and empty and dark.

Hendricks had gone cold.

"You have to walk away, Eliah. Linda's not going to help you. Tippity is surrounded by cops. You're on your own."

"But you have all your friends, don't you? The Sunder police. Everyone else on the Niles payroll." He rolled the heart of the Fire Sprite between his fingertips. "I can't let this happen again. This time, I have to stop it."

"And I can't let you." My face was wet from steam and blood. "Eliah, I will take on the world with you. I will follow you anywhere.

I will fight till every bone in my body is broken so that we can make things better. I *will* make things better. But we cannot force the people of this city to pay the price."

He shook his head. I watched his hand, begging him not to let go.

"Eliah, please. Stop."

"I was High Chancellor of the Opus, tasked with protecting all the magical creatures of this world. But I failed. I gave away our secrets, to you, and now it's gone." He sighed, and the firelight danced in the tears that formed in the bottom of those black eyes. "It was supposed to be forever."

"It can be! Hendricks, please. We can fix this. Together. There has to be a way."

He stopped. His shoulders relaxed and the tight grimace on his face melted away.

"You're really going to do it?" he asked. It was a real question this time. Nothing snide or disbelieving about it. No lesson. He really wanted to know. "You're actually going to try to fix it? Even after everything you've seen?"

I saw it. The chance to get through to him. He just needed to believe it.

"Yes. I am. I have to. So please, don't make me do it alone."

He smiled. Warm and a mile wide. Every part of Mr Deamar evaporated away and it was just my old friend, High Chancellor Eliah Hendricks, staring at me with those all-seeing green eyes.

"I told you," he said. "We're all alone."

He lifted up his hand. He didn't have to. He could have just let the orb tumble from his fingers. But he gave me one last chance to make the right choice.

So, I made it.

The machine bellowed out a crack that seemed louder than ever before. Full of triumph, as if its own desires had finally been fulfilled. I dropped it and ran.

Hendricks had a hole in his chest. He stumbled back and smeared a line of blood down the pillar. His fingers unwrapped from around the orb. I jumped to catch it, scraping my body across the floor and letting Hendricks crumple in a heap.

I caught the orb in both hands. Acid burned through my sleeves and I scrambled back, keeping the Faery power as far away from it as possible. I tucked it inside my coat pocket and turned back to Hendricks.

There was blood all down his shirt but it wasn't flowing anymore. His fingers had stopped shaking. His mouth was hanging open. His tongue was lying motionless over his teeth.

I started wailing.

I grabbed his body and pulled it close. I held him, sobbing into his shoulder between painful, heaving breaths of hot air.

Why hadn't I done that when he first came back? The moment I knew it was him, why didn't I just wrap him in my arms and tell him that I missed him? That I'd missed him for every day he'd been gone. Why could I only do it now, when he wasn't even here and it was all too late?

"Fetch!" It was Richie. His burned clothes were falling off him and he was all flushed and wheezing. "Are you okay?"

I wasn't, but I nodded anyway.

"Shit," he said, "is that . . .?"

I nodded again. Richie knelt down and examined the face of his old leader, perhaps looking for anything familiar in the near-Human face of the dead man on the floor. I searched for some way to explain.

"He was—"

Richie looked back over his shoulder. Under the roar of the fires, there were other sounds. Voices and footsteps.

"You gotta get out of here. Tippity is dead. All his men are down. Now Niles is taking the city. They want Deamar but they want you too."

I looked down at my friend. To everyone else, he would just be Mr Deamar, the mad rebel who tried to kill them all.

"Richie, we can't let them have him. We need to look after him and—"

He grabbed me by collar.

"I'll handle it. I promise. But you have to go." There was shouting now. Lights. "They're all coming in from the tunnels under the stadium. We need to sneak you out."

He was so worried. About me. I pushed his hand from my collar and hugged him.

"Thanks, Rich. Don't worry. I know another way."

82

I ran back to the elevator and used the crates as a staircase to climb up through the hole in the roof and past the broken wire. I went out through the room with the metal floors where I'd first looked down and seen the fires, and got into the other cage. I rode it up, went out past the decomposing body of the Dragon and through the newly built tunnel into the foreman's office.

I had no lighter and the sky was full of clouds. I kicked my way out, guessed which way was south, and tried to plot a path from memory, bouncing off walls and tripping over my own toes.

There were screams in the distance. Excited conversations close by. People shouted out of windows and over fences. Radios were turned up loud so neighbors could follow along with the news. I crossed over Main Street with the faint intention of heading east.

There was so much commotion going on that I risked a trip home. Nobody was waiting for me so I packed a few belongings and kept moving. I went past the Steeme household and took anything that seemed valuable: gold cufflinks, an old clock and some expensive-looking silverware. I wanted to lie down so badly. I needed to close my eyes, but I knew that if I did, I'd never get up again. If I stopped moving, all of reality would come tumbling in.

Get out of town. Go east.

At the city limits, I found a cramped carriage that was loading up with travelers. The driver agreed to swap the silverware for a day's ride. Then I went to sleep.

At noon, my spot on the carriage was handed over to someone paying proper fare in coin instead of cutlery. After that, continuing my journey on foot, I understood what Thurston had warned me about.

He was right. Sunder had been keeping me safe.

I'd ventured outside the city since the Coda, but not far. Not far enough to know how the rest of the world now worked.

Sunder had a Human mayor, Human business owners and a Human population who were stronger than most of the creatures around them. Other species avoided picking fights with us for fear that the rest of our kind would have something to say about it afterwards. I'd convinced myself that we were all just trying to move on. That the damage was done. But as soon as I left the local areas that were within Sunder's influence, I found out that the rest of the world wasn't quite so forgiving.

Out on the road, two Elven farmers took one look at me and started throwing stones. An hour later, I went into a Dwarven tavern by the side of the road. It only took ten minutes for the place to turn. Everyone had machetes and axes and I only escaped by running out the back, into the woods, and hiding under a tree trunk in a marsh until morning.

I stayed on my own after that, stealing food from storehouses or going without. I washed myself in muddy streams and slept as far from the road as I was brave enough to wander, always paranoid that someone might stumble upon my sleeping body and stop me from waking up.

Eventually, I made it to Lipha, but I didn't know where Carissa was staying or if she was even there. I was too nervous to ask the locals for directions so I found a watchtower near the main square and spent a week hiding in the turret, peering out between the wooden boards till I finally spotted her walking through the market.

She took me in. I hadn't given her much of a choice. We stayed in her cousin's guest house and she patched up my clothes and my wounds. I was weak, starving, and still in shock. Carissa didn't seem to mind having someone to care for. I did my best to be quiet and gracious and accept her generosity.

When I was healthy enough, I asked her to bring me some

books from the library and as many newspapers as she could find. Then, I began my work.

The books were for history. The newspapers were for the present. I cut out any clippings in which a bold journalist dared to consider the possibility that some kind of magic had returned to the world. The juiciest snippets were contained in cheaper gossip rags or letters to the editor. Occasionally, a real news story would quote some civilian who thought they saw the magic of old, but the papers would always clarify that this was opinion rather than fact.

It kept my mind busy but, over time, I became increasingly restless. I didn't like being cooped up in a bedroom, too afraid to step outside in case somebody spotted my species or the telltale tattoos on my arm.

As I got stronger, the old, rougher parts of my personality crawled back out. Carissa became frustrated with my obsessive fixation on my stories. I snapped when she tried to help me and I kept saying stupid things that rubbed her up the wrong way.

Then, one day, she brought me something special: a week-old edition of the *Sunder Star*. She thought I might be interested in seeing how life back home was progressing. She wasn't wrong. The power wasn't on yet but the Niles Company had been continuing their work. There was an interview with Eileen Tide about her plans for a new library and a half-page advertisement for the Succubae Surgery (I guess they'd decided to do away with discretion). The article that most caught my attention was an update on the construction of a new high-security prison to replace the Gullet, complete with a picture of the original damaged building.

Carissa couldn't have known what seeing that image would do to me, but over the next week, I became even more irritable. The thing about self-loathing is that when it has you in its talons, you'd better be alone. If you're with someone else, you might start to think those feelings have something to do with them, connecting your melancholy to whoever dares to be close to you at the time.

Carissa didn't deserve that. If I was going to be a surly, hot-headed, drunken, two-bit man-child, then I needed to be somewhere that could take that kind of abuse. Somewhere that was just as full of black smoke and bad deeds as I was. A place made of fire where dreams came to die and nightmares weren't afraid to face the day.

"You're going back?" she asked, when she saw me packing my bag.

"I am."

"I thought you said you were done with Sunder for good."

"I know. But I need to get to work and I can't do it from here." She tried her best not to look relieved.

"If you need anything, you can always write me."

"Thanks. When I'm putting together a team of heroes to go and save the world, I'll make sure to send you a telegram."

I'd given Carissa a lot of bronze to get her out of Sunder. She used some to buy me a ticket back. I kept my head down the whole way. Throughout the entire journey from Lipha to Sunder, the driver was the only other soul who saw my face.

It was late afternoon when I walked up Main Street. Nobody sized me up. Nobody cared who I was or what I was. Nobody cared at all. When I passed a cop, she didn't bat an eye, but I did notice the pistol swinging from her hip.

Niles had been busy.

Back at the office, I put down my bag and looked around. There were letters by the door: pamphlets, the telegram from Hildra, and one small blue envelope with a return address from the Isle of Mizunrum.

To the idiot who somehow convinced me not to kill him,

I'm guessing that you must have skipped town too, but if you ever read this, send a letter to Keats. The headmaster will make sure it gets to me. Unless you're dead, which wouldn't surprise me. If you're not, you better hold up your end of the bargain or I'll come looking for you. I've already got a couple of leads. Nothing solid, just a few interesting stories that might put some fire under your flabby ass. I won't put them down in writing but come find me if you want to know more.

Don't be a fuck-up.

Linda

PS Remember that Reptilian woman who came by my office? I found a way to help her. The mortician, Portemus, has some cream he uses on the stiffs that preserves their flesh. Worked wonders on her. Make sure you give some to Simms. I have a feeling you'll need some help smoothing things over.

I put the letter back in the envelope and dropped it in the drawer. Then, I went over to the Angel door and opened it. Winter had almost moved on. I stood on the doorstep and felt the wind swim through my uncut hair and jaggedy beard.

Then, I stepped out.

Finally.

But I didn't fall.

"It's called a fire escape," said the voice behind me.

I spun around. Thurston Niles was standing in my office.

Under my feet there was a set of steel stairs that zigzagged all the way up the side of the building. There was even a little barricade to stop me from accidently stumbling off the edge.

I hated it.

"The Mayor wanted these staircases installed all along Main Street: partly as a safety precaution, but also so we can put those Angel doors back in use. Drive up business, raise real-estate prices, show the world that we still have a future."

Thurston reached into his jacket and pulled a pistol out of its holster. It was Victor's prototype. My machine.

"If you're here to kill me, can you at least let me jump? It's been my thing for a while."

Thurston stepped forward.

"Why would I kill you? You did the job I asked you to do, right? You found my brother's killer and stopped him from hurting anyone else. A job well done."

There was that knowing smile again. I was sick of it, but I had a bad feeling it wasn't going anywhere. He dumped the machine on the desk.

"A gift. We have plenty more. My factories have been working non-stop since you left. More pistols. More construction. For a hard-working man like yourself, I see prosperous times ahead."

I was really, really sick of that smile.

"As long as I stay in line, right?"

He shrugged. "I'm not your enemy, Fetch. When you've got yourself settled back in, I know you'll be able to see that. After all, a man can never have too many friends."

He left, and I waited as long as I could before I picked up the pistol. I hated how good it felt to have it back in my hand.

The phone rang.

"Fetch Phillips."

"Yes, are you the investigator? The man who looks for ways to bring back the magic?"

I turned and looked back out the barricaded Angel door.

"Yes, ma'am. That's exactly who I am."

She told me some story about a Giant who broke into her kitchen and ate all her food. Nobody had seen Giants in this part of the world for over six years, so I made some notes and booked her in for an appointment the next day.

Then, I grabbed my coat and my hat and I went outside.

There was a festival exploding onto Main Street. It was going to be a special night and I'd arrived just in time to catch the excitement. Shiny topless automobiles beeped their horns happily as they weaved through a parade of dancers. Street-food vendors sold bottles of ale and bags of Swine-o's. Musicians were up on the fire escapes singing in celebration as women threw paper petals from their windows.

I pushed my way through. As hard as I tried, I couldn't stop the festive spirit from forcing its way into my soul. The drumming. The smell of the fryers. The laughter of the children who ran freely through the knees of the crowd. This was Sunder City, the way Hendricks had always seen it, but it had never been real until now. If he was beside me, I wouldn't have been able to move. He would have brought us to a standstill every ten seconds as he tried some new delicacy or sparked up conversation with every person on the street.

But that wasn't me. It never would be. I cut through them like running water and went all the way uptown.

There were no clouds overhead, and the freshly grown leaves went translucent when they caught the light of the sunset, turning every shade of green. The twisted branches were painted with fluffy patches of moss and wrapped in dainty loops of vine. Dewy pink flowers, white buds, and shoots of long grass sprouted from the stringy bark. The whole place shimmered with butterfly wings and buzzing bees.

The trunk of the tree had exploded out of the dirt and lifted up the concrete wall of the Gullet, cracking it into untold pieces. They could build here again, if they cut down the tree. But why bother? There were plenty of other silos, already built, that they could use to make another muddy dungeon.

I pressed the palm of my hand against her trunk. She was cool to the touch. Rough. There was a bend in one of the branches. When I put my hand around it, it felt like she was holding me too. I squeezed. She was strong. I put my forehead against her bark and closed my eyes. Under the bees and the wind and the hum of the factories, I swear I could hear her breathing.

I grabbed hold and pulled myself up. I wrapped around her, climbing through her arms as high as I could go. I leaned into her trunk and she cradled me like I was back in her leaf-filled bed.

The sun set and the sky turned a deep, twilight blue. I could see all the way down Main Street as it pulsed with impossible energy. Everybody was standing outside, on their doorsteps, looking up into the sky.

It started at the southern end of town. A ball of light in the distance. People cheering. Then another light. Closer. Louder. Then more, coming block by block up Main Street.

Then I saw it. Two lamps exploding in flame, reaching up to touch the stars. Then two more. Then two more. The flames painted the buildings, the cobblestones and the faces of the crowd until the whole city was bright and full of fire.

The lights were back, and with them came hope that all the other things we thought were lost might one day come back too. I leaned my head against the branches and wished that Amari could see what we'd done.

The people of Sunder squealed with joy. The music got louder and the whole city cheered.

Then there was another sound. An explosion, but not like the others. It was a machine. One of the mass-produced pistols out on the street, joining in the celebration. The music stopped. People screamed. The crowd scattered in all directions. Another pistol fired back. Chaos. It was an orchestra of anger and panic as people were trampled under the feet of their neighbors, fleeing some new horror.

But the fires kept on roaring. Dancing, wild and bright. They didn't care about what happened below. The cries didn't matter to them at all.

A gust of wind went through the city, bringing the smell of smoke and sulfur up to the top of the tree.

And it was warm.

Acknowledgements

As I'm writing this, *The Last Smile in Sunder City* is still a couple of months away from release so it's impossible to separate this book from the experience of bringing my debut into the world. Thank you to everyone who has been a part of this adventure so far.

First, my friend in the review column, Jenni Hill. A lot of the anxiety is taken out of writing when you know such a sharp mind will be looking over it all before it heads out the door.

To my agent Alexander Cochran for his patience and enthusiasm as I do my best to learn about a whole new industry on the fly.

To everyone at Hachette, Orbit and Little, Brown in the UK, US and Australia. So many lovely people working on covers, publicity, sales and everything in between. I can't thank you enough for your hard work, most of which I never see and likely wouldn't understand.

A special thanks to Toby Schmitz and Laurence Boxhall for hosting the launches of *The Last Smile* in Australia. By the time you're all reading this there will surely be many other people I should add to this list, so thank you to you too.

To Mum and Dad, again and always.

Thank you to everyone who read my first book and came back for more. Thank you to everyone who spread the word online or recommended it to a friend, and thank you to the other authors who welcomed me into their world with open arms.

Writing is a solitary profession so it means the world that when I come back out of the shadows with my pile of pages, so many people are excited to help me share them.

Thank you, all.

extras

orbit

meet the author

LUKE ARNOLD was born in Australia and has spent the last decade acting his way around the world, playing iconic roles such as Long John Silver in the Emmy-winning *Black Sails* and his award-winning turn as Michael Hutchence in the INXS mini-series *Never Tear Us Apart*. When he isn't performing, Luke is a screenwriter, director, novelist, and ambassador for Save the Children Australia.

Find out more about Luke Arnold and other Orbit authors by registering for the free monthly newsletter at www.orbitbooks.net.

if you enjoyed
DEAD MAN IN A DITCH

look out for

SPELLSLINGER
Spellslinger: Book One

by

Sebastien de Castell

Kellen is moments away from facing his first duel and proving his worth as a spellcaster. There's just one problem: His magic is fading.

Facing exile unless he can pass the mage trials, Kellen is willing to risk everything—even his own life—in search of a way to restore his magic. But when the enigmatic Ferius Parfax arrives in town, she challenges him to take a different path. Daring, unpredictable, and wielding magic Kellen has never seen before, she may be his only hope.

1

The Duel

The old spellmasters like to say that magic has a taste. Ember spells are like a spice burning the tip of your tongue. Breath magic is subtle, almost cool, the sensation of holding a mint leaf between your lips. Sand, silk, blood, iron ... they each have their flavour. A true adept—the kind of mage who can cast spells even outside an oasis—knows them all.

Me? I had no idea what the high magics tasted like, which was why I was in so much trouble.

Tennat waited for me in the distance, standing inside the seven marble columns that ringed the town oasis. The sun at his back sent his shadow stretching all the way down the road towards me. He'd probably picked his spot precisely for that effect. It worked too, because my mouth was now as dry as the sand beneath my feet, and the only thing I could taste was panic.

"Don't do this, Kellen," Nephenia pleaded, quickening her step to catch up with me. "It's not too late to forfeit."

I stopped. A warm southern breeze shook the flowers from pink tamarisk trees lining the street. Tiny petals floated up into the air, glittering in the afternoon sun like particles of fire magic. I could have used some fire magic just then. Actually, I would have settled for just about any kind of magic.

Nephenia noticed my hesitation and unhelpfully added, "Tennat's been bragging all over town that he'll cripple you if you show up."

I smiled, mostly because it was the only way I could keep the feeling of dread crawling up my stomach from reaching my face. I'd never fought a mage's duel before, but I was fairly sure that looking petrified in front of your opponent wasn't an especially effective tactic. "I'll be fine," I said, and resumed my steady march towards the oasis.

"Nephenia's right, Kel," Panahsi said, huffing and puffing as he struggled to catch up. His right arm was wrapped around the thick covering of bandages holding his ribs together. "Don't fight Tennat on my account."

I slowed my pace a little, resisting the urge to roll my eyes. Panahsi had all the makings of one of the finest mages of our generation. He might even become the face of our clan at court one day, which would be unfortunate, since his naturally muscular frame was offset by a deep love of yellowberry sweetcakes, and his otherwise handsome features were marred by the skin condition that was the inevitable result of the aforementioned cakes. My people have a lot of spells, but none that cure being fat and pockmarked.

"Don't listen to them, Kellen," Tennat called out as we approached the ring of white marble columns. He stood inside a three-foot circle in the sand, arms crossed over his black linen shirt. He'd cut the sleeves off to make sure everyone could see he'd sparked not just one, but two of his bands. The tattooed metallic inks shimmered and swirled under the skin of his forearms as he summoned the magics for breath and iron. "I think it's sweet the way you're throwing your life away just to defend your fat friend's honour."

A chorus of giggles rose up from our fellow initiates, most of whom were standing behind Tennat, shuffling about in anticipation. Everyone enjoys a good beating. Well, except the victim.

Panahsi might not have looked like the gleaming figures of ancient war mages carved into the columns in front of us, but he was twice the mage Tennat was. There was no way in all the hells that he should have lost his own duel so badly. Even now, after more than two weeks in bed and who knew how many healing spells, Panahsi could barely make it to lessons.

I gave my opponent my best smile. Like everyone else, Tennat was convinced I'd challenged him for my first trial out of recklessness. Some of our fellow initiates assumed it was to avenge Panahsi, who was, after all, pretty much my only friend. Others thought I was on some noble quest to stop Tennat from bullying the other students, or terrorising the Sha'Tep servants, who had no spells of their own with which to defend themselves.

"Don't let him goad you, Kellen," Nephenia said, her hand on my arm.

A few people no doubt suspected I was doing all this to impress Nephenia, the girl with the beautiful brown hair and the face that, while not perfect, was perfect to me. The way she was staring at me now, with such breathless concern for my well-being, you'd never have guessed that she'd hardly noticed me in all the years we'd been initiates together. To be fair, most days no one else had either. Today was different though. Today everyone was paying attention to me, even Nephenia. Especially Nephenia.

Was it only pity? Maybe, but the worried expression she wore on those lips that I'd longed to kiss ever since I'd first figured out that kissing wasn't just two people biting each other made my head spin. The feel of her fingers on my skin...was this the first time she'd ever touched me?

Since I really hadn't picked this fight just to impress her, I gently removed Nephenia's hand and entered the oasis.

I once read that other cultures use the word "oasis" to describe a patch of fertile terrain in a desert, but a Jan'Tep oasis is something completely different. Seven marble columns towered above us, one for each of the seven forms of true magic. Inside the enclosed thirty-foot circle there were no trees or greenery, but instead a glimmering carpet of silver sand that, even when stirred by the wind, never left the boundary set by the columns. At the centre was a low stone pool filled with something that was neither liquid nor air, but which shimmered as it rose and fell in waves. This was the true magic. The Jan.

The word "tep" means "people," so it should tell you how important magic is to us that when my ancestors came here, like other peoples before them, they left their old names behind and became known as the Jan'Tep, the "People of True Magic."

Well, in theory, anyway.

I knelt down and drew a protective circle around myself in the sand. Actually, "circle" might have been a bit generous.

Tennat chuckled. "Well, now I'm really scared."

For all his bluster, Tennat wasn't nearly as imposing a figure as he imagined. True, he was all wiry muscle and meanness, but he wasn't very big. In fact, he was as thin as I was and half a head shorter. Somehow that just made him meaner.

"Are you both still determined to go through with this duel?" Master Osia'phest asked, rising from a stone bench at the edge of the oasis. The old spellmaster was looking at me, not at Tennat, so it was pretty clear who was supposed to back out.

"Kellen won't withdraw," my sister declared, stepping out from behind our teacher. Shalla was only thirteen, younger than the rest of us, but already taking her trials. She was a better mage than anyone present except for Panahsi, as evidenced by the fact that she'd already sparked the bands for breath, iron, blood and ember magic. There were mages who went their whole lives without ever being able to wield four disciplines, but my little sister fully planned on mastering all of them.

So how many bands had I sparked? How many of the tattooed symbols under my shirtsleeves would glow and swirl when I called on the high magics that defined my people?

Zero.

Oh, inside the oasis I could perform the practice spells that all initiates learn. My fingers knew the somatic shapes as well or better than any of my fellow initiates. I could intone every syllable perfectly, envision the most esoteric geometry with perfect clarity. I was skilled at every aspect of spellcasting—except for the actual magic part.

"Forfeit the duel, Kellen," Nephenia said. "You'll find some other way to pass your tests."

That, of course, was the real problem. I was about to turn sixteen and this was my last chance to prove that I had the calibre of magic worthy of earning my mage name. That meant I had to pass all four of the mage's trials, starting with the duel. If I failed, I'd be forced to join the Sha'Tep and spend the rest of my life cooking, cleaning or clerking for the household of one of my former classmates. It would be a humiliating fate for any initiate, but for a member of my family, for the son of Ke'heops himself? Failure was inconceivable.

Of course, none of that was the reason why I'd chosen to challenge Tennat in particular.

"Be warned, the protection of the law is suspended for those who undertake the trials," Osia'phest reminded us, his tone both weary and resigned. "Only those whose calibre gives them the strength to face our enemies in combat can lay claim to a mage's name."

Silence gripped the oasis. We'd all seen the list of past

430

initiates who'd attempted the trials before they were ready. We all knew the stories of how they'd died. Osia'phest looked to me again. "Are you truly prepared?"

"Sure," I said. It wasn't an appropriate way to speak to our teacher, but my strategy required that I project a certain confidence.

"'Sure,'" Tennat repeated in a mocking whine. He took up a basic guard position, legs shoulder width apart and hands loose at his sides, ready to cast the spells he'd use for our duel. "Last chance to walk away, Kellen. Once this starts, I don't stop until you fall." He chuckled, his eyes on Shalla. "I wouldn't want the tremendous pain I'm about to inflict on you to bring any needless suffering to your sister."

If Shalla had noticed Tennat's childish imitation of gallantry she gave no sign of it. Instead she stood there, hands on her hips, bright yellow hair billowing gracefully in the wind. Hers was straighter and smoother than the dirt-coloured mop I struggled to keep out of my eyes. We shared our mother's pale complexion, but mine was exacerbated by a lifetime of intermittent illnesses. Shalla's accentuated the fine-boned features that drew the attention of just about every initiate in our clan. None of them interested her, of course. She knew she had more potential than the rest of us and fully intended doing whatever it took to become a lord magus like our father. Boys simply weren't part of that equation.

"I'm sure she'll weather my screams of agony just fine," I said.

Shalla caught my glance and returned a look that was equal parts bemusement and suspicion. She knew I'd do anything to pass my trials. That was why she was keeping such close watch on me.

Whatever you think you know, Shalla, keep your mouth shut. I'm begging you.

"As the student who has sparked the fewest bands," Osia'phest said, "you may select the discipline of magic for the duel, Kellen. What is your weapon?"

Everyone stared at me, trying to guess what I'd choose. Here in the oasis, any of us could summon some tiny portion of the different forms of magic—just enough to train in spell-work. But that was nothing compared with what you could do once you'd sparked your bands. Since Tennat had iron and breath at his disposal, I'd be crazy to choose either of those two.

"Iron," I said, loud enough to ensure that everyone heard.

My classmates looked at me as if I'd lost my mind. Nephenia went pale. Shalla's eyes narrowed. Panahsi started to object, but a glance from Osia'phest shut him up. "I did not hear you correctly," our teacher said slowly.

"Iron," I repeated.

Tennat grinned, a greyish glow already winding itself from the iron band on his forearm, slithering around his hands as he began summoning the power. Everyone there knew how much Tennat loved iron magic, the way it let you tear and bludgeon at your enemies. You could see the excitement building up inside him, the thrill that came from wielding high-calibre magic. I wished I knew what it felt like.

Tennat was so eager that his fingers had already begun running through the somatic shapes for the spells he'd be using against me. One of the first things you learn in duelling is that only an idiot shows his hand before the fight starts, but since there was no possible way I could beat Tennat in iron magic, he probably figured there was nothing to lose.

That was the real reason why I was smiling.

See, for the past several weeks I'd watched every single duel Tennat had fought against the other initiates; I'd noticed how even those students with more power—those who should have been able to beat him with ease—always ended up forced to yield.

That was when I'd finally figured it out.

Magic is a con game.

The oasis was quiet, almost peaceful. I think everyone was waiting for me to giggle nervously and announce before it was too late that it had all been a joke. Instead, I rolled my shoulders back and tilted my neck left then right to make it crack. It didn't help my magic any, but I thought maybe it would make me look tougher.

Tennat gave a confident snort. It sounded like his regular snort only louder. "You'd think someone who can barely light a glow-glass lantern without giving himself a heart attack would be a little more cautious in his choice of opponent."

"You're right," I said, rolling up my sleeves to let him see the flat, lifeless inks of my own six tattooed bands. "So you've got to ask yourself, why would I challenge you now?"

Tennat hesitated for a second before he said, "Maybe you've been having death-dreams and you know I'm the best person to help usher you into the grey passage and end your suffering."

"Could be," I conceded. "But let's say for the sake of argument that it's something else."

"Like what?"

I had a whole speech planned about how I'd banded myself with shadow—the seventh and deadliest of magics, the one forbidden to us all. If that didn't scare him I had a different bit about how the truly great mages among our ancestors could wield the high magics without sparking their bands at all. Just as I was about to speak though, I saw a falcon flying overhead and decided to switch tactics.

"You don't need to spark your bands if you've found your power animal."

Everyone looked up to see. Tennat's smirk was just angry enough to tell me he was getting nervous. "Nobody bonds with familiars any more. Besides, how would someone with as little magic as you ever attract a power animal? And a falcon? No way, Kellen. Not in a thousand years."

I noticed the falcon was about to swoop down on a smaller bird. "Dive, my darling," I whispered, just loud enough for everyone to hear. There was a sudden nervous intake of breath all around me as the falcon's claws took merciless hold of its prey. It occurred to me then that I might have made a decent actor if it hadn't been a forbidden profession among the Jan'Tep.

"All right, all right," Osia'phest said, waiving his hands in the air as if trying to cast a banishing spell on all our nonsense. I was fairly sure the old man knew I hadn't acquired a familiar, but I guess it's bad form to reveal another mage's secrets, even when they happen to be lies. Or maybe he just didn't care. "I recognise that it's traditional for there to be a certain amount of…posturing prior to a duel, but I think we've all had just about enough. Are you ready to begin?"

I nodded. Tennat didn't bother, as if the implication that he might not be ready were an insult.

"Very well," Osia'phest said. "I shall commence the counting." The old man took in a deep breath that was probably excessive given that all he said next was, "Seven!"

The breeze picked up and my loose linen shirt flapped noisily against my skin. I dried my hands on it for the tenth time and cleared my throat to get rid of the tickle. *Don't start coughing. Don't look weak. Whatever you do, don't look weak.*

"Six."

Tennat gave me a wide grin as if he had some big surprise

waiting for me. I would have been more scared if I hadn't seen him give every opponent that same look prior to each duel. Also, I was already as terrified as I could possibly be without collapsing to the ground.

"Five."

The bird swooped overhead again so I looked up and winked at it. Tennat's smile wavered. Evidently he was capable of simultaneously believing I was a weakling and yet had also acquired a power animal. *Moron.*

"Four."

His left hand formed the somatic shape necessary for his shield spell. I'd never seen him prepare the shield before the sword. He looked down at his hand to check the form. Tennat was just a little worried now.

"Two."

Two? What happened to three? *Pay attention, damn it.* Tennat's right hand made the somatic shape for the iron attack spell we informally call the *gut sword*. His fingers were perfectly aligned to cause the maximum pain in his opponent. His head was still down, but it was starting to look as though he might be smiling again.

"One."

Okay, Tennat was definitely smiling. Maybe this hadn't been such a good idea.

"Begin!" Osia'phest said.

The next thing I felt was my insides screaming in pain.

Like I said, magic is a con game.

Mostly.

To an observer, it wouldn't have looked as if anything was happening. There was no flash of light or roar of thunder, just the early evening light and the soft sounds of the breeze coming from the south. Iron magic doesn't create any visual or auditory effects—that was why I'd picked it in the first place. The real fight was taking place inside our bodies.

Tennat was reaching out with his right hand, carefully holding the somatic form: middle fingers together making the sign of the knife, index and little fingers curled up—the shape of pulling, of tearing. The horrifying touch of his will slipped inside my chest, winding itself along my internal organs. The pain it created—more slithering horror than anything blunt or sharp—made me want to fall to the ground and beg for mercy. *Damn, he's fast, and strong too. Why can't I be strong like that?*

I responded by letting out the barest hint of a laugh and smiling effortlessly. The look on Tennat's face told me I was creeping him out. I was probably creeping everyone out, since confident smiles weren't exactly my customary expression.

I let the corners of my mouth ease down a bit as my gaze narrowed and I stared straight into Tennat's eyes. I thrust out my hand as if I were stabbing the air—a much more pronounced gesture and by all rights much too fast for an initiate like me to do while holding on to the shielding spell. Where Tennat's hand formed the somatic shape with care and precision, mine was looser, almost casual, something few would dare because of the risk of breaking the shape.

At first nothing happened. I could still feel Tennat's will inside my guts, so I let my smile grow by a hair—just enough to let him see how sure I was that he was completely screwed. The painful pulling at my insides began to subside just a little as Tennat's gaze lingered on me for several agonising seconds. Suddenly his eyes went very, very wide.

That's when I knew I was going to win.

The other reason I'd chosen iron magic even though I couldn't wield it myself was because when a mage uses the gut sword to attack, he has to use a second spell—the heart shield—to protect himself. But it's not a shield the way you might think of a big round thing that acts as a wall. Instead, you use magical force to maintain the shape and integrity of your own insides. You have to picture your heart, your liver, your... well, everything, and try to keep them together. But if you start to panic—say, if you think the other mage is beating you and nothing you're doing is working—you can inadvertently compress your own organs.

That was how Tennat had beat Panahsi. That was how he'd hurt him so badly, even though nobody but me—not even Tennat himself—had realised it. Pan had been trying so hard to protect himself that he'd actually ended up crushing his own internal organs. Now it was Tennat who was so convinced that his spells were failing that he was pushing them too hard. I was still in blinding pain, but I'd expected it. I was ready for it. Tennat wasn't.

He struggled for a while, increasing his attack on me even as he unconsciously tore at himself with his own shield spell. I felt my legs shake and my vision start to blur as the pain became too much for me. It had seemed like such a good plan at the time, I thought.

Suddenly Tennat stumbled out of his circle. "Enough!" he shouted. "I yield...I yield!"

The fingers of his own power disappeared into nothingness. I could breathe again. I tried my very best to keep my tremendous sense of relief from showing on my face.

Osia'phest walked slowly over to Tennat, who was on his knees gasping. "Describe the sensation," our teacher demanded.

Tennat looked up at the old man as if he were an idiot, which was a fairly common impression of our teacher. "It felt like I was about to die. That's what it felt like!"

Osia'phest ignored the belligerent tone. "And did it feel the same as with the other students?"

A jolt of fear ran through me as I realised Osia'phest was testing his suspicions. Tennat looked over at me, then at the old man. "It...I suppose not at first. Usually it feels hard, like a strong hand grabbing at you, but with Kellen it's different... worse, like tendrils insinuating themselves all around my insides. By the end I could feel him crushing my organs."

Osia'phest stood in silence for a long time as the breeze picked up and drifted off again around us. The other initiates were still staring at me, wondering how someone who hadn't broken any of his bands had beaten the best duellist in our class. But they'd all seen Tennat falter and heard him describe what sounded like someone being overwhelmed by superior magic. Finally Osia'phest said, "Well done, Kellen of the House of Ke. It would appear that you've passed the first test."

"I'll pass the other three too," I declared.

I did it, I thought, as a surge of joy erupted inside me. *I beat him. I won.* No more spending hours and hours staring at the bands on my forearms, praying without success to break the bindings between the sigils to spark them. No more sitting awake at night wondering when I would be sent away from my family home, doomed to become Sha'Tep and take a position as a tradesman, clerk or, ancestors help me, Tennat's personal servant.

A few of the other initiates applauded. I doubted any of them other than Panahsi and maybe Nephenia had wanted me to best Tennat, but among my people? Let's just say everyone loves a winner. Even Tennat bowed to me, with about as much grace as you'd expect given the circumstances. I hadn't hurt his standing in the trials. Every initiate was allowed three attempts at the duel and he'd already won several.

"All right," Osia'phest said. "Let's have the next pair and—"

"Stop!" a voice called out, cutting off our teacher and, with more force than any spell I could imagine, shattering everything I had done and everything I would ever do. I watched with a sinking heart as my sister pushed past Osia'phest and strode forth to stand in front of me, hands on her hips. "Kellen cheated," she said simply.

And, just like that, all my hopes and dreams came crashing down around me.

if you enjoyed
DEAD MAN IN A DITCH

look out for

SENLIN ASCENDS
The Books of Babel: Book One

by

Josiah Bancroft

Mild-mannered headmaster Thomas Senlin prefers his adventures to be safely contained within the pages of a book. So when he loses his new bride shortly after embarking on the honeymoon of their dreams, he is ill-prepared for the trouble that follows.

To find her, Senlin must enter the Tower of Babel—a world of geniuses and tyrants, of luxury and menace, of unusual animals and mysterious machines. He must endure betrayal, assassination attempts, and the illusions of the tower. And if he hopes ever to see his wife again, he will have to do more than just survive.... This quiet man of letters must become a man of action.

Chapter One

The Tower of Babel is most famous for the silk
fineries and marvelous airships it produces, but
visitors will discover other intangible exports.
Whimsy, adventure, and romance are the Tower's real trade.
　　—*Everyman's Guide to the Tower of Babel*, I. V

It was a four-day journey by train from the coast to the desert where the Tower of Babel rose like a tusk from the jaw of
the earth. First, they had crossed pastureland, spotted with
fattening cattle and charmless hamlets, and then their train
had climbed through a range of snow-veined mountains where
condors roosted in nests large as haystacks. Already, they were
farther from home than they had ever been. They descended
through shale foothills, which he said reminded him of a field
of shattered blackboards, through cypress trees, which she said
looked like open parasols, and finally they came upon the arid
basin. The ground was the color of rusted chains, and the dust
of it clung to everything. The desert was far from deserted.
Their train shared a direction with a host of caravans, each a
slithering line of wheels, hooves, and feet. Over the course of
the morning, the bands of traffic thickened until they con-
verged into a great mass so dense that their train was forced to
slow to a crawl. Their cabin seemed to wade through the boisterous tide of stagecoaches and ox-drawn wagons, through the

tourists, pilgrims, migrants, and merchants from every state in the vast nation of Ur.

Thomas Senlin and Marya, his new bride, peered at the human menagerie through the open window of their sunny sleeper car. Her china-white hand lay weightlessly atop his long fingers. A little troop of red-breasted soldiers slouched by on palominos, parting a family in checkered headscarves on camelback. The trumpet of elephants sounded over the clack of the train, and here and there in the hot winds high above them, airships lazed, drifting inexorably toward the Tower of Babel. The balloons that held the ships aloft were as colorful as maypoles.

Since turning toward the Tower, they had been unable to see the grand spire from their cabin window. But this did not discourage Senlin's description of it. "There is a lot of debate over how many levels there are. Some scholars say there are fifty-two, others say as many as sixty. It's impossible to judge from the ground," Senlin said, continuing the litany of facts he'd brought to his young wife's attention over the course of their journey. "A number of men, mostly aeronauts and mystics, say that they have seen the top of it. Of course, none of them have any evidence to back up their boasts. Some of those explorers even claim that the Tower is still being raised, if you can believe that." These trivial facts comforted him, as all facts did. Thomas Senlin was a reserved and naturally timid man who took confidence in schedules and regimens and written accounts.

Marya nodded dutifully but was obviously distracted by the parade of humanity outside. Her wide, green eyes darted excitedly from one exotic diversion to the next: What Senlin merely observed, she absorbed. Senlin knew that, unlike him, Marya found spectacles and crowds exhilarating, though she saw little of either back home. The pageant outside her window was nothing like Isaugh, a salt-scoured fishing village, now many hundreds of miles behind them. Isaugh was the only real home she'd known, apart from the young women's musical conservatory she'd attended for four years. Isaugh had two pubs, a Whist Club, and a city hall that doubled as a ballroom when occasion called for it. But it was hardly a metropolis.

Marya jumped in her seat when a camel's head swung unexpectedly near. Senlin tried to calm her by example but couldn't stop himself from yelping when the camel snorted, spraying them with warm spit. Frustrated by this lapse in decorum, Senlin cleared his throat and shooed the camel out with his handkerchief.

The tea set that had come with their breakfast rattled now, spoons shivering in their empty cups, as the engineer applied the brakes and the train all but stopped. Thomas Senlin had saved and planned for this journey his entire career. He wanted to see the wonders he'd read so much about, and though it would be a trial for his nerves, he hoped his poise and intellect would carry the day. Climbing the Tower of Babel, even if only a little way, was his greatest ambition, and he was quite excited. Not that anyone would know it to look at him: He affected a cool detachment as a rule, concealing the inner flights of his emotions. It was how he conducted himself in the classroom. He didn't know how else to behave anymore.

Outside, an airship passed low enough to the ground that its tethering lines began to snap against heads in the crowd. Senlin wondered why it had dropped so low, or if it had only recently launched. Marya let out a laughing cry and covered her mouth with her hand. He gaped as the ship's captain gestured wildly at the crew to fire the furnace and pull in the tethers, which was quickly done amid a general panic, but not before a young man from the crowd had caught hold of one of the loose cords. The adventuresome lad was quickly lifted above the throng, his feet just clearing the box of a carriage before he was swung up and out of view.

The scene seemed almost comical from the ground, but Senlin's stomach churned when he thought of how the youth must feel flying on the strength of his grip high over the sprawling mob. Indeed, the entire brief scene had been so bizarre that he decided to simply put it out of his mind. The *Guide* had called the Market a raucous place. It seemed, perhaps, an understatement.

He'd never expected to make the journey as a honeymooner. More to the point, he never imagined he'd find a woman who'd have him. Marya was his junior by a dozen years, but being in his midthirties himself, Senlin did not think their recent marriage very remarkable. It had raised a few eyebrows in Isaugh, though. Perched on rock bluffs by the Niro Ocean, the townsfolk of Isaugh were suspicious of anything that fell outside the regular rhythms of tides and fishing seasons. But as the headmaster, and the only teacher, of Isaugh's school, Senlin was generally indifferent to gossip. He'd certainly heard enough of it. To his thinking, gossip was the theater of the uneducated, and he hadn't gotten married to enliven anyone's breakfast-table conversation.

He'd married for entirely practical reasons.

Marya was a good match. She was good tempered and well read; thoughtful, though not brooding; and mannered without being aloof. She tolerated his long hours of study and his general quiet, which others often mistook for stoicism. He imagined she had married him because he was kind, even tempered, and securely employed. He made fifteen shekels a week, for an annual salary of thirteen minas; it wasn't a fortune by any means, but it was sufficient for a comfortable life. She certainly hadn't married him for his looks. While his features were separately handsome enough, taken altogether they seemed a little stretched and misplaced. His nickname among his pupils was "the Sturgeon" because he was thin and long and bony.

Of course, Marya had a few unusual habits of her own. She read books while she walked to town—and had many torn skirts and skinned knees to show for it. She was fearless of heights and would sometimes get on the roof just to watch the sails of inbound ships rise over the horizon. She played the piano beautifully but also brutally. She'd sing like a mad mermaid while banging out ballads and reels, leaving detuned pianos in her wake. And even still, her oddness inspired admiration in most. The townsfolk thought she was charming, and her playing was often requested at the local public houses. Not even the bitter gray of Isaugh's winters could temper her vivacity. Everyone was a little baffled by her marriage to the Sturgeon.

Today, Marya wore her traveling clothes: a knee-length khaki skirt and plain white blouse with a somewhat eccentric pith helmet covering her rolling auburn hair. She had dyed the helmet red, which Senlin didn't particularly like, but she'd sold him on the fashion by saying it would make her easier to spot in a crowd. Senlin wore a gray suit of thin corduroy, which he felt was too casual, even for traveling, but which she had said was fashionable and a little frolicsome, and wasn't that the whole point of a honeymoon, after all?

A dexterous child in a rough goatskin vest climbed along the side of the train with rings of bread hooped on one arm. Senlin bought a ring from the boy, and he and Marya sat sharing the warm, yeasty crust as the train crept toward Babel Central Station, where so many tracks ended.

Their honeymoon had been delayed by the natural course of the school year. He could've opted for a more convenient and frugal destination, a seaside hotel or country cottage in which they might've secluded themselves for a weekend, but the Tower of Babel was so much more than a vacation spot. A whole world stood balanced on a bedrock foundation. As a young man, he'd read about the Tower's cultural contributions to theater and art, its advances in the sciences, and its profound technologies. Even electricity, still an unheard-of commodity in all but the largest cities of Ur, was rumored to flow freely in the Tower's higher levels. It was the lighthouse of civilization. The old saying went, "The earth doesn't shake the Tower; the Tower shakes the earth."

The train came to a final stop, though they saw no station outside their window. The conductor came by and told them that they'd have to disembark; the tracks were too clogged for the train to continue. No one seemed to think it unusual. After days of sitting and swaying on the rails, the prospect of a walk appealed to them both. Senlin gathered their two pieces of luggage: a stitched leather satchel for his effects, and for hers, a modest steamer trunk with large casters on one end and a push handle on the other. He insisted on managing them both.

Before they left their car and while she tugged at the tops of her brown leather boots and smoothed her skirt, Senlin recited the three vital pieces of advice he'd gleaned from his copy of *Everyman's Guide to the Tower of Babel*. Firstly, keep your money close. (Before they'd departed, he'd had their local tailor sew secret pockets inside the waists of his pants and the hem of her skirt.) Secondly, don't give in to beggars. (It only emboldens them.) And finally, keep your companions always in view. Senlin asked Marya to recite these points as they bustled down the gold-carpeted hall connecting train cars. She obliged, though with some humor.

"Rule four: Don't kiss the camels."

"That is not rule four."

"Tell that to the camels!" she said, her gait bouncing.

And still neither of them was prepared for the scene that met them as they descended the train's steps. The crowd was like a jelly that congealed all around them. At first they could hardly move. A bald man with an enormous hemp sack humped on his shoulder and an iron collar about his neck knocked Senlin into a red-eyed woman; she repulsed him with an alcoholic laugh and then shrank back into the swamp of bodies. A cage of agitated canaries was passed over their heads, shedding foul-smelling feathers on their shoulders. The hips of a dozen black-robed women, pilgrims of some esoteric faith, rolled against them like enormous ball bearings. Unwashed children loaded with trays of scented tissue flowers, toy pinwheels, and candied fruit wriggled about them, each child leashed to another by a length of rope. Other than the path of the train tracks, there were no clear roads, no cobblestones, no curbs, only the rust-red hardpan of the earth beneath them.

It was all so overwhelming, and for a moment Senlin stiffened like a corpse. The bark of vendors, the snap of tarps, the jangle of harnesses, and the dither of ten thousand alien voices set a baseline of noise that could only be yelled over. Marya took hold of her husband's belt just at his spine, startling him from his daze and goading him onward. He knew they couldn't very well just stand there. He gathered a breath and took the first step.

They were drawn into a labyrinth of merchant tents, vendor carts, and rickety tables. The alleys between stands were as tangled as a child's scribble. Temporary bamboo rafters protruded everywhere over them, bowing under jute rugs, strings of onions, punched tin lanterns, and braided leather belts. Brightly striped shade sails blotted out much of the sky, though even in the shade, the sun's presence was never in doubt. The dry air was as hot as fresh ashes.

Senlin plodded on, hoping to find a road or signpost. Neither appeared. He allowed the throng to offer a path rather than forge one himself. When a gap opened, he leapt into it. After progressing perhaps a hundred paces in this manner, he had no idea which direction the tracks lay. He regretted wandering away from the tracks. They could've followed them to the Babel Central Station. It was unsettling how quickly he'd become disoriented.

Still, he was careful to occasionally turn and construct a smile for Marya. The beam of her smile never wavered. There was no reason to worry her with the minor setback.

Ahead, a bare-chested boy fanned the hanging carcasses of lambs and rabbits to keep a cloud of flies from settling. The flies and sweet stench wafting from the butcher's stall drove the crowd back, creating a little space for them to pause a moment, though the stench was nauseating. Placing Marya's trunk between them, Senlin dried his neck with his handkerchief.

"It certainly is busy," Senlin said, trying not to seem as flustered as he felt, though Marya hardly noticed; she was staring over his head, a bemused expression lighting her pretty face.

"It's wonderful," she said.

A gap in the awnings above them exposed the sky, and there, like a pillar holding up the heavens, stood the Tower of Babel.

The face of the Tower was patched with white, gray, rust, tan, and black, betraying the many types of stone and brick used in its construction. The irregular coloration reminded Senlin of a calico cat. The Tower's silhouette was architecturally bland, evoking a dented and ribbed cannon barrel, but it was ornamented with grand friezes, each band taller than a house. A dense cloudbank obscured the Tower's pinnacle. The *Everyman's Guide* noted that the upper echelons were permanently befogged, though whether the ancient structure produced the clouds or attracted them remained a popular point of speculation. However it was, the peak was never visible from the ground.

The *Everyman's* description of the Tower of Babel hadn't really prepared Senlin for the enormity of the structure. It made the ziggurats of South Ur and the citadels of the Western Plains seem like models, the sort of thing children built out of sugar cubes. The Tower had taken a thousand years to erect. More, according to some historians. Overwhelmed with wonder and the intense teeming of the Market, Senlin shivered. Marya squeezed his hand reassuringly, and his back straightened. He was a headmaster, after all, a leader of a modest community. Yes, there was a crowd to push through, but once they reached the Tower, the throng would thin. They would be able to stretch a little and would, almost certainly, find themselves among more pleasant company. In a few hours, they would be drinking a glass of port in a reasonable but hospitable lodging on the third level of the Tower—the Baths, locals called it— just as they had planned. They would calmly survey this same human swarm, but from a more comfortable distance.

Now, at least, they had a bearing, a direction to push toward.

Senlin was also discovering a more efficient means of advancing through the crowds. If he stopped, he found, it was difficult to start again, but progress could be made if one was a little more firm and determined. After a few minutes of following, Marya felt comfortable enough to release his belt, which made walking much easier for them both.

Soon, they found themselves in one of the many clothing bazaars within the Market. Laced dresses, embroidered pinafores, and cuffed shirts hung on a forest of hooks and lines. A suit could be had in any color, from peacock blue to jonquil yellow; women's intimate apparel dangled from bamboo ladders like the skins of exotic snakes. Square-folded hand-kerchiefs covered the nearest table in a heap like a snowdrift.

"Let me buy you a dress. The evenings here are warmer than we're used to." He had to speak close to her ear.

"I'd like a little frock," she said, removing her pith helmet and revealing her somewhat deflated bronzy hair. "Something scandalous."

He gave her a thoughtful frown to disguise his own surprise. He knew that this was the kind of flirtation that even decent couples probably indulged in on their honeymoon. Still, he was unprepared and couldn't reflect her playful tone. "Scandalous?"

"Nothing your pupils will need to know about. Just a lit-tle something to disgrace our clothesline back home," she said, running her finger down his arm as if she were striking a match.

He felt uneasy. Ahead of them, acres of stalls cascaded with women's undergarments. There wasn't a man in sight.

Fifteen years spent living as a bachelor hadn't prepared him for the addition of Marya's undergarments to the landscape of his bedroom. Finding her delicates draped on the bedposts and doorknobs of his old sanctuary had come as something of a shock. But this mass of nightgowns, camisoles, corsets, stock-ings, and brassieres being combed through by thousands of unfamiliar women seemed exponentially more humiliating. "I think I'll stay by the luggage."

"What about your rules?"

"Well, if you'll keep that red bowl on your head, I'll be able to spot you just fine from here."

"If you wander off, we'll meet again at the top of the Tower," she said with exaggerated dramatic emphasis.

"We will not. I'll meet you right here beside this cart of socks."

"Such a romantic!" she said, passing around two heavy-set

women who wore the blue-and-white apron dresses popular many years earlier. Senlin noticed with amusement that they were connected at the waist by a thick jute rope.

He asked them if they were from the east, and they responded with the name of a fishing village that was not far from Isaugh. They exchanged the usual nostalgia common to coastal folk: sunrises, starfish, and the pleasant muttering of the surf at night, and then he asked, "You've come on holiday?"

They responded with slight maternal smiles that made him feel belittled. "We're far past our holidays," one said.

"Do you go everywhere lashed together?" A note of mockery crept into his voice now.

"Yes, of course," replied the older of the two. "Ever since we lost our little sister."

"I'm sorry. Did she pass away recently?" Senlin asked, recovering his sincere tone.

"I certainly hope not. But it has been three years. Maybe she has."

"Or maybe she found some way to get back home?" the younger sister said.

"She wouldn't abandon us," the older replied in a tone that suggested this was a well-tread argument between them.

"It is intrepid of you to come alone," the younger spinster said to him.

"Oh, thank you, but I'm not alone." Tiring of the conversation, Senlin moved to grip the handle of the trunk only to find it had moved.

Confused, he turned in circles, searching first the ground and then the crowd of blank, unperturbed faces snaking about him. Marya's trunk was gone. "I've lost my luggage," he said.

"Get yourself a good rope," the eldest said, and reached up to pat his pale cheek.

Follow us:

f **/orbitbooksUS**

🐦 **/orbitbooks**

▶ **/orbitbooks**

Join our mailing list
to receive alerts on our
latest releases and deals.

orbitbooks.net

Enter our monthly
giveaway for the chance
to win some epic prizes.

orbitloot.com